THE
ASHFORD
AFFAIR

ALSO BY LAUREN WILLIG

THE
ASHFORD
AFFAIR

LAUREN WILLIG

ST. MARTIN'S PRESS
NEW YORK

THE ASHFORD AFFAIR. Copyright © 2013 by Lauren Willig. All rights reserved. Printed in the United States of America. For information, address St. Martin's Press, 175 Fifth Avenue, New York, N.Y. 10010.

www.stmartins.com

Design by Kathryn Parise

ISBN 978-1-250-01449-8 (hardcover)
ISBN 978-1-250-03893-7 (international trade paperback)
ISBN 978-1-250-02719-1 (e-book)

St. Martin's Press books may be purchased for educational, business, or promotional use. For information on bulk purchases, please contact Macmillan Corporate and Premium Sales Department at 1-800-221-7945 extension 5442 or write specialmarkets@macmillan.com.

First Edition: April 2013

10 9 8 7 6 5 4 3 2 1

To James,
now and always

THE
ASHFORD
AFFAIR

PROLOGUE

Kenya, 1926

A ddie's gloves were streaked with sweat and red dust.

It wasn't just her gloves. Looking down, she winced at the sight of her once pearl-colored suit, now turned gray and rust with smoke and dust. Even in the little light that managed to filter through the thick mosquito netting on the windows, the fabric was clearly beyond repair. The traveling outfit that had looked so smart in London had proved to be a poor choice for the trip from Mombasa.

She felt such a fool. What had she been thinking? It had cost more than her earnings for the month, that dress, an unpardonable extravagance in these days when her wardrobe ran more to the sensible than the chic. It had taken a full afternoon of scouring Oxford Street, going into one shop, then the next, this dress too common, that too expensive, nothing just right, until she finally found it, just a little more than she could afford, looking almost, if one looked at it in just the right way, as though it might be couture, rather than a poor first cousin to it.

She had peacocked in her tiny little flat, posing in front of the mirror with the strange ripple down the middle, twisting this way and that to try to get the full effect, her imagination presenting her with a hundred tempting images. Bea coming to the train to meet her, an older, more matronly Bea, her silver-gilt hair burned straw by the equatorial sun, her figure softened by childbearing. She would see Addie stepping off the train in her smart new frock with her smart new haircut and exclaim in surprise. She would turn Addie this way and that, marveling at her, her new city sophistication, her sleek hair, her newly plucked brows.

You've grown up, Bea would say. And Addie would smile, just a wry little hint of a smile, the sort of smile you saw over cocktails at the Ritz, and say, It does happen.

And, then, from somewhere behind her, Frederick would say, Addie? and she would turn and see surprise and admiration chasing each other across his face as he realized, for the first time, just what he had left behind in London.

Sweat dripped between her breasts, dampening her dress. She didn't need to look down to know that she was hopelessly splotched, with the sort of sweat stains that would turn yellow with washing.

Addie permitted herself a twisted smile. She had so hoped—such an ignoble hope!—that just once she might look the better by comparison, that even a poor first cousin to couture might come off first in comparison to the efforts of Nairobi's dressmakers. Instead, here she was again, an utter mess, a month and a week away from all that was familiar and comfortable, chugging across the plains of Africa—and why?

David had asked her that before she left. Why?

He had asked it so sensibly, so logically. Her first impulse had been to bristle, to tell him it was no business of his. But it was; she knew that. The ring he had given her hung on a chain around her neck, a pre-engagement rather than an engagement. *Put it on when I come back,* she had told him. *We can make the announcements then.*

But why wait? he had asked. *Why go?*

Because . . . she had begun, and faltered. How could she answer him when she didn't quite know why herself? She had mumbled something about her favorite cousin, about Bea needing her, about old affections and old debts.

All the way to Africa? he had asked with that quirk of the brow that his students so dreaded as they sputtered their way through their explications of Plato's *Republic* or Aristotle's *Politics.*

Perhaps I want to go because I want to go, she had said sharply. Hadn't he thought of that? That she might want to travel beyond the borders of the country, just once in her life? That she might want to live a little before donning an apron and cooking his dinners?

It was a cheap shot, but an effective one. He had been apologetic immediately. He was very forward-thinking, David. It was one of the things she liked about him—no, one of the things she loved about him. He actually found it admirable that she worked. He admired her for throwing off her aristocratic shackles—his terms, that—and making her own way in the world.

He didn't realize that the truth was so much more complex, so much less impressive. She had less thrown than been thrown.

Poor David. Duly chastised, he had made it his business to plot her trip to Africa, appearing, each evening, with a new guilt offering, a map, a travel guide, a train schedule. He had entered into the planning for her trip as though he were going instead of she. Addie had nodded and smiled and pretended an interest she didn't feel. To do otherwise would be to acknowledge that the question was still there, hanging between them.

Why?

She jolly well wished she knew. Beneath her cloche, her hair was matted to her head with sweat. Addie yanked it off, dropping it on the narrow bed. The movement of the train ought to have created a bit of breeze, but the screens were tightly fitted, their mesh clogged with the red dust that seemed almost worse than mosquitoes. With the screens down, the car was dark and airless, more like a cattle car than a first-class cabin, the clatter of wheels against track broken far too frequently by the high-pitched wail of the whistle.

Kneeling on the bed, she wrestled the screen open. The train chugged steadily along on its slim, single track—the Iron Snake, they had told her the natives called it, in Mombasa, as she had struggled to see her belongings from ship to train, jostled this way and that in the bustling, busy harbor. In the distance, she could see a flock of beasts, rather like deer, but with thin, high horns, startled into flight by the noise of the train. It was nearly mid-day, and the equatorial sun made the scene shimmer in a kind of haze, like a glaze over glass, so that the fleeing beasts rippled as they ran, like an impressionist painting.

She had never imagined Africa being so very green, nor the sky so very blue.

Her imaginings, such as they were, had been in shades of sienna and burnt umber, browns and oranges, with, perhaps, a bit of jungle thrown in, as a courtesy to H. Rider Haggard. Perhaps she ought to have paid more attention to the books and maps David had brought, instead of watching him, his thin face animated in the lamplight, feeling a familiar mix of obligation and guilt, affection and dread. She hadn't bothered to think much about Africa at all. There were books she could have read, people she could have quizzed, but she hadn't bothered, not with any of it. When she had thought of coming to Africa, it hadn't been of Africa she had thought.

The wind shifted, sending a plume of wood smoke directly at her.

Addie slammed the screen down again, coughing in acrid haze. Her handkerchief came away black when she pressed it to her face. She stumbled to the little lavatory, scrubbing herself as clean as she could, avoiding the sight of her own face in the mirror.

Such a plain little face, compared to Bea's glowing loveliness.

The Debutante of the Decade, they had called Bea, the papers delighting in the alliteration of it. She had been photographed, not once, but a dozen times, as Diana, as Circe, as a beam of moonlight, as a bride, in lace and orange flowers.

Addie tried to remember Bea, remember her as she had been, her face bright with movement, but all she could conjure up was the cool beauty of a photographer's formal portrait, silver-blond hair sleeked forward around a fine-featured face, lips a Roman goddess would envy, pale blue eyes washed gray by the photographer's palette. She kept the photo on the mantel of her bed-sit, the silver frame an incongruous touch against the peeling paint and damp-stained walls, relic of a life that seemed as long ago as the "once upon a time" in a child's story.

Addie wondered how that pale loveliness had held up under the equatorial sun. It was six years since they had seen each other. Would she be changed? Lined, weary, burned brown?

It was impossible to imagine Bea as anything but what she had been, dressed in silk and fringe, a cigarette holder in one hand. Try as she might, Addie couldn't picture her on a farm in Kenya, couldn't reconcile her with dirt and sun, khaki and mosquito net. That was for other people, not Bea. She found it nearly as hard to believe, despite the evidence of her cousin's pen, that she was a mother now, not once, but twice over. Two little girls, her letter had said. Marjorie and Anna.

Addie had gifts for the two girls in her trunk, French dolls with porcelain faces and sawdust arms. She had bought them at the last minute, grabbing up the first ones she had found, just in case the children were real and not one of her cousin's elaborate teases. Motherhood and Bea were two concepts that didn't go together. Rather like Bea and Kenya.

Addie worried at the finger of her glove. She should stop it and stop it now, before she got to Nairobi. She was being unfair. Bea might be a wonderful mother. She had certainly been a wonderful mentor to a lonely cousin, the best of guides and the best of friends. Careless sometimes, yes, but always loving.

People changed, Addie reminded herself. They did. They changed and learned and grew, just as she had.

Perhaps Kenya was what Bea had needed to bring out the best in her, just as emancipation had brought out the best in Addie. This might, Addie told herself hopefully, be all for the best. They could meet as equals now, each happy and secure in her own life, no more tangles of love and resentment and obligation. She wasn't the charity girl in the nursery anymore.

She was twenty-six, she reminded herself. Twenty-six and self-supporting. She had been making her own living for five years, paying her own way and making her own decisions. The days of living in Bea's household, trailing in Bea's footsteps, were over, long over.

If anything, Bea's letter had made it clear she needed her, not the other way around.

Addie slid Bea's letter out of her travel wallet. It was stained and crumpled, read and reread. *Do come*, she had written, sounding like the old Bea, no hint of everything that had passed before she left. *I am utterly lost without you.*

Distilled essence of Bea, thought Addie. Not just the sprawling letters, but the words themselves. Nothing ever was simply what it was; it was always utterly, terribly, desperately. Love or hate, Bea did neither by halves. Excellent when one was loved, not so entertaining when one was hated. Addie had seen both sides.

We should all so dearly love to see you.

"We." Not Marjorie and Anna, they didn't know her to miss her. Addie had sat up, night after night, parsing that one word like a professor with a poem, twisting and turning it from every angle. We. Was it only another example of Bea's hyperbole? A kindly social gesture? Or—

Addie put the letter abruptly away, cramming it back into her travel wallet. It would be what it would be. And then she would go back to David, David who thought he loved her and perhaps even did. He seemed very sure on the point.

Was he sure enough for both of them?

Yes, she told herself. Yes. David belonged to her new life, the life she had built for herself, piece by painful piece after—well, after everything had gone so hideously, dramatically wrong. The rest was all history, lost in the mists of time. She and Bea could laugh about it now, on the porch of the farm. Did the farm have a porch? Addie assumed it must. It sounded like a suitably rustic addition.

That was why she was going, she told herself. To make her peace. She and Bea had been each other's confidantes for so long, closer than sisters. These last five years of silence had gouged like a wound.

She wouldn't think about Frederick.

The whistle gave one last, shrieking cry and the train jolted to a halt. "Nairobi!" someone shouted. "Nairobi!"

It seemed utterly impossible that she was here, that the train journey wasn't going to go on and on, jolting and smoky, the sun teasing her eyes through the blinds.

"Nairobi!"

Jolted into action, Addie scooped up her overnight bag, scanning the room for stray possessions. Her hat still lay abandoned on the bed. She plonked it back down on her head, skewering it into place with a long steel pin. Here she was. No turning back now. Straightening her suit jacket, she took a deep breath and marched purposefully to the compartment door.

Wrenching it open, she squinted into the brightness. Her silly little hat was no use at all against the sun; she had a confused impression of light and dust, people bustling back and forth, unloading packages, greeting friends in half a dozen languages, calling out in Arabic, in English, in German, in

French. Poised on the metal steps, Addie shaded her eyes against the sun, ineffectually searching for a familiar figure, anyone who might have been sent to greet her. Car horns beeped at rickshaws drawn by men in little more than loincloths, tires screeching, while the sound of horses' hooves clattered over the excited chatter of the people at the station. In the hot sun, the smells seemed magnified, horse and engine oil and curry, from a stand by the side of the station.

Over the din, someone called her name. "Addie! Addie! Over here."

Obediently she turned, searching. It was Bea's voice, husky and lovely, with that hint of laughter even when she was at her most reserved, as though she had luscious secrets she was longing to tell. *A mouth made for eating strawberries,* one of her suitors had rhapsodized, lips always pursed around the promise of a smile.

"Bea?" Dust and sun made rainbows over her eyes. Dark men in pale robes, Europeans in khaki, women in pale frocks, all swerved and shifted like the images in a kaleidoscope, circling around one another on the crowded rail side.

A gloved hand thrust up out of the throng, waving madly. "Here!"

The crowd broke and Addie saw her. Time fell away. The noises and voices receded, a muted din in the background.

How could she have ever thought to have outdone Bea?

Two children hadn't changed her. She was still tall and slim, her blond hair gleaming golden beneath the hat she held with one hand. It was a slanted affair that made Addie's cloche seem both impractical and provincial. Bea's dress was tan, but there was nothing the least drab or dowdy about it. It fit loosely on the top and clung tightly at the hips, outlined with a dropped belt of contrasting white and tan that matched the detail at sleeves and hem. It made Addie's suit seem both fussy and cheap.

Addie felt a familiar wave of love and despair, joy at the joy on her cousin's face, so beautiful, so unchanged—so unfairly beautiful, so unfairly unchanged. She knew it wasn't fair to resent Bea for something that was so simply and effortlessly a part of her, but she did, even so. Just once . . . Just once . . .

"Dearest!" Bea had never been one to shy from the grand scene. She swooped down with outstretched arms as Addie clambered clumsily down the metal stairs, stiff and awkward from a day and night in a steel box. "Welcome!"

Addie put out a hand to fend her off. "Don't touch me—I'm a mess."

"Nonsense," Bea said, and embraced her anyway, not a social press of the cheek, but a full hug. For a moment, her arms pressed so hard that Addie could feel the bones through her dress. She was thinner, Bea, thinner than she had been in London. Her arms grasped Addie with wiry, frenetic strength. "I have missed you."

Before Addie could reply, before she could say she had missed her, too, Bea had already released her and stepped back, poised and confident, every inch the debutante she had been.

Looking Addie up and down, she grimaced in a comical caricature of sympathy. "That dreadful train. What you need," she said, with authority, "is a drink."

Addie looked ruefully down at herself, at her carefully chosen traveling dress, soiled and sweat stained. So much for her grand entrance. So much for competing with Bea. She had lost before she'd begun. "What I need is a bath and my things."

"We'll get you both. And a drink." Bea linked her arm through Addie's in the old way, drawing her effortlessly through the crowd. "Travel is always ghastly, isn't it? Those hideous little compartments and those nasty little people crowing about tea from the sides of the track." Bea had always had a gift for mimickry. She did it unconsciously, twisting herself into a pose and just as quickly twisting out again.

"It wasn't so ghastly," said Addie, struggling to keep up. Her overnight bag was heavier than she had remembered, her shorter strides no match for Bea's. She scrounged to remember some of David's lectures. "I gather it's much easier now that the railroad's been put in."

"Much," said Bea absently. She smiled and waved at a man in a pale suit. "That," she said out of the side of her mouth to Addie, "is General Grogan. He owns Torr's Hotel. We don't go there."

"Oh?" Addie's bag banged painfully against her knee. "Is it—?"

"Common," said Bea dismissively. "Of course, you wouldn't be staying there anyway, since you'll be with us, but if we're in town, it's Muthaiga. Or the Norfolk. *Never* Torr's." She gave the unfortunate owner a broad smile that made him trip over his own feet.

"Right," said Addie, although the names meant nothing to her. "Of course."

She craned her neck to look behind, but the man was already gone, and Bea was imparting more wisdom, something about race meetings, and drinks parties, and this couple and that couple, and whose farm had failed and who was worth knowing.

"—don't you remember, Euan Wallace's first wife? You must have met them, surely?" Fortunately, Bea didn't wait for an answer, plunging on, even as she plowed through the crowd. "She divorced him ages ago—or maybe he divorced her. It's so hard to keep track. Joss is her new one, although not so new anymore. It's been—seven years now? Eight?"

"Mmm," said Addie, trying desperately to keep from panting too obviously. Sweat blurred her eyes, half-blinding her, but she couldn't get to a handkerchief to wipe it off. She blundered determinedly on, trying to ignore the nasty sinking feeling deep in the pit of her stomach, the one that told her that this had been a terrible mistake.

Instead of being the worldly one, she was, instead, the neophyte, being introduced by Bea into the mysteries of her world, mysteries Addie would never perfectly understand, and which would, once again, render her dependent on Bea's leadership and guidance.

In short, straight back to the same old pattern.

"How much farther?" she blurted out, breaking into Bea's recitation.

"Not so very far," said Bea, looking at her in surprise. "Oh, darling, you do look done in. It's the heat, isn't it? It does take people by surprise in the beginning."

It hadn't done anything to Bea; she looked perfectly cool and fresh. But, then, she wasn't the one carrying a bag that seemed to have gotten considerably heavier over the past ten minutes. Nor had she spent the past twenty-four hours in a closed train car.

"Don't worry, darling," she said, "we'll be at the car in a tick. Oh, look! There's Alice de Janzé." Bea waved languidly at a woman dressed as smartly as anything you would see in Paris. "American, married to a Frenchman. I can't think what she's doing in Nairobi. She's usually off at Slains."

The social catalog grated on Addie's nerves. It was like being back in London, back in their deb year, Bea constantly surrounded by people, effortlessly making friends and friends of friends. What had happened to "we live quietly on our little farm"?

Addie asked breathlessly, "Where are your girls?"

Bea's pace picked up. Addie had to practically run to keep up. "They're at the farm. They're happy there. Like Dodo with the stables. There's no accounting, is there?"

Addie sensed the edge of an argument, one not to do with her. Unsure how to respond, she said, instead, "Dodo sends her love."

Dodo was Bea's older sister, the only one of the clan officially on speaking terms with her. With Dodo, though, it was hard to tell the difference between speakers and non-speakers; the only things she ever talked about were her beloved horses. She came down to town once a month, always to the Ritz, where her battered tweeds made an odd contrast to the other women's tailored suits and Paris frocks. Perhaps that was the nicest thing about Dodo; she always was what she was.

"Pity she couldn't send cash," said Bea flippantly. "You have no idea what it costs to run a coffee farm, no idea at all. No crops for the first four years and then whatever the market will bear. It's vile."

"Is Frederick at the farm?" No need to worry about tone. Her voice came out in gusty pants.

Bea winced sympathetically and slowed down. "No, he's with the car. He'd have come to meet you, but he was waylaid by D."

"Dee?" Addie's imagination conjured up a vamp with long, red fingernails.

"Lord Delamere. Frightful old bore."

Addie laughed breathlessly. "Not one of the blessed?"

That was how they used to refer to people they liked, she and Bea, back in the nursery days, part of their own private code. It felt rusty and raw on her tongue.

Impulsively Bea turned and hugged her, nearly knocking her off her feet. A wave of expensive French perfume blotted out dust and sweat. "Oh, I *have* missed you! Are you hungry?"

Addie swayed and caught her balance again. She set her bag down with a thump. She was hungry, she realized, hungry and a little dizzy with the heat and sun.

"They fed us at Makindu." There had been a British breakfast of eggs and porridge, looking oddly foreign in that setting, with strange, striped beasts grazing in the distance. Addie scrunched up her nose, trying to remember how long ago that had been. It felt like a different lifetime already. "But that must have been—oh, hours ago. Just about dawn."

"Don't worry, we'll see you fed, once we get you out of that frightful frock."

Addie tensed, instantly on the defensive. "What's so frightful about it? Once it's been washed and pressed . . ."

Bea looked her up and down with an expert eye. "Oh, my dear, no."

Addie suddenly saw herself as Bea must see her, frowsy and wilted, in an off-the-peg dress that had lurched at fashion and missed. Bea had always been, and was, even now, effortlessly and glamorously fashionable. She could make a pair of men's trousers look like a Worth gown. Addie had no doubt that on her that sad little traveling suit would look like Lanvin.

"Don't worry," she said, as one might to a child, and suddenly Addie was back at Ashford again, six and shy and unprepared, harkening unto the Gospel according to Bea. "We'll find you something much better." Her expression turned speculative. Her pale blue eyes glinted as she looked at Addie from under her lashes. "And, perhaps, a man?"

"I already have one of those," Addie said tartly. She picked up her bag again, taking a firmer grip on the handle. "David Cecil. He's a lecturer at University College. In Economics."

"My dear," Bea said. "How frightfully clever."

"He is," Addie said loyally, as though he hadn't, over the course of the trip, become little more than a mirage in her imagination, David, whom she was supposed to love, and whom she might love, if only she could convince herself that the past was past.

Wasn't that what David was always telling her? The world of her youth, with its house parties and servants, Lord This and Lady That—that world was gone. She had been in it but not of it, not really. It was David with whom she would build a life, share a flat, share a bed, grow old and grow roses—or whatever other plant it was among which they would gently potter, surrounded by children and grandchildren, all as clever as he.

"We're to be engaged when I get back," she said, and it came out more belligerently than she had intended.

"So you're engaged to be engaged?" It did sound rather ridiculous when put that way. Bea smiled a crooked little smile. "Isn't that funny. I had thought— well, never mind. Look. Here we are."

"Here" appeared to be a monster of a car, a massive square thing that re- minded Addie of the estate cars back at Ashford, designed for moving both men and game. There were two men standing by the side, deep in conversa- tion, in which she could hear "elevation" and "fertilizer." The one on the right was shortish, on the wrong side of middle age, with a face like an amiable turtle beneath a round hat with a wide brim.

The other man had his back to them, but Addie would have known him just the same. He had always been thin, too thin the last time she had seen him, but the casual clothes of the colony suited him; he looked rangy rather than lanky, the short sleeves of his shirt displaying skin that had acquired a healthy glow. Unlike his companion, he wore no hat. The sun had burned lighter streaks into his dark hair.

"Look who I've found!" called Bea, and he turned, his face breaking into a smile of welcome.

"Addie," he said. "It is. It's really Addie."

He smiled, and Addie's heart turned over with a sickening lurch, five years gone in five minutes.

Addie felt suddenly cold, cold despite the warmth of the day. She looked at Bea, shining in the sun, at Frederick. The mustache he had once sported was gone; he was clean-shaven now, his face tan where it had once been pale. There were lines by his eyes that hadn't been there before, white in the brown of his face, but they suited him. The circles of dissipation were gone, burned away by sun and work.

From far away, she could hear David's voice. *Why?*

This was why. This had always been why. Addie fought against a blinding wave of despair and desire, all mixed up in sun and sweat, dust and confusion. She wanted to curl into a ball, to cry her frustration out into the dust, to turn, to flee, to run away.

David was right; she should have left well enough alone. She stood have stayed home in the cool of England, in her safe flat with her safe almost fiancé, instead of poking at emotions better left buried.

Frederick held out a hand to her, and there it was, glinting in the sun, the gold ring that marked him as Bea's.

"We didn't think you'd come," he said.

I can still go away again, she wanted to say. Forget that I was here. But that was the coward's path. There was, as Nanny used to say, no way out but through.

Addie set her bag carefully down by her feet, flexing her sore hand. By the time she had straightened, she had her pleasant social smile fixed firmly on her face.

"Well, here I am," she said, and took Frederick's hand. His ring pressed against her palm, a reminder, a warning. "How could I stay away?"

PART ONE

ASHFORD

ONE

New York, 1999

Clemmie hurried beneath the awning of her grandmother's building, panting a quick hello in response to the doorman's greeting.

He started to say something, but she kept on going, heels click-click-clacking on the marble floor. She tossed a "hello" over her shoulder, flapping her hand in a wave.

It was Granny Addie's ninety-ninth birthday party and Clemmie was late.

She steamed through the foyer, loosening her coat and scarf as she went. Despite the November cold, she felt sweaty straight through, clammy with perspiration beneath the layers of bra, blouse, suit jacket, and coat. She'd meant to change into a dress, but there hadn't been time, so here she was, disheveled and blistered, hair any which way and lipstick a distant memory. Her mother would be appalled, but she wouldn't say anything. She would just telegraph her distress with tightened lips and raised brows. She was good at that. Clemmie's mother's brows were better than sign language, complicated concepts conveyed with a minimum of movement.

Clemmie jabbed at the elevator button and made the mistake of glancing at her watch. Eight fifteen. Cocktails had started forty-five minutes ago. They might, in fact, already be sitting down to dinner. No wonder the doorman had looked at her like that. Her mother had probably been calling down every ten minutes to ask if she had been spotted yet. She was past the realm of acceptably late and well into the kingdom of unpardonably tardy.

Shifting her large Longchamp bag from one shoulder to the other, she mentally mustered her arsenal of excuses, none entirely a lie, but none entirely true either: a meeting at the last minute, the BlackBerry in her bag that wouldn't stop buzzing, that damn deposition in Dallas that needed to be prepped before she flew off on Thursday. Then there were all the standard-issue disclaimers: no cabs, delayed subways, the impossibility of getting directly from her office, all the way west on 49th and 8th, to Granny Addie's, safe in the fastness of the Upper East Side, on 85th and 5th. That, at least, was pure, unvarnished truth. Clemmie had wound up walking most of the way, half-speedwalking, half-running, slipping and sliding in her high-heeled pumps as she scanned for cabs, all of which seemed to be full, their occupants smug silhouettes in the backseats, inside while she was out.

Clemmie shifted feet, discreetly easing her left foot out of her black pump. Matte black leather, now slightly scuffed, with a three-inch heel. These shoes looked very nice under a conference table, but they had not been made for walking.

Her stocking clung stickily to her heel. Lovely. Not just a blister, but a burst blister. It was going to hurt like hell tomorrow when she limped into work.

The elevator pinged, the doors opening.

Clemmie jammed her foot back into her shoe and hobbled inside. The elevator was lined in rosewood, the buttons set in polished brass. It hadn't changed much over the past thirty years. She hit the 8, her finger finding the number by rote, and the elevator began its ascent. As she always did, she glanced at the shield-shaped security mirror in the corner. As a child, she used to entertain herself by moving her head this way, then that, watching as her features moved in and out of focus, like a Barbie head when you took the rubbery features between your fingers and squeezed.

Now she checked for obvious signs of wear and tear, applying a hasty coat of lip gloss from the blunted stick in her bag. Mascara? There was still more over her eyes than under them. Good enough. The wind had taken the part of blush, pounding her pale cheeks into color. Unfortunately, it had also encouraged her hair to make a desperate bid for liberation, standing up any which way.

She hadn't had this problem when it was long; then she could just bundle it back, clipping it up with a slide or holding it back with a headband.

It was such a cliché, wasn't it? End a relationship, cut your hair.

She had had it chopped off last week, ostensibly so it wouldn't keep getting caught under the strap of her bag, defiantly taking a whole hour away from the office in the middle of the day. Screw it, she had told herself. She had spent the better part of six years in the office, eating meals at her desk, taking personal calls on her office phone, watching the seasons change from behind the thick glass windows. If she wanted to take an hour to go to Fekkai, she had damn well earned it. One hour away wouldn't cost her the place in the partnership for which she had so desperately worked, the partnership she was so close to achieving; while the stylist clipped away Clemmie had kept her BlackBerry in her lap, typing away with two fingers on the miniature keyboard.

Her hair was supposed to be easier to manage like this, the hairdresser had said, but the short, fine strands seemed to have a mind of their own, sticking up any which way and flying into her eyes. She missed being able to pull it back, the comforting nonsense task of bundling it up and letting it down again. She found herself constantly reaching for hair that wasn't there anymore.

The elevator doors opened onto the eighth floor, a small landing decorated with burgundy silk flowered paper and a spindly gilded table beneath an equally spindly and gilded mirror. A bronze bucket provided a home for stray umbrellas. Grandpa Frederick's walking stick still stuck out in pride of place in the middle. Clemmie touched it lightly with her fingers. The head was shaped like a terrier. Grandpa Frederick used to make it yip and bark for her as Clemmie would shy back, alarmed and delighted.

Grandpa Frederick had died when Clemmie was six, but she remembered him, just vaguely, a seamed face and white hair and a lopsided grin and a lifelong smoker's hacking cough. It was odd to think that he had died that long ago; even gone, he had been a presence throughout Clemmie's childhood, like Victoria's Albert, always there in memory. Granny Addie's apartment was still full of him, even thirty years on. There were pictures of him in grainy black and white, wearing the comical clothes of the 1920s, pictures of him bending over the plants on their coffee plantation in Kenya, and then, later, shiny color photos of a much older Grandpa Frederick, with Granny Addie, with children, with grandchildren, clothes changing to suit the era.

They were, Clemmie had always thought, rather an inspiration. They had met when Granny Addie was still, as they quaintly put it, in the schoolroom, and married when she was in her twenties. Together, they had taken a little farm in Kenya and turned it into a thriving coffee company. The business had been sold back in the seventies, swallowed up by Maxwell House, but the back hallways of Granny Addie's apartment were hung with old posters, now framed, advertising KENYAN COFFEE—FOR THE DISCRIMINATING PALATE. Some even featured a younger-looking Granny Addie, poised and impossibly aristocratic, a coffeepot in one hand, a cup and saucer in the other.

They had been together so long, Granny Addie and Grandpa Frederick.

Even if Clemmie met someone tomorrow, even if by some miracle she stumbled upon her dream man in an elevator or on the subway, she would still never be with anyone as long as Granny Addie had been with Grandpa Frederick. It was an incredibly depressing thought. The idea of starting over, having to go on the same awkward first dates, recite the same tired personal stories, made her want to curl into a little ball and whimper.

Why was it so easy for some people and not for others?

Birthday, she reminded herself. She was meant to be celebratory. She couldn't go in and mope all over Granny Addie. Not with all the cousins watching, at any rate. Clemmie's mother was a big believer in Keeping Their End Up, which generally seemed to boil down to smiling whether you wanted to or not and never ever telling Aunt Anna how you really felt about anything.

Mother had a thing about Aunt Anna. Clemmie had never been able to discover any malevolent tendencies on her aunt's part—yes, she was kind of ditzy and a little phony, but evil?—but Clemmie's mother remained convinced that Aunt Anna lived to exploit the chinks in her armor. Clemmie tended to think that Aunt Anna lived for Aunt Anna, which was a very different thing.

Clemmie hung her coat on the rack in the hall, shoving it in between a fur-trimmed cashmere cape that could only belong to Aunt Anna and someone else's well-used Burberry. Someone had left the door to the apartment slightly ajar. Through it, Clemmie could hear the unmistakable noises that denoted a cocktail party: the staccato rhythm of voices, the click of heels against hardwood, the soft-soled shuffle of the waiters bearing crab cakes or smoked salmon squares.

"There you are!" Her mother must have been lying in wait; she pounced as soon as Clemmie opened the door. "You're the last one here."

"I had a meeting," Clemmie began, but her mother was frowning at her left hand.

"You didn't wear your ring."

"It's not mine anymore." She viewed its continued presence in her apartment as a bailment rather than ownership. It was going back to Dan the next time she saw him, along with his *Star Wars* video, his Penn sweatshirt, and his spare sneakers. The toothbrush she had already thrown out. She had thought of keeping it for cleaning grout, but that seemed just a little too vindictive, a little too voodoo doll–esque. She didn't want to be vindictive. They had parted friends, at least theoretically.

Could one part friends in such a situation? There had been things said. . . . She had given as good as she got, but some of Dan's observations about her character still stung. Like he should talk about being emotionally unavailable. Pots and kettles, Dan, pots and kettles.

Her mother shot a furtive glance over her shoulder, checking to make sure there were no relatives in earshot. "I don't see why you couldn't have kept it on just for tonight."

God forbid the cousins realize that her engagement had imploded, that she was single again at thirty-four, Marjorie's unwanted spinster daughter. It was like something out of Jane Austen. Weren't they meant to be past this as a society? It stung even more coming from her mother, the woman who had always given her a hard line on putting career first. Until she hit thirty and the tune suddenly changed.

Clemmie gave her mother a long, hard look. "It's not like you liked Dan."

Her mother bristled. Mother did a good line in bristle. "I never said that."

"How else would you define 'perhaps it's time to reconsider your options'?"

"I never meant— Never mind. We'll discuss this later."

Mother's response to everything: deny, deny, deny. If we pretend it's all okay, it is!

"Fine," said Clemmie, moving past her mother into the foyer. "Sure. Whatever."

That was the problem with being a menopause baby; the usual generation gap was multiplied by two. Her mother had been a young woman during the Blitz and the mentality had stuck. Clemmie had been born when her mother was forty-four, the last gasp of a failing marriage. It had been hugely embarrassing for her mother, who had thought her childbearing years were long since over.

It had been even more embarrassing when Clemmie's father had left, three years later, having had enough of diapering and burping with the first round—that being practically a verbatim quote. He had left her mother for a journalist named Jennifer, twenty years younger, Californian, and blond.

Clemmie didn't blame him for leaving, but she did blame him for being a cliché.

"Now you're upset with me," said her mother with gloomy certainty. Even after fifty years in the States, Clemmie's mother still clung to her veddy veddy British accent, relic of a childhood spent between Kenya and London. It gave even her most mundane pronouncements a certain ring of authority.

"I'm not upset with you," Clemmie lied. "Let's just leave it, okay? It's Granny Addie's birthday! Woo-hoo!"

"Hmm," said Mother. Her face suddenly changed. She stood straighter, almost moving up to her toes in her flat, sensible shoes. "Anna!" she said brightly. "Look who I found."

Rescued by the cavalry. "Hi, Aunt Anna," said Clemmie, keeping her left hand behind her. "Long time, no see."

"Clemmie, sweetie!" Aunt Anna still wore her hair long. It was fair, like Clemmie's, cunningly cut so that it curved forward in a way that made her seem to be leaning forward in perpetual anticipation. She had to have been seventy, at least, but the good people at Frederic Fekkai had spun silver back into gold, keeping her hair the same pale blond it had been in the wedding photos on Granny Addie's piano. There were many wedding photos. Aunt Anna had been married no fewer than eight times. Her hair brushed against

Clemmie's cheek as Aunt Anna enveloped her in a Chanel-scented hug. "We were afraid you'd been eaten by wolves!"

"Nope, just my desk," said Clemmie, disengaging herself.

"Your mother was getting worried about you," said Aunt Anna.

"Nonsense," said Clemmie's mother stiffly. No Fekkai magic for Clemmie's mother. She wore her hair cut short, in an uncompromising gray. "Clementine works very hard."

"How is everyone?" Clemmie asked hastily. It was the conversational gambit of least resistance. "Do you still have Shoo-Shoo?"

"Oh, goodness, you are behind!" said Aunt Anna.

Clemmie's mother looked pained. She generally did when Aunt Anna talked. After years on the transatlantic scene, Aunt Anna's accent wasn't quite anything anymore, not quite English and not quite American. Affected, Clemmie's mother called it, which was rather rich coming from someone who sounded like the upstairs of *Upstairs Downstairs*.

"—darling little Pekinese," Aunt Anna was saying. "Jonathan got the Columbia job, so he's apartment-hunting. Won't it be nice to have him back in the city? Millie was staying with me for a bit, but she's moved in with her boyfriend now."

"Isn't she, like, ten?" Millie was one of Aunt Anna's stepchildren, one of the younger batch, relic of her third husband—or was it her fourth? It was so easy to lose track. Clemmie could see her mother pursing her lips. It drove Clemmie's mother crazy that Aunt Anna dragged her stepchildren to family events when they weren't, in Clemmie's mother's view, family at all.

"Oh, sweetie!" Aunt Anna laughed her tinkly laugh. "She's twenty-three now! I know, I know, it's too awful. But she seems very happy with her Sean. They have a place in Yorkville."

"Isn't she a bit young to be living with someone?" asked Clemmie's mother.

"Better young than never," replied Aunt Anna cheerfully.

Clemmie didn't think it was meant to be a dig, but it stung all the same. Her left hand felt very, very bare after the weight of Dan's ring.

Her mother sniffed. "Not everyone makes a career out of matrimony."

Aunt Anna winked at Clemmie. "We can't all be lawyers, can we? How's tricks, kiddo?"

"Busy," said Clemmie quickly. "Really busy. I'm in Dallas on Thursday for a deposition and then London the week after that. It's been crazy. How's Granny Addie holding up?"

"Come see for yourself," Mother said before Aunt Anna could say anything. She put a hand on Clemmie's arm and propelled her forward toward the living room, where the cocktail hour was in full swing.

Behind her, Aunt Anna shrugged and waved. Clemmie grinned back at her.

The living room was crowded with men in Brooks Brothers suits and women in black sheath dresses, colorful scarves at their necks. Most were friends of the family of various varieties, rather than relatives. Clemmie's two older brothers had settled in California with their families. She recognized one of her nieces, now in her twenties, interning with some fashion designer. Clemmie's second-oldest brother seemed to have sent his wife as emissary, but, for the most part, their side of the family was underrepresented. Uncle Teddy, Mother's younger brother, had died relatively young, a victim of a heart attack in his forties, but his children and grandchildren had come out in force, doing their bit to honor Granny Addie.

There was only one thing missing from the scene. "Where's Granny Addie?" Clemmie asked.

Her mother looked tired. "She's resting a bit," she said. She had moved in with Granny Addie a few months ago, ostensibly because her lease had run out, but Clemmie suspected it was because she was worried about her. Granny Addie had professional care, a team of nurses who came in shifts, but Clemmie's mother was of the "if you want it done right, do it yourself" variety.

Mother nodded towards the bar. "Get yourself a drink and I'll take you over to her."

"How stiff a drink do I need?" asked Clemmie, but her mother had already turned away, exchanging an air-kiss with one of Uncle Teddy's offspring.

Clemmie made for the bar.

It was set up like all of Granny Addie's parties, going back as far as Clemmie could remember. She presumed that the bottles had been drunk out and replaced over time—and the bartenders tended to change party to party—but otherwise it all looked exactly the same. A folding table had been placed in a corner with a white cloth over it, crowded with bottles and glasses. It was always in the same corner, a little alcove between a window facing out onto 85th Street and the door to the den. On the far side of the room, a wall of windows showcased the apartment's glory, a view out over Central Park.

One of the catering staff was behind the makeshift bar, briskly squeezing a wedge of lime into a tall glass filled with ice and clear liquid. Even from yards away, Clemmie smelled gin. The bartender must be mixing them strong. Good.

There was a man waiting for his drink, his back to Clemmie. He took his drink from the bartender, slipping a few dollar bills discreetly across the cloth.

If she hadn't been sure who it was before, that would have clinched it. You weren't supposed to tip at private parties, but Jon had always ignored that, wanting to make sure the waitstaff got a fair deal.

Clemmie resisted the childish urge to flee, wishing she still had Dan's ring as armor. Not that she needed armor. They were adults now, past that sort of thing.

Clemmie waited until he turned, gave him a chance to see her. She nodded at him in greeting. "Hey, Jon."

"Hey," said Jonathan, raising his gin and tonic. "One for you?"

"Please."

She waited while he relayed the request to the bartender. Unlike the other men in the room, Jon was dressed in khakis and a blazer, rather than a suit, although he had chosen a traditional blue blazer, rather than going all professorial with tweed and patches. She remembered him here in this same room, years ago, in pretty much the same uniform, an awkward adolescent in khakis and bow tie. She would have been in patent-leather shoes, sulking over being put in a little-girl dress at twelve, the two of them trying to sneak drinks from the bar while their respective parents weren't watching. Of all Aunt Anna's "offspring," Jon had been around the most, at least until he went off to Stanford for his Ph.D.

They'd bickered incessantly as teenagers, each trying to one-up the other. Jon was three years older, an advantage he had employed mercilessly. But

Clemmie was the actual daughter—well, granddaughter—of the house; she belonged to Granny Addie, Jon was there by accident. It had evened the scales.

They hadn't stayed in particularly good touch, but there had been vacations and odd overlaps, including that embarrassing weekend in Rome, when she had puked all over his shoes. She didn't particularly care to remember either the state of Jon's shoes or the random—and entirely unprecedented—events that had followed.

They had made a deal never to talk about Rome.

She had always thought Jon looked a bit like Val Kilmer. Val Kilmer or Harrison Ford in his early Indiana Jones days. Jon had the sun-streaked brown hair, the wiry build, the spectacles. Not her type, of course; she was more of a Kevin Costner girl, but she could see how it made Jon popular with his students, especially the female ones. The Val Kilmer resemblance was still there, but Jon looked tired. Tired and older. There was gray in his light brown hair that hadn't been there before.

Clemmie murmured her thanks as he passed her a glass, resisting the urge to toss back the contents.

She lifted her glass, trying for cool. "Aunt Anna said you got a job at Columbia. Congrats. I know how few and far between those are."

"Thanks." Jon's smile didn't reach his eyes. "How's Dan?"

Clemmie silently held up her left hand. "If you say 'I told you so,' I'll punch you."

After a beat, Jonathan smiled a crooked smile. "If I get to say 'I told you so,' then so do you."

"Caitlin?" Caitlin was Jon's wife of three years. They'd been grad students together at Stanford, Caitlin doing something to do with intellectual history, Jon focusing on modern Britain. By a miracle, they'd gotten jobs together at one of the UNCs. Not Chapel Hill, but one of the other ones. "Is she—I mean, are you . . . ?"

Jon clinked his glass against hers. "Got it in one."

"I'm sorry," she said, and meant it. Well, sort of. She had never been a Caitlin fan. "Pretentious" didn't even begin to cut it.

"Yeah, so am I. She's keeping the house."

"What do you get?"

"Shame and rage?"

"Oooh, fun." For a moment, they grinned at each other, united in the land of the love lost. Clemmie dropped her gaze first. Playing with the condensation patterns on her G&T, she said, "Hey, Jon, if you want to talk about it . . ."

He looked pointedly at her left hand. "Do you want to talk about it?"

Fair point. They'd never had that kind of relationship. It was probably too late to start now. "So what do you think about those Jets?" she said heartily.

Jon gave her a look. "You know who the Jets are."

They had been like this as teenagers, engaged in a constant game of one-upsmanship. "There's no need to sound so skeptical. They're a sports team," said Clemmie briskly. "Duh."

A gleam lit in Jon's eyes. "Which sport?"

Oh, crap. This was what she got for not going on any of the firm's sports outings. Clemmie took a stab. "Basketball?"

The lines around Jon's eyes crinkled. For the first time since she'd seen him, his shoulders relaxed. He braced a hand against the bar and looked down at her, which was pretty impressive, given that, thanks to her heels, they were roughly the same height. But, then, he must have had a lot of practice intimidating undergrads.

"They play football," he said, enunciating the word very clearly. "Foot. Ball. Which, in case you didn't know, is not actually played with much ball to the foot. It's the sport where the men in the big shoulder pads hurl an oblong object at each other. Just in case that helps."

"Oh, ha, ha. I knew it had to be something involving a projectile," she said. "Cut me a little slack here."

Jon raised an eyebrow. "A projectile?"

Clemmie lifted her nose in the air. "If I have to define the word for you, you shouldn't be teaching at Columbia."

"Thanks, Clem," he said. "I mean, really. Thanks. You've just made my life suck a little bit less."

High praise indeed. But she knew what he meant. "Hey, that's what family's for." She could see her mother trying to catch her eye from across the room. "I should go say happy birthday to Granny Addie."

Clemmie had thought he would say something snarky, but he didn't. "Yeah," Jon agreed. "She's a pretty special lady."

As accolades went, it might not have been the most poetic, but it was the more meaningful for clearly being meant.

Clemmie got a firm grip on the slippery sides of her glass. "See you around?"

Jon looked at her for a long, thoughtful moment before saying, "Take care of yourself, Clem."

It felt like a dismissal.

It was stupid to feel rebuffed. But she did. Served her right for forgetting that Jon was still Jon. Served her right in general, for wandering around being all needy in public. Especially with Jon.

"You, too," she said lightly, and plunged back into the throng, accidentally elbowing a third cousin.

She was just . . . off tonight. Off-balance, off-kilter, off. She felt strangely vulnerable, as though her protective coating had been peeled away, leaving only a mass of nerves and fears painfully visible to anyone who could see. Clemmie caught a glimpse of herself in the Venetian mirror over the mantelpiece and was surprised to see how normal she looked, how put together, her hair in a sleek, blond bob, the collar of her shirt folded neatly down over her suit collar, pearls at her throat and her ears. The pearls were real, as was the Cartier watch at her wrist. She looked like someone's image of Lawyer Barbie: Professional. Expensive.

That was the good thing about dark suits; no one could see the coffee stain on the sleeve or the perspiration splotches beneath her arms. Like Mother's English accent, suits conferred an automatic air of authority.

"There you are," said her mother, and took her back under her wing, expertly muscling her way through the crowd to Granny Addie's chair. Clemmie followed along behind like an unlikely duckling, taller than her mother in her heels, slender where her mother was solid. She had inherited Grandpa Frederick's build, tall and slim.

In contrast, Granny Addie had always been diminutive, all of five foot two at best. But Clemmie had never thought of her as small. There was something about the way she held herself that had always belied her inches, an air of authority, of solid sense. Competence, that was it. Competence. Clemmie still remembered how Grandpa Frederick, taller and older, had deferred to Addie, taking her word as the final word.

It was, as always, a shock to see her as she was now. In Clemmie's head, Granny Addie was frozen permanently at seventy-something, old, yes, but curiously ageless. Not like this, shrunken and frail. Her knit suit was too large for her wasted frame; Grandpa Frederick's ring seemed to weigh down her hand.

There was a nurse standing behind Granny Addie's chair. She did it very discreetly, managing to do a fairly good impression of a piece of furniture, but she was still there, watching. The chair itself was a hospital chair, on wheels, incongruous among chintz and rosewood that had been unchanged in Granny Addie's living room for as long as Clemmie could imagine.

Clemmie felt a sudden surge of panic. It had always been Granny Addie to whom she had turned for security, Granny Addie who represented the constant and the permanent. The idea of a world without her . . . It wasn't to be thought of.

But she was ninety-nine. Not many people made it as far as ninety-nine. Even fewer people made it past it.

"Is she okay?" Clemmie asked the nurse, trying not to sound as anxious as she felt.

The nurse nodded. "She's just nodded off for a bit." Her voice was the soothing singsong of nurses and nursery-school teachers. "It's nothing to be alarmed about."

If anyone could make it to a hundred and ten, it would be Granny Addie. She'd show death.

Clemmie knelt by her chair, feeling the close-woven wool of the carpet driving her stockings against her knees. "Granny?" she said softly, resting a hand on the arm of her grandmother's chair. "Happy birthday, Granny."

Granny Addie stirred, blinking. She wore spectacles, thick, unlovely things that seemed too big for her shrunken face. It took a moment for her eyes to focus on Clemmie's face. Her eyes were filmed, vague, and distant.

A lump rose in Clemmie's throat. She forced it down. "I'm sorry I'm late," she said. "I would have been here sooner, but I stupidly wound up walking."

Her grandmother frowned down at her, confusion and alarm chasing across her face. She looked, thought Clemmie, so lost. Lost and confused. So utterly unlike herself.

"I'm so sorry, Granny." Clemmie took her grandmother's veined hand in hers. "I'm sorry I haven't been back sooner. Work has been nuts."

As soon as she said it, she wished she hadn't. It sounded so inadequate. Work. So petty and selfish. It didn't matter about work. She ought to have made the time for Granny Addie. She just hadn't realized how frail she had become, how much she had deteriorated in the past months.

Granny Addie's throat worked. Her lips moved, producing the barest breath of sound.

Clemmie leaned forward. "Granny?"

She could feel her grandmother's fingers flex, gripping hard at hers. *"Bea,"* she said.

TWO

New York, 1999

I t's Clementine, Mother," Clemmie's mother said sharply. "Your grand-daughter. Clementine."

"She's not really awake yet," said the nurse soothingly. "She's had a long day. That lunch party tired her out."

Granny Addie looked from Clementine to her mother and back again, giving herself a little shake, like someone coming out of a long sleep.

"Clem-en-tine," Granny Addie repeated slowly. She sounded out the syllables like someone repeating a lesson learned by rote a long time ago, only half-remembered. "Clem . . . ?"

Clemmie nodded vigorously, not trusting herself to speak.

"Have a sip of water," said the nurse, and held a glass to Granny Addie's lips, helping her drink. When the nurse made to pat her lips with a cloth, Granny Addie objected.

"'s fine," she slurred, and took the cloth from the nurse in a hand that shook just enough to belie her words. She put the napkin down in her lap and contemplated Clemmie, studying her through her spectacles as though attempting to work out a puzzle.

Granny Addie's lips moved. Someone had made an effort to put lipstick on her. It looked unnaturally bright against her pale face, caking in the cracks. "Bobbed," she said. "You've bobbed your hair."

Clemmie put her hand self-consciously to the bottom of her bob. "Yes. It kept getting all over the place the old way."

Dan always used to say that having her around was worse than keeping a cat. Her hair got everywhere. On the sofa, on his suits. He had been joking, of course.

At least, she had thought he was.

"Bea . . ." Granny Addie's voice was slurred and unsteady. "What . . . will . . . say?"

"What?" Clemmie looked to her mother for guidance, but she looked away. "Who?"

"Won't like it," Granny Addie mumbled. "Bea . . ."

"It's the new medication," said the nurse quietly, over Granny Addie's head. "It doesn't agree with her."

Clemmie stroked her grandmother's thin hand, feeling the veins, like cording. "I love you, Granny." As if that could bring her back to herself. "I've missed you."

It was the wrong thing to say. "Miss . . ." echoed Granny Addie. "Miss you . . ." A slow tear rolled down the side of her face, first just one, then another, making a track through the lined and papery skin of her face. She cried soundlessly, her eyes open and her mouth closed.

"Granny." Clemmie chafed her hands. "Granny, please don't cry."

The tears continued, soundlessly.

"Excuse me." Shifting Clemmie out of the way, the nurse leaned over Granny Addie, efficiently blotting her tears, saying, "There, there. You're just all tired out, aren't you? Time for your nap, Mrs. Desborough."

"I'll talk to her doctor tomorrow morning," said Clemmie's mother, her voice strained.

Clemmie stumbled awkwardly to her feet. "Will she be okay?"

The nurse spared Clemmie a glance over her shoulder. "Don't worry, miss. It's just these new pills. It's not anything you did." She leaned back over Granny Addie, arranging a pillow behind her, making sure her diamond brooch wouldn't poke her in the cheek.

The woman in the wheelchair didn't look like Granny Addie. Her face was slack in sleep, the skin hanging loosely from the bone. Like laundry, thought Clemmie, laundry left out in a heap, discarded. It was as if Granny Addie, the Granny Addie she knew, had gone away, leaving her body behind like so many old clothes. All the character that had animated her was gone.

"That's right, Mrs. Desborough," said the nurse in a singsong. "You take a nice rest."

Clemmie cleared her throat. "Is she like this a lot?"

The nurse exchanged a glance with Clemmie's mother. "It's the first time she's been this bad," said the nurse. She put the wheelchair smoothly in gear. "It's probably just these new pills, nothing to worry about. Don't worry, we'll tell her you were here."

As Clemmie watched, she wheeled the chair away, through the living room, past the oblivious, chattering guests, Granny Addie asleep now, her face still damp with tears.

"How long has she been on those pills?" Clemmie demanded.

"I'm not one of your witnesses, Clementine," said her mother crossly. "There's no need to interrogate me."

"Sorry," Clemmie mumbled.

"I'll call the doctor tomorrow. She was a little disoriented earlier, but the doctor said it would pass." Mother clicked her tongue against her teeth. "Clearly, he was wrong."

"Why did Granny keep calling me Bea?"

"For heaven's sake, Clementine, do you think I know everything? I need to talk to Donna. Get people into the dining room, will you? It's just a buffet. I thought something like this might happen."

Her mother disappeared through the den, in the direction of Granny Addie's bedroom. It took Clemmie a moment to realize that Donna must be the nurse.

This was not good.

Clemmie clung to the nurse's soothing words, that the day had been too much, that this was just an aberration, nothing to worry about, but, deep in the pit of her stomach, she knew that it wasn't true. Granny Addie was fading fast. She hadn't been like this the last time Clemmie had seen her. When had that been? Two months ago? Three? No, more. It had been August. She remembered because she had been complaining about the heat, her shell clinging stickily to her suit jacket. Nearly four months. Clemmie's conscience smote her. She lived in the same damn city. She really had no excuse.

Especially since it was Granny Addie, to whom she owed so very much. They had lived here briefly—very briefly—when Clemmie and her mother had moved from California after the divorce. Clemmie had been only four, too young to remember it well, but she did remember the strangeness of it. Her mother had been gone most of the time, and when she was around she was busy studying, cramming for the paralegal course that was meant to be their ticket to independence.

Grandpa Frederick, long since retired, had taken Clemmie for walks in the park, buying her illicit ice-cream cones from the Mister Softee truck. Granny Addie had been busier, occupied with her boards and committees, but she had still found the time to take Clemmie to the Museum of the City of New York, to the dollhouses, a hundred different households in miniature. Most nights, Clemmie's mother wouldn't get home until after bedtime, but Granny Addie was always there to tuck her in, sometimes in going-out clothes, petticoats rustling as she sat down on the side of Addie's bed, bringing with her the scent of expensive powder and old, dried flowers.

She would, Clemmie thought, have been perfectly happy to have had them stay, but Clemmie's mother had found a job and an apartment of her own, a tiny apartment in Yorkville, a second-floor walk-up. The only financial help Mother would accept from Granny Addie had been the cost of Clemmie's private-school tuition. It was arranged between them that in those awkward after-school hours Clemmie would come to the apartment on 85th and 5th. She had done her homework there, had friends over for sleepovers, traded stickers, gossiped on the phone about Buckley boys and Nightingale girls, filled out her college applications at Granny Addie's kitchen table.

Clemmie couldn't imagine a world without Granny Addie in it.

Clemmie swiped at her hair, pushing it back out of her face. Enough. Mother had told her to start herding. She made her way over to Aunt Anna and one of the assorted family-friend group. Granny's accountant, maybe? He looked familiar, but she wasn't sure.

"Sorry to interrupt," she said, baring her teeth in a fake social smile. "I'm supposed to be herding people into the dining room. It's a buffet."

"Oh, goody, no place cards," said Aunt Anna. "I always seem to get stuck next to the biggest bores. You'd think someone was doing it deliberately."

And by "someone" she meant Clemmie's mother.

"No, no place cards this time," said Clemmie. "Will you excuse me? I should go herd people."

Aunt Anna tapped her companion on the shoulder. "Save me a spot, Phil? I just want a word with my niece." Having neatly disposed of Phil, Aunt Anna turned back to Clemmie, her perfectly manicured brows drawing together in concern. "You all right, sweetums? You look like someone's been tap-dancing on your grave."

Clemmie could hear her mother's voice in her head. *Don't tell Aunt Anna anything. You don't know how she'll use it.* Silly. Aunt Anna was Granny Addie's daughter, too. And she'd always been sweet to Clemmie. A little phony, yes, but fundamentally okay.

Clemmie bit her lip, shaking her head. "It's Granny. She's . . . not all there. The nurse says it's normal, that it's just because she's tired, but—"

Suddenly it was all too much, the day, Dan, Granny Addie. A week ago, everything seemed so firmly in place, fiancé, future, family. And now, poof! Where had it all gone? No fiancé, which meant no family; her mother pissy; her grandmother losing her marbles; everything falling apart all around her. The only thing that was constant was her damn BlackBerry. She hated that BlackBerry.

Partner, she told herself; she was going to make partner. Her name on the firm letterhead and a brass plaque outside a corner office. That was supposed to make up for it all. At the moment, she couldn't remember why.

"She didn't even know who I was," Clemmie blurted out. "She called me Bea."

Wine sloshed over the top of Aunt Anna's glass as she juggled to keep her grip. "Fuck," she cursed, swiping at the splotch on her champagne silk sheath with her cocktail napkin. "I just had this dry-cleaned."

"Here." Clemmie took the wineglass from her as Aunt Anna mopped at the damage. "At least it's pretty much the same color?"

"Ha," said Aunt Anna bitterly, retrieving her glass from Clemmie. She looked, Clemmie thought, much older suddenly. Older and harder. Her eyes weren't green like Grandpa Frederick's or brown like Granny Addie's, but a clear, pale blue. "Your mother hasn't told you anything, has she?"

Clemmie's ears pricked up. "About Granny Addie?" Those pills . . . She didn't like this. She didn't like any of it.

Aunt Anna's lips pressed together. "This is *so* like Marjorie." Aunt Anna tapped her Prada-shod foot against Granny Addie's Axminster carpet. "I can't *believe* she didn't tell you."

Fear made Clemmie's skin prickle. "Tell me what?"

Aunt Anna tapped a nail against her arm. "What time do you go into work?"

"Nine thirty," said Clemmie automatically. "Usually. Why?"

Aunt Anna rolled her eyes. "I suppose I'm just lucky you're not a banker. All right. Come see me tomorrow morning, around eight. You have the address?"

"Um, yes, I think so." Her mother was giving them the fish-eye. If there was something about Granny Addie's condition, Clemmie wanted to know it now. "But—"

"Good. We can talk then. Without scrutiny." She smiled broadly at Clemmie's mother, giving a little wave for good measure. Mother did not look pleased. "Tomorrow."

"Aunt Anna—" But her aunt had already drifted away on a fog of expensive perfume. "Damn."

Across the room, Aunt Anna caught Clemmie's eye. *Tomorrow morning,* she mouthed.

And Clemmie nodded "yes."

Trust Aunt Anna to insist on unnecessary melodrama.

Clemmie limped her way over to Aunt Anna's late and annoyed, last night's blister biting into her heel. Aunt Anna's apartment was all the way over on East End Avenue, near the Asphalt Green, about as far away from Granny Addie as she could get and still remain on the East Side. Aunt Anna's was the fifth door down on a long, narrow hallway. Clemmie hit the buzzer harder than she had to.

The door opened, but it wasn't Aunt Anna.

"What are you doing here?" demanded Clemmie.

"Good morning to you, too," said Jon. He was wearing boxers with snow-men on them and a worn T-shirt with the words YALE UNIVERSITY in cracked blue lettering. His legs were bare, lightly fuzzed with brown hair. Clemmie hadn't seen this much of Jon since their childhood days swimming at Aunt Anna's fourth husband's country house. "Anna is letting me stay until I find an apartment."

"Right," said Clemmie slowly. He'd said last night Caitlin had gotten the house. Clemmie wondered if he had been thrown out. "I forgot. Columbia."

"Yep," said Jon. He made a sweeping gesture, reminiscent of Sir Walter Raleigh. "Would you like to come in, or would you prefer to continue dis-cussing my job prospects here on the stoop?"

"In," said Clemmie, squeezing past him. "I wouldn't want you exposing your unmentionables to the world any longer than necessary."

"They're called snowmen," said Jon mildly, closing and locking the door behind her. "And there's nothing unmentionable about them."

Clemmie decided to quit while she was arguably ahead. She unwrapped her maroon cashmere scarf from around her throat. "Is Aunt Anna around? I came to see her."

Jon raised both brows. "I didn't think you were here to see my humble self. Or my snowmen." Clemmie could feel her cheeks heating, the curse of fair skin. Before she could retort, he said, "Anna is still asleep. So you're stuck with me for the moment."

"Oh." So much for *I'll see you at eight.* "Do you think she'll be long?" There was work piling up back at the office.

Jon grimaced. "She took a sleeping pill last night. She's going to be dead to the world for a while."

Her mother would tell her it served her right, listening to Aunt Anna. Clemmie felt like an idiot on multiple levels, standing here, in Aunt Anna's hallway, holding her scarf in her hands with her coat half-unbuttoned. "Look, Jon, if Aunt Anna said anything to you about Granny—"

"Let me take this," said Jon, and relieved her of her scarf. He held out the other hand for her coat.

Clemmie moved back. "I don't really have time. Aunt Anna was going to be tell me about—"

"Bea," said Jon. He took her coat from her and dumped it on a chair, her scarf trailing out below, classic guy hospitality. "I know."

"And I suppose you know who this Bea person is?" Clemmie said sharply.

Jon crossed his arms over his chest, obliterating the lower half of YALE. "What do you know about where your grandmother came from?"

"She came from England," said Clemmie haughtily. She had no idea what this had to do with Granny's medication, but she certainly wasn't going to admit that to Jon. Or his snowmen. "By way of Kenya."

"That's it? 'From England?'"

"Don't forget the Kenya bit. Don't give me that look. You know Granny Addie wasn't exactly big on the childhood reminiscences." Clemmie squeezed her eyes shut, hating herself. "I mean isn't. Crap. Isn't."

Jon raised a brow. "Did you ever ask her anything? About herself? Or her youth?"

"I am a horrible, self-centered, ungrateful granddaughter and I am going straight to hell," said Clemmie through her teeth. "Point taken. She's dying and I suck."

"Clemmie—" Jon scrubbed a hand through his hair. "I'm sorry. I didn't mean it that way. Really."

She could feel the tension crackling between them, old rivalries and complications. And, if she was being honest, old attraction. She could feel the ghosts of their old selves between them, twenty-one and fearless.

That had all been a long time ago. Before Dan. Before Caitlin. Before any of this.

Clemmie took a safe step back, breathing in through her nose, employing all those tricks she had learned to stay calm during difficult depositons. "I'm sorry I snapped at you. I'm just— I really wasn't prepared for how much she's changed."

"Yeah," said Jon. "I know what you mean."

For a moment, they stood in silence, united by mutual memories. Granny Addie playing grandmother to them both, making sure they did their homework, got their applications in on time.

"Does Aunt Anna know anything?" Clemmie asked urgently. "About her condition? She said she had something to tell me and I thought—"

"It's not that," said Jon quickly. "Nothing like that." Clearing his throat, he said, "Would you like some coffee or anything? I know where Anna keeps the good stuff."

"No, that's okay. I'll hit the coffee machine at work. It's not very good, but it's there." Clemmie glanced down the hallway. "I should probably get going anyway. Tell Aunt Anna I was here? Honestly, I'm not really sure why I came."

Mostly to piss off Mother. It wasn't a terribly noble thought, but there it was.

"Last night was tough," said Jon quietly. "For everyone. Anna doesn't usually take sleeping pills."

"What are we going to do when she goes?" Clemmie hadn't meant to say the words, but there they were, stark and cold. She looked down at her hands. "And you're right. I don't know anything about her. I never bothered to ask."

"She didn't volunteer," said Jon.

Clemmie grimaced at him, trying to keep her cool. "Are you being *nice* to me?"

"Don't get used to it." Jon looked at her for a moment, head tilted, considering. He said, slowly, "Can I show you something?"

"That depends on what it is."

"Don't worry," said Jon. "You're not going to get that lucky." Clemmie snorted. Jon jerked his head sideways. "This way."

She followed him into a room that looked like it was ordinarily a study of some kind. The walls were lined with built-in bookcases in a dark wood. There was squishy chair in one corner and a table that looked like it could double as a desk. The room also obviously doubled as the guest room. Clemmie avoided looking at the rumpled sheets on the daybed. There was something weirdly intimate about it. Jon's suitcase, a plain black wheelie, lay on the floor next to the chair, closed but unzipped, the corner of a pair of khakis bulging out of one side.

Last night's blazer was tossed over the arm of the desk chair, still smelling faintly of Granny Addie's apartment: potpourri and lemon oil.

Clemmie nodded to the daybed. "I thought you said I wasn't going to get that lucky."

"Control yourself, you animal you. I'm still a married man. Technically." Kneeling on the bed, Jon scanned the bookshelves, his finger moving from one spine to the next.

Clemmie stood awkwardly behind him, just far enough back to keep her knees from bumping into the bed. "What are you looking for?"

Aunt Anna's library ran heavily towards glossy hardcover coffee table books on art and architecture. She had gotten her degree in art history, Clemmie dimly remembered that. It had been one of the bones of contention between Aunt Anna and Clemmie's mother, that Aunt Anna had gotten her degree and Mother hadn't. And, then, as Mother saw it, Aunt Anna had thrown it all away, pursuing first one man, then another. It was something that had been drummed into Clemmie from an early age, the importance of picking a career and sticking with it, of being self-driven and self-supporting. Being a success. Like Granny Addie.

"This." Jon pulled a large folio-sized book from the shelf, his T-shirt stretching across his back with the movement. For a professor, he kept in pretty good shape. There was something to be said for those free university gym memberships. "Clem? Clemmie?"

"What?" She looked down at the book he was shoving under her nose. There was a castle on the front of the book, atmospherically shot in the midst of a fantastical garden of topiary, the sun setting behind the battlements. *Great Houses of England*?

"She reads!" said Jon.

"I do card tricks, too," said Clemmie. She sat down with it on the daybed, bracing the heavy pages on her knees, trying not to think of her Black-Berry buzzing away in her bag. "What exactly am I meant to be seeing here?"

Jon flipped through the pages with a sure hand, his eyes on the book. "There."

The makers of the book had spared no expense; the paper was glossy and double-weight, with more pictures than text. The page on the left featured a glamour shot of a square building built of golden stone, its dome both echoing and dominating the hills beyond.

"ASHFORD PARK," read the heading on the right-hand page, all big black letters. Beneath it, in a prissy, curly script, was inscribed:

Thou still unravished bower! Token of England's greatest hour!
Ne'er knew I true beauty ere I saw Ashford.
—JOHN KEATS, 1795–1821

Clemmie hadn't realized that the Romantic poets had been for hire for marketing and publicity.

Although the Earls of Ashford trace their heritage back to a Sir Guillaume de Gillecote, the lands comprising the Ashford family seat were first acquired in 1486, following a successful bid on the correct candidate during the Wars of the Roses.

Successive generations of Gillecotes enlarged and expanded the initial structure, turning a Jacobean showhouse into a neo-classical fantasyland. With 135 rooms . . .

"It's pronounced 'Gill-cott,'" said Jon helpfully. "The *G* is hard."

Clemmie looked up from the text. "I don't get it. What does this have to do with the price of tea in China? Or Granny Addie?"

Jon plonked down on the daybed beside her. She could feel the mattress sag, tilting her towards him.

"This," he said, tapping a finger against the dome. "This is where Granny Addie grew up."

THREE

London, 1906

Impossible!" said a female voice. "Simply impossible."

Addie huddled in the hall closet, buried among the coats. The heavy leather coat her father used for motoring formed a wall to her left, the cracks and seams in the leather tracing their own peculiar geography. Her mother's brown duster brushed Addie's cheek, still smelling vaguely of her scent, soap and lilac. Addie scrunched herself up small between the bootjack and a set of old fire irons that someone had meant to be taken to be mended and forgotten.

Usually those fire irons became a castle portcullis or sometimes a garden gate, but today her imaginary worlds had failed her. Camelot with its bright pennants, the hidden gardens of the Hesperides with their golden fruit, Goblin Market with the goblins clucking and clacking, moping and mowing, all were flat and cold. Wrapping her arms around her knees, she squinched her eyes shut, trying to pretend that she wasn't there.

They were coming to take her away, Fernie had told her. An aunt and uncle she had never met, who lived in a place of which she had never heard.

"You'll like it there," Fernie had said tearfully, packing up Addie's dresses, her boots, her pinafores, and, on the very top, where she could reach it easily, her copy of *The Tale of Mrs. Tiggy-Winkle*. Addie was very attached to Mrs. Tiggy-Winkle. "You'll have cousins to play with. Won't that be nice?"

"I'd rather stay with you," Addie had said, wrapping her arms around Fernie's waist.

Fernie was properly Miss Ferncliffe and her governess, but there was nothing governess-like about Fernie. She wrote poetry and sometimes tried it out on Addie, who didn't understand most of it but liked the cadence of Fernie's voice and the way she tilted her head as she read. She was only twenty-two, Fernie, and very pretty, with long red hair that she wore piled on top of her head in loops and puffs that she promised she would teach Addie to make just as soon as Addie was old enough. Her dresses all had pretty flounces on the bottom, and lace trim, and she always smelled of rosewater. Addie wanted to be just like her when she grew up.

"I'd rather that, too," said Fernie gently. The flounce on her dress swished gently against the wood floor as she moved from dresser to bed, tucking Addie's brush and comb, the ones with her initials on them, into the corner of the bag. "But where would I keep you?"

"We can stay here! I'll be a laundress like Mrs. Tiggy-Winkle."

"Oh, sweetheart." Fernie squeezed her in a quick, rose-scented hug. Her lips brushed Addie's hair. "You haven't much luck keeping your own pinafores clean. I wouldn't trust you with anyone else's."

Addie bit her lip, bunching together the front of her pinny to hide the telltale smudges on the fabric. "I'll try harder?"

But Fernie had been obdurate. Usually, she could be wheedled and cajoled, but not on this. Addie's aunt and uncle were coming for her and she was to go with them and be a good girl and *always remember I love you*, Fernie had said, *and that your mother and father loved you, too*.

If they loved her, why had they gone away?

It had been an omnibus, they said, coming around a sharp corner. The night had been dark and wet. Addie's parents, heads lowered, one umbrella shared, had been picking their way back from a concert across the rain-slick streets. They had decided to walk, rather than take a cab; it was like them, everyone agreed. Like them, too, to be too absorbed in their discussion to know where they were going or see the vehicle before it was upon them.

Father had died instantly; Mother had lived long enough to be taken to hospital, but not long enough for Addie to see her. By the time Addie had been told, it was over; they were both gone. Everyone agreed that she wasn't to come to the funeral, that it was too much for a child her age. Instead, she had sat at home, watching the endless rain weep outside the window as Cook sobbed into her pots and Mary, the one maid, clattered up and down, setting out tea and cakes for Mother's and Father's friends who had come to say their final good-byes.

That had been yesterday, and the house was empty again, cold and empty. Mother's papers were still where she had left them, on her writing table in the parlor; Father's pipe was in its saucer. But, already, they had an air of abandonment about them, as though they knew their owners weren't to come back.

It was cold in the closet, cold and damp, surrounded by musty coats that no one would ever wear again.

"*Is* there anyone in this ridiculous house?" There were people in the front hall, a woman and a man. The woman's voice dropped. "I have a bad feeling about this, Charles, a very bad feeling."

"What else is to be done? We are her family." It was a man's voice, clipped, aristocratic, unutterably weary.

"There are places. . . ." It was the woman's voice again.

"Would you have it said that a Gillecote of Ashford was sent to the poor-house?"

"Don't be pompous, Charles," said the woman irritably. "You make me sound like something out of Dickens! Hideous, underbred man. I wasn't suggesting we send her to the poorhouse. But, surely, there are options other than taking her ourselves. What about her mother's people? She must have come from *somewhere*."

"Vera—"

"Or the cousins in Canada. They have so many, they'd scarcely notice another. Good hearty, colonial air. Just the thing, surely."

"I'm not putting a little girl alone on a boat," said the man. Uncle Charles. Addie didn't know anything about him, other than that he was Father's brother and they hadn't seen each other since Father had married Mother. "She'll come to us and that's an end to it."

Addie could hear the click of shoes against the tile of a hallway, the swish of a skirt navigating the narrow corridor between closet and hall table. "I don't like the idea of her in the nursery with our girls. When you think of her parents—"

"My brother," Uncle Charles interjected.

"Half brother. And *that woman*. Do you really think I'd have that woman's child—"

"Child, Vera," said Uncle Charles tiredly. "That child. She's only—what was it? Six? Seven? Young enough to be taught. I have no doubt," he added dryly, "that if anyone can do it, it will be you."

"Addie? Addie?" It was Fernie calling. "Are you hiding?" Addie heard her quick steps come to an abrupt halt. "Oh, I'm so sorry. Have you been waiting long?"

"There was no one to answer the bell." It was the woman's voice, heavy with disapproval.

"I let the servants go. Since—" Fernie's voice caught. She went on determinedly. "You must be Lord and Lady Ashford? Thank you so much for coming for Addie. She's—well, she's as you can imagine. It's been very hard for her. For all of us. It was all so sudden, so unexpected—" Her voice broke.

"Do you have the child ready?" said the woman, breaking off further confidences. "We have the car waiting."

"Yes, everything is ready," said Fernie distractedly. "But Addie— She likes to hide in the closet when she's upset. It's her private place."

The door opened, letting in a pale triangle of light. Addie made herself as small as she could, scrunched up against the back wall of the closet.

"Addie," Fernie said, and there was a pleading note in her voice. "Addie, come and meet your uncle and aunt, Lord and Lady Ashford. Please, darling, do come out."

Reluctantly, Addie unfolded herself from her snug corner, wiggling out between old boots and discarded umbrellas. Her hair had come out of its ribbon and there were dark smudges on her face where she had wiped at her cheeks with dirty hands.

The first person she saw was the aunt, Lady Ashford, who stared at her as though she were a bug caught crawling out of the wainscoting. She wasn't precisely tall, but she seemed to take up a great deal of space. Her hat went up at the sides and down in the middle. There was a feather sprouting from one side, too impossibly purple to have come from any bird Addie could imagine. Lady Ashford wore a fur stole around her shoulders, over a traveling costume of purple and black. Her collar was high and pointy and went up right under her chin, which might be, Addie thought, why she held it quite so high.

Next to her, Uncle Charles seemed faded in comparison, as if he were a watercolor that had been caught in the rain. Addie's father's hair had been blond, too, but Uncle Charles' was several shades lighter, pale blond blending to silver, his eyes a pale blue that looked as though the color had been bleached out of them. Everything about him was tall and thin, from his long, narrow nose to the long, thin hand on his wife's arm.

They were both staring at her. Addie scrunched her shoulders, wishing she had stayed in her closet. They weren't at all like her parents' friends, who bribed her into good humor with gifts of sweets or stood her on a chair and made her recite Fernie's poetry for them, applauding vigorously as she did.

"Say hello to your aunt and uncle, Addie," Fernie said nervously.

"Young ladies," said Lady Ashford, "do not lurk in cupboards."

Addie tucked her chin in. "Then I won't be a young lady," she said defiantly. "I'd much rather be a hedgehog."

It was the sort of remark that made Fernie shake her head and kiss Addie on the cheek and her parents' friends laugh.

The aunt and uncle weren't amused. Lady Ashford looked triumphant. Lord Ashford looked grave.

Lady Ashford gave Lord Ashford a significant look. "Grubbing in the dirt, I see," she said meaningfully.

"Oh, no," said Addie quickly, amazed at this lack of comprehension. "Mrs. Tiggy-Winkle doesn't grub. She washes Lucie's handkerchiefs for her and makes them nice and clean. She washes Henny-penny's stockings and Tabby Kitten's mittens and—"

"Addie," said Fernie, very softly.

"But she does!"

"*Completely* ungoverned," said Lady Ashford. She turned to Fernie. "Have you packed her things?"

Fernie nodded. "I've packed Addie's clothes, but there are still—there are still Mr. and Mrs. Gillecote's things. I didn't know what you would want to do about them, if you want to bring them, or save them for Addie, or—" She looked anxiously to Uncle Charles. "The house was let furnished, but there are, oh, little things. And all their books, of course."

"We shan't be wanting any of that," said Aunt Vera dismissively. "There are books enough at Ashford."

"If you would like to have any of it as a keepsake..." added Uncle Charles to Fernie diplomatically.

Fernie dumbly shook her head. "No, I couldn't. But, surely, Addie should have her mother's books—not to read now, of course, but for when she's older...."

Aunt Vera ignored her. "I assume the child has a coat?"

Addie opened her mouth to protest, but Fernie put her hand on her shoulder and squeezed, hard. Addie glanced up at Fernie and Fernie shook her head, warning her to silence. Addie looked at the aunt and uncle and back at Fernie and held tight to Fernie's hand. She wanted to cry, but she couldn't, not in front of the new aunt with the hard, cold eyes or the uncle who ought to look like her father but didn't.

As Aunt Vera and Uncle Charles' chauffeur fetched Addie's bags, Fernie buttoned Addie into her coat. "Don't worry, darling," she whispered. "Just pretend you're a princess in a tower."

Addie wrapped her arms around Fernie's neck, squeezing as hard as she could, breathing in her rosewater scent for the very last time. "A very high tower."

"But a very brave princess." Fernie squeezed back, then let her go, gently untangling Addie's arms from around her neck. "Wait. Wait here for a moment."

She disappeared in a swirl of skirts and came back again a moment later, breathless, her cheeks pink with exertion.

"Take this," she said, and pushed a thin volume into Addie's hand, cheaply bound in pink, speckled paper.

It was Fernie's own copy of Christina Rossetti's *Goblin Market*.

It was Addie's favorite poem, with all the clucking and clacking and mopping and mowing. She had made Fernie read it to her again and again, acting out the goblins, alternately playing the parts of Lizzie and Laura, the daring sister and the prudent one.

"There." Fernie closed Addie's hands around the book. "Read that and think of me." She leaned forward, lowering her voice. "But if I were you, I wouldn't let your aunt and uncle see it."

Addie tucked it away under her coat. Somehow, she had the feeling that Fernie was right. Quiet and subdued, Addie took her place in Uncle Charles' car.

"Ashford," she heard him tell the driver.

The word echoed in her ears with the thrum of the engine and the rumble of the tires as they pulled away from Guilford Street, rolling their way mile by mile towards the home from which her father had so pointedly run away.

Ashford.

New York, 1999

"Isn't that *Brideshead Revisited*?" Clemmie looked at the image on the page. It was *Masterpiece Theatre* come to life.

"Nope," said Jon. "That was Castle Howard. But close. Same architect."

The golden stone of Ashford Park gleamed in the sunshine, the dome dominating the landscape for miles around. A multitiered flight of stairs led up to the front entrance, a massive doorway dwarfed by its frame of matched columns, overshadowed by a triangular portico. Long wings stretched out on either side, pilaster after pilaster, window after window, all in perfect symmetry. Even squished flat on an eleven-and-a-half-by-eight-inch piece of paper, the house had an imposing feel to it, the sort of place that was designed to overawe the peasantry and impress visiting monarchs.

It didn't look like anyone actually lived in it. It was a showplace, not a home, and certainly not Granny Addie's home.

"You're pulling my leg," Clemmie said. "Unless you're going to tell me that she was a housemaid who made good or something like that."

Jon choked on a laugh. "What have you been reading? Barbara Taylor Bradford?"

"What's wrong with Barbara Taylor Bradford?"

Jon made a face amply illustrative of his feelings.

"Yeah, yeah, whatever. And Terry Pratchett is high literature?" That was the danger: they knew way too much about each other; they always had. That was why they hadn't . . . well. Clemmie poked at the picture. "Can you really see Granny there? I can't."

"Why not?" asked Jon.

Clemmie leafed through the pages. After the big glamour shot of the façade, the next five pages were dedicated to interiors, some whole rooms, others detail shots of intriguing bits of masonry. She couldn't picture Granny Addie there, playing hide and go seek on that great double staircase, with the elaborately carved gallery that ran all around, taking meals in that long, red-walled dining room with the massive silver epergne on the center of the table. There was a detail shot of the epergne, the base made of trumpeting elephants.

There were no private areas, no bedrooms or nurseries. That wouldn't have interested the author of the book.

"She had to grow up somewhere, didn't she?" said Jon reasonably. "Where did you think it was?"

Funny, Clemmie had never really thought about her grandparents coming from anywhere in particular. They just were. Like pillars on a building. You never stopped to ask where the marble had been quarried and how it had been carved. It just was.

Granny sometimes talked about Kenya, about their early days there, getting the hang of the farm, learning how to run a business, but that was all. That was as far back as it went and Clemmie had never thought to inquire further.

"If it makes it better," said Jon, "she wasn't a housemaid, but she was a poor relation. She was the daughter of the sixth earl's younger brother."

Clemmie was reminded of that line from *Spaceballs*, the bit about the father's brother's nephew's cousin's former roommate. *What's that make us? Absolutely nothing!*

Jon was in full lecture mode. "When her parents died in an omnibus accident in 1906, the earl and his wife took her in."

Clemmie did the genealogical math. "So that would make Granny Addie the earl's niece."

"Yup."

Clemmie shook her head. "It doesn't wash, Jon." She pointed at the book. "According to this, it says the Earl of Ashford and his family still live there. If Granny Addie grew up there, why don't we have any contact with them? Why wouldn't she say that she still had family left in England?"

"I gather," said Jon carefully, "that she parted ways with them. There was a falling-out. Why do you think she doesn't talk about this stuff?"

Maybe she would have if Clemmie had been around more. Clemmie shoved that thought aside, wiggling out from under the book. It made her feel better to stand. "In case you haven't noticed, we're not exactly the Brady Bunch. No one in my family is big on talking about their personal lives." Except maybe Aunt Anna, and even she had managed to perfect the art of talking a lot while saying very little. "We don't do the whole sharing thing."

Jon looked up at her from his comfy sprawl on the daybed. "There's a difference between letting it all hang out and normal information flow. I don't know much about my grandparents, but I do know the basic things, like where they grew up"—his face turned grim—"and where they died."

Clemmie tilted her head in inquiry. All this looking down was making her neck hurt. She perched, gingerly, on the corner of the bed.

"Auschwitz. Both my dad's parents." Jon tapped a finger against the corner of the book. "Trust me, I'd trade you."

"It's just—it's too weird," said Clemmie. "It's like something out of a Frances Hodgson Burnett novel."

Jon grinned. "You make a very cute Little Lord Fauntleroy. Especially with the new haircut . . . What was that kid's name?"

Clemmie held up her hands. "Search me. I was always more a *Secret Garden* girl."

Jon plopped the book back in her lap, leaning over her arm to turn the pages.

"You see that?" He was pointing at the massive epergne, the one with all the elephants.

"It would be hard to miss it." He smelled of generic dandruff shampoo, Old Spice, and laundry detergent. Guy smells. Lazy Sunday morning hanging out in bed smells.

She really needed to get back out there on the dating market. Clemmie forced her attention back to what Jon was saying.

"Apparently, Granny Addie's uncle was almost appointed Viceroy of India." At Clemmie's blank look, he explained, "The viceroy was the Governor of India. It's basically playing king on behalf of the king. The viceroy had semi-regal powers. Hence the name. Vice. Roy. Roy from the French, *roi*. Demi-king."

"Your students must love you," said Clemmie dryly. "So what happened?"

Jon grinned. "They appointed someone else. But apparently, Lord Ashford never really got over being passed over. He picked up any Indian knick-knacks he could, to remind people that he might have been there."

"That's quite a knickknack." Clemmie pushed her hair back behind her ears, asking the question that was eating at her. "Jon, how do you know all this?"

"Because I asked."

Clemmie gave him the stare she used on annoying junior associates.

"This is my time period," he reminded her. "Modern Britain. I stumbled on some stuff about the family—your family," he corrected himself, "when I was working on my dissertation. So I asked Granny Addie about it."

"When?" Clemmie asked.

Jon did some mental computation. "It was right after I did my research year in London. That would have been . . . nine years ago? Awhile."

"So you've known this for a long time." Clemmie moved the book away from him and closed it, resting her palms on the cover.

Jon sighed. "Look," he said, and, for a moment, he sounded eerily like Aunt Anna, her favorite expression in her favorite tone. "I think it was easier for Granny Addie to talk to me. I wasn't part of the family. It made things . . . simpler."

Clemmie nodded slowly. "Okay," she said, "I get that." Although she didn't, really. "And you asked."

Jon leaned towards her, bracing an elbow on the bookshelf. "It's not a unique art," he said, his hazel eyes intent on hers. "You can ask, too. If you really want to."

Yes, but would Granny Addie still be able to answer? "That sounds like a dare."

"It wasn't meant to be." Jon levered himself up off the daybed. It felt, somehow, colder without him there. He stood, looking down at her. "Knowledge can be a double-edged sword. You need to decide whether it's worth cutting yourself on it."

"Did you get that out of a fortune cookie?" Clemmie got clumsily to her feet, her legs stiff from sitting. "You have my coat somewhere, right?"

"On the chair. In the hall." Jon followed her out into the hallway as she retrieved her coat. She felt his hands take the back of her coat, relieving the pressure as she tried to struggle into the sleeve. "Are you sure you want to go poking around in the past, Clem?"

Clemmie tugged sharply on the lapels of her coat, pulling it into place. "You do."

"Yes, but I do it for a living." His breath was warm on the back of her neck. "And about people who aren't related to me. You love Addie. Addie loves you. That's the important thing."

She turned, awkwardly, at the wrong moment, so that they bumped together and had to disentangle themselves. "Thanks, so much, Dr. Phil," she said, shoving her hair out of her face. "I'll bear that in mind."

Jon leaned over to fish out her scarf from under the chair, thigh muscles showing to good advantage beneath his snowmen. "I think the appropriate answer to that is probably something along the lines of 'yeah, right.'"

"Strange as it is," said Clemmie, taking the scarf from him, "I think I'm actually glad to have you back."

"Strange as it is," said Jon, reaching around her to unlock the door, "I think I'm actually glad to be back. I'll let you know once I've found a place."

Clemmie wrapped her scarf around her neck, shaking her too-short hair out of the way. "Good luck with the apartment-hunting. Tell Aunt Anna I stopped by."

"Will do." He held the door for her with exaggerated courtesy. "And, hey, if you need me for anything—"

"—I'll think of someone else to call," said Clemmie.

He gave her a thumbs-up and the door swung shut behind him.

It was only after the door had closed that she realized: He had never told her what Aunt Anna meant to tell her. And he had never explained about Bea.

FOUR

Ashford, 1906

Is it true that you were raised by heathens?"

It was Addie's first night at Ashford. She lay wide-awake, her covers pulled up to her chin, doing her very, very best not to cry. She was afraid that if she did, her tears would freeze on her face. The fire in her room had long since burned down and it was bitterly cold. There was no Fernie to fix it for her, no Mother to come kiss her on the temple and tuck the edges of the blanket around her chin.

Addie rolled onto her side, but the creak of the mattress sounded uncomfortably loud in the silence. It was darker than she had ever imagined it could be. The white-painted wardrobe and nightstand were gray shapes in the general gloom. Addie missed the light of the gas lamps shining through her window through the chink in the drapes. She missed the comforting sounds of London, the creak of carriages, the dull rumble of automobiles. There were other sounds here, strange creaks and rustles that made her shrink beneath the sheets for safety.

Imagination was all very well in the daylight, but it was an uncomfortable thing late at night. This was the sort of house where ghosts seemed less a superstition and more a certainty, white ladies and phantom cavaliers and carriages that thundered down the lane with no one driving. Her parents' friends used to have competitions to see who could tell the ghastliest tales, but it had been one thing in the well-lit drawing room of the little house on Guilford Street, quite another here at Ashford, with the strange, keening cry of an unknown animal coming from the woods.

They had arrived at Ashford late, late enough that Addie's only image of the house was a confused impression of burning torches at the entrance and gray stone walls that had seemed to go on forever. There had been servants lined up, waiting for them outside, but Addie hadn't been introduced to them, just shooed along the row, up an endless flight of stairs, and into a hall bigger than her parents' entire house, with a ceiling that went up and up. Addie had craned her head to look back at it, bending back as far as her neck would let her to goggle at the painted people cavorting in tiers so far, far above her.

Don't gawk, had said Aunt Vera.

Aunt Vera was full of don'ts. Don't run, don't fidget, don't disturb your uncle.

Uncle Charles had, in his own way, tried to be kind. *Your father and I used to race up that,* he told her, pointing to the double staircase, although Addie couldn't imagine Uncle Charles racing anywhere.

Don't encourage her, said Aunt Vera. *That's the last thing we need, the children racing around like heathens.*

Uncle Charles patted Addie distractedly on the shoulder and told her he hoped she would be happy at Ashford, then disappeared somewhere behind the curve of the staircase, followed by an imposing personage in a black suit whose conversation was larded with *Your Lordship.*

Yes, yes, Badger, said Uncle Charles. *Have it brought to me.*

She wasn't allowed to climb the curving stair. Addie looked longingly at it over her shoulder as Aunt Vera took her out of the hall along a side way, through room after room, paintings hanging off the silk-hung walls, one on top of the other, in big gilt frames. Despite Aunt Vera's admonition not to gawk, Addie couldn't help it. She had never seen anything like it before, the pictures hung from wires, tilting slightly forward so that they all seemed to be leaning towards her, bowls of fruit and smirking ladies and birds sprawling with their feathers hanging limp over the ends of rustic tables.

There was one picture of two boys that made her stop and pause. The older, tall and thin and blond, gazed solemnly out at the viewer, one elbow resting on a stylized pillar. He was quite old, at least ten, and seemed to feel all the dignity of his advanced years.

But it was the boy next to him who caught Addie's attention. His hair was blond, too, but it was a darker blond, the color of taffy chews. Instead of lying sleek, like the older boy's, it curled in ringlets around his face. He wore a black velvet suit with a lace collar, but his collar had pulled slightly at the side, rumpling. His head was tilted away from the viewer, his attention caught by a butterfly that flapped its wings just out of reach.

His cheeks were flushed and deeply dimpled, his round child's face alight with happiness and interest as he lunged for the butterfly.

It was Father, quite unmistakably Father, even though he was unimaginably young, younger than Addie.

LORD MALTRAVERS AND THE HONORABLE HENRY GILLECOTE, said the brass plaque below, in curly script. Behind Father's shoulder, Addie could see the dome of Ashford Park.

Don't dawdle, said Aunt Vera over her shoulder, and Addie scurried to catch up, her buttoned boots slap, slap, slapping against the floor. It felt somehow comforting to know that Father had lived here, that he had walked these same corridors, chased butterflies in the garden. It made him seem less far away.

At least, it had, just for a moment. But then Aunt Vera had tugged her along again and Addie had found herself spiraling up, up, and up, along a twisty staircase that went around and around for what seemed like forever, pale stone blending into pale stone.

Addie had only the most confused impression of the schoolroom before Aunt Vera herded her into a room she called the day nursery. It was long and rectangular, with windows on two sides and a dollhouse whose sides were open, spilling out a confusion of dolls and furniture, of different eras and sizes.

It seemed, to Addie's tired eyes, to be full of people. There was a girl sprawled across a chair, her feet over one side, and another lying on her stomach by the hearth, flipping through fashion papers and disputing their possession with a rosy-cheeked toddler who seemed to think that they were made to be stepped on. They were all very tall and very blond, except for the baby, who was very small and very blond.

Aunt Vera cleared her throat and they all shot to attention, except the youngest, who was snatched up by a wiry woman in a white pinny.

Nanny, said Aunt Vera. *This is Miss Adeline. You've prepared a room for her? Good. I leave her to you. Diana, your top button needs buttoning.*

Addie thought of Hans Christian Andersen's Ice Queen, turning the world to winter. While Aunt Vera was there, the entire room stood frozen. It wasn't until she said her good nights and sailed out again that the ice cracked and the inhabitants of the room could move and speak again.

The one who had been flipping through the fashion papers started forward. *We've been waiting forever for you to arrive! Did you drive all the way down in the car? Did you—*

Bedtime! said Nanny, clapping her hands. She took the cousin by the shoulders and turned her firmly in the direction she wanted her to go. *No dawdling, Miss Bea. Go along with you.*

The cousin—Bea?—made a comical face over her shoulder at Addie, shrugged, and skipped off.

The older cousin, the one who had been sitting on the chair, nodded at Addie. *See you in the morning!* she said, and was gone, too.

Nanny hoisted the toddler up to her shoulder, where she wiggled, agitating to be put down. *As for you, Miss Adeline,* said Nanny, *you'll sleep here.*

There was something very ominous about the way she said it.

Nanny took her down the same hallway into which Bea and the other cousin had disappeared. There was a cluster of doors and a curious half stair that paused briefly at a landing with two doors before meeting up with another, longer stair. Addie had never seen so many doors. Their house in London had been constructed on far simpler lines; this hallway alone had more rooms than the entirety of Addie's old home put together. And this was just a tiny corner of Ashford. Her mind boggled at it.

Nanny had made sure Addie scrubbed behind her ears and said her prayers, performing the tasks with a sort of grim determination. Then Nanny had shut the door and Addie had been alone. She slipped Fernie's book under her pillow, touching it as though it were a sort of talisman.

If this were home, Fernie would have kissed her good night. If this were home, Mother would be poking her head around the door to see if she were asleep.

That was when the door opened and a slender figure slipped through.

"Is it true that you were raised by heathens?" she demanded, plunking herself down on the foot of Addie's bed. "It did seem unfair that you came in so late, we never got to talk to you. I've been half-dead of curiosity."

She didn't seem half-dead. She seemed incredibly alive and making a large dent at the bottom of Addie's bed. Addie could see her only as a combination of shadows, but she recognized the voice; it was the fashion-paper cousin, the one who had been waiting forever for her to arrive.

Addie wiggled herself up. "You're Bea, aren't you?" she said, unsure what the etiquette was under the circumstances.

"Beatrice, if we're being formal. I was named after a particularly dreary aunt. One of Mother's sisters, so you needn't worry, she's not one of yours. She gave me a miserable little spoon as a christening gift, not even an apostle on it. I do call that mean. Don't you agree?"

At this point, Addie would have agreed to anything. "I suppose," she hedged.

"If one is to be named after dreary aunts, they should at least give good presents," said Bea with authority. "Dodo's left her a tiara, not that it does Dodo any good."

"Dodo?"

"Diana. You met her just now—well, not met, really, but she was there. She's the older of us. Goodness, no one has told you anything, have they?"

Addie shook her head, feeling the tears prickle at the backs of her eyes.

"Well, you needn't worry," said Bea. "I'll take care of you. It's all very dull, really. There's four of us, only Edward is off at school most of the time. Dodo likes horses better than people and Poppy is still at the babbling stage, so she's not terribly much of a conversationalist. How old are you?"

"Almost six." Somehow, Addie had the sense that it was very important to be almost six rather than five. One wouldn't want to be dismissed as still at the babbling stage. "How old are you?"

"I'm just past seven." Bea considered her. "I must say, you don't *look* like a savage."

She sounded deeply disappointed.

"What does a savage look like?" asked Addie.

"Oh, you know, feathers and paint and that sort of thing. Nanny said you were raised by heathens," said her cousin, bouncing on her bed. "Lucky old you. I was raised by Nanny and you can imagine what that's been like. Dull, dull, dull."

It was hard to imagine anywhere Bea was ever being dull; she crackled with energy, like the sky before the storm. She looked more like Uncle Charles, but something about her exuberance reminded Addie just a little bit of Father. The thought made Addie feel warm inside.

"Have you lived here all your life?" she asked shyly.

"Yes, isn't it awful? If we're lucky, they take us to Aunt Agatha in Scotland in August, and it's all grouse grouse grouse. I've only been to London once. You lived in London, didn't you?"

Addie nodded.

"I *am* jealous. What is it like? Is it terribly exciting?" Without waiting for Addie to answer, she leaned forward and confided, "When I am older, I'm going to be a marchioness and live in London and have walnut cake for breakfast *every morning.*"

Addie sensed that she was meant to be impressed by this, but she was missing some key information. "What's a marchioness?" she asked humbly.

Bea wrinkled her brow at her. "The wife of a marquess, of course. A marquess," she said with satisfaction, "is grander than an earl, which means that I will outrank Mama. What's this?" She had found Fernie's copy of *Goblin Market.*

"A book," said Addie warily.

"Silly, I know that! I can tell that much. But what *is* it?"

Addie wiggled herself up into a sitting position. "It's a poem, called *Goblin Market.*"

"Read it to me." There was a rustling as Bea heaved herself off the bed, rummaging for a candle and matches. There was electricity at Ashford, but it hadn't yet made it as far as the nursery. "Here." Bea struck a match and the candle blazed into life.

Addie looked anxiously at the door. "Won't someone see?"

"Nanny sleeps like the dead. Snores, too," confided Bea. "We'd hear her long before she got here."

"All right," said Addie. It was Bea's house; she should know. And it seemed nice to be the one who knew something when she was so ignorant about Ashford and marsh—well, whatever it was. She held up the blanket so Bea could scooch in next to her. "It's about two sisters, Lizzie and Laura. That's Laura."

She tilted the book to show Bea the frontispiece, Laura leaning forward, scissors in hand, preparing to cut off a lock of her long blond hair to barter for the goblin feast. Even in black and white, you could tell that her hair was moonlight pale, like Bea's.

Bea leaned over Addie's shoulder to study the picture. "Are those goblins?" said Bea. "They look more like badgers. You wouldn't believe the trouble we have with badgers."

"I've never seen a badger," Addie admitted shyly. "Only pictures."

Bea frowned. "They don't have them in London, do they? What does it say underneath?"

Addie traced the text with her finger. "It says: 'Buy from us with a golden curl.'" She looked at Bea's blond braid, silver-gilt in the candlelight. "Like yours."

Bea punched the pillow into a more comfortable shape. "What happens?"

"Every day, the goblins march by, shouting 'come buy, come buy.'" Addie didn't need to look at the text to know. It was written on her memory, the goblins marching two together, clucking and clacking, mopping and mowing. "They come with apples and quinces, damsons and blueberries. Laura and Lizzie know they're not supposed to eat it, but Laura can't resist."

"Can't resist *fruit*?" said Bea.

"It's magical fruit," said Addie. She permitted herself a delicious shiver. "Goblin fruit."

"Hmm," said Bea.

"Laura wants it so badly that she cuts off a lock of her hair in exchange for just one peach. But mortals aren't supposed to eat goblin fruit." The poem was very clear on that point. The yearning for it could drive a mortal mad. "Laura gets sicker and sicker, only yearning for goblin fruit she can't have."

"How does it end?"

"Lizzie saves her." Scrunching up her eyes, Addie quoted from memory, "'For there is no friend like a sister / In calm or stormy weather; / To cheer one on the tedious way, / To fetch one if one goes astray, / To lift one if one totters down, / To strengthen whilst one stands.'"

Bea was much struck by this. "How lovely," she breathed. "How perfectly lovely."

In the candlelight, her tilted face looked almost uncannily like Laura's in the woodcut, the shadows making Bea's face older, creating planes and hollows that weren't yet there.

"I used to pretend I had a sister," Addie confided. She caught herself on a yawn. "I called her Lizzie, after the poem."

"You don't need to have a make-believe sister." Impulsively Bea took Addie's hand and squeezed. "You can be my sister."

"You've already got sisters," Addie felt compelled to point out. The day was beginning to catch up with her. She had to cover her mouth to stifle a yawn. "Real ones."

"Dodo?" Bea wrinkled her nose. "She doesn't care for anything but her horses. And Poppy? She's just a baby. No," she said decidedly. "We'll be sisters. Real sisters. We'll be the kind of sisters who save each other from goblins."

Addie liked the sound of that. "From goblins," she said sleepily, "and from aunts."

The last thing she heard before she drifted off to sleep was Bea's laughter, like fairy music in the darkness.

New York, 1999

For all of Clemmie's good intentions, it was more than two weeks before she found the time to see Granny Addie.

It was work again, always work. Reply briefs on the Dallas matter had been due yesterday, so the junior associates had been scurrying, scrounging for case law to refute the opposition's last round. And then there was the London trip, coming up far faster than Clemmie had expected, with too much to prepare in too little time, too many binders and not enough time to read them. Her office looked like a war zone, half-filled coffee cups everywhere, shreds of lettuce under her desk from last night's SeamlessWeb salad, those weird little white circles left by hole punchers blanketing the floor like snow. The cleaning lady who came around the floor at midnight had taken one look inside, seen Clemmie still at her desk, waved, and gone away again.

It felt like heaven to be out of the office.

While she had been working, the seasons had changed, the post-Halloween warm snap giving way to winter. The sky was that chalky gray peculiar to December and there was the scent of wood smoke and roasting pretzels in the air.

On an impulse, she cut down to Madison and bought a bunch of flowers for Granny Addie. She wasn't quite sure what they were, but they were purple and they smelled nice.

Donna took them from her at the door, mmming approvingly. "Your grandma will like these," she said. And, "You can go on in."

"Is she doing better?" asked Clemmie, and was reassured when Donna nodded.

"Better enough to argue with me," said Donna.

Clemmie grinned. "That sounds like her."

Donna went off on rubber-soled shoes to the kitchen, to put the flowers in water, and Clemmie did as she had told her and went on in, through the den and the tiny bathroom that had once been intended for a maid and into Granny Addie's bedroom. The light paper and the chintz-covered chaise longue were still the same, as were the white-painted woodwork and the photographs on the walls, not family pictures, but landscapes, of sunsets somewhere out west. They had always struck Clemmie as slightly incongruous, not at all in Granny Addie's usual taste. Where Granny Addie's sleigh bed had once been there was a hospital bed instead, complete with official-looking buttons and a tray contraption that went back and forth so that she could take her meals in bed.

"Granny?" said Clemmie, hovering in the doorway.

Granny Addie put aside the book she had been reading. "Clemmie!"

Clemmie felt her chest unclench. Granny Addie's voice was weak, but she sounded like herself again. And she knew her.

"Forgive me if I don't get up, darling," she said apologetically. "Donna would have my head."

"Don't move, I'll come to you." Clemmie picked her away across the carpet. "May I?" She indicated the wheelchair next to the bed.

Her grandmother's eyes crinkled. "You always did like chairs with wheels on them. Your grandfather used to wheel you around and around on the chair in his office."

"I'd forgotten about that."

His "office" had really been the room that was now the den, then his study. He had an old swivel chair and he used to spin her around, like the teacups at an amusement park. Clemmie wondered what had happened to that old chair. Thrown out, probably.

She leaned over her grandmother to kiss her wrinkled cheek. "How are you feeling?"

"Like ninety-nine," said Granny Addie. "More importantly, how are you?"

Clemmie bit her lip. "I'm . . . okay. Working hard. You know." She seated herself carefully in her grandmother's wheelchair, smoothing her suit skirt down over her knees. "Granny, the other night, when you weren't yourself . . . you called me Bea. Who was she?"

Granny Addie closed her eyes, and, for a moment, Clemmie was afraid she had nodded off. "My cousin. Bea was my cousin." She considered for a moment, thinking, before saying, abruptly, "We grew up together."

"Were you very close?" Clemmie asked tentatively.

It took Granny Addie a long time to answer. "Very," she said at last. "We were very close. Closer than sisters."

Then why did she never speak of her? Why hadn't Clemmie heard of her before last week?

Because you never asked, said Jon's voice in her head.

"Jon told me you grew up someplace called Ashford," said Clemmie awkwardly. "He showed me a picture. It looked very . . . intimidating."

"It was," said Granny Addie frankly. "It was absolutely terrifying." She touched the back of Addie's hand with one finger. "Open my night-table drawer. No, not that one. The other one. I want to show you something."

"*The Sheik*?" Clemmie held up the first thing she found. It was a lurid 1970s edition with a bare-chested man on the cover. He appeared to be wearing far too much eye makeup. "Granny, really!"

"Don't be such a prude, darling; it's a classic now. Keep looking."

"I'm not sure I should," joked Clemmie. "What else am I going to— Oh."

It was a picture, in black and white. It looked as though it had been folded at one point; there was a crease running down the middle. It was a large picture, nearly the size of a piece of paper from a legal pad. Clemmie recognized the building in the background. Even faded, with bits rubbed off, it was unmistakably Ashford Park.

Unless it was Brideshead, but she didn't think so. That wasn't Jeremy Irons out front.

"That," said Granny Addie, "is Ashford."

"May I?" said Clemmie, and drew the picture out from the drawer. On closer consideration, it had to be a reprint of an older picture; the glossy paper felt too thick to be anything but modern and the picture had the blurry quality of an old photograph enlarged and remastered.

There was a whole grouping of people in the foreground, posed around a man and a woman, the man seated, the woman standing.

"That's Uncle Charles," said Granny Addie, pointing.

The sixth Earl of Ashford. He looked the part: tall, thin, and imposing, immaculately garbed in a dark suit.

"Where are you?" Clemmie asked loyally.

Granny Addie readjusted her glasses. "There I am," she said, pointing at a dark blur off to one side. "Behind Bea. That's Dodo there on the side, and Poppy in the front—she was the youngest—and Edward right behind Uncle Charles. This was taken in 1908. Two years after I came to Ashford."

Two years after, but Granny Addie still looked curiously out of place in the family portrait. It took Clemmie a moment to realize why: Addie's was the only dark head among the lot. It made her look as though she were blending into the shrubbery in the background. It didn't help that she was standing off to the side, half-hidden behind her cousin.

Clemmie tried to get a look at the famous Bea, but her grandmother's favorite cousin had turned at the last moment to say something over her shoulder, giving only an impression of blond, blond hair and a profile blurred by movement.

"Why didn't you frame it, Granny?" The piano was covered with family pictures, but none before Kenya. "You look cute."

Clemmie slid the picture back into the drawer. There was another underneath it, a studio portrait of a woman, her head tilted. Her pale hair was crimped in stylized waves around her face and her pale eyes gazed soulfully into the distance. She looked, somehow, strangely familiar, her cheekbones, the shape of her lips, as if Clemmie had seen her somewhere before.

"I should have told you more." Her grandmother's voice was scratchy. Clemmie looked up in surprise. "I've been selfish."

Dropping the picture, Clemmie bumped the drawer closed. "No! I've been selfish. It's always me, me, me. I never really asked you about you. And I should have, years ago."

Granny Addie touched her cheek with a shaky finger. "I like you, you, you."

"You have to like me. You're my granny."

"I would have liked you anyway. You were such a solemn little girl, so hardworking. So quiet. You reminded me of me." She smiled a crooked little smile. "But your face is pure Bea. The world does work in strange ways."

"I have Grandpa's eyes," Clemmie said quickly. It was always a family party game, who had someone's nose or someone else's chin. It was freely acknowledged that any green eyes came from Grandpa Frederick.

"So you do."

"Did you meet Grandpa Frederick at Ashford?" asked Clemmie. She felt like a toddler trying out a new word. Ashford. Ash-ford.

"Yes. Yes," said Granny Addie. "I suppose I did."

"How?" asked Clemmie. "You never told me." Just Jon. Clemmie pushed aside the uncharitable thought. What was it he had said? *I asked?* Well, she was asking now.

Not like it was a competition or anything.

"It's a rather silly story," said Granny Addie.

Clemmie scooted the wheelchair closer. "I like silly," she said encouragingly. Goodness only knew, she could use some silly.

"Let's see." Granny Addie settled back against her pillows, trying to figure out where to begin. "It was the night of my cousin Dodo's coming-out dance. Aunt Vera picked a date late in the Season. Dodo's ball would be the end of the Season and the one everyone remembered afterwards. And so it was, although not quite as Aunt Vera intended."

After all this time, Granny Addie looked rather maliciously pleased at the memory.

"I take it you didn't overly adore Aunt Vera?"

"The feeling was mutual," said Granny Addie. "Aunt Vera had the dance at Ashford. I think she thought Dodo would make less of a cake of herself in the country. Dodo," Granny Addie confided, "wasn't the most graceful of girls."

"With a name like Dodo . . ." Clemmie muttered.

"Her real name was Diana, but I don't think anyone ever called her that—except Aunt Vera. She wasn't one for pet names."

"So you went to the ball . . ." Clemmie prompted.

Granny Addie shook her head. "Bea and I weren't allowed to go. We were—how old were we? I was only thirteen, nearly fourteen, but Bea was fifteen and thought herself very grown-up. Oh, how she raged!"

"If you weren't at the party, how did you meet Grandpa Frederick?"

Granny Addie's lips turned up at the corners. "It was all the fault of Binky, the nursery mouse. . . ."

FIVE

Ashford, 1914

Ⅰt *is* unfair," said Bea, dropping onto the sofa hard enough to make dust rise from the cushions.

It was the night of Dodo's ball. Left out of the fun, Addie and Bea were moping in the nursery. They had watched the preparations over the preceding weeks: crates of champagne motored in from Berry Bros., ices from London, linens from Harrods. They had benefited from the bounty as Cook experimented with new recipes, dainties to please the most jaded London palates. But today the junior members of the nursery had been summarily banished from the kitchens, their trick of begging for treats being deemed rather less adorable than usual. Cook was usually a friend and ally; today she had dismissed them with a crisp *Lady Ashford wouldn't like your being down here.*

The gardens were swarming with footmen hanging Chinese lanterns; Josh, their favorite groom, had his hands full with the sudden influx of strange horses down for tomorrow's hunt; even the summerhouse wasn't safe, having been colonized by a string quartet planted there like the last outpost of empire for those stragglers who braved the chill of the gardens.

It ought to have felt impossibly gay, like something out of a fairy tale. It didn't. All week long, as Aunt Vera had been meeting with Cook and Badger, Uncle Charles had been having his own meetings, tense ones, private ones, with other members of the Cabinet. They weren't supposed to know about that, up in the nursery, but Addie had watched the cars come and go, a long trip from London for a few hours' meeting, their hats tipped low over worried faces. She had recognized some from the papers. Others she didn't know at all; she only knew they were important from the way Uncle Charles greeted them, from the worry lines on their faces.

Just last week, she had heard Uncle Charles and Aunt Vera quarreling, a rare circumstance. *It's a bloody ball,* she had heard Uncle Charles say, and that had been shock enough. Uncle Charles never cursed in front of Aunt Vera. *A bloody ball when—*

For heaven's sake, Aunt Vera had said, in much the same tone she had used, all those years ago, when trying to have Addie dispatched to the Canadian cousins, *it's not as though it was an English duke killed. The Continent is overrun with princelings. They'll scarcely miss one.*

They've missed this one, Uncle Charles had said darkly, and Aunt Vera had made a snorting noise and reminded him that princes were princes, but daughters were daughters and had to be launched, regardless of the inconvenient posturings of foreign powers.

Aunt Vera hustled Dodo to the dressmaker, but the foreign powers continued to posture, the telegrams mounted on Uncle Charles' desk, and, up in the nursery, Bea continued to sulk.

"It's not fair," Bea said again. "All that fuss and us up here."

"We'll have our turn," Addie said, although she knew that wasn't entirely true.

Bea would have her turn. Addie knew herself to be the poor relation, the charity girl in the nursery, and although Bea might not realize it, she had a fairly shrewd idea that Aunt Vera wasn't going to be donning the family tiara for her benefit. When the time came, it was Bea who was destined for chiffon and diamonds, not she. Aunt Vera made no secret of her feelings about Addie's presence at Ashford.

She had been at Ashford for eight years now, more than half her life. It was hard now to remember how strange it had all been when she had first arrived, the scale of it, the assumptions, the rules. Bea had been her map and her guide, taking Addie under her wing as a sort of prized pet. If her situation was a comfortable one, she owed that, in large part, to Bea.

They lived, mostly, in the nursery, a large, sunny room at the top of the house. The walls were papered in a faded print of flowers, climbing roses that they used to pretend would grow and flower when they weren't looking. There were carpets scattered across the floor, rejects, mainly, from the main house, as were the squishy sofa with its snagged silk upholstery, the wide, chintz-covered chairs, and a particularly impractical stool with gold legs that was frequently pressed into service as a makeshift throne.

Along one wall, they had their menagerie: a hedgehog named Tiggy, a rather drowsy rabbit named Lapin, and the nursery darling, a white mouse unimaginatively titled Bianca, although, in the nursery argot, her name had long since been shortened to Binky. Next to Binky's cage presided Rosinante, the nursery rocking horse, who gazed nearsightedly out at the nursery through filmed glass eyes.

Sometimes, it felt like forever, as if the nursery were its own little island, cut off from the rest of the world, rather like Ashford itself, unchanged and unchanging.

It was that very quality that chafed at Bea. Bea kicked out at Rosie with a booted foot, sending him rocking back and forth. "They might at least have let us come down for dinner," she groused.

"With thirty at table and two of them dukes? Not very likely! Think of this as practice," Addie suggested. "If they get it wrong for Dodo, they can get it right for you."

Despite all the fuss over Dodo, they all knew the truth, that Dodo was only a rehearsal for Bea. Bea had all her mother's drive, as well as that elusive quality her mother lacked, the quality known in men as charisma and in women as charm.

"Dodo," brooded Bea. "It's not as if she even enjoys it. She'd be happier if they let her make her debut from the back of a horse!"

Addie giggled. "Think of it. Poor old Euclid slipping and sliding on the ballroom floor. Badger would have a fit."

Badger was the butler, and a very grand personage. His real name was Battinger, but subsequent generations of Ashford children had shortened it to Badger and Badger he remained.

Bea permitted herself, reluctantly, to smile. "It would be a sight, wouldn't it? They're just lucky they got her out of her habit and into a gown. And in the meantime we're left moldering up here."

"It's hardly the Château d'If."

Bea gestured tragically towards Binky's cage. "We even have a mouse. What more proof do you need?"

Addie was unmoved. "Get a teaspoon. We'll dig our way out."

"Oh, ha, ha. You want to go to the ball, don't you, Binkers?" Bea crooned, bending over Binky's cage. She scooped Binky up out of her comfortable nest of shavings. "I think it's utter rubbish that Edward gets to go and we don't."

"He is almost eighteen. And he does look so very grown-up." She felt again that little shiver of unease. She'd heard Uncle Charles speaking with Edward, quite seriously, about the possibility of a war. At almost eighteen, Edward would be fighting. It was impossible to think of Edward, Edward just out of Eton, leading battalions, urging men into battle.

"I look at least as old as he does," protested Bea.

"Truuuuue," said Addie slowly. They were only a year and a half apart, but at fifteen Bea looked far older than Addie's still childish thirteen. "But your mother would throw you out on the spot."

"We could dress ourselves up as footmen," Bea said with relish, "and go that way."

"Very short footmen."

"Only you." Bea lessened the sting with a hug. "Traveling musicians, then."

Addie tucked her legs up under her, hugging the mangled pillow. "With long, loopy mustaches. You mustn't forget the loopy mustaches."

Outside the window, she could hear the sounds of the musicians practicing, warming up their instruments for the dance that would follow Dodo's grand descent to the ballroom and adulthood.

Pushing up off the sofa, Bea wandered towards the window. The nursery looked over the back, across the gardens, where Chinese lanterns sparkled like little stars, making up constellations never dreamed of by any astronomer. She stood there, slowly stroking Binky's back, looking out over the gardens.

Addie joined her there, resting her elbows on the sill. It had been a miserably cold and rainy summer, but it was clear tonight, the breeze bringing with it the smell of flowers from the garden. "Do you think it's true they've got the Prince of Wales to come?" she asked idly.

"Why don't we go find out?" Bea's face was alight with mischief. "They just said we couldn't come to the dance. They didn't say we couldn't *watch* it."

Addie had a bad feeling about this. "Bea, but what—"

"They'll never see us." She was already moving towards the door. "If we hide behind the balustrade, they'll have no idea."

"Aren't we a little old for that?"

Bea waggled her eyebrows. "If we're too young for the ball, we can't be too old for looking through the railings, can we?"

Addie sensed that there was something to be desired in her logic. "If we're caught..."

"We won't be," Bea said with assurance.

Addie let out her breath in a long sigh. "At least leave Binky, then."

"Nonsense," said Bea. "Binky wants to see, too, don't you, Binkers?" She lifted her up to Addie. "See, she's even worn white for the occasion, poor thing."

Binky blinked pathetically, her little red eyes darting first one way, then the other.

"If you keep doing that, she will make a mess in your hand," Addie warned, holding out a hand for her. "You know she doesn't like to be waved about."

Bea slipped Binky into her pinafore pocket. "Here. Now she has a tidy little balcony view, like a dowager at the opera. All she needs are the opera glasses."

Binky's face just poked out over the pocket flap. Bea was right; she did look rather like one of the dowagers of Aunt Vera's acquaintance.

Addie giggled. "I've never noticed it before, but Binky is the spit of Lady Rushworth. She has the same nervous, whiskery look."

"Good blood," said Bea solemnly. "It does show."

They both convulsed with giggles. "Good blood" was one of Aunt Vera's favorite topics.

"Onward?" said Bea.

Addie nodded. "Onward."

Still giggling, they tiptoed out of the nursery. They had done this before, when they were smaller, during Aunt Vera's house parties, hiding themselves behind a bust of the second earl that conveniently blocked them from view on the gallery that stretched above the Great Hall. The scent of flowers reached them even before they arrived at the gallery. Aunt Vera had denuded hothouses for miles around, ordering in blooms from as far away as London. On top of that were the perfumes of all the guests, some laid on with a heavy hand to disguise other, more natural scents.

The girls settled themselves behind their old friend the second earl, one to each side.

"Can you see?" Addie whispered.

"Yes. You?"

Aunt Vera and Uncle Charles presided from the landing in the center of the staircase as guests, announced by Badger, processed up one side and then back down the other, earning themselves a glass of champagne for their labors. They did look very grand up there, Aunt Vera in her diamonds, Uncle Charles in his medals, various orders of this and that. The signs of fatigue were there, in the new silver at his temples, the lines on either side of his mouth, but nothing could take away from the straightness of his spine, the air of authority he wore as naturally as his dinner jacket.

But the real surprise was Dodo.

Dodo had been transformed. Aunt Vera had wrestled her out of her tatty old riding habit and into a frock of white satin, overlaid with a silvery sort of tulle that gave her a deceptively ethereal air. She didn't look like someone who was happiest mucking out a stall; she looked like she dined on ambrosia and slept on thistledown. Like all the Gillecotes, she was tall and thin; the cleverness of Aunt Vera's dressmaker had contrived to make Dodo elegant rather than angular.

She was still Dodo, though. Addie heard her "haw-haw" laugh all the way up from the balcony and saw Aunt Vera stiffen beneath her layers of diamonds and lace.

At precisely the stroke of eight, Aunt Vera nodded to Badger, who closed the great doors. This served as a signal to the musicians, who struck a slightly ragged fanfare, and the guests settled into an expectant hush. Addie had a slight advantage over the guests; she had seen this all performed in rehearsal. She knew what was to come next.

At least, she thought she knew.

A footman appeared next to Uncle Charles, with crystal glasses on a silver tray. Downstairs, in the hall, identically garbed footmen were circulating with identical trays, handing champagne out to the guests in preparation for the toast, in preparation for the moment when Dodo, dull, horsey Dodo, so unexpectedly brushed into beauty, would be officially launched into the World.

Uncle Charles raised his glass and the room fell silent. Once on the public stage, Uncle Charles, who ceded so much in private life to Aunt Vera, had what could only be called a presence. Next to him, Aunt Vera looked small and fussy.

"I should like to thank you for joining us here today," he said, and it was as if he were personally speaking to each person in the room.

Next to Addie, Bea slipped Binky out of her pocket. She had that look on her face again, the one that meant deviltry was afoot.

Addie gave her a warning look. "Don't," she whispered.

Bea looked at her with limpid, innocent eyes. "Don't what? Binkers just wants a better view, don't you, Binks?"

"—to raise a toast—" Uncle Charles was saying.

"Oh, bother! She's made a mess." Bea shook her hand and Binky went flying.

"—to my daughter—"

"Bea—no!" Binky hit the ground running. "Binky!"

"—Diana—"

"Binky," Addie hissed, but it was already too late. Binky was off like a shot, charging straight for the stairs. "Binky, no!"

It was unclear who saw her first. By the time Uncle Charles instructed his guests to raise their glasses, the first shriek had already occurred, then another. Glass shattered as champagne glasses dropped to the ground, one after the other. Ladies rushed for chairs, for the stairs, for any higher ground they could find. At a gesture from Aunt Vera, the musicians struck up "Rule, Britannia!" of all things, but their distracted plucking, rather than masking the disaster, only added to the general cacophony.

Someone had to get Binky back. Addie didn't look to see if Bea followed. She set off after the mouse, dodging startled party guests, tracking her progress by the sound of shrieks and shattering champagne glasses.

"Binky!" she called, interspersed with "So sorry!" and "Pardon me!"

Perhaps it was stupid; it probably was; but Binky was her mouse and she couldn't let her be squished.

"I assume this is what you're looking for?"

She skidded to a halt as a hand stretched out before her, a bit of black sleeve, a white cuff with a carnelian cuff link. There was an oval signet ring, a heavy thing of very yellow gold, deeply carved. Above it poked out a familiar small, pink nose.

Addie looked up and saw a male face, lips creased with amusement beneath a narrow mustache. His eyes were a curious mix of green and brown, like moss and peat mixed together. Winded, she gaped stupidly up at him.

"Yours, I presume?" he said, and held out Binky to her.

SIX

New York, 1999

So it was love at first mouse?" said Clemmie.

Granny Addie didn't answer. She had slipped into the easy sleep of old age, her lids purple and swollen, her mouth slightly ajar.

Carefully, making sure not to bump the bed, Clemmie leaned over her, making sure that her breathing was regular, her color still good. Clemmie's mother said this happened more and more these days, that Granny Addie would doze off mid-sentence, waking up again to pick up where she'd left off—or talking about something else entirely, finishing a conversation begun in a dream.

Clemmie sat herself gingerly back down in the chair. Even though it had been dark for hours, it was relatively early yet, not quite eight. She could give it a little time before going home to pack.

It felt good just to sit.

The shades were still up and through them she could see the lights of the building across the way. Through the windows, scenes in miniature were being played out, people coming home from work, families sitting down to dinner. Clemmie wrapped her arms around herself, leaning her head against the side of the chair. There was a strange sort of melancholy that came of looking into other people's lives, watching them from the outside. It made her miss Dan.

Well, maybe not Dan himself. She was surprised at how little a gap he had left in her life, how little she thought of him, of him as him. But she missed the idea of him. She missed what he had represented.

Was it so wrong to want someone? Someone to call when she was stuck at the office, someone to snuggle up against on cold nights, someone who would remind her that there was a life outside of work. For a moment, she had thought she had that with Dan, even if Dan himself was, well, Dan. But he had seemed so sure, sure enough for both of them, and just having someone else in her life, even if she wasn't entirely sure it was the right someone else, had made her feel more complete, more comfortable in her own skin.

He had shown up at a time when she was beginning to feel a little panicky, suddenly aware that her friends weren't just marrying around her, they were having children already, and here she was, married to her desk, without a date in sight.

She had dated in college and law school, but none of them had seemed to last. At the time, it didn't matter; she had plenty of time, years and years for that. Her mother had pounded into her the importance of being self-motivated and self-supporting. Marriage was the kind of thing that just happened; a career was something you had to work at.

But it hadn't just happened, not for her. There had been a brief fling with another associate her second year at the firm and then nothing. Nothing for a long, long time. She had gone on the odd blind date, set up by college friends and colleagues, some awful, some okay, but none accompanied by a blinding clap of thunder. She had gone to cocktail parties—when her work schedule permitted—and been seated awkwardly next to the token single man at married friends' Saturday night dinner parties, but, at the end of the day, she'd always found herself going home alone.

And then along came Dan.

Dan was an expert witness called in to advise her team on an IP case. As a fifth year, Clemmie was the most senior associate involved, and she didn't know her UNIX from her eunuchs. Dan had found that hysterically funny, far funnier than the weak joke warranted. He had invited her for coffee, and

Clemmie, more for the caffeine than for the company, had said yes. She hadn't realized that when he said "coffee" he meant *coffee*.

They'd gone downstairs to the Starbucks next door and he'd told her all about himself. He had his PhD in computer science from Yale, he told her, and his computer start-up was creating—something or other. Clemmie, who already knew all this from his bio, wondered why he was telling her until, hesitantly, he'd asked her what she thought about dinner.

Mine generally comes from a plastic bag delivered to the lobby, she'd said.

Want to do something wild and crazy and have some with me? he said.

So she had.

His life couldn't have been more different from hers. As CTO of an Internet start-up, he'd knock off half a day to play foosball, then work forty-eight hours straight, not because he had to, but because he wanted to. He got her out of the office on weekends, taking her places she hadn't realized existed within reach of Manhattan: apple-picking, Renaissance fairs, Scottish games. His friends threw *Lord of the Rings* parties and brewed their own beer.

Bemused, Clemmie had come along for the ride. It was entirely out of the blue, and she had never thought it would last, but one month turned into two, and then into a year, and somehow, she had a toothbrush at his apartment and contact-lens solution under his sink. He had proposed with a candy ring, a big cherry one.

She had looked at it and thought, Is this it? Not the ring, but Dan, everything. Shouldn't she feel . . . more? Not the rapturous passion promised by romance novels, but some sort of deep joy and conviction.

Sometimes, she wondered if everyone else was just faking it, if they felt this way, too, and were just better at hiding it, or fooling themselves. But then there were Granny and Grandpa, and however much Clemmie might allow for rose-colored glasses or selective retelling, the look on Granny's face when she talked about Grandpa Frederick—Grandpa Frederick and that silly mouse—couldn't be feigned.

How did one go about finding a true love? If such a thing existed, that was. Everything else in Clemmie's life she had been able to work for or study for, but not this. It seemed like it happened completely at random—or sometimes not at all.

Elsewhere in the apartment, a clock chimed, eight high, metallic pings, one after the other.

Clemmie pushed the chair back carefully. Her grandmother was fast asleep, her white head against the pillows. Leaning over, Clemmie pulled up the covers, tucking in her grandmother as her grandmother used to tuck her.

"Good night, Granny," she said softly. "Sleep well."

Her grandmother slept on, smiling slightly in her sleep. Clemmie wondered if she was dreaming about Grandpa Frederick.

Maybe Clemmie needed a mouse.

Ashford, 1914

"It made a jolly crash," said Bea with relish. "Did you see the look on Aunt Agatha's face?"

It wasn't the look on Aunt Agatha's face that had stayed with Addie but Aunt Vera's. It was a look that promised murder, or at least some sort of sufficiently gruesome retribution. Addie counted herself lucky that racks and thumbscrews had gone out of fashion.

It had taken the footmen quite some time to restore order, sweeping up the broken glass, administering hartshorn to those who had fainted. Aunt Vera had dealt with the whole affair like a viceroy's wife. Without faltering for a moment, she had swept the entire party off to the long drawing room that spanned the back of the house. It wasn't ideal for dancing, being too narrow, but with the rapid removal of unnecessary furnishings and some of the party spilling over into the gardens she had managed to create the impression that this had been her intent all along. With a smile on her face, she had chatted up dignitaries, pushed awkward young men in the direction of Dodo, and agreed that, yes, it really was too amusing.

This they had heard via Edward, who had stopped off at the nursery to report and commiserate. Although perhaps "commiserate" wasn't quite the right word. *Jolly glad I'm not in your shoes* was the phrase that had been used.

Addie didn't particularly want to be in her own shoes either.

"Poor Dodo," she said. "And when she was looking so pretty."

"Nonsense," said Bea. "It's done her a favor. People will be talking about her ball for months. Years, even."

"Yes, but not in the right way." The fact that poor Dodo herself had had nothing to do with the disaster wouldn't factor into it; the story would grow and spread and Dodo would be the debutante with the mouse from now unto the ends of the earth. Addie knit her fingers together. "I do wonder what Aunt Vera is going to do with me."

Bea's face softened. "Poor you," she said. "I hadn't thought. I'll tell them it's my fault. It was."

Addie shook her head. "They'll never believe it. Your mother still thinks of me as a cuckoo in the nest."

"A very creditable cuckoo," said Bea encouragingly.

"Not at the moment," said Addie glumly. "Your mother will say it just shows. She's always waiting for me to sprout socialist tendencies and bring shame upon the family name." No matter how she tried to make a joke of it, they both knew it was true. No matter how hard she tried, she would always be suspect.

"I'm so sorry," said Bea. "I shouldn't've—well, never mind." She chewed on the side of a nail, her only unlovely habit.

"I doubt they'll hang, draw, and quarter me," said Addie, trying to make her cousin feel better. "The worst that can happen is that they'll stop my pocket money again. I can make do without penny bars for a week."

"You can have all mine," said Bea. "All mine with interest."

"Bea," said Addie slowly. "I was wondering . . ."

"What?"

"Never mind." It was a foolish question. Of course Bea hadn't let Binky go on purpose. Instead, she said, "I'm going to go for a walk. It's too maddening being cooped in here, waiting for my fate."

"What if you run into *them*?" said Bea, sitting up on the sofa, the ends of the shawl dangling across her legs.

"They shouldn't be back for ages." Since Dodo showed to best advantage on horseback, Aunt Vera had got together a hunt, on the theory that Dodo's good seat might win her what her dancing wouldn't.

"Shall I come with you?" A clear sign that Bea was feeling remorseful. She hated country walks.

Addie glanced out the window. The morning's rain had turned into a fine mist. Perfect walking weather.

"That's all right." She slid into an old beige coat, a long, narrow duster that had once been worn by Dodo. It was too long on her and the sleeves flapped over her hands, but it would keep the mist off. "I'd rather be alone."

Bea subsided against the sofa cushions. She looked up over the edge of a month-old *Tatler.* "If you change your mind . . ."

"I'll be back in a bit," said Addie. "Happy reading."

Bea's head disappeared behind the magazine.

Addie took the side stairs down. After eight years at Ashford, she knew all the ins and outs, all the twists and turnings. Nursery life at Ashford felt a bit like being in the wings of a theatrical production; all their doings took place around the main stage set and seldom in it. She and Bea and Poppy roamed free around the outskirts of the house, through the back ways and the kitchens, seldom penetrating into those grand rooms on the first floor that had so overawed Addie on her first evening at Ashford.

Now that Dodo was "out," she had graduated from the nursery to a bedroom on the second floor; Bea would follow in a little more than a year. Addie tried not to think about that. It was impossible to imagine the nursery without Bea. Whatever Bea thought, Addie knew that Aunt Vera was unlikely to include her in any of her plans; she had grand designs for Bea, designs in which a tagalong cousin had no place.

There had been talk recently of sending Bea to Paris for a year, for polish, to learn a little French, spend some time copying Great Works at the Louvre, and generally do whatever one did on one's pre-debutante year abroad. Dodo had gone to Munich, but with the news in the papers what it was, it seemed unlikely that Uncle Charles would send Bea to Germany.

"You'll come with me, of course," Bea had said when she told Addie about the Paris plan, but, more than ever, it seemed unlikely.

Not after last night's incident.

Addie let herself out through a side door, into the kitchen garden, rich with the scents of lavender and thyme. Addie lifted her face to the sky, relishing the feel of the light mist against her skin. Skirting the stone-walled kitchen garden, she crunched her way down the graveled path to the boxwood maze, breathing in the familiar scents of damp earth and old stones.

Mist lay heavy over the hedges. The gardens appeared to be deserted, except for a bird that perched on a yew hedge, regarding Addie with beady black eyes. With a scornful glance, it cawed and flapped away.

Obviously, it had heard about the mouse incident, too.

Addie stuck her hands in the pockets of Dodo's coat, kicking at the pebbles with the toe of her boot, trying not to think about just how furious Aunt Vera had been and just how serious her retribution might be. The delay was an additional form of torture, although, Addie knew, not by design. It was simply that with a household full of guests, punishing a wayward niece was a pleasure to be delayed until one's duty as hostess had been done. There had been telegrams this morning, too, telegrams that had sent Uncle Charles into his study with a frown that boded worse troubles than mice in the offing.

What would her punishment be? Not the pocket money; for all her brave words to Bea, that was for minor infractions. Every now and again, Aunt Vera liked to threaten to send her to the cousins in Canada, but that was unlikely.

She rounded the side of the maze and skidded to avoid plunging directly into someone coming from the opposite direction.

She had only a vague impression of a tweed jacket and brass buttons as a pair of hands grasped her shoulder, setting her straight. "Steady on, there," said a friendly male voice.

"I'm so sorry. I didn't mean to barge into you." Addie hastily extricated herself. "I should have been looking—"

"I think I was the one who bumped into you."

It was the man from last night. The man who had rescued Binky for her. He was in tweeds today, not evening dress, but she recognized those laughing green eyes.

He recognized her at just about the same time. "I say, you're the girl with the mouse!"

Addie ducked her head. "To my eternal shame and discredit."

She heard him chuckle. "I don't believe we met properly last night," he said. "So we might as well introduce ourselves improperly now. I go by Frederick Desborough."

He pressed a hand to his chest and bowed with a mock formality that made Addie giggle despite herself.

"Mr. Desborough." She knew she ought to match his gesture with one of her own, that she ought to sweep into a mock court curtsy, but instead she stuck her hands into her pockets and jerked her chin in an awkward little bob that was almost a nod, but not quite. "I'm Adeline Gillecote."

"Miss Adeline." He looked at her quizzically, taking in her rumpled hair, Dodo's old coat. "You're not Miss Gillecote's sister?"

"Oh, no," said Addie quickly. There was Dodo, tall and blond like Uncle Charles, and Bea, and Gillecotes going back unto the ends of the earth—or at least the Norman Conquest. And then you had her. Little and brown, Aunt Vera called her. "That's Bea and Poppy. I'm just the cousin."

Mr. Desborough raised an eyebrow. "*The* cousin? Is that a title or a position?"

"More the latter." Addie tried to make a joke of it. "I'm a sort of a feature of the nursery. Like the rocking horse. Every nursery needs a cousin. Just think of *Jane Eyre*."

"I hope it's not that kind of nursery," said Mr. Desborough.

"I'm only locked up in the Red Room once a week now," Addie said, and was amazed at her own nerve. There was something about Mr. Desborough, though, that made him terribly easy to talk to, not like an adult at all. "Shouldn't you be out with the others?" she asked shyly.

"You mean the hunting party? I can't. Doctor's orders."

He flapped an elbow and Addie realized, for the first time, that his left arm was in a silk sling, cleverly hidden under the drape of his jacket.

"What happened?'

"I had a disagreement with a fence at Melton. It won." Addie was duly impressed. Melton. How terribly grown-up and grand. Before she could ask him to elaborate, he smoothly changed the subject. "Speaking of accidents, how is your little friend?"

"My little—oh! You mean Binky."

He smiled. "That was the name you were calling last night, although it was hard to hear through all the crashing crockery. Have you been raked over the coals?"

Addie shoved her hair back behind her ears, wishing it didn't always go so woolly in the rain, wishing it were sleek and shiny like Bea's. "No, but I expect I shall be."

"Bread and water?" Pebbles crunched beneath their feet as they plodded along the path.

"The very moldiest bread," she said, getting into the spirit of it. "And the most brackish water. But it's the flogging that's the worst."

He stopped, looking down at her, so she was forced to look at him. "You are joking, Mouse?" he said quietly. "Aren't you?"

"Of course," she said quickly. "They would never actually beat me— only as often as they lock me in the Red Room, that is. I expect I shall have my pocket money stopped for a week or two. That's what they usually do. Only this time, they'll probably stop it till I'm eighty. What do you think the going rate is for a ruined debut?"

She was talking too much, too fast, but there was something about the expression in his face that unnerved her, something serious and intent that made part of her, ignobly, wonder just what he would have done if she had said she were being beaten, something that made her pulse quicken.

He slid his hands into his pockets and strolled forward, setting the pace for both of them. "I'm glad to hear it." Somewhere nearby, a bird called, loud in the quiet of the garden. "I was afraid I was going to have to charge to the rescue."

The words were said lightly, but something about the way he said it, the way he glanced over at her, so casually, and yet . . . Addie could feel her cheeks flushing, despite the morning chill, but her hands were cold and tingling.

"Like Perseus and Andromeda," she blurted out, just to say something.

He looked at her quizzically. "Don't tell me you have a pet sea serpent in your menagerie, Mouse?"

"No." She shook her hair down over her face. "I just meant, it seems to be what heroes do. Rescuing princesses from ghastly predicaments and all that sort of thing."

Through her hair, she could see that he was smiling and trying not to. "I can't promise anything princely," he said gravely, "but if you find yourself in a ghastly predicament, give a holler and I'll come charging. I make no promises about the sea serpents, though."

"Thank you," said Addie shyly. "That's very kind of you."

"Except about the sea serpents," he said with a smile that showed off a dent in one cheek that wasn't quite a dimple but could have been.

Addie buttoned and unbuttoned the top button of Dodo's coat, trying to muster up something halfway intelligent to say, or at least something that wouldn't come out in an awkward squeak. If Bea were here, she would know just what to say; she always did. She would laugh and say something light and charming and not chew her hair like a cow while the silence went on and on and surely he must think she was a half-wit mute, the sort of cousin people kept in attics for a reason.

Oh, dear, she should have made some joke about the sea serpents, shouldn't she, about not being near water. But now it was too late, too much time had passed, and it would just sound like she'd spent all this time thinking it up, which she had, but—

She snuck a glance sideways. He caught her eye and grinned back. Addie flushed and ducked her head.

She was saved by the crunch of gravel and the sound of her own name.

"Miss Adeline? Miss Ad— Oh, thank the Lord." Ivy, the upper housemaid, came to an abrupt halt, resting her palms against her knees as she caught her breath. "I thought I'd never find you, miss. I've been looking for you for *hours*."

She spotted Mr. Desborough and broke off in confusion.

"Forgive me, sir," she said, and dropped a curtsy. "I didn't mean to interrupt. Her Ladyship wants to see Miss Adeline. In His Lordship's study."

Addie braced herself for trouble. The study was never good. The morning room was for light reprimands and general inspection, the study for more serious infractions. Aunt Vera would be even angrier at being kept waiting.

Hours? It couldn't have been that long. Addie snuck a shy glance at Mr. Desborough. Her entire sense of time was in disarray; she felt like they'd been talking for only minutes. She felt like she'd known him for years. She was a mess of contradictions—and in a mess, once Aunt Vera got to her.

"Thank you, Ivy. I'll be there in a moment." She turned to Mr. Desborough and wrinkled her nose in exaggerated distress. "It seems I'm for it now."

"Courage, Mouse," he said. "And remember—"

"I know," Addie said. "No sea serpents."

Astonished at her old boldness, she ducked her head and hurried after Ivy through the hedge, to face whatever penalty awaited her. At the moment, she would have called any well worth it. Mouse, he'd called her. But it was rather sweet, really, like a pet name. She knew Aunt Vera wouldn't launch her as they would Bea—especially not after Binky—but, perhaps, just perhaps . . .

She could picture herself grown-up and grown elegant, in a shimmering white gown, and Mr. Desborough stepping towards her, champagne forgotten in his hand, a wicked glint in his green eyes. Why, Mouse, he'd say. You've grown up.

And then he'd whisk her away, far away, from Aunt Vera and Ashford and Uncle Charles' study door.

It was the study door that did it. She wasn't a debutante anymore; she was a grubby schoolgirl in an elderly shirtwaist and a skirt with a mud splotch on it. Addie took a deep breath and knocked on the door. Servants went right in; poor cousins learned to knock.

"What?" It wasn't Aunt Vera but Uncle Charles, sounding uncommonly sharp and cross.

Worse than she'd thought! Uncle Charles seldom participated in punishment. When he did—well, she was for it now. She spared a thought for Perseus. Fictional sea serpants were one thing, aunts and uncles quite another.

Addie stuck her head around the door, sidling the rest of her body reluctantly through. Uncle Charles was seated at his desk, Aunt Vera behind him, her face set and white.

Addie gathered all her courage. "Ivy said you wanted to see me—about the mouse?"

"An hour ago," said Aunt Vera, and stopped, as though she didn't trust herself to say more.

"A mouse," said Uncle Charles. There was a telegram in front of him, the ink smudged as though it had been snatched off the press and delivered too soon. He looked at her, but she had the impression he wasn't seeing her, not at all. "It might as well have been. One mouse to make everything fall."

It hadn't quite been everything, but Addie had learned long ago that she mustn't speak in her own defense. That only made matters worse, generally.

"It's not as bad as all that," said Aunt Vera, and Addie looked at her in surprise; she hadn't thought to hear her aunt speak in her defense. It was on Uncle Charles' clemency that she had been relying, Uncle Charles who occasionally remembered that she had been her father's daughter. Aunt Vera looked at Addie and said harshly, "What are you still doing here?"

Nothing made sense this morning. Addie swallowed hard. "The mouse?"

"No one cares about a mouse, you daft girl!" Her aunt's voice broke. "Go back to the nursery."

Addie went, but she stopped at the kitchen first. It was Cook who told her, Cook who had given a cup of tea to the postman's boy and had heard the news: Germany had declared war on France.

Within a day, England was at war.

SEVEN

New York, 1999

Fatigue kicked in in a big way by the time Clemmie let herself back into her apartment.

She dumped her coat on a chair and today's pile of mail on the bookcase that doubled as a hall table. She didn't need to open any of it to know what it was. Credit card offer, credit card offer, bill, bill, bill.

Her apartment was what was optimistically referred to as a "junior one bedroom," which really meant a studio with an alcove, an alcove too far removed from a proper room to justify a door. The people who had lived here before had hung a beaded curtain over the doorway; the hooks were still there on the ceiling, like an outré art installation. Clemmie had never bothered either to remove them or to hang anything on them, although sometimes she used them for drying laundry.

There was room in the alcove for only a twin bed and a narrow chest of drawers. All other life activities took place in the living room, which housed a couch, bookshelves, and a card table that doubled as kitchen/dining room table/desk and general dumping ground for briefs, binders, mail, and whatever else happened to find its way there.

The light on her answering machine was blinking. There were four messages. All of them were from Dan.

Oh, damn. They had told her in the office that he had been calling, but she had been buried with work and—that was what he had complained about when they were together, wasn't it? That she had never made time for him.

What time? When?

It wasn't like she was sunning herself on a beach somewhere. Not everyone could earn a living playing competitive foosball with people who communicated in ones and zeroes.

Oh, God. She wouldn't be this bitchy if she didn't feel, on some level, that he was right. She hadn't made time for him. She wondered, tiredly, if that was because she hadn't wanted to make time for him, if, deep down, it was because she had just never wanted him enough in the first place.

And what kind of horrible human being did *that* make her?

She was dragging her suitcase out from under the bed when the phone rang again. She paused for a moment, then let it go to the answering machine. In the mood she was in she was either going to tear Dan to bits or beg him to take her back, and neither of those was good.

"Hey, Clemmie. This is Jon. I just wanted to let you know I found a place. I'll be heading back to Greensboro next week, but I'll be back in New York for good as of—"

Clemmie snatched up the phone. "Hey!"

"Oh, hi." In the background the answering machine continued to do its thing. "I didn't realize you were home."

"I was screening. Dan."

Bleep. "End of message," announced the answering machine.

"Gotcha," said Jon. "Anyway, as I was saying, I just wanted to let you know that I'll be back in town as of December twentieth."

Clemmie wedged the phone under her ear and began folding shirts into her suitcase. "Shouldn't you be teaching somewhere?"

"I'm on sabbatical this term."

Sabbatical or post-divorce meltdown time? She knew just enough about academia to know that people generally had to apply for these things way in advance.

"Does that make it easier or harder?" she asked.

He didn't ask her to explain what she meant. "Easier," he said, "in that I don't have to be in Greensboro for the rest of the year. But, generally? Harder."

"When do you start teaching again?" Clemmie wandered over to the dresser. Flying out Wednesday, getting in Thursday. That meant she needed underwear for Thursday through Sunday.

"Next term. But only one class. I'm supposed to be working on a book right now. *Decline and Fall*—question mark. *The English Aristocracy in the Aftermath of the Great War.*"

"Catchy." She bypassed the sensible underwear, the whites, the beiges, and went for the impulse buy: hot-pink silk with lace trim. Why not, after all?

"I got it from Evelyn Waugh. It's not exactly original."

She dumped the underwear in the suitcase and went back for pajamas. "If you're going with Waugh, how about *Brideshead Regurgitated*?"

She heard Jon take a bite of something, chew. "You stole that from Stoppard," he said thickly.

"And you stole yours from Waugh, so we're even." Her pajamas were flannel, with fluffy pink sheep on them. She tossed the matching T-shirt on top. "So you really are writing about Granny's people."

She heard him take a swig of something and swallow. "So you don't think I'm making it up?"

Clemmie kicked her suitcase to the side so she could navigate around it to get to the bathroom, where there were strange and exotic cultures growing in the grouting. If she couldn't make a living as a lawyer, perhaps she could sell her bathroom to science?

She flipped the light switch, trying not to look too closely at the soap rings on the sink. "I went to the horse's mouth—although that's not the most flattering way to put it, is it? Especially since it makes me a horse by extension. Of the lineage of the horse, at any rate."

Jon ignored the humor. "What did she tell you?"

"Pretty much what you did." Clemmie clamped the phone under her ear as she reached up for her makeup bag, way up on the top shelf of her bathroom organizer.

"Oh?" Jon's voice was carefully neutral.

"She showed me a picture of the gang at Ashford Park." The name still sounded strange on her tongue, the fact that Granny had lived there stranger still, a world away from a ninth-floor studio on 52nd and 8th. "Who calls a kid Dodo? It's worse than Clementine."

"They had some weird nicknames," Jon agreed. "It was part of the whole shtick, the feeling of being part of a small club. They created their own slang and changed it whenever it looked like the proles were catching up."

"Is that part of what you're writing about?" She tugged on the makeup bag, and the pile of washcloths next to it began to slide forward. Clemmie hastily shoved them back. Crap.

"Part of it." He sounded decidedly cagy.

"Hey, don't worry. I'm not going to steal your ideas." A pile of terry cloth slid slowly but inexorably in her direction. Damn, damn, damn. Clemmie slapped the washcloths down on the toilet lid. She'd put them back up later. "I just didn't realize that was what you, well, did."

She had never really thought much about it. She had a copy of Jon's first book, pristine and unopened, a Christmas present from Aunt Anna. Signed by the author, of course. There was even a little SIGNED BY THE AUTHOR sticker on the front to prove it. She couldn't remember what the title was or, for that matter, where she had put it.

"It's okay," said Jon dryly. "You've been busy."

"I know, but . . ." Why was she beginning to dislike that theme? Goodness only knew, she used it often enough, but something about hearing it parroted back at her made her squirm. On an impulse, Clemmie said, "Will you do me a favor? You're around for the rest of this week, right?"

"What kind of favor? Am I going to regret this?"

"Now who's thinking like a lawyer?" jibed Clemmie. "Don't worry; it's nothing too scary. Would you mind checking in on Granny Addie for me? She looked a lot better today, but . . . I don't know."

"No problem," was all he said, but there was a quiet assurance to it that made Clemmie feel about a thousand times better.

Funny how things turned out. Ten years ago, if anyone had told her she would be looking to Jon for reassurance she would have told them they were on crack.

She tucked her makeup bag into a corner of her suitcase and straightened, stretching the aching muscles in her back.

"Thanks, Jon. Really. It's good to have you back." Silence. Awkward silence. Damn. Raising her voice, Clemmie said jokingly, "After all, you're the closest thing I have to a brother."

There was a pause, then a snorting sound. "What does that say about your real ones?"

"Dad got them in the divorce," said Clemmie. She bit her lip. "I mean—"

"It's okay, Clem." Clemmie flushed at the mockery in his tone, clear even through the static of her cordless, which tended to get cranky outside a two-foot radius. "I'm not going to start blubbering every time someone mentions the word 'divorce.'"

"Of course. I know that. Anyway, thanks for keeping an eye on Granny Addie for me."

"Stop thanking me. I would have gone anyway."

He probably would have, too. "Keep that halo shiny, Jon."

"I intend to. Get some sleep."

"You, too," said Clemmie, and hung up.

Way to go, Saint Jon, patron saint of grandmothers. What did it say that he was a better grandchild than she was—and he wasn't even actually related?

Aside from that one comment the other day, she didn't know anything about Jon's real grandparents. He didn't talk much about his family. Instead, he had mostly hung around with hers. For the first time, Clemmie wondered what that felt like, being on the fringes of someone else's family, always being reminded that you didn't quite belong.

Like Granny Addie at Ashford. Well, without the whole earldom bit.

Clemmie had been six when Aunt Anna had married Jon's father, too young to view him as a romantic interest but old enough to resent the inclusion of a competitor in the family circle. Until then, Clemmie had been the only grandchild in the immediate area, the center of grandparental attention. Her brothers were so much older; they were both in their late twenties, with wives of their own, and all the way off in California besides. Uncle Teddy was out in Greenwich, not so very far away, but Uncle Teddy's kids were that half generation older than she was, already applying to colleges, going other places, getting married.

Besides, Uncle Teddy and Aunt Patty didn't leave Greenwich much.

Clemmie knew, as children know, without being told, that there wasn't much love lost between Granny Addie and Aunt Patty, Uncle Teddy's wife. Granny found Aunt Patty pedestrian, dull, and unambitious. A housewife, Granny called her, with a dismissiveness that was worse than active criticism. In return, Aunt Patty kept her kids as far from Granny as Metro-North would allow.

And then along came Jon. Aunt Anna and Jon's father had moved into an apartment near Columbia, enrolling Jon at Collegiate. Not only was he close in age to Clemmie, but he was bright and he knew it, with that arrogance that Collegiate boys donned along with their blazers. Suddenly it wasn't just Clemmie who was Ivy bound, there was Jon, too, and he was three years ahead of her, three years closer to success and grandparental approbation. He had mocked her indifferent Chapin Latin, criticized her calculus, raised his eyebrows over her recreational reading. She had retaliated with clannish-ness—*her* aunt, *her* mother, *her* grandmother—deliberately engaging him in reminiscences he hadn't been there to remember.

God, she had been a brat. But, then, so had he. They had each known how to hit where it hurt, struggling to find a place for themselves.

They'd had truces, too. Jon had helped her with her college applications. Grudgingly, but he'd helped her all the same. And she hadn't said anything when he kept on coming to Granny Addie's, even after Aunt Anna had moved on, ditching his father for husband number three—or was it four? And then, of course, there had been Rome.

They didn't talk about Rome.

Sighing, Clemmie flipped the lid of her suitcase closed, zipping it up the sides. Good thing they'd grown out of all that. So weird to think how old they were now. If she was thirty-four, that made Jon thirty-seven, well on his way to forty. He a professor, she a lawyer. What would the teens squabbling in Granny Addie's kitchen have made of that? What would they have made of any of it? Clemmie would never have imagined Jon divorced. She would never have imagined herself alone and childless at thirty-four.

Okay, that was enough of that. Clemmie shoved her suitcase into the living room and shut the lights. Retreating into her alcove, she shrugged into a nightgown. Something moved in the mirror above the dresser, and she had a moment of disorientation before realizing that it was her own reflection, rendered unfamiliar in the meager light of the bedside lamp, her hair still short and strange.

For a moment—it was stupid, but there it was—for a moment, she thought she had seen the woman in the picture in Granny's night-table drawer. Bea.

Clemmie shook her head and the woman in the mirror shook her head, too, hair swinging around her face in a flapper bob. It was the haircut; that was what did it. The haircut and a trick of light and coloring. She didn't really look that much like the woman in the photo.

She wished she had taken a better look at it when she'd had the chance. She wondered what had happened to her, that Bea. Had she married her marquess? And why had Granny never spoken of her before?

All long ago and far away.

Clicking shut the bedside lamp, Clemmie clambered into bed, pulling the quilt up around her shoulders. The sheets were cold, and she curled herself up as small as she could, waiting for her body heat to warm the bed.

On the nights when Dan had stayed over here, they had fit themselves together like puzzle pieces to keep from falling off the bed; she had bitched about it in summer, when heat made it irksome. Right now, it would have been rather nice to have someone cuddled up next to her, sharing his warmth.

Maybe she should have married Dan.

What if she had used up her chances? What if he was her last ever man? Clemmie rolled over onto her other side, shivering as she hit a cold patch. True, she hadn't really loved him, but she had been fond of him. On a cold night, in a narrow bed, it was very easy to come to the conclusion that it was better to be with someone, even a wrong someone, than not to be with anyone at all.

Clemmie buried her head in her pillow, feeling her strange, short hair tangling around her face. She fell shiveringly into an uneasy sleep, in which images of Dan warred with the remote face of the woman in the picture in Granny's nightstand.

London, 1919

Her mother caught her as she was making her way to the powder room.

Bea telegraphed her excuses to Camilla and Mary with a smile and a roll of the eyes. "Yes, Mother?"

Her mother motioned her off to the side of the room. Her stiff social smile was firmly in place, nearly as stiff as her posture, but her voice indicated that she was Not Amused. "Did you just refuse Rivesdale a dance?"

Bea had and quite deliberately, too, but she didn't think her mother would appreciate the finer points of her grand strategy of flirtation. "Topper Bingham trod on my train. I need to pin it up."

Her mother was not appeased. "You don't want to go putting Rivesdale off," she warned. She looked around the ballroom, dismissing the progeny of her peers with one damning sniff. "You're not going to do better."

Ah, those loving, maternal words that warmed the cockles of one's heart. Bea stretched luxuriously, chest forward, shoulders back. "Maybe I can do worse."

"Beatrice," said her mother sharply.

"Yes, Mother." It was easier to humor her than to fight with her. God, she was gagging for a gasper, but her mother didn't approve of smoking; she'd be horrified if she knew Bea did.

But, then, Mother was horrified right and left these days, ever since the War had turned the world topsy-turvy, decimating an entire generation of eligible gentlemen, loosening the old codes and rules. For other people, that was. Mother had staunchly refused to bend. Corseted like Queen Mary, she made the round of the same drawing rooms in the same houses, turning a blind eye on the missing faces, the bright lipstick, the new music. If she didn't choose to acknowledge it, it wasn't there. The new fashions hadn't touched her. Jazz was "that caterwauling," nightclubs someplace other people's wayward children went.

She wouldn't hear of Bea taking any part in the war effort; that was for other people's daughters, people whose lineage was lesser, whose marital prospects were scarcer. She had received the news that the Duchess of Rutland's daughter had been allowed to train as a nurse with horror and indignation. Consort with the wrong sort of people, handle strange men, expose oneself to infection—most certainly not!

Addie had gone instead. Addie was expendable. Her mother hadn't said so in so many words, but Bea knew that was what was meant. It didn't matter if Addie picked up coarse expressions from the troops or came down with Spanish flu; she wasn't expected to uphold the family honor by making a grand marital alliance. Dodo had mucked in, too, poulticing wounded soldiers as though they were sick horses, clicking and clucking over them, tireless and cheerful. Dodo had been more popular in the sickroom than she had ever been in the ballroom; she had received a number of proposals. Most were unsuitable. Some, surprisingly, were not.

Who would have thought that Dodo could land the son of an earl? An Irish earl, but still an earl. He had been a younger son when Dodo snagged him, but a well-placed shell had fixed that. Dodo was now the future Lady Kilkenny. Bryan was shorter than Dodo and short an arm, but he had the best stables in Ireland. He and Dodo spoke an incomprehensible argot of hocks and withers. They had settled at Melton, setting a fashion for being fashionable by being unfashionable.

Meanwhile, Bea had fidgeted and fumed back at Ashford. Always Ashford. Someone was needed to keep an eye on the home farm, her mother had said. Her father had greater matters on his mind and heaven only knew what those land girls might get up to.

Bea knew that was rot. Her mother's instructions contained an endless list of don'ts. Don't spend too much time in the sun; don't get brown; don't ruin your hands. She wasn't contributing to the war effort, she was being rolled up in cotton wool, stored away to be taken out after the war, like a precious china figurine or a very old bottle of port, too valuable to be jostled.

This. Bea regarded the ballroom with a decided sense of ennui. They were halfway through the Season and Bea felt as though she had been to the same dance again and again and again—the same people, the same clothes, the same music, the same tired streamers, the same gilt chairs tenanted by the same drowsing dowagers.

This was what they had been saving her for. This was what she had been waiting for all those long years, all those endless hours in the nursery at

Ashford. This was supposed to be life! Romance! Adventure! And what did she get? Tepid ices from Gunter's, girls in droopy pastel dresses, and a ballroom full of graying men her father's age and boys just out of the schoolroom, pulled in to make up the numbers. The band plunked dispiritedly at a waltz. Even though it had been eight months since the Armistice, London still hadn't quite recovered from the exigencies of the war. Paper streamers and some dispirited vines hung limply in the place of the flowers that had once filled the ballrooms. The hothouses and flower gardens of five years ago had been plowed up for vegetables while would-be debutantes wilted on the vine, aged past their prime as the war raged on.

Out there, Bea knew, beyond these ice-blue walls, there was music and dancing, real dancing. The few able-bodied men in the room, meekly fetching lemonade, being polite to the dowagers, would bolt before the evening was over, seeking out their real entertainment in smoky clubs in the remote hinterlands of the city where there were no chaperones to monitor them, no endless rules and restrictions.

God, she was bored. Damnably, painfully, unutterably bored.

But it didn't do to show it. The trick, she had learned, was to always look as though one were having the best of all possible times, as though one were reveling in a delightful secret that one just might, with the correct inducements, be willing to share.

She did it now, sending a little half smile over her shoulder at Marcus.

Marcus, Marquess of Rivesdale, center of all her mother's hopes and ambitions. Six foot two, with the broad build of the born sportsman. Dark blond hair. Ruddy cheeks. Quick laugh. Passable dancer; decent kisser, at least from what she'd been able to discern from a few stolen moments behind a potted palm. They said he played an excellent game of golf.

He wasn't a bad egg, Marcus. In fact, he was really rather . . . well. One didn't go thinking of such things. Love was for the middle classes, her mother said, a sop to their sensibilities. One wasn't supposed to pay any attention to the little tingles at the back of one's neck when he smiled; one wasn't supposed to go weak or woozy or race to the door to see if the flowers that had just been delivered might be from *him*.

Catching her eye, Marcus grinned. He cocked his head towards the

French doors, the French doors leading out onto the ever so convenient balcony.

Bea smiled at him and turned away. Promising nothing. Denying nothing.

"You see?" she said to her mother. "I know what I'm about."

"I hope you do," said her mother darkly. And then, as Bea knew she would, she added, "You're not getting any younger."

"Really?" drawled Bea. "Time moves so slowly here, I thought I could make it run backward."

"If you don't get him," said her mother severely, "Lavinia ffoulkes will."

Lavinia ffoulkes? The woman couldn't even manage an uppercase letter in her last name!

"I have to fix my train," Bea said, and fled. Only her mother had the power to rout her like that. Only her mother had the power to make her feel like a disorderly schoolgirl, all braids and bruised knees.

Lavinia ffoulkes indeed!

Bea pushed open the door to the powder room. Camilla and Mary had gone; only one girl lingered at the dressing table, dispiritedly readjusting a slightly wilted blossom in her dark hair.

"Thank goodness," Bea said. She dropped down on the stool next to her cousin. "I'm so glad it's you. Mother's been having a go at me. Too shame making."

"What about?" Addie shifted on her stool, and the flower promptly fell down again.

Bea rolled her eyes. "What else? Marcus. Mother would propose to him herself if she could. Poor Mother. Such a blow to her not to be able to betroth me in my cradle. She would have loved that. Here. Let me." She plucked the flower out of her cousin's hand, pinching off the broken part of the stem. "Turn just a bit. . . ."

"Do you think he will propose?" Addie's voice was slightly muffled by Bea's arm.

Bea shrugged. "Why wouldn't he? Aren't I prize enough?"

Lavinia ffoulkes, whispered her mother's voice. That was nonsense. Lavinia was at least as old as she and had a laugh like a squeaky hinge.

"There. Isn't that better?" She leaned back so Addie could see herself, flower now firmly moored between two carefully placed waves of hair. It had been a good choice; the white flower showed to good advantage in Addie's dark hair. "I do wish you would let me do something about your eyebrows. I know the cleverest little woman. . . . Oh, the look on your face! Don't worry; I'm not going to come after you with a tweezer."

"Please don't." Addie made a comical face. "Besides, you know what they say about silk purses and sows' ears."

"You're hardly a sow's ear—" Bea broke off, shaking her head at her cousin, feeling the familiar mix of affection and irritation. "The cream shades suit you, and as long as you don't load yourself down with flounces . . . You could be such a success if only you'd try a little harder."

Addie poked at the flower in her hair. "It depends on what you mean by 'success.'"

Addie had a way of doing that, of taking simple things and making them complicated. It had been worse since the War. Sometimes, Bea didn't understand her cousin at all.

"What everyone means," said Bea firmly. "Stop that! You'll undo all my good work."

Addie turned her big brown eyes on Bea. She had such lovely brows and lashes; Bea had to resort to kohl to achieve the same effect. "You mean marrying?"

Bea shrugged and opened her bag, wishing desperately that she had a cigarette. "What else is one to do? Stay on with Mother and wind her wool? Run a dreary little shop?"

"It needn't be dreary." At Bea's look, Addie said, "Oh, all right. All I mean is, you don't have to marry Marcus. If you don't want to. I know your mother is trying to push you into it. . . .'"

Bea turned away, shoving at a pin that threatened to fall out of her hair. "Don't be silly. Of course I don't *have* to." That implied all sorts of other things, whispers and scandals and babies who came too soon. "Why wouldn't I want to marry Marcus?"

She could practically see the wheels turning in her cousin's head. "He's a bit—well, he's a bit ordinary."

"Ordinary?" Bea was offended on Marcus' behalf. Didn't Addie realize how thin on the ground titled men of a comparable age with all their limbs in place had come to be? "Hardly! Look at him. Next door to a duke and not even doddering."

"Yes, but do you love him?" her cousin persisted.

Sometimes she thought she did, sometimes when Marcus looked at her just so, or slipped his hand beneath her chin to tilt up her face to kiss. It was both exciting and terrifying. Love has no place in great alliances, her mother had always told her; marriage was a contract, not a novel. People did foolish things for the sake of the madness called love; better not to entertain the notion.

But, even so, sometimes . . .

Addie just didn't understand, that was all. Her parents had married for love; they had lived in bohemian abandon in Bloomsbury. She could afford to ask questions about the meaning of success and the value of marriage. Bea didn't have those options.

They had read their novels together in the nursery, she and Addie, passing them back and forth, sighing over the heroines and heroes, but there was a difference. In fiction, a Rochester could marry a Jane Eyre. In real life, Bea knew, it was the Blanche Ingrams who prospered. She wasn't being hard; she was just being a realist.

Even so, Addie's disapproval bothered her.

Bea shoved up off her chair, her bag making a slapping sound as it bounced off the glass top of the dressing table. "You're being bourgeois, darling. Don't let Mother hear you talking like that." At her cousin's expression, her voice softened. "Don't worry, dearest. Once I marry my marquess, you can come live with me and marry whomever you like, even if he's the lowliest chimney sweep."

"What if I don't mean to marry?"

Bea shuddered. "Don't let Mother hear you say that!" Taking Addie's hand, she tugged her off the stool. "Come along, darling. Come watch me work my wiles."

Back in the ballroom, the band had switched to a Scottish reel, trying to feign some measure of gaiety. A few couples vainly skipped their way through the forms. Marcus was in one of the couples on the floor, dancing with Lavinia ffoulkes, she of the insufficient capitalization. Lavinia was nearly as old as Bea, another casualty of the Great War, only just making her debut at twenty-one. There was a desperate gaiety in the way she tossed her head, a forced pertness in her exaggeratedly girlish dress. Bea didn't miss the way she clung to Marcus' arm when the dance brought them together.

Marcus caught Bea's eye over Lavinia's head and grimaced.

There was a group of men hovering, as always, by the refreshment table. Bea nudged Topper Bingham with her elbow. "Go ask my cousin to dance."

Topper staggered just a bit. "Why can't I ask you to dance?" he asked thickly. Bea smelled something stronger than champagne on his breath.

Bea assessed him with an expert eye: just drunk enough to be docile, not too drunk to dance.

"Because you already mangled my hem," she said. "It's someone else's turn. Now *go*. And tell Tommy I expect him to dance with Addie after you."

There. She had done her bit, and now it was up to Addie. Not that either Topper or Tommy were real prospects; Topper was well on his way to dipsomania and Tommy was the younger son of a younger son, but popularity bred popularity. Popularity drove away disquieting thoughts.

"So that's where you got to." She looked up to find Marcus standing there, Marcus, tall and handsome. He was handsome, in that very wholesome English way. He would run to fat in old age, but at the moment he was still a fine specimen. Besides, Bea thought flippantly, he had all his limbs and what more could a girl ask, these days? "I've been looking for you."

"Maybe you just weren't looking hard enough." She drew away in a feigned retreat. "Shall I go away and you can try again?"

He chuckled belatedly. "No need for that."

Bea could hear Addie in the back of her head, clucking.

What if he wasn't the quickest knife in the drawer? He had other qualities to recommend him. He was handsome. Handsome and reasonably kind. He had picked up a glass for her when she knocked it over the other day. He had put his jacket around her when she had lost her wrap. The memory of it made her fingers tingle, the intimacy of it, the male smells of cologne and tobacco snuggled up around her, the wool of his jacket scratchy against her bare arms.

Marcus looked around, at the rows of dowagers dozing on their chairs. "Fancy a breath of fresh air?"

Was it her imagination, or did he seem just a bit nervous? If he proposed . . . Marriage, Bea thought. The Rivesdale town house in Mayfair, the Rivesdale sapphires around her neck, a coronet on her stationery.

And Marcus.

"Yes," she said. It felt like a rehearsal. She smiled up at him, under her artificially blackened lashes, and tried it again. "Yes."

EIGHT

London, 1999

The firm's travel agent had booked her into someplace called the Rivesdale House Hotel.

A country house hotel in the heart of London! exclaimed a framed magazine cover, placed discreetly to one side of the front desk. The reception desk sat incongruously in an oval entrance hall that made Clemmie think of a wedding cake, with stucco ornamentation for icing. Her battered black wheelie looked particularly scruffy against the white marble floor. Fortunately, there were no mirrors in the entryway. After seven hours in the air, Clemmie knew she looked worse than her suitcase, still wearing yesterday's suit with the coffee stain on the right sleeve, where someone had accidentally bumped the stewardess mid-reach.

Even without the coffee stain, her pin-striped polyester Tahari skirt suit looked painfully cheap and American in the hushed dignity of the Rivesdale House lobby.

This had to be Paul's latest find. Paul was the partner for whom Clemmie worked. Every partner had his own hotel and restaurant preferences. Some liked ultramodern; others preferred brand-name chains. No communing with the vulgar hordes at the Ritz for Paul; he was the disciple of the undiscovered gem, some of which were less gem-like and more discovered than Paul had anticipated.

This one, however, seemed to live up to Paul's exacting standards. There was no piped-in music, no squabbling families with fanny packs, no courtesy coffee table. A Roman emperor in a roundel looked disapprovingly down his nose at Clemmie from above the fireplace, his toga slipping slightly over one shoulder.

Toga, toga, thought Clemmie, and fought down a chortle of jet-lagged laughter. She hadn't slept much on the plane. She'd had strange dreams, dreams of flaming planes and shingled flappers with bloodred lips and ice-blue eyes, dancing to the tune of the clickety-clack of shotguns firing in double time. The shotguns had turned out to be the laptop keyboard of the person in the seat next to her, who was clearly far more disciplined than she was. Clemmie had woken up with a crick in her neck and a dent in her cheek where she'd fallen asleep facedown on the binder she was meant to be reviewing.

After two cups of coffee, one on the plane, one snatched at Terminal 4 on the way to the Heathrow Express, she had the floaty feeling she used to get just around finals time in law school, the one where she would go off on laughing jags for no reason in particular because her body had to do something to keep itself awake.

She'd better hope she could pull it together before meeting up with Paul. Paul was the partner on the case, which made him eligible for toga and laurel leaves in the strict hierarchy of law firm life. As a senior associate, she wasn't quite a gladiator to his imperator, but she was still definitely subject to the imperial will.

Him emperor, her viceroy. The thought of Paul in a toga was enough to make her choke on giggles again.

Must. Not. Lose. It.

"Yes?" The man behind the desk had tired brown eyes and a voice like Hugh Grant in *Four Weddings and a Funeral*.

"Evans," Clemmie said, more brusquely than she had intended. Her eyes were watering from sleep deprivation and suppressed laughter. "Clementine Evans. You should have a reservation for me."

The clerk must have been used to dealing with Americans. If he thought her rude, he didn't show it, just consulted a surprisingly modern computer, hidden behind the fronds of a potted palm.

"Room three-oh-two," he said. "Will you need help with your bag?"

"No, I can manage," Clemmie said, before remembering that in London "three" meant "four." She'd be very surprised if Rivesdale House had anything so vulgar as an elevator. Damn. The bag, which wasn't that heavy when rolled along, could be very heavy indeed when lugged up three flights of stairs.

It would be just like Paul to make sure his juniors were stuck away three flights up, where the servants used to live. It was the sort of petty put-down in which he delighted.

The man behind the desk was already doing something arcane to the computer. "Passport, please?"

She slid it over. "Has Paul Dietrich checked in yet?"

The desk clerk paused over her passport, looking distinctly wary. "Would you like to leave him a message?" he asked.

She didn't look like an international hit man, did she? But, then, neither had John Cusack in *Grosse Pointe Blank*. Or maybe he thought she was an angry wife, tracking down her husband's suspected infidelities. Or something like that.

"I don't need his room number or anything." Clemmie took her passport back. "I just need to know if he made it in. I'm supposed to meet him here. We work together."

The clerk visibly relaxed. "Right." He said apologetically, "I've just started, you see. Still learning the ropes."

"No problem," said Clemmie, and smiled at him to show there were no hard feelings. "I can't even begin to imagine."

"Neither did I," said the clerk with a wry smile.

Now that she looked at him, really looked at him, he looked nearly as tired as she was, with purple circles under a pair of warm, brown eyes. It wasn't just the voice that was Hugh Grant–ish; he looked a bit like the actor, too, with the same floppy-hair thing going, although there was something about the eyes that was more reminiscent of the goofy friend from *Four Weddings*, the one with the country estate who wound up marrying the woman dressed like Little Bo Peep.

"How long ago did you start here?" Clemmie asked.

"We've been open for just over six months now." He nodded towards the framed *Country Life* cover. "That helped rather a lot."

"Mmm," said Clemmie.

He must be just about her age. Or maybe a little younger. She was constantly forgetting how old she actually was. Her mental age was permanently stuck at twenty-seven, just past law school, before she had descended into a never-never land of depositions and doc review. It was like a reverse Rip van Winkle; time had gone by and she had aged without being aware of it.

The desk clerk tap-tapped on the computer, with the awkward, two-fingered typing of the self-taught. He was rather cute, really. In that slightly inbred English public-school way.

If this were a novel, she would rediscover her Inner Woman by having a fling with the cute desk clerk.

If this were a novel, it would be Tuscany in summer rather than London in December and she wouldn't have a run in her stocking and yesterday's mascara under her eyes. Besides, weren't Brits supposed to make lousy lovers?

God, she was tired. Clemmie suppressed a yawn. The last of her caffeine buzz had worn off, leaving her entirely drained. Their first meeting was supposed to be at noon, which should leave time for a change of clothes and, if she was very lucky, a hot shower. That was if the plumbing had been updated more recently than the décor. The lobby screamed old money. Unfortunately, in Britain, that also often meant old plumbing.

With any luck, maybe Paul had gotten detained and they'd have to push back the meeting. Screw the shower; she would sell her soul for a nap.

The clerk looked up from the computer. "Mr. Dietrich did check in last night."

Damn. So much for that.

The lock of hair flopped down over his eyes as he frowned at the keyboard. "Wait a minute. I think he left a note. . . ."

He rummaged among a pile of papers behind the desk, a gold ring on one hand catching the light. A wedding ring? No. A signet.

That was all right, then, thought Clemmie sleepily. Even in purely imaginary flings, she did draw the line at adultery.

"Miss Evans?" The clerk was holding out a note to her expectantly.

"Oh! Thanks." Clemmie's hand bumped against his as she snatched at the note. She mumbled, "Sorry, jet lag," and hastily opened the note.

Paul used only a fountain pen. It didn't make his chicken-scratch handwriting any more legible, but Clemmie had had lots of practice deciphering it, usually in an effort to decode crucial words in the margins of key documents at three in the morning, long after Paul had gone home to his homestead in Westchester. This note was scrawled on Rivesdale House stationery, *RHH* with a crest over it.

Paul hadn't wasted time on unnecessary amenities. *Lunch meeting moved to breakfast. Nine at—* The Hill? No, *The Grill.* The Grill Room at the Dorchester.

Oh, lovely.

He did realize her plane hadn't gotten in until seven, right? Of course not, that would have meant that Paul had actually read the e-mail she'd sent him with her itinerary. It was already eight forty-five now. Clemmie's knowledge of London geography was hazy, but she was pretty sure the Dorchester wasn't exactly next door.

And he couldn't have e-mailed her because? If she'd gotten the e-mail on her BlackBerry, she could have gone straight from the airport to the Dorchester. What sucked the most was that she couldn't even complain; like the customer, the partner was always right. She'd have to simper and apologize, even though it was Paul's own damn fault.

Clemmie cursed. "Sorry," she said to the desk clerk.

"I've heard worse," he said mildly.

There was no time to go up and change, no time for that shower she'd been fantasizing about since Heathrow. "Do you mind if I leave this with you?" She indicated the suitcase. "I've got to run."

"It will be waiting for you in your room."

"Thanks," she said, and meant it. "How far is it from here to the Dorchester?"

"When do you need to be there?"

Clemmie grimaced. "Five minutes ago?"

The clerk took in her skirt suit and high-heeled pumps. "You'll want a cab."

He came out from behind the desk, walking briskly past her to the doorman, who was dressed in a dark blue, vaguely military-looking uniform, with gold around the collar and cuffs. In contrast, the clerk looked as though he'd just come down from Oxford, in gray flannels and blue blazer. A few quick words, one sharp blast on the doorman's whistle, and there was a cab waiting for her. In her fatigued state, it all felt rather like magic.

"Thank you," said Clemmie sincerely. "You've just saved my ass. I mean—"

The clerk's lips quirked in a smile. "All part of the service," he said, forestalling any other idiotic remarks she might make. "Good luck."

He closed the door behind her and Clemmie resisted the urge to bang her head against her knees. No wonder she had been single for years before Dan. Hell, she would have done better with *I carried a watermelon*. Not that she'd really been planning to hit on the desk clerk. But it would be nice to able to open her mouth without jamming a three-inch heel down her throat.

"Where to, love?" demanded the cabdriver.

"Dorchester House," said Clemmie, and wiggled her BlackBerry out of the side pocket of her bag. She still had a fighting chance of making it on time, but best to e-mail Paul, just in case.

She typed in *D* for "Dietrich," and before she could get to the *e* Dan's e-mail popped up instead, still auto-programmed into her BlackBerry. DanG@cosine.com.

That was "cosine" as in the MIT cheer or the trigonometric principle, pronounced "co-sign." They'd had a joke about it being chic to refer to Cosine as "Co-zeen," the same way some people said "Tar-zhay" instead of "Target."

How are things at Co-zeen? she would ask during their daily late-night call. *Magneefick!* he would say, his version of *magnifique*. Or sometimes, if the day had gone poorly, *Tres mal*, pronounced "tremmle." Dan had taken French at school, just as she had, but he was functionally tone deaf. His mispronunciations had trod that uncomfortable line between annoying and endearing. Like so much else about Dan.

The familiarity of it all—DanG@cosine—hit her with a sharp pang of nostalgia. She couldn't count the thousands of times she had done this, the thousands of times she had BlackBerried him from curbs and cabs and conference calls with a "hey, late for dinner tonight," or, "Chinese food good for you?" or just an "Argghh, still in office."

On an impulse, Clemmie typed: "Sorry to have missed your calls; work's been nuts. In Dallas last week, in London now. Any chance you're free for dinner next week?"

It seemed weird to sign it "love," the way she used to, so she didn't sign it at all. She just clicked "send" quickly, before she could overthink or change her mind. The BlackBerry sent her message spinning off into the electronic aether.

It wasn't that she was reconsidering or anything, she told herself. They were friends. They had said they would stay friends. And if she was a little tired . . . and a little lonely . . . well, that was beside the point.

Clemmie settled back against the seat. The cab was round roofed, capacious, with jump seats across from the banquette, the sort of cab they used to have in New York when she was a little girl. There was something pleasantly antiquated about it. Outside the cab window, London zigzagged past, Hyde Park on her left, the dignified buildings of Mayfair on her right, men in dark suits with furled umbrellas, newspaper sellers on the corners. Only the more modern buildings among the older edifices betokened the ravages of the Blitz.

The women in their own dark suits, the SUVs doubled-parked at the curb, the ubiquitous white paper coffee cups were the only telltale signs of modernity. Otherwise it might have been eighty years ago, white houses blending to gray in the incipient gloom of a rainy winter day. Even 5th Avenue didn't have this sense of history, this sense that if one blinked, one would find oneself in the same place at another time, ponytails replaced by cloche hats, bare heads covered by bowlers.

In the rush-hour traffic, the cab's motion had slowed to a crawl. It was warm in the cab, the heater working double time, a fine film of condensation frosting the car windows, silvering the scene outside, like an old photographic plate, faded by time to gentle shades of gray. Clemmie could feel her tired eyelids beginning to droop, past blending into present in the mist of the morning.

Her BlackBerry lurched in her hand, jarring her awake. It buzzed angrily. High priority. Whoever had invented the high-priority message deserved to be condemned to a circle of inferno populated by constantly buzzing Black-Berries. The BlackBerry buzzed again. Groaning, Clemmie hauled herself upright and clicked open the message.

Paul's message was succinct and to the point. "Where the fuck are you?"

Somewhere nearby, a car horn blared. Someone responded with a long stream of profanity.

So much for once upon a time.

Shoving her hair back behind her ears, Clemmie bent her head over her BlackBerry. "In traffic. On way."

She was so not looking forward to this meeting.

London, 1920

Addie hated these meetings.

She perched awkwardly on the edge of a heavily embroidered Louis XV chair, legs crossed at the ankles, her skirt riding up just enough to make her feel like a schoolgirl again, still in short skirts, being called in for a ticking off.

There was a lavish tea set out, iced cakes and bread spread with real butter, as if rationing were a thing only imagined, once upon a time. A piece of bread and butter sat on Addie's plate, the edges beginning to curl. The day was warm for September, warmer in the overcrowded room, with its heavy, brocade drapes. Addie could feel a little bead of sweat inching down her back, just below her shoulder blades.

Little chats, Aunt Vera called the weekly torture. *Just to see how you're getting on.*

Ever since Addie had moved under Bea's roof, Aunt Vera had shown a surprisingly un—Aunt Vera—like solicitude. Addie wasn't fooled. It wasn't Addie Aunt Vera wanted to know about; it was Bea. She wanted to know where Bea and Marcus dined and with whom, whom they entertained, how they lived, and, most important, whether Bea showed any signs of increasing.

Not that she asked straight out, of course. It was all done by indirection, by questions that didn't seem to lead anywhere until they did. There was always something, some nugget of information that seemed entirely innocuous until Aunt Vera leaned forward, piercing Addie with that look, the same look she'd given her years ago when Addie had told her she wanted to be a hedgehog when she grew up.

Addie was always left feeling obscurely guilty, not quite sure what secrets she was meant to be keeping but sure she had failed Bea all the same.

Aunt Vera took a cake from the tray, licking icing from her fingers with the complete unconcern of the socially secure. "When do they go to Haddleston?"

Haddleston was one of Marcus' family properties. "I don't know. That is, I don't think they mean to go," she amended. "At least, not that I've been told."

Aunt Vera leaned forward in her chair, both her stays and her chair creaking in protest. "Lady ffoulkes said her girls were going."

If Lady ffoulkes had said it, it was probably true. Bea wasn't going to like that. She wasn't particularly fond of Lavinia ffoulkes or her younger sister, Bunny. Bea had grown even less fond of them ever since Marcus had taken to inviting them up to Haddleston for house parties, Saturday to Mondays that sometimes became Friday to Tuesdays, or even to Wednesdays.

Sometimes, Bea motored down to join him. Other times, Addie would hear crashing and stamping from Bea's sitting room and raised voices when Marcus came back. Aunt Vera didn't need to know about that, or about the telephoning that happened in hushed voices, the smell of cigarette smoke where there shouldn't be, gramophone music from the garden long after the rest of the household had gone to bed.

"Maybe they just haven't invited me," said Addie, trying to make a joke of it.

"I shouldn't be surprised if they hadn't," said Aunt Vera with annoyance. "Sit up straight, girl! No one wants a Drooping Dolly."

Addie shot up, her teacup rattling in its saucer.

Aunt Vera sighed.

"Dodo came to visit last week," volunteered Addie, as a peace offering. Surely that was neutral enough. "She needed some things from Fortnum's, so she came down herself."

"I know," said Aunt Vera grumpily. "I saw her. She's brown as a savage. As for that creature she's married—"

She broke off, constrained by her own social code. He was an earl, after all, even if he was an Irish one.

"They do seem happy," offered Addie. The earl in question was ten years older and half a head shorter than Dodo, but the difference didn't show on horseback, and since that was where they spent most of their time, Dodo didn't seem to mind the discrepancy in the slightest. Dodo was as fond of her husband as Addie had ever seen her of anyone. *Best damn seat I've ever seen on a woman* was his lover-like assessment of his beloved, but it was plain to everyone that he adored her. They spent their year half in Ireland and half in Melton, and, in her own undemonstrative way Dodo was happier than Addie had ever imagined Dodo could be.

It had been rather a source of awkwardness when she had come to tea last week, her glowing happiness when Bea and her marquess were so very clearly not.

"Happy," sniffed Aunt Vera. "What a child you are."

At least, thought Addie, sneering seemed to buck her up a bit. Aunt Vera had been the bogeyman of her childhood, able to quell her with a glance, but, these days, the lines on her cheeks were graven a little too deeply, the shadows beneath her eyes too pronounced.

They never talked about the reason for it, just as they never talked about Uncle Charles' hours in his study, hours and hours, late into the night, until he looked nearly as insubstantial as the pieces of paper on his desk, a thin sheet of aristocratic ivory parchment. They were very good at carrying on, at pretending that everything was as it had been, but Addie knew what the truth of it was; she could read it in the color of Aunt Vera's dress, in the empty patch on the wall where a portrait had once hung, in the missing pictures among the clutter of silver frames on the boule table by the door.

There were Bea and Marcus on their wedding day, Aunt Vera's tremendous lace veil incongruous with Bea's skimpy, wartime dress, accompanied by a very satisfied Aunt Vera; Dodo and her husband at Melton, Dodo hanging on to the reins of a large horse and grinning like anything; and Edward in his uniform, posed so that one would never notice the empty sleeve where his left arm used to be. There were pictures of friends and family connections, the closer to royal the better, with minor princelings given pride of place, glittering in all their regalia.

There were no pictures of Poppy.

Addie could mark out the empty places where they used to stand, Poppy stiff and posed in her best taffeta dress, Poppy chasing butterflies with her nurse napping nearby, Poppy with a tennis racket in her hand, nearly fifteen and bursting with life. There was a family grouping from Bea's wedding, Marcus and Bea in the middle, Uncle Charles and Aunt Vera to one side, Edward on the other. Addie could tell where the photo had been bent, as though Poppy had never been.

But she had; Addie still remembered the photographer's pleas to *look this way, Lady Penelope, just for a moment,* as Poppy laughed over her shoulder at Bea or clutched at her hat to keep it from blowing away in the breeze or held up a hand to catch an imagined raindrop, never still, always in motion.

It seemed impossible to think of her eternally still, not racketing down the stairs with a *Hullo, Addie!*—never again nagging Bea into a game of tennis, or coaxing Edward out for a ride.

It had happened a little over a month after Bea's wedding, while Bea and Marcus were still off on their wedding tour. Poppy had come back from a trip to the village complaining of a sore throat and an aching head. Nanny—Nanny was still Nanny—had put her to bed, prescribing a good night's rest and some lemon and honey. But in the morning Poppy's temperature had risen, and by evening they knew: It was the influenza.

Addie could still remember the smell of the sickroom: barley water and vinegar and the cloying smell of the dried lavender sachets Nanny scattered around the room to try to make the other smells go away. Nursing at Guy's Hospital during the War had been hard, but, somehow, this was harder, because it was Poppy and there was nothing, nothing at all, she could do to save her. The influenza had hit the village hard. The postmistress was taken, and the butcher's son, and a score of others, some connected to the estate, others not. The doctors hadn't come for them, but they came for Poppy, and their verdict was the same; everything that could be done had been done. The disease took its course as it would.

It took Poppy.

For that, Addie was willing to put up with Aunt Vera's sniffs and sneers. She was, Addie suspected, lonely. Not that Aunt Vera would ever admit to it. But she had no more daughters for whom to plan or scheme. Bea and Dodo were both married, out of her charge. And Poppy was gone.

Sometimes, despite the doctors, Addie wondered what would have happened if they had realized just a little bit sooner that Poppy's sore throat was more than just a sore throat; if she had looked at Poppy that first night instead of leaving her to Nanny; if she had done something, anything, differently. The doctors said no. They cited statistics, so many deaths to the months, so many other people's daughters, sisters, cousins gone. But those girls weren't Poppy. They hadn't been in Addie's charge.

"A whole Season and nothing," said Aunt Vera fretfully, looking Addie up and down. "I don't know what we are to do with you. Of course, you haven't any fortune. . . ."

Addie had heard this before, frequently. Uncle Charles made her an allowance, although Addie was never quite sure how much had come from Uncle Charles and whether any might be out of the small amount her parents had left. She was afraid to ask.

"I had thought . . ." Addie said tentatively. "I had thought about a job."

The word sat strangely in Aunt Vera's sitting room, somehow inappropriate among the rose and gold, the china fine as lace.

Aunt Vera's stays creaked. "A job? Nonsense! Modern nonsense," she said. Then, as if to herself, "A younger son. Or a clergyman. That would serve nicely. . . ."

On the mantel, a clock of malachite and gold chimed the hour, five delicate pings.

Addie let out her breath in a silent sigh of relief.

"Five o'clock already?" Aunt Vera hauled herself out of her chair. "Tell Beatrice I expect to see her Tuesday."

"Yes, Aunt Vera." Addie set her plate down on the tray. There was something terribly forlorn about the uneaten bread and butter, half-shriveled on a Spode plate painted in flowers and edged in gold.

"Adeline?" Addie shot to attention as Aunt Vera turned in the doorway. "No more of this nonsense about a 'job.' Do try to remember who you are."

Who she was? She'd had it pounded into her for years: She was a Gillecote, even if—there was always the "even if"—she didn't look like one. It was one thing for Bea to stay out half the night or Aunt Vera to lick icing sugar from her fingers or Dodo to talk about breeding at dinner. They could. They didn't have an errant father and a middle-class mother to make up for. She was, Addie had been told again and again, meant to be twice as correct, try twice as hard to make up for her unfortunate origins. The others were Gillecotes by right; she had to work to be one.

What if, just what if, that wasn't what she wanted to be? Addie felt a tiny spark of rebellion tingling as she passed through the hall beneath the massed portraits of Gillecotes, all up the sides of the vast mahogany staircase, pale and blond like Bea and Dodo and Uncle Charles. Jacobean Gillecotes, Georgian Gillecotes, Regency Gillecotes.

Addie had no pictures of her mother, other than the blurry images in her own brain, more daydream than memory. All these years, she'd had no contact with her mother's people. All she knew of them was that her mother's father had been a country doctor. Addie had only learned that from Aunt Vera during the War, when she'd announced her intention to go to Guy's Hospital and train as a nurse. Aunt Vera had seen it as a sign that blood will out—although the fact that the Duchess of Rutland's daughter was also at Guy's had quelled some of her objections.

For the past fourteen years, Aunt Vera had done everything she could to refine any hint of her mother's people out of Addie, leaving her pure Gillecote, unalloyed by baser stuff. It had been a relief to escape from Aunt Vera's house to Bea's, where one didn't have to worry about having one's clothes, one's mannerisms, one's habits picked at, one's movements scrutinized.

A maid handed Addie her hat and gloves and she stopped by the mirror to set the hat on her own head, her hair just a shade lighter than the wood paneling in the hall. Fernie told her that she took after her mother—except about the smile. That, said Fernie, was her father's.

Addie drew on her gloves, hugging her secret to her like a charm. Fernie! After all these years she had seen Fernie, an older, sadder Fernie, but still Fernie, with her red hair streaked with gray now, no longer masses and masses of it piled on top of her head, but daringly shingled, in a short bob that made her seem younger and older all at once.

Addie had visited her in her little office in a rickety building in Bloomsbury, not so very far from where Addie had grown up, with a dying potted plant on the windowsill and a typewriting machine on the desk and people rushing in and out with open collars and ink-damp pages in their hands and a smell of cigar smoke about their rumpled clothes, a world away from the hushed grandeur of Gillecote House.

The maid—once it would have been a footman, but the War had put an end to that—opened the door. Addie stepped out into a blaze of September sunshine, the dying sun concentrated for one last hurrah, shining right into her eyes.

Addie felt a burst of exhilaration. Such heaven to be free of Aunt Vera for another week! There needn't be any younger sons or earnest young clergymen. She had a plan of her own. Yes, Aunt Vera would hate it, but she didn't need Aunt Vera's permission. She'd be properly twenty-one in just two months, and then—

"Ooph!" Sun-blind, she had blundered right into someone's path, her shoulder connecting with an arm, sending a package tumbling onto the pavement. She could hear the dull thud as it landed.

"Oh, good heavens, I am sorry!" Addie held up a hand in front of her eyes. All she could see was the silhouette of a man, dark against the light.

"Not at all," he said. He bent to fetch his fallen package, his gray homburg hiding his face. "It's as much my fault."

Which was very generous of him when Addie was quite sure it was nothing of the kind. She stooped slightly. "I hope that wasn't anything breakable."

"Just a book," he said, straightening, so that she could see, for the first time, not just the hat but the face beneath it.

For a moment, she thought it was a trick of the light, the rainbows still chasing their way across her eyes. It seemed impossible that it could be otherwise.

"Mr. Desborough?" she said breathlessly, and he looked up sharply, surprised. Addie couldn't blame him; she was equally surprised, surprised and giddy and delighted. She clasped her hands together. "It's Captain Desborough now, isn't it?"

He looked at her quizzically, his eyes intent on her face. Addie wondered what he saw; with the sun falling full in her face, did he see her haloed in rainbows or simply a bleached-out blur?

"Do I—?" he began, but caught himself. His face broke into a smile as he let out a shout of laughter. "Good Lord! It's the girl with the mouse."

NINE

London, 1920

I haven't one at the moment," said Addie. She held out a hand. "Adeline Gillecote."

"I remember now," said Captain Desborough. "You do have a talent for a dramatic entrance."

Addie winced. "I don't usually make a practice of knocking people over, I promise."

"Just unleashing livestock?" he said, and then, "Which way are you walking?"

"This way," she said, pointing vaguely down the street, only half-aware of what she was saying, still boggling over the unreality of it all, that she was talking to Frederick Desborough, that he was standing in front of her, alive, older, real. "I live with my cousin now, in Wilton Crescent."

"I'm just going that way as well," he said. "Shall I see you there?"

She must have nodded or shown some sign of consent, because, somehow, she was walking beside him, through the rows of white-walled houses with their wrought-iron grilles, the sun shining up from the pavement and the varied sounds of motorcars and horse-drawn carts muted to dullness against the roaring in her ears.

She snuck a glance sideways, checking that she hadn't imagined him, but he was quite definitely there, still, surprisingly corporeal in his gray flannel suit. He didn't know, thank goodness, how often she had walked with him in daydream over the years. In the Ashford days, she had spun ridiculous fantasies about her debut, walking down the staircase of Gillecote House in Bea's wake, all eyes on Bea—except for one set of green eyes. His. He would lift a glass to Addie, silently, and she would float down the stairs and spend the rest of the night dancing in his arms, a fairy-tale princess freed from her tower.

Later, in the war years, she would go, exhausted, to bed in the nurses' dormitory at Guy's, wondering whether, in the next round of patients she would find a lean, dark-haired man who would struggle to a sitting position, exclaiming, Miss Gillecote! He was never badly wounded, of course, just enough to justify his being invalided home. You've turned nurse, he would say, admiration in his eyes. Something—it changed from daydream to daydream—would occur, a fire in the hospital, a bombing, an operation of the utmost delicacy, in which her unflappable calm would carry the day, at which Captain Desborough would take her hand and say, I've never known a girl like you.

And they would live happily ever after.

It was silly, she knew. But it was fundamentally harmless, this little dream of love, based on a fine pair of eyes and a passing kindness, just something to send her to sleep with a smile after a particularly trying evening of toting bloody basins or swallowing Aunt Vera's maxims. Although Addie had half-guiltily followed his career where she could, searching for his name in the papers, she had never expected to meet Frederick Desborough again. He had become, to her, almost as fictional as Mr. Rochester, someone to be sighed over and then tucked away again.

"Whatever happened to it?" he asked conversationally.

"To—?" Addie looked up at him from under her hat brim, hoping that he couldn't tell half of what she was feeling.

"The mouse," he said smilingly.

"Oh, you mean Binky!"

"Was that its name?"

"Short for Bianca." She tried for a tone of proper worldly boredom, clenching and unclenching her hands to stop them tingling. "She was a white mouse, you know. We thought we were so very clever."

"Was she put down for crimes against the state?"

"You mean for spoiling Dodo's ball? No. She died a perfectly natural death at the ripe old age of five." How ridiculous it all seemed now, how absurd that once they had cared about such things as a mouse let loose at a ball. "It seems a very long time ago, doesn't it?"

"Yes. It does." His voice didn't sound quite as she remembered. There was more of a drawl to it, an undercurrent of ennui. His face was thinner than it had been, thinner and wearier. "Are you in town for the Season?"

"No. I wasn't much good at it, so I decided to give it up."

"You gave it up?" Captain Desborough gave a little snort of amusement. "What do you mean?"

"You mean aside from being an awful wallflower?"

Somehow, it felt like a triumph to have made him laugh, to bring a smile to his too-thin face.

Emboldened, she said, "It just seemed such a waste, all that, when so much has happened. The going to parties and standing about and just pretending that everything is all the same as it was when it can't ever be again." Addie glanced at him, trying to see his expression, but his face was shrouded by the brim of his hat. "And, of course, there's the not liking the parties. So, really, I'm just making a virtue out of necessity."

"What shall you do with yourself now that you've given up society?" he asked politely, but Addie had the sense he wasn't really there anymore, that whatever pleasure he might have taken in her company had been leached away.

A bird trilled from an iron railing. In the street, an omnibus rumbled past.

Addie clasped her hands together in front of her. "Look, don't tell anyone, will you? It's just that I'm bursting to tell someone. I've got a job. Well, not really a job. It's more of an accidental unpaid apprenticeship—on probation—but at least it's *something*."

"Let me guess," said Captain Desborough. "You've got a place at a fashion house. No. Wait. Writing tittle-tattle for the tabloids."

Addie made a face. "No, nothing like that. I wouldn't know one cut from another. As for tittle-tattle—by the time it got to me, it would be old news."

"What, then?" he asked lazily.

The sun was shining full in her eyes, over the white-painted walls of the Georgian houses. Addie held up a hand to her hat brim. "*The Bloomsbury Review*," she said with satisfaction.

"Good Lord." Captain Desborough didn't ask her what it was, as Marcus would have. His eyebrows went up, more intrigued than shocked. "*The Bloomsbury Review?*"

"It hasn't the reputation yet of *The Mercury*, but it's got such a lot of interesting people," said Addie earnestly. "It looks to newer writers and critics, the ones who can't get into the *Mercury*. I know there's *Wheels* for that, but they only publish once a year, and only poetry. We have short fiction, as well, and criticism and philosophy and . . . oh, all sorts."

"Subversive reading material for a young lady. Does your family know you're reading that?"

Addie all but danced down the street. "I won't just be reading it, I'll be editing it! Well, if I'm lucky. Mostly, I'll be fetching tea and whatever it is that the most junior of the junior are made to do."

"Isn't Bloomsbury a bit off the beaten path?"

"Not for me." She thought about the narrow house in the narrow street, haloed in memory with rosy light and the smell of biscuits and pipe smoke. Over the years, it had flattened and softened in memory until it looked like an illustration out of a children's book, all pastels and rounded corners. "I grew up in Bloomsbury, you see. Right off Russell Square."

He was looking at her, really looking at her, like an appraiser presented with a painting that had turned out to be rather more interesting than he had first surmised. "I thought you were a Gillecote of the Gillecotes. They aren't precisely . . ."

"They're frightfully county. I know," Addie agreed. "Horses and hounds and footmen at dinner. My father was the family scandal. He fell in love with a novelist and ran off with her. My uncle and aunt didn't at all approve."

"No," murmured Captain Desborough. "I can see where they wouldn't. Who was she?"

"Helen Layton. She wrote as H. R. Layton."

That stopped him dead in his tracks. "You *are* full of surprises."

Addie did her best to look glamorous and Bohemian, hoping he wouldn't realize that none of the glamour was inherent to herself. While it might be rather dashing to have a mother who had written scandalous novels, they weren't Addie's novels any more than the articles in *The Bloomsbury Review* would be her articles. But, maybe, by association . . .

He resumed walking, book swinging easily by his side. "You haven't any uncles named Picasso, have you?"

His voice sounded different than it had when they met, no longer avuncular, but playful, teasing. If she didn't know better, she'd think he was . . . Was he flirting? Addie's pulse picked up as excitement warred with doubt.

"No, and I haven't the least relation to any of the dancers in the Russian ballet," she said, striving for the same sophisticated, bantering tone. "It's just my parents, really. My father wrote, too. Histories."

Subversive, Aunt Vera called them, although not when Uncle Charles was there to hear. Uncle Charles wouldn't have anything said against Addie's father, whether from affection or from a sense of family propriety she wasn't quite sure. In effect, it had meant that no one said anything at all. Addie wished they had. There was so little she remembered and it was so long ago that she had long lost track of that fragile dividing line between memory and invention.

Reading her mother's books was like seeing the world turned inside out, familiar refrains and ideas turned on their heads. Only, reading her mother's words, Addie couldn't help feeling that it was the world as she had known it that had been inside out all along and she was only now seeing it right way up. She had never seen the beauty in poverty or the poorness in riches until her mother laid it out for her. She had never thought to question Aunt Vera's codes or strictures, or to ask whether being correct was the same as being good.

Aunt Vera had taught her what one did and, more forcefully, what one did not. Her mother had forced her to ask "why?"

"Have you read my mother's books?" she asked.

"Yes. Before the War . . ." His face darkened, his lips narrowing into a thin line, as though he didn't trust himself to say more. Addie had seen that look before, on the men in the hospital, somewhere between anger and loss.

"And what did you think?" Addie asked hastily.

Captain Desborough blinked, his eyes focusing on her with difficulty.

"About . . . Oh yes. Your mother's books. There's no good way I can answer that question, is there? I think she had a rare talent for seeing both the best and the worst in human nature and portraying them both faithfully. We see all the petty hypocrisies of both rich and poor."

"But also their power for redemption," said Addie eagerly. If her mother's books had taught her anything, it was that inevitability was only inevitable if one allowed it to be so. The best of her mother's characters seized life on their own terms, made their own destinies. Addie only wished she had the courage to do the same.

An automobile backfired and Captain Desborough flinched, his entire body snapping with tension.

"Redemption," he said heavily. There were dots of sweat on his brow that hadn't been there a moment before. He began walking again, much faster than before. "You don't really believe that rot, do you?"

"It's not rot!" Addie scurried to match her shorter stride to his. "Isn't that the best part of the human experience? Our ability to learn from our mistakes and rise to a higher plane of consciousness?"

"You've been attending free lectures, haven't you?" He made it sound like a bad thing. "If you'd bothered to read anything in the papers other than poetry, you'd know that higher consciousness is hardly a human gift. We scurry like rats back into the same poisoned gutters . . . Like rats . . ."

"That's absurd." Addie struggled with her skirt, hobbling herself. "We're hardly rats. It's the power of reason that distinguishes man from the animals."

Captain Desborough gave a short, humorless bark of laughter. "I've seen precious little evidence of that."

"But that's why poetry is so important," said Addie excitedly. She hadn't been able to discuss this with anyone from her ordinary life, not Bea, not Dodo, and certainly not Aunt Vera. "It forces people to think—to reevaluate. Surely, if we all make a concerted effort, we can change the world for the better."

"One cup of tea at a time?" he said derisively.

She looked at him in dismay. He was mocking her, she realized. Put that way, her job at *The Bloomsbury Review* did seem remarkably silly, as silly as working for a fashion house or a gossip column. Shame made her cheeks heat. So much for flirtation or sophistication. She'd made an utter fool of herself, and all for what? The memory of a mouse?

She held out a hand with all the dignity she could muster. "Thank you for seeing me home, Captain Desborough. It was very good of you. I do hope I did not incommode you too greatly."

It was a horrible, stilted little speech.

Captain Desborough didn't take her hand. He stood, looking down at her, his lips pressed tightly together. "No, it wasn't good of me," he said baldly. "That was beastly of me. And entirely uncalled for."

Addie shrugged uncomfortably. "You were only being honest. It is rather silly when you look at it that. To be so proud of getting to make the tea . . ."

"Don't forget the old saw about oaks and acorns. All great things come from small beginnings—and poetry from a pot of tea." Captain Desborough tilted her hat back until he could see her face. "I didn't mean to belittle your new venture. Forgive me?"

She blinked up at him, afraid to move, to break the spell. "There's nothing to forgive," she said breathlessly.

His eyes were very, very green in his pale face, like jade, ancient and earnest. He was still standing too close, close enough that her skirt brushed against his trousers, close enough that Addie could practically hear the kitchen maids whispering about it through the railings.

"Look," he said. "I feel like the worst sort of cad. Let me make it up to you?"

"There's no need," said Addie, feeling suddenly shy again. She stepped back, her skirt whispering against the iron railings. "There's nothing to make up."

Captain Desborough's gaunt face lit with a sudden smile. "But I want to," he said. "And I want to hear more about your excursion into bohemia. Can I stand you supper?"

London, 1999

Clemmie ate supper at Rivesdale House.

It was only seven o'clock London time, still early for dining, as the almost empty dining room attested. Right now, Clemmie didn't care about being fashionable; she was just glad she was still awake. They'd had a full day of meetings, going from Dorchester House to co-counsel's office on Silk Street to the PharmaNet offices in trendy Docklands. Clemmie didn't like to think how long she'd been wearing the same clothes.

She had to hand it to Brooks Brothers; their non-iron shirts really did hold up well. Especially after—she did the mental math—twenty-seven hours of continuous use. Weird to think that she'd put it on yesterday morning in her own apartment and hadn't changed since. Yesterday felt like a million years ago. International travel did strange things to both one's sense of time and one's billable hours. Paul liked to brag that he frequently billed more than twenty-four hours in a day, with a little help from the Concorde.

"Not exactly the firm cafeteria, huh?" whispered Harold, the junior associate.

"Huh?" said Clemmie. "Sorry. What did you say?"

Harold poked her in the arm. "This. Pretty impressive."

There was no arguing with that. The walls were hung in a rich mulberry brocade, although it was hard to see the fabric beneath the paintings, row upon row of them, hanging from cords from the moldings. There wasn't much of a theme to them. It looked like someone's ancestors had gone on a rummage in Rome circa 1700 and picked up whatever was going cheap: battle scenes, biblical scenes, landscapes, portraits of smirking courtiers. There were the requisite dead fowl and large bowls of fruits and spaniels with liquid brown eyes, as well as a brawny woman holding someone's head suspended over a silver platter.

There were two fireplaces, one on either side of the room, bracketed by recessed pillars that looked, to Clemmie's untrained eye, like real marble, rather than its painted imitation. Large portraits hung above each, one of a woman in the tight-waisted garb of the late nineteenth century, the other in one of the waistless creations of the twenties. They appeared to be glowering at each other across the room, locked in a timeless generational battle. Even preserved in paint, Edwardian Woman didn't approve of Flapper Girl.

What was it the magazine cover had called the place? A country house hotel in London? Yup, she could see that. The menu bore that out. Printed on a single sheet of heavy card stock, deeply embossed, it boasted mostly fowl in various forms: partridge, grouse, pheasant. For the pescatarians, there was a fish option: wild Scottish salmon. For the price, it ought to come dressed in a kilt and dancing a reel.

"Perhaps a nice Château Lafite," murmured Paul, who was perusing the wine list with an attention he seldom applied to client documents. "Or a white Bordeaux."

Clemmie leaned back in her chair, letting her eyes roam around the room. Only two of the other tables were tenanted. There was a young couple, looking bored, by the far wall—honeymooners, maybe? At the far end of the room, beneath Flapper Girl, two elderly ladies were carrying on an animated conversation over their wild Scottish salmon.

"She looks kind of like you," said Harold.

"Who?" If he meant one of the octogenarians, she was going to be seriously offended.

"The woman in the painting." He nodded at the picture of the Flapper Girl.

"It's just the hair," said Clemmie dismissively, but she gave the portrait a second look all the same.

The portrait was slightly blurry, either from accumulated candle smoke or by design Clemmie couldn't tell. It gave the woman a slightly dream-like look, her eyes smudged and sultry. She sat on a bench, one thin hand resting on the velvet cushion, as if she had just sat down or were about to get up again. There were pearls looped around her neck, strands and strands of them, and more at her ears and wrists. A black band circled her pale hair, lending her a somehow rakish air. Or maybe that came from the cock of her hip, the quirk of her lips. There was a decidedly come-hither air about her, but it was more of a challenge than an invitation.

She looked, thought Clemmie, as though she ate men up and spat them out again.

There was something strangely familiar about her. Not the expression, but the facial features. Clemmie knew she had seen her before, but in a different setting, with a different tone. She grasped after the memory.

Paul drew in his breath in a long hiss. "You know who that is, don't you?"

"Bea," said Clemmie, realizing suddenly where she had seen her before. It was the woman in Granny Addie's drawer.

Paul looked at her as though she were stupid. "What? That's the *owner*," said Paul impatiently in a whisper that wasn't. "The Marquess of Rivesdale."

"Huh?" Clemmie came down with a crash from her own thoughts. "Where?"

"There." Paul nodded to the far side of the room, where a man had paused to say hello to the two elderly ladies, bending to kiss one of them on the cheek. He had changed out of his gray flannels and into the regulation black and white of evening wear, but Clemmie recognized him as the man at the desk.

"Seriously? I thought he was the desk clerk. He was very sweet about getting me a cab this morning," she added as Paul's eyes bugged out in horror.

As if he knew they were talking about him, the marquess looked up, saw her, and smiled. Catching sight of Paul, he just as quickly turned away again. He didn't, thought Clemmie, look terribly marquess-like, or at least not what she would have imagined a marquess would look like. He looked like a junior professor or someone's cousin at a wedding, the one whom you didn't mind getting seated next to.

Paul looked a bit like the time he had accidentally swallowed that cocktail olive at a post-trial party. "You made him get you a cab?"

"He offered."

Paul raised a hand. "Marquess!"

The marquess slowly disengaged himself from his elderly admirers. "Mr. Dietrich," he said politely. Then he turned to Clemmie. "I see you found your party."

"My colleagues," corrected Clemmie. Just in case he thought she was hanging out with Paul for fun. "Thanks for the cab this morning. You were a lifesaver."

"It was my pleasure," he said gravely, as though he lived to hail convey-
ances for pesky American businesspeople—which, if he was running a hotel,
he probably did. "I hope you enjoy your stay at Rivesdale House."

"I'd enjoy it more if you'd have some extra towels sent up," said Paul.

"Certainly," said the marquess. Clemmie gave him points for not going
after Paul with the wine list. "I'll see that it's done. Good evening." His polite nod expertly encompassed them all.

"Excuse me." Clemmie's voice caught the marquess mid-step. "Excuse me,
er—" What did one call a marquess? Your Lordship? My lord? Jon would
know.

He turned, slowly. "Yes?"

He probably thought she was going to ask him for more towels. Clemmie
shoved the menu out of her way, planting her elbows on the table. "The
woman in the picture? Was her name Bea—I mean, Beatrice?"

"What?" said Paul.

The marquess blinked at her.

Clemmie waved her hands in the air. "Forget I asked. Silly question. It's
just . . . Never mind."

"No," The marquess cleared his throat, shaking back his shock of brown
hair. "Not at all. It's not a silly question. She was born Lady Beatrice Gillecote." He pronounced it the way Granny had, making the G hard and the
vowels flat. "Are you a student of the period? We do get many Americans
with an interest in our history . . ."

Ha. She could hear Jon hooting with laughter at the very suggestion. Her
knowledge of history was limited to Mel Brooks' *History of the World: Part I*,
with a side of Ken Follett. She didn't even watch BBC costume dramas.

"Not really. It's just that she's a—well, a sort of cousin. She was my
grandmother's first cousin."

"That makes us cousins then, too. Of a sort," he corrected himself. He
added, almost apologetically, "Lady Beatrice was my grandfather's first
wife."

"So there's no real relationship," said the practical-minded Harold.

"Do we get the family discount?" cracked Paul.

The marquess' smile went a bit stiff around the edges. "It's a fairly distant connection. Lady Beatrice was the first wife of the fifth marquess."

It sounded like an LSAT logic problem. If the first wife of the fifth marquess was going fifty miles an hour and the second wife of the fourth marquess was going sixty miles an hour, whose tiara would fall off first?

"Did she live here?" Clemmie asked tentatively.

It was hard to imagine Rivesdale House as a private home, much less as a private home in which her grandmother might have been a guest. In Clemmie's world, such places existed only as hotels or as museums. She wondered if Granny had come to tea here, if she'd exchanged confidences with her cousin in the bedrooms upstairs or stood back to admire or comment on the location of the new portrait of her cousin as the workmen hoisted it onto the dining room wall.

"Lady Beatrice did live here," the marquess said, sounding more reserved than the question warranted. "For a time."

"For a time?" Clemmie echoed.

The marquess glanced back at the portrait, preserved in eternal chic. "They were only married two years."

TEN

London, 1920

"Were you going to tell me you were off?" asked Bea sweetly. "Or were you just planning to go?"

"Dash it!" Marcus blundered into a pedestal holding a high Chinese vase, catching it just before it toppled.

Leaning back against the doorframe, Bea watched him coolly as he grappled with it. She had caught him in his country tweeds, hand on the knob of the dressing door, preparing to slip away for yet another Saturday to Monday without her.

"Oh, dear," she said with false concern. "Did I startle you?"

Giving the vase a final pat, he flashed her a strained smile. "Er, just a bit."

Bea didn't say anything. She just waited, idly flicking the ash from her Turkish cigarette. The thin line of smoke created a hazy trail between them.

In the beginning, he used to ask her before he went away. Just a brief jaunt with a few friends for the shooting, she didn't mind, did she? After awhile, the asking had turned into an announcement and, from announcement, nothing at all. She wouldn't have known Marcus was leaving if she hadn't seen his valet, earlier, packing up his shaving kit, the special one with his initials in silver that she had had commissioned for him in Paris on the occasion of their one-month anniversary.

It baffled her that she had been reduced to this, spying on servants, stalking her husband's movements, snatching his correspondence off the tray in the hall.

"I didn't see you there," he added.

"No," said Bea acidly. She took a long drag on her onyx cigarette holder, the one Marcus had bought her in Paris, with her initials inlaid in diamonds. "You wouldn't, would you?"

She couldn't remember the last time he had looked at her instead of through her or around her. She was as much of a fixture as that blasted vase on its stand, something to be navigated around, something to be steadied before it smashed.

Bea wondered what he would do if she took the vase in both hands and flung it down, flung it down onto the floor so that it smashed into a thousand tiny shards at their feet.

It wouldn't, though. The carpet would cushion the fall, muffling the sound, and the servants would sweep up the pieces. And Marcus would go blithely on.

"Having a pleasant afternoon?" Marcus ventured, doing his best to brazen it out. "Lovely weather we're having, what?"

The weather? That was the best he could do? The weather? But, then, thought Bea, grinding ash into the Axminster carpet, he never had been much of a conversationalist, not even in the halcyon heyday of their courtship when his eyes, his thoughts, his roving hands had been only for her, when he had followed her, fascinated, from ballroom to balcony.

She had told herself that it didn't matter, that what he didn't say was as important as what he did. So what if he couldn't woo her with poetry? He was a man of action, not a man of words, and he hadn't been the least bit chary about indulging his impulses.

She had never stopped to consider what might occur should those impulses lead him somewhere else. Her husband stray from her? The idea was laughable.

Until it wasn't.

Bea took a long drag at the tip of her onyx cigarette holder, leaning lazily against the doorframe. "Who is it this weekend? The luscious ffoulkes sisters?"

"Lavinia and Bunny will be joining the party, yes. Among others," he added hastily.

Bea raised a carefully manicured brow. "You mean Stuart Trevis and Dick Penhallow and that tiresome Curzon girl with the nasal voice?"

"Yes," said Marcus defensively. "They will be in attendance."

"Of course they will," murmured Bea. "Your precious Gang."

And wasn't it just too too? They called themselves something absurdly twee, the Gorgeous Gang or the Gruesome Gang or the something equally sick making, even worse than Diana Manners and her Corrupt Coterie. Stuart had been best man at Marcus' wedding. Dick—or Deadly Dull Dick, as Bea had dubbed him—was a ffoulkes cousin, firmly in the enemy camp. His presence lent a spurious pall of respectability to Lavinia's painfully obvious attempts to snag Bea's husband.

The Gang hadn't been in existence in the golden days of their courtship. Then, it had been all laughter and champagne. Their engagement had been a whirlwind of fast motor rides, breathless embraces in gardens, sneaking off to dance at Rector's, where there was a jazz band who wore fireman's helmets, and dizzy-making drinks in thick, cheap cups. It would wear off eventually, Bea knew. At some point when they were old and stodgy with three children in the nursery, when her waist had thickened and Marcus' looks had gone. But not now, not while she was still beautiful and admired, not while men still threatened, half-jokingly, to take their own lives if she wouldn't throw Marcus over and take them instead. She was the Debutante of the Decade and Marcus was puffed with pride at having won her.

As for Lavinia, she was a thing of fun, she and Deadly Dull Dick. Passing a hidden flask back and forth under the cover of a potted palm, Marcus and Bea had mocked them, stodgy, managing old Lavinia and slack-lipped Dick, their witticisms becoming wittier with each swig of cherry brandy or whatever vile concoction of the moment.

Paris had been even better, no chaperones, no disapproving dowagers. Bea's adoring husband had given her carte blanche to indulge her fancies in the newly reopened shops of the Paris couturiers. He had taken her to the Folies Bergeres, let her experiment with absinthe, gone with her on the rounds of the nightclubs of Paris. They had found friends, Old Etonians posted to Paris, young couples on holiday, roving the restaurants and clubs in a great, laughing gang, making up laughing groups for cards or picnics. And each night, she and Marcus would tumble into bed in their room at the Ritz, making the bed rumble and creak. She had laughed at him for his enthusiasm. Like a puppy, she had told him, and he had pounced, just because, making her laugh and squeal and squirm.

And then the cable had arrived, and it was all over before it had begun.

She wanted it back, she wanted it all back, she wanted the laughter and the admiration and the squealing. But, somehow, between mourning and bed rest, she had lost it all; she had been supplanted by the Gang. By the Gang and by Bunny.

It would almost be funny if it weren't so awful. There was Lavinia, organizing impromptu picnics, theatre tickets, punting parties, weekends at Haddleston, so triumphant at finally having snagged the man she'd lost, never once realizing that the real threat wasn't Bea but her own little sister. Bunny hadn't had to delay her debut; she was just out, right on schedule, eighteen and untouched—and as scheming as they came.

Bother Bunny. Bother Bunny and bother the Gang. Marcus was still married to her, wasn't he? It was time he remembered that. She would make him remember that.

Bea reached a painted fingernail to touch her husband's cheek, once so familiar, now so foreign. She could smell the special shaving lotion his valet made up just for him, bay rum and citrus. That, at least, hadn't changed. "Another weekend with Deadly Dull Dick. Poor darling. I do feel for you."

Marcus held himself stiffly. "He's a good chap," he said, not quite meeting her eyes.

Bea trailed her finger down his cheek. "You used to find it amusing when I called him that," she said softly. "You used to laugh."

He caught her hand and drew it away from his face. "Well, yes," he said awkwardly. "I didn't know him so well then. He gets better once you know him."

Once one knew Bunny, he meant. "Oh, and he improves so much on acquaintance, does he?"

Marcus didn't rise to the bait. He stood there, looking down at her, a small furrow between his brows. "What do you want, Bea?"

I want my husband back.

She wanted his eyes to light up as she entered the room; she wanted his front pressed to her back at night, his arms tight around her; she wanted someone to tell her what had gone so hideously, horribly wrong, what Bunny ffoulkes had that she lacked.

"Stay," she said fiercely. "We'll go to the clubs, see a show, have a laugh. It will be just like before. You'll see. And then . . ."

She reached out to him, twining her arms around his neck, pressing her body against his. How long had it been since they had last slept together? Months, at least. She nuzzled his ear with her nose, breathing in the familiar scent of him, splaying her fingers across his back to hold him close.

"Stay," she murmured.

She felt Marcus' muscles tense beneath her fingers, but not in the right sort of way. He patted her awkwardly on the back before untangling himself from her embrace. "Sorry, old thing. I promised Vinnie I'd be at Haddleston by supper. Maybe another time?"

Pride and rage boiled up together, choking her. Bea's hands curved into fists, her nails digging into her palms. She wanted to fly at him, to shove him, to rake her nails across his smug face. It took every ounce of her training to restrain her.

"Of course," she said nastily. "You couldn't possibly go back on your word to Lavinia. What *was* I thinking? It doesn't matter that you see the Gang four nights out of five; how could you possibly miss a day of them?"

Marcus looked wary. "I know you don't like my friends. . . ."

"Wherever did you get that idea?"

"Dislike" was far too mild a term. Bea hated, loathed, and reviled them. They were like a pebble in one's slipper, insignificant but maddening and nearly impossible to dislodge.

Bea waved a languid hand, trying not to let him see how it was shaking. "Go off. Have a ripping old time. I'll be enjoying myself here in London."

Let him just imagine how she might be entertaining herself in London without him. It would serve him right.

"Would you like to join us?" said Marcus hastily. "You're more than welcome."

"Thank you so very much," said Bea with heavy sarcasm. "I can't tell you how flattered and thrilled I am by your invitation. I imagine it will be utterly divine. Such a pity you didn't ask me sooner. I would have simply *expunged* everything else from my calendar. But as it is . . ."

"That's a pity," said Marcus, with obvious relief. "Some other time, then."

He turned to go and Bea felt panic well up in her chest. He was walking away from her; he was turning and walking away and there was nothing she could do about it. This wasn't the way this was supposed to end. Not now.

"What other time, Marcus?" asked Bea tautly. "What other time?"

He sighed and scratched his left cheek with his right hand. She used to tease him about that gesture; it was what he did when he was tired or distracted, a strangely childish gesture. Seeing it caused a lump to form at the base of her throat, like the first stages of the influenza. He looked at her, looked down, and shook his head.

That was all, just a shake of the head and a little shrug of his shoulders.

"I'll see you on Tuesday," he said, and closed the door behind him.

Bea felt herself shaking as though with cold, shaking so hard that her teeth chattered with it. He wasn't . . . He hadn't . . .

But he had. He had walked out on her, just turned and walked out. Any moment now, she would hear the motor of the car in the courtyard, and off he would go, off to Haddleston and Bunny, who would stroke him and tell him not to worry about that hag of a wife. He hadn't even bothered to stand and fight with her. He had just walked out.

Oh, God.

She drew in a long, choking breath, resting her wrists on the windowsill, her forehead against the cool glass pane. She had told herself again and again that this would pass; men had their flirtations, they strayed, they returned. But this, this had been going on too long now, was too entrenched, too public, too obvious.

How had it come to this? They'd been married little more than a year ago, a year and four months, hardly enough for the bloom to have worn off. In the early fall twilight, Bea could already see her own shadowy reflection in the window glass, turning her into a shadow of herself, older, paler. Only a year and a half ago, she had been the most sought-after woman of her Season. How had she gone from that to this?

Her pride smarted with it and, beneath the wounded pride, an undercurrent of fear. It had been one thing in her parents' day, when divorce was a scandal, a sort of social Black Death. But now . . . there had been Idina Gordon and others, new wives like her, divorced, handed off for younger, more complaisant brides. If he had to dally, why couldn't he have found a nice, married woman, someone who would play the game as it used to be played, someone who would pose no threat to Bea?

Bea's hands clenched into fists, her nails biting into her palms. No. She refused to allow herself to be reduced to a drab domestic creature, sitting idly by while her husband dallied. If Marcus could find his amusements elsewhere, so would she.

She wasn't going to go gently.

London, 1999

"Only two years?" echoed Clemmie.

She glanced back at the portrait, no longer a generic flapper, but Granny's cousin, rendered tragic by this new information.

That would explain Granny Addie's reluctance to talk about the mysterious Bea. Clemmie wondered what had happened. Childbirth? She had a vague idea that people frequently died from childbirth in the bad old days.

"Why is she still on the wall?" asked Harold, earning a dirty look from Paul. Junior associates were meant to be seen and not heard.

"Why is she still on the wall?" asked Paul loudly.

The marquess directed his answer to Clemmie. "She was said to be one of the great beauties of her time. I've always wondered if the old boy wasn't still just a little bit in love with her."

Clemmie contemplated the portrait. Yes, Bea was pretty enough, but it wasn't her porcelain-perfect features that caught the eye; it was her attitude. The woman in the portrait simmered with raw sex appeal. Despite the restrained color palette of the portrait, the black dress, the pale pearls, the silver-blond hair, the painting crackled with vitality. It was almost as if the woman in it were bound to the canvas only by the strips of paint and at any moment she would break free, stand up, and undulate her way into the room, snapping those long, tapered fingers for someone to bring her a cigarette.

"That's so sad," said Clemmie. "He lost her in life so he kept her in paint?"

"And the plaster was cracking on that part of the wall," added the marquess prosaically. "It would have been a job to find something else to cover that spot. Not that the broken-heart theory isn't more fun."

Clemmie tilted her head up at him. "I'm sorry if my great-great, er, cousin broke your grandfather's heart."

"Don't be," said the marquess. "I, for one, am rather glad that his second marriage came off." At their blank looks, he clarified, "His second wife was my grandmother."

"So he did marry again?" Clemmie wondered what the second wife had thought of having the first one still hanging on the wall.

The marquess smiled, looking rather adorably dopey. "Went forth and was fruitful and multiplied. So, you see, I owe your great-great-cousin rather a debt."

"In that case," said Clemmie, "I'm glad?"

The marquess' eyes met hers, the corners crinkling with amusement. "I won't tell your great-great-cousin that you said that."

Clemmie felt her lips quirk into a grin. "You're the one who has to live with her."

His eyes were the color of melted milk chocolate; it made her think, somehow, of winter days and ceramic mugs and her old stuffed bunny, the one she used to trail around by one leg.

"Hey!" Paul drummed his fingers against the tabletop. "This is all very interesting, but can you send the waiter over? We need to get moving. Early meetings tomorrow," he added, as though that explained everything.

"Certainly," said the marquess, doing, Clemmie thought, an admirable job of hiding his irritation. His nod neatly encompassed the entire table. "Enjoy your evening."

Clemmie wasn't quite sure, but she thought he might have winked at her. She reached for the roll on her bread plate, nibbling on a corner, trying to shake a sudden wave of vertigo.

As Paul snatched up his BlackBerry, Harold leaned towards Clemmie. "That's so cool that you're related to the owner."

"Not really," said Clemmie dismissively. She didn't like the way Paul was frowning over his BlackBerry. This boded ill. "I mean, we're not really re-lated. It's just one of these weird things." She leaned towards Paul. "What's up?"

Paul didn't look up from his BlackBerry. "Gordon isn't happy," he said.

Gordon was the general counsel at PharmaNet, the man directly respon-sible for the fact that Clemmie had been wearing the same suit for the past twenty-eight hours. PharmaNet was a United Kingdom company, but they were being sued in the United States, in the Eastern District of Pennsylva-nia, over an anti-depressant that the class-action plaintiffs claimed had been deliberately mislabeled and mismarketed. After a two-week crash course and four exhausting hours in the PharmaNet headquarters, Clemmie knew more than she had ever expected to know about the pharmaceuticals industry, the inner workings of PharmaNet, and SSRIs.

"Why isn't Gordon happy?" asked Clemmie. "We've got a strong case for limiting their scope of discovery."

She should know; she'd been up until four in the morning working on the brief just two nights ago. Only two nights ago?

Paul shook his head over his BlackBerry, sending it back to the main screen with one quick jab. "He didn't like the questions you were asking the marketing VP. Too much about the nursing homes."

The FDA approved drugs only for specific uses and populations, in this case for the treatment of depression in those over eighteen. The class-action suit claimed that the company had been illegally marketing the drug for teens, despite lack of FDA approval, as well as pushing it on old-age homes and hospitals as a cure for unspecified geriatric ills. It was the teen marketing that was the heart of the case, fueled by a few spectacular suicides of teens on the drug, but it was the geriatric issue that had caught Clemmie's attention.

"It could come back to bite them," argued Clemmie. "It has come back to bite them. I know it's a side issue, but the opposition will use it to go to our overall probity. If they can show that it was mismarketed for seniors, they have an easier time convincing the jury that we went off-label for teens."

"Look," said Paul. "If some reps got a little overzealous in their sales pitch, that's not the company's fault. They can't help it if a few guys get a little overenthusiastic."

"But what if it's not just a few guys?" asked Clemmie. "Those marketing boards they showed us—that's a clear paper trail leading back to the central management team. You can't write that off as a few rogue salesmen."

"There was *nothing*," said Paul forcefully, "nothing in those training slides that specifically directed off-label marketing."

Is your patient feeling anxious? Lost? Confused? That had been the wording on one of the slides. Beneath was a picture of a white-haired woman in horn-rimmed glasses, holding a cane. *Try Soprexa!*

It was the picture that had struck Clemmie. The cartoon figure on the screen, shapeless house dress and permed blue hair, didn't look anything like Granny Addie in her signature Chanel suits. But there was a vulnerability about the image that went straight to Clemmie's gut. She could picture Granny Addie's eyes, unfocused, as they had been that day at the birthday, hear the nurse soothingly saying, *It's just something wrong with her meds.*

"Anxious, lost, and confused" covered a frighteningly broad amount of ground. Hell, Clemmie felt anxious, lost, and confused half the time.

"Not explicitly, no," said Clemmie, "but the implications . . ."

"What are you, working for the plaintiffs? Making their argument for them?"

"No, but we should be prepared to refute—"

"We don't refute it unless they argue it," said Paul dismissively. "Until then, the last thing you want to do is build a paper trail for them or get the PharmaNet people talking about things they shouldn't be. What?"

It was the marquess again, standing hesitantly next to their table, looking as if he didn't want to be there. Clemmie couldn't blame him. She didn't want to be there either.

"Miss Evans?" he said, avoiding looking at Paul. "You have a call. From the States."

Clemmie scraped back her chair. "It's probably the Cremorna matter." Another way in which real lawyering differed from the television version: they didn't have cases, they had "matters." Dropping her napkin on the seat, she looked to Paul. "Will you excuse me?"

"Mmph," said Paul. He was assiduously clicking into his BlackBerry, using only his thumbs, probably placating Gordon by promising he had had the offending associate whipped and how did Gordon feel about a round of golf on Sunday?

"Do you want me to order for you?" asked Harold, with a wary glance at Paul.

"Thanks. I'll have the Scottish salmon, done however the chef wants to do it." Trying not to trip on the strap of her computer bag, which was protruding from beneath her chair, she turned to the marquess. "Thanks for waiting."

"This way," he said, ushering her towards the lobby with ceremonial care. Lowering his voice, he said, "I take it that was an opportune interruption?"

"Very," said Clemmie, with feeling.

By the time she got back to the table, Paul would be tucked into his bottle of Sancerre and feeling more mellow. She'd worked directly for Paul for more than a year now and learned that while he had a reputation for being a screamer—firm parlance for abusive partners—it tended to blow over quickly. He hadn't thrown a stapler at anyone since that second-year associate had threatened to sue.

"Thanks, again. This is the second time today you've come to my rescue." Struck by a sudden thought, she said, "Wait—is there actually a phone call?"

"There is," he said apologetically. But, then, everything he said seemed to come out as half an apology, a sort of self-deprecatory style entirely foreign to Clemmie. "You don't mind taking the phone call at the desk? Or we can have it put through to your room...."

Three flights up? "That's okay," she said quickly. "I don't mind taking it at the desk. It should be quick."

The fourth-year associate dealing with the Cremorna matter while she was away was the nervous type. He was probably just calling to make sure he'd dotted all the appropriate *i*'s, with anxious questions about the exact circumference of the ideal dot. Clemmie kept trying to explain to him that there were times when any dot would do.

"As you wish," said the marquess courteously, sounding rather like Wesley in *The Princess Bride.* Clemmie wondered whether it had been intentional. She suspected not.

On a whim, she leaned towards him. "I have to ask. What did happen to my great-great-whatever? Was it childbirth?"

"Childbirth?" He frowned down at her, a floppy lock of hair grazing one eye. "I'm afraid I don't..."

"I mean, how she died. The woman in the portrait." It sounded very crass put that way. But, then, there was something about talking to the English that made Clemmie feel crass by default, cross and very stridently American. It was a reflex her mother used to advantage. "You said they were only married two years."

"Ah." The marquess looked at her in surprise. "They were, but she didn't die. Not then, at least."

Clemmie's brows drew together in confusion. "Then—?"

"She didn't die; she bolted." Taking pity on Clemmie's American ignorance, the marquess translated, "She ran off with another man."

ELEVEN

London, 1920

U tter rubbish," said Frederick.

"Really?" Addie glanced up at him from under her hat, trying to unmoor a pin that had gotten stuck in her hair.

They were just back from a lecture at the London Literary Society and she had, feeling quite bold about it, invited him back to Rivesdale House for a drink. It still amazed and thrilled her whenever she thought about it, that he was standing here next to her in Bea's entryway, that he had escorted her to a lecture, that she could think of him as Frederick now, instead of Mr. Desborough.

They had fallen, over the past few months, in the habit of attending talks and lectures together. No other suppers had followed that first, impromptu one, but there had been long walks in the park and rock-hard cakes at Lyons and any number of improving talks and ear-shattering concerts. In accordance with the strictures of *The Bloomsbury Review*, Addie was trying to improve her ear with modern music, but she found some of it very hard going. Frederick liked it more than she did.

There was something so giddy making, so intimate, about that knowledge, that she knew his musical tastes as he knew hers. She could imagine herself saying it to someone: Frederick has more patience for atonality than I, don't you, darling? It implied a sort of ownership.

Today they had been to a talk on poetry and politics. Addie had had to poke him in the arm to make him stop snorting. That, too, had made her thrill.

Oh, heavens, she was being a ninny, wasn't she? Miracle enough that her hero had become her friend; she shouldn't go spoil it by going all infatuated.

Even if she was.

"I didn't think it was as bad as that," she said, struggling with her hat. The footman blandly looked the other way. Addie suspected she was the source of a certain amount of merriment in the servants' hall. Better not to know, really. "I thought there was something to it."

Frederick handed his hat and gloves to the footman standing by the door. "Music soothes the savage beast?"

"You can mock all you like," said Addie, exerting her will on the blasted pin, "but isn't there a truth to it? Music *does* soothe us, and poetry is just music by another name."

"Yes," said Frederick, "but this notion of fostering world peace by sending anthologies of verse to world leaders—how would one know if Mr. Lenin likes Keats? He might be a blank-verse sort of man. It seems a shame to precipitate another war all for the wrong sort of poetry."

"Now you're just making fun," protested Addie, craning towards the mirror to try to get a better view of the offending pin. "That wasn't what they were saying at all. Not really."

"If I didn't make fun," said Frederick flatly, "I might be offended by it. As it is, I can write it off as good-natured idiocy. Here, let me help you with that. No, stay still."

His hands pressed briefly on her shoulders, indicating that she should stay where she was. It was no more intimate a caress, Addie told herself, than stroking the neck of a horse to make it stay. Even so, she could feel the tingle of it straight down her spine.

He was poking at her hat now, doing something with the brim. Her eyes sought his in the mirror, but he was blocked now by the absurd feather on her hat.

"It's the pin," she said as he examined the back of the hat, resisting the urge to wiggle. "It seems to have got caught on—ouch!"

"I think I've found the problem," said Frederick.

"I think I felt the problem," said Addie, managing to sound quite credibly insouciant and only the slightest bit breathless.

"There," he said, and stepped back, away from her. He held up a tapered metal pin. "There's a nick. That was the culprit. Your hair must have caught on it."

Addie turned it over, glad to have something to do with her hands. "Where?"

Bea had given her a pretty hat pin for her birthday, with a bezel shaped like a flower and leaves, all inlaid with tiny, sparkling gemstones. Addie had kept it to admire and gone on using her old ones.

"There." Frederick's ungloved hand settled on hers, inching her hand down on the pin. "Can you feel it?"

"Mmm?" Addie kept her eyes glued on their joined hands.

"The nick," said Frederick. "It's right there, towards the bottom."

Addie cleared her throat. "Yes, yes, that's it. I can feel it." There was a practically infinitesimal gouge at the bottom of the pin, scarcely visible, but just enough to snag her hair, which tended to snag at the least opportunity. "I should have noticed before."

She started to retrieve it, but Frederick neatly snagged it from her. "I'll take that, or you'll forget and use it again," he said.

"Most likely," she admitted, turning away to remove her hat, which hadn't been the least bit improved by the struggle with the pin. "Did you see the notice about Mr. Hardy's appearance next week? He'll be reading from his *Collected Poems*."

Frederick looked down at her, his lips turning up at the corners in a rueful sort of smile. "You should go to university and read Literature," he said, tweaking a lock of her hair as though she were a little girl. "I can just see you as a female don in a black gown with your hair all tucked away beneath a cap."

She hated it when he did that, treated her like an adult one moment, like a woman, worthy of admiration, and then the next like someone's little sister, chucking her under the chin and tugging her hair. It was maddening.

"I should have liked to go to university," she said, "but Aunt Vera wouldn't countenance it."

Bea had needed her, too. She could remember how Bea had looked after Poppy's funeral, so thin and pale.

"And must you always listen to what your aunt Vera says?"

"She pays my allowance," said Addie pragmatically. "Or, at least, Uncle Charles does, which is really the same thing."

"You still haven't told them about *The Bloomsbury Review* yet, have you?"

"Noooo," admitted Addie. "It hasn't come up." The only periodicals Aunt Vera read were the *Tatler* and the Court Circular. And thank goodness for that.

"If you liked," said Frederick thoughtfully, "I still have a few chums at Oxford. One of them could have a natter with the Dean of Somerville, drop a word in her ear."

Addie chewed on her lower lip. Frederick might think she was an attractive candidate, but she knew the truth, that she had almost no education other than that provided by making free of the Ashford library. Their governess had been primarily concerned, per Aunt Vera's strictures, with such niceties as matters of precedence when seating a party for three hundred at a vice-regal palace.

Addie couldn't admit that, though, not to Frederick, not when she so particularly wanted him to think well of her. He had been a Balliol man and, although he hadn't told her so himself, had taken a first in History. How could she confess the inadequacies of her education to him?

"Maybe later," Addie said, and was aware of how weak it sounded. "I don't want to leave the magazine just when it's all going so well! Besides, it would be a shame to leave London just when I'm beginning to enjoy it."

"All right," he said. "As long as it's your decision, and not Aunt Vera's."

"It is," she assured him. "I really do mean it about the *Review*. I'm beginning to feel like I might be useful to them." She looked earnestly up at him. "Frederick, it's the most harum-scarum sort of place, I can't even begin to describe."

His lips twitched. "I think I can imagine."

"Nothing is ever ever where it's meant to be. They have tradesmen's bills all muddled up with proofs of poetry. We're supposed to be a monthly, but the last edition came out seven weeks ago!"

"Not terribly surprising," said Frederick, following her into one of the smaller, less baronial drawing rooms. "I've seen a number of these periodicals come and go."

"Not this one," said Addie determinedly. "Not if I have anything to say about it."

She had, she had been told by the rest of the staff, quite appallingly outmoded ideas about literature, but she had discovered in herself an unexpected talent for organization. She might make the faux pas of preferring Tennyson to Brooke, but when she had had the revolutionary idea of putting printers' bills into one pigeonhole and incoming receipts—should there ever be such a thing—into another, she had been treated as a bringer of wonders and toasted with champagne in a chipped ceramic mug. She had begun, tentatively, putting forward ideas about how things might be done, advertising secured to fund their efforts, universities canvassed to increase their circulation. For the most part, these suggestions were cheerfully ignored, philosophy being preferable to practicality, but she was beginning to work out her own plans as to how to get them done.

"You sound very fierce," said Frederick with amusement.

"Do I? I'm sorry. I don't mean to. It's just that I do so want to make this work—the magazine, I mean."

He crooked a finger beneath her chin, tilting her face up towards his. "Don't apologize," he said, his green eyes intent on hers. "Not to me."

She stared up at him, voiceless, not wanting to breathe, to blink, to do anything to upset their precarious balance. The room felt suddenly charged with electricity; she could feel it crackling between them. She hung suspended, waiting breathlessly, for him to lean forward, to—

"You didn't tell me we had visitors." A voice sliced through the silence, shattering it like glass.

Addie jumped back. Frederick dropped his hand and stepped away, as remote as if he had been on the moon. It was as if she had imagined it all, the way he was looking at her, how closely he had been standing, all something out of the pages of a book or a particularly vivid waking dream.

It was Bea in the doorway, looking cool and poised, one eyebrow raised, cigarette holder propped in one hand. The thin stream of smoke seemed to trace a question mark in the air.

Addie could feel herself flushing. "Oh, Bea, this is—I mean—"

It was absurd to feel as though she had been caught out in something when there was nothing at all to have been caught out in.

"I've seen you before, haven't I?" Strolling into the room, Bea gave Frederick a frank once-over. She paused, cigarette holder aloft. "At Oggie's."

Frederick's eyes shifted. "I'm sure I would have remembered. . . ."

Bea gave a husky laugh. "You were with Dora Palliser. I'd be surprised if you remembered anything at all."

Addie looked anxiously from Bea to Fredrick, wondering what they were talking about. She knew of Dora Palliser, vaguely. Her picture was constantly in the papers, usually paired with slightly lewd headlines. She was notorious for both her support of the more avant-garde arts and her very well-publicized affairs with several of the artists.

The jangle of Bea's bracelets interrupted Addie's train of thought. Bea flicked her wrist imperiously. "Darling, aren't you going to introduce me?"

Addie belatedly did her duty. "Mr. Desborough, may I present you to my cousin, Lady Rivesdale?" It still felt odd referring to Bea as Lady Rivesdale, as though she were someone's mother. Turning to Bea, she added, "We were just at a lecture on prosody and politics."

"How frightfully interesting," murmured Bea. She held out a hand to Addie's companion. "Mr. Desborough."

He bowed over it. "Lady Rivesdale."

Bea twined her fingers through his before releasing them again. "Why so formal? Any friend of Dora's is a friend of mine." She glanced back over her shoulder. "Drink?"

Frederick glanced towards Addie. She felt, as always, that little spark of recognition, as if it were just them, cut off from all the world. But then he looked back at Bea again, and the moment was lost. "Yes, thank you."

Bea meandered towards the drinks cart, originally Marcus' toy, now hers, equipped with a complicated mess of bottles and shakers and strange implements that looked, to Addie, like something out of the Inquisition's midnight imagination.

"Ring for more ice, will you, darling?" Addie obediently rang as Bea began expertly assembling ingredients in a shaker. "You must tell me all about this fascinating lecture."

"You'd have been bored stiff," said Addie frankly. "It wasn't really your sort of entertainment."

"Nonsense," said Bea stoutly. "I simply adore . . . prosody."

She rolled her eyes and Frederick laughed softly. He took the ice bucket from the servant and handed it over to Bea. "Your ice."

"Your drink, you mean," she said, and handed the shaker to Frederick. "Do the honors?"

Addie stood back, feeling entirely cut out. Not that Bea had done it on purpose, of course; she just had a way of attracting the attention of a room, like iron filings to a magnet. She was always telling Addie that there was no magic to it, that it was just a matter of asserting oneself. Addie watched Frederick shake the drinks, watched Bea taste and make a face and dump it out and start again. She knew she should say something, do something, but what? She hadn't anything at all interesting to say, just prosody, which, on Bea's lips, sounded quite as stodgy as it was.

Bea handed her a drink, the sapphire ring on her finger clanking against the side of the glass. Addie took it tentatively. It smelled strongly of gin. Addie set it quietly down on the marble top of a small, gilt table.

Bea took a hearty swig of her own drink. "Do the two of you have something frightfully fabulous planned for tonight? No? Then you must join me. There's a party going to Claridge's and then on to the Golden Calf. Haven't you heard of it, Mr. Desborough? I would have thought you would."

"I thought they'd closed," said Frederick.

"This is the *new* Golden Calf," said Bea blandly. "Isn't it too utterly biblical? They killed the fatted calf only to have it rise again. Or am I confusing myself? It's all terribly hush-hush, secret knocks and curtains and all that sort of thing. You must come."

"I'm not sure . . ." Addie began, galvanized into speech at last.

"Don't fuss; you'll adore it. I have a frock that will fit you perfectly."

"Only if you chop it off at the knees," protested Addie.

Bea wafted her objection aside, spattering gin in the process. "I've been remiss. As your chaperone, I ought to have seen that you got out more—and not to lectures!"

"You're hardly my chaperone," protested Addie, trying to catch Frederick's eye and failing. "We're scarcely a year apart."

"Hush, child," said Bea, tossing back the rest of her drink. "Don't you know you're not meant to speak that way to an elderly matron? It's past time I took your social education in hand." She looked at Frederick over the rim of her glass. Her pale lashes had been darkened, making them even more dramatic. "Especially if you insist on taking up with such degenerate characters as these."

"Isn't taking your charge to worship at the Cave of the Golden Calf quite the opposite of the usual work of a chaperone?" asked Frederick.

Taking the shaker from the tray, Bea deftly topped up his drink. "Not at all, Mr. Desborough. It's the work of a good chaperone to make sure her charge is prepared for *all things.*"

She stressed the last two words in a way Addie didn't entirely understand. There were circles within circles here, going around and over Addie's head.

Looking up, Addie found Frederick's eyes on her. "To the pure," he said quietly, "all things are pure."

She felt herself flush without quite knowing why. "I'm hardly as unworldly as all that," she protested, taking up her drink.

"Aren't you, darling?" said Bea lightly, and touched Frederick on the arm. "Would you be an utter angel and find my cigarette case? I left it on the chaise in the morning room, there's a dear."

"Your servant," drawled Frederick, in a very different voice from the one he used with Addie.

Addie looked to her cousin with confusion. She could see Bea's cigarette case sitting in plain sight next to the portable gramophone. "Why did you do that?"

Shamelessly Bea clicked the case open, drawing out a Turkish cigarette and tapping it against her palm before inserting it into the long, ebony holder. "Is this what's been taking up all your time, darling?"

"Not all of it," hedged Addie. She hadn't told Bea about *The Bloomsbury Review* either. It wasn't that she didn't trust her; it was just that Bea tended to be . . . a bit effusive sometimes. And sometimes there was a sting beneath it, especially when she was unhappy, as she was unhappy now. "But some. Don't you remember Mr. Desborough? He was the one who rescued Binky."

For a moment, Bea looked blank. Then she burst into a coughing laugh. "Good heavens, that ridiculous mouse!" For a moment, she sounded much more like her old self. "Will you ever forget the look on Mother's face?"

"Never," Addie agreed.

Stripped of her affectations, Bea looked more like her old self. But she also looked painfully tired. Addie was reminded of the way Bea had looked just after Poppy's death, gutted and trying to hide it.

Cautiously, Addie touched her cousin's wrist. "Is there something the matter? When you came in, I thought—"

"There's nothing the matter." Bea twitched her wrist away, prowling restlessly across the room. "I'm perfectly all right. I'm not the one racing about to lectures with strange men."

Yes, because lectures were so very compromising. Addie refused to let herself be deterred. "Have you had another fight with Marcus?"

Bea's lips tightened. "Marcus is Marcus," she said carelessly, but her hands betrayed her, her fingers digging into her palms. "We're talking about *you*. You and that Mr. Desborough. You sly old thing, you. When were you going to tell me?"

"There wasn't anything to tell," said Addie. "He's a friend."

Bea gave her a look. "Darling, you need someone to find out what your Mr. Desborough is about. You can't take a mouse as a reference."

Addie felt her chin setting. "He isn't about anything. He just likes to go to the same sorts of lectures I like to go to." Bea's blond brows rose. Addie stumbled over her words. "He's—he's a *chum*."

"Oh, darling. You can tell yourself that all you like. I saw the way you looked at him, all sun and moon and stars. I'm quite jealous, you know," she said in her bantering tone. "It's terribly lowering to be eclipsed. But if I must be," she said, and there was steel beneath her tone, "I intend to make sure it's someone worthy. If you're going to abandon me, you can't go throwing yourself away on just anyone."

"I don't think Mr. Desborough thinks about me that way," said Addie, succumbing to the horrible, overwhelming temptation to confide. She shook her head. "There's really no need, Bea."

"Don't be silly," said Bea, brisk as only Bea could be once she'd set her mind on something. Those were the moments when Addie was reminded, disconcertingly, of Aunt Vera, all that imperiousness beneath the evanescent overlay of Bea's beauty. "Wouldn't you rather make sure he's not goblin fruit?"

She smiled at Addie and Addie found herself smiling back at the memory of that old poem, of two little girls linking their pinkies and promising devotion. She'd always fancied herself more Lizzie than Laura, the sensible one, not the giddy one. "Are you afraid I'll go off into a decline?"

"Don't worry, darling." Bea's lips curved in a wolfish smile. "I'll take the bite on your behalf."

Addie knew she was only joking, but she couldn't help it, she had a sudden, horrible image of Bea smiling up at Frederick, the way he had laughed only for her. She had never minded Bea's beauty or her charm; it had only seemed fair that Bea should have first crack at their toys, at games, at men.

She was happy to cede the first place to her, but not in this, not Frederick, not even if Frederick wasn't hers to lose.

Bea hastily put down her drink. "Don't look like that, dearest! I was only joking." She looked speculatively at the doorway. "I seldom bite."

London, 1999

"I thought she looked like a slut," Clemmie said without thinking.

The marquess gave a shocked chuckle. "I thought she looked rather like you. Not like that," he added quickly. "I mean . . . That is . . ."

And he didn't even know about the hot-pink underwear. "Thank you?" said Clemmie.

The marquess was still trying to recover from his faux pas. "She was a great beauty," he said quickly. "They called her the Debutante of the Decade. My great-grandfather was quite chuffed to have caught her."

Something about the way he looked at her as he said it made Clemmie's cheeks warm. "Men wanted her, women wanted to be her?" she quipped.

"Yes," the marquess said quite seriously. "That's it exactly. Before the scandal, that is."

"Scandal, hmm?" Clemmie wondered whether Paul had gotten his

Sancerre yet and, if so, whether he would have arrived at an appropriate stage of mellow before she got back to the table.

"Oh, yes," said the marquess. "It was all dragged through the courts, divorce for adultery. Headlines in the paper, people lining up outside the courtroom." He gave a polite little cough. "Or so I understand."

"Wow," said Clemmie. And yet they kept her on the wall. Clemmie would never understand the English. "I'll have to ask my grandmother about it."

She wondered, vaguely, whom Granny's cousin had run off with, if they'd been happy together. There was something about that restless woman in the portrait that didn't go with happy. She looked like the sort who toppled kingdoms and sunk ships, good fodder for poetry, but not necessarily material for a happy life.

Dan had accused her of adultery, too. Only in her case, with the law firm rather than another man. He had said he was tired of never knowing when he was going to see her, of always coming second. "What do you care about more?" he had asked.

It was, thought Clemmie, one of those idiotic questions. If you had to ask, it meant you probably didn't want to know the answer.

"Where's the phone?" asked Clemmie.

She must have sounded more brusque than intended, because the marquess gave her a cautious, sideways glance. "Right through here," he said.

They were back in the lobby where she had registered. It felt like decades ago. And she still had to deal with Scott, the nervous associate, placate Paul, find her room, review a pile of documents . . . The very thought of it made her want to curl up into a little ball, but it had to be done; there was no way any of it could not be done. But it would all be worth it in the end when she made partner. That was what she kept telling herself. She hadn't busted her butt like this not to make partner.

Take that, Dan.

"Pamela will take care of you," said the marquess, indicating the young woman on the other side of the desk. "Line three?"

The woman nodded, her ponytail bouncing, and pressed a button, handing the receiver across to Clemmie.

Clemmie covered the mouthpiece with one hand. "Thank you," she said to the marquess. "And sorry about the whole cousin thing."

He smiled fleetingly.

Clemmie put the phone to her ear. Back to real life.

"Clementine Evans," she said briskly.

"Hello?" said a voice on the other end. It was a male voice, but it didn't sound like Scott, the nervous fourth year. "Clemmie?"

There was static and honking on the other end. "Hello?" she said. "Who is this?"

For a crazy moment, she wondered if it was Dan, tracking her down to England. Not that it would be a very Dan sort of thing to do.

"It's Jon. *Jon.* Can you hear me?"

"Just barely," said Clemmie. What was he doing calling? Clemmie propped an elbow against the side of the desk. "What's up?"

There was a sound that might have been a deep breath, or just the poor connection. "I'm sorry to call you on a business trip." The bad phone line made his voice sound much deeper than its natural tenor, the words slurring together. "Granny Addie is at the hospital—Mount Sinai."

"What?"

In the background, she could hear the sound of sirens. The line was breaking up again; she heard only: "... mother ... there ... didn't want ... call ... yet."

Clemmie seized on that one word. "What do you mean by 'yet'?" said Clemmie sharply. "What are they saying? How is she? What happened?"

There was a string of unintelligible gibberish.

Clemmie clutched the phone cord. "Jon. Jon! You're breaking up. I can't hear you."

It sounded like a hurricane blowing in the background, all whistling winds and crackling noises, like trees going over.

"Clemmie?" The static turned his voice to Darth Vader's electronic crackle and heavy breathing. "Sorry. I'm—"

More static. This was absurd. They could put a man on the moon, but they couldn't maintain a decent cell-phone connection. She wasn't sure whether it was Jon's cell phone or the little gizmos straining to make their way across the Atlantic, but whatever it was, she wanted to punch something.

"Jon," she shouted into the phone. "Jon! How bad it is?"

"Hang on." He almost sounded clear. "I'm moving."

On the other end, Clemmie fumed, wrapping the cord again and again around her hand until it left angry red marks on her fingers. She saw the desk girl looking at her and hastily shook it off, stretching her lips in an unconvincing smile.

Not bad, thought Clemmie. Don't let it be bad.

"Clemmie?" It was Jon again, still faint, but there. "You still there?"

"Yes!" she snapped. "What's going on? What happened? How bad is it?"

From very far away she heard his voice. "It's not good, Clem." And then, "I think you should come home."

TWELVE

London, 1920

All Addie wanted was to go home.

Without clocks or watch, she couldn't tell what time it was, but it might have been any time between midnight and five in the morning, an artificial world of nighttime gaiety that began well past sundown and stretched on until dawn, populated by a revolving crowd of men in white tie and women in jewels, a blur of shrill voices and half-known faces.

The evening had begun with the by now traditional cocktails at the Ritz, then on to a vertiginously high fifth-floor loft, reached via stairs and then ladder, done up in a sort of Arabian Nights theme with a band in turbans and a woman with a grating cockney accent wearing rather unconvincing gauze pants and a veil that kept getting tangled in her lipstick who took their wraps and gave them glasses of a dubious concoction that she called Turkish Delight but that tasted to Addie rather like turpentine mixed with raspberry jam. From there, they had made their way to the crowded, underground confines of Rector's, where the overwhelming scent of the cheap face powder in the powder room made Addie's stomach churn and the brass band made her ears ache. The band wore policeman's helmets—Addie wasn't quite sure why—but Geordie Pillbrook pinched one, which had led to trumpeting and squawking and the whole group piling hastily out of the club and into taxis, not, alas, to go home, but to go on to this next place, as frigidly cold as Rector's had been stiflingly hot.

This one was called The Garden of Eden, the garden represented by a few bare flagstones of outdoor space done up with a handful of desolate-looking potted shrubs and hanging lanterns made to look like apples.

It was official. Addie detested nightclubs,

She had been to enough of them to make a survey. For the last month, she had racketed from one end of London to the other with Bea's set. She had painted her lips an unbecoming red in a fruitless effort to blend in, pinning back her modest dresses to achieve the requisite low-backed effect. It always looked wrong on her, somehow. She looked wrong. She couldn't mimic their drawling slang, their casual hyperbole. "Too, too utterly shame making!" shrieked one of Bea's friends. They spoke of topics that bored Addie and of people she didn't know.

Addie knew they thought her boring. She couldn't blame them. She was boring with them. All of her enthusiasms stuck in her throat. They wouldn't want to hear about Fernie's experiments in spiritualism (Fernie had been quite convinced that she had got a message from her dead fiancé on the Ouija board the other day, although no one, including Fernie, had been able to make the least bit of sense out of it), or Addie's success in persuading the printer to allow the *Review* more credit or the hilarious spectacle of the office cat getting snarled in a typewriter ribbon, yowling furiously and leaving streaks of ink over everything and everyone as he led them a merry chase around the office until finally brought to bay behind the junior poetry editor's desk. They didn't want to hear about the lecture she had been to on political economy or "The Love Song of J. Alfred Prufrock."

How could anyone hear the mermaids singing each to each among this din?

It was her deb year all over again. Bored and boring, she trailed in Bea's wake yearning to go home. She knew everyone thought Bea a perfect martyr for taking her on. So dull, darling! Too, too yawn making!

In the midst of the fray, she could see Frederick making his way through, creating little eddies as he passed.

He did look very handsome in his evening togs, Addie thought wistfully. Not in the way Marcus was handsome, full and fair and English, but with a wiry, dark poise, as if he were made out of paper stretched over wire, intricate and precarious. He had some of that quicksilver quality she had always envied in Bea, that odd combination of vitality and grace.

Bea's friend Rosita leaned close to shout something in his ear. Addie saw the flare of his lighter as he held it to Rosita's cigarette. That was Frederick, lighter always at the ready, always game for another glass.

Gone was the man who had debated poetry with Addie, and sat rapt through a concerto that sounded to Addie like the pounding of feet on the stairs of a bus. This was a different, worldlier Frederick, a Frederick whose smile touched only one side of his mouth and whose slightest statement was double-edged and honed to cut. He fit in beautifully with Bea's set so beautifully that it was easy to forget he had originally been Addie's discovery and not Bea's.

Addie wasn't sure she liked this Frederick.

"Here you go." Frederick shouldered his way into her protected alcove. She had found a bit of high ground above the dance floor, two steps up, in the lee of a stone embrasure, guarded by a screen of those silly pots. There was a rickety wrought-iron table and chairs, uncomfortable and rust tinged but better than nothing. "Your libation, fair lady."

He had picked up their habit of speech, the insouciant, mocking tone; or maybe that had always been his and she just hadn't realized it, hearing only what she wanted to hear.

Was this what Bea had meant about the goblin fruit? That with exposure Addie would realize it tasted only of ash?

"Thank you." Addie took the cup from him, some sort of dubious mixture with a lemon peel floating on top. It looked as though they had haphazardly dropped in the contents of half a dozen bottles and stirred. If this was goblin fruit, it tasted not of ash but of very strong liquor, inexpertly mixed. She took a sip and tried not to gag. "It's lovely."

"They call it an Adam and Eve." He propped an elbow on the stone embrasure behind him, uncorking the silver flask that lived in the inside pocket of his jacket. "Designed to bring you straight back to a state of nature."

Addie hunched her shoulders. Her wrap had been designed for the interior of a warm ballroom, not a December garden. "I wouldn't mind a few extra fig leaves right now."

Frederick blinked, then frowned. "Devil take it, you're half-blue. Why didn't you say anything?"

Addie gamely lifted her glass. "I'm sure this will warm me right up!" If it didn't lay her flat out in the process.

"Don't be ridiculous," he said briskly. "You're all over gooseflesh."

He shrugged out of his jacket and set it around her shoulders. Still warm from his body, it smelled of tobacco, brandy, and Frederick.

"Thank you." Addie pulled the coat close around her shoulders, fighting an entirely unreasoning sense of pride at wearing *his* jacket. Idiot, she told herself. It meant nothing at all, other than rudimentary good manners. "But won't you be cold?"

Frederick unlooped the white silk scarf from his neck and draped it around hers. "Me? I'm steaming. Bloody hot for December." He staggered a bit as he stepped back, and Addie noticed that his color was high, his eyes bloodshot. "Too much dancing."

"Perhaps you ought to go home," Addie suggested tentatively.

"And miss all the fun?" He gestured out at the dance floor. There was the inevitable jazz band blaring away on the other side, trombones and trumpets and someone making an unconscionable rattle with a pair of cymbals.

Bea was in the midst of it all, ethereal in an ice-blue silk frock. She was modeling the policeman's helmet Geordie had pinched from Rector's, posing with it, evading mock attempts to pinch it back. Addie could hear her laugh, too high-pitched, too loud, just a little bit drunk. Addie would have gone over and hugged her, but she knew her sympathy wasn't wanted, that it would destroy the impression Bea was trying to create.

It was all about Marcus, of course. Addie had spotted him as soon as they came in, everyone fighting over the policeman's helmet, elbowing one another back and forth. Bea had been laughing and jostling with the rest, until suddenly she wasn't. It was only the briefest pause, a, *What, darling? It's the band—too deaf making!* but Addie had looked where Bea had looked and seen him there, in an alcove with Bunny.

Would you like to go? Addie had whispered to Bea quietly, so the others couldn't hear.

Why would I? Bea had said haughtily, and sailed off into the thick of the fray to make a spectacle of herself, a spectacle entirely wasted on her husband, cozy in his corner with Bunny.

"I'm not sure 'fun' is quite the word," said Addie, thinking of Bea watching Marcus watching Bunny.

"You don't like this, do you?" Frederick said suddenly. He peered at her with the concentrated stare of the inebriated. "Why?"

Because I don't fit in, she wanted to say. Because my pearls are paste and my dress looks wrong and you only dance with me because you have to.

"I don't like places where you can't hear yourself speak," she said priggishly. "As for the drinks—have you tasted them?"

"Toss 'em down faster," he said. "Then you don't have to bother with the taste."

Addie looked with distaste at her Adam and Eve. "But if you don't like something, why have it in the first place?"

"If you don't want it, I'll have it," he said, and took her drink from her.

"It's not just the drink," said Addie unhappily. "It's all of this. I just don't see the *point*. Going from place to place, complaining that it's just too boring or too hot or too crowded, only to go on to another just like it, and then doing it all again the night after that."

"The point, my dear girl," Frederick said, "is enjoying oneself. Enjoying oneself right into oblivion. Or, if the do-gooders are right, straight into damnation." He eyed the liquid in his glass skeptically, shrugged, and downed a hearty swig. "But, then, damnation is waiting for us whether we will or no. At least we'll have trod our measure along the way. A measure, a measure, a measure full of pleasure. Are you sure you wouldn't like it?"

He offered her the glass. Addie batted it away, and Frederick laughed. It was a singularly unpleasant laugh.

Addie wiggled upright in her seat, grabbing at his jacket as it started to slide from her shoulders. "I just don't see how one can countenance the idea of living purely for pleasure—especially when most of it isn't so pleasant at all! Cocktails that taste like petrol and dancing to music that's hardly music and laughing like loons at jokes that aren't the least bit funny and then waking up with a bad head the next morning. It's a waste."

"Oh?" said Frederick lazily, stretching an arm out across the back of her chair. Even through the jacket, his touch made her skin prickle. She hated herself for that, for wanting him despite all of this, all of these wasted, miserable evenings.

"Yes," she said sharply. "It's a waste. It's a waste of time and energy and intellect."

Frederick rolled his head slightly to the side so he could look at her. "You left out money," he drawled.

"I'm not concerned about money," she said primly. "It's the waste of talent that concerns me."

Frederick rummaged in his pocket for his cigarette case. "Don't moralize," he said. "It doesn't suit you."

"What does suit me, then?" she demanded. "Pinning back the backs of my dresses in the middle of December? Making conversation I can't remember a moment later—and wouldn't care to if I did? Competing for the attention of buffoons in dinner jackets who think it's the height of wit to pinch a policeman's helmet?" She could hear her voice rising and she didn't care. She'd had enough, enough of being patronized and ignored and made to feel small. "I never knew before what Shakespeare meant by an expense of spirit in a waste of shame, but now I do. I see it right before me, night after night, and I don't like it and I won't pretend I do, not for anyone."

So there. She'd had enough, enough of this, enough of him, enough, enough, enough.

Frederick leaned both hands on the metal table. The table gave under his weight, causing him to stagger slightly, but his eyes didn't leave hers.

"You haven't the slightest idea, have you?" he said softly. "You want Shakespeare? I can give you Shakespeare. 'I could be banded in a nutshell and count myself king of infinite space, but that I have bad dreams.' Do you know what it is to have bad dreams, mouse?"

"I don't see what that has to do with anything," she said with frustration.

"It has everything to do with everything." He pushed abruptly away, making the table rock. Addie's drink sloshed over the edge of the glass, spilling through the slats of the table, staining the crepe de chine of her dress. "See that man over there? The one coughing into his companion's handkerchief?"

"Yes? What of it?" She knew him, vaguely, and didn't think much of him. He'd married an American heiress and gone on to spend her money on cigarette girls.

"He got a dose of gas in Bethune. Not by the Bosh, by our side. They'd brought the wrong sort of spanners. The cylinders cracked. Do you know what it's like to be trapped in a trench with a lungful of yellow gas? Do you know what a man looks like after he's been gassed? You can't even begin to comprehend the stench of it."

Addie blinked at him, confused. He never spoke of the war. She had alluded once or twice, tentatively, to his war record, but each time he had changed the subject quickly enough to make her head spin, turning her question to the side with a joke or an observation about the scenery.

"But didn't you have masks?" asked Addie timidly.

Frederick's face was a study in bitterness. "Our masks were a mockery. You'd like the resonance of that, wouldn't you? A mere masque of a mask, all form and no function. They looked well enough for the papers back at home, but they didn't do a bally thing to keep out the fumes." He fished her abandoned drink up from the table and knocked it down. "A nice sort of poetic justice all around. We unleashed it and it killed us."

"But now that we know," ventured Addie, feeling on firmer ground here—hadn't *The Bloomsbury Review* printed an article on just this topic?— "we know better. The League of Nations—"

"The League of Nations is a sham. It's not worth the paper on which its charter is written." He stared into the empty glass, looking up with sudden violence. "No, it's worse than a sham. It's a scam. The idealists bustle around it like so many deluded ants while the realists go and stockpile their weaponry in private."

"But now that we've learned how horrid war is, surely people will want peace—"

Frederick's voice was like a lash. "People don't want peace; they want revenge. You thought the last war was bad? Just wait and see. They'll come up with more and better. More gas, more trenches, more maimed men screaming." His face twisted. "There's a peculiar sound a shell makes just before it's about to fall. A whistling noise. Can't you hear it, Addie? That's where we are now, just waiting for the next shell before the screaming begins."

She felt cold, cold straight through in a way that had nothing to do with the temperature. She swallowed hard. "But—but, surely," she said, "if we can just make sure people *remember*." She could feel herself beginning to babble. "There was the moment of silence, and you have all those articles in the papers, and statesmen and philosophers and poets all working to—"

"Words," he said flatly. "Nothing but words. Words can't protect you. They can't protect any of us."

"Oh, but you're wrong!" The table rocked as she leaned forward, clutching at it to make it still. "Words are the most powerful things there are. If we only—"

"Don't be naïve." His words hit her like a slap in the face. "It will happen again, and worse. All your poetry is nothing more than ribbons, a pretty package to wrap the basic bestiality of man. But the bestiality will out and all your free verse can do nothing to hold it. Nothing at all." He raised his glass to her, offering it in mock salute. "Drink tonight, Miss Gillecote. For tomorrow we die."

Addie knocked his hand away. "Don't be horrid," she said fiercely, standing with a scrape of metal on stone. His coat fell from her shoulders. She made no effort to retrieve it.

"You call it horrid; I call it honest." His eyes glittered like green glass. "That's not horrid. Horrid is coming back to your cot to find a couple of rats scrapping over a human hand. Horrid is men waist-deep in mud, with sores that never heal. Horrid is sharing a cigarette with a man who two minutes later has no face. You want true horrors? I could a tale unfold to harrow up your linen-white little soul. This." He pointed unsteadily at the dance floor. "All this that you so despise is the panacea that makes the horror of living just barely bearable."

"Surely," said Addie, "you can't mean that."

"Which would you prefer? Would you rather I mouth polite social nothings to you? Would you rather I lie? You probably would," he said meditatively. "Most of us prefer lies to truth, because the truth is too bloody awful. We say that we want truth. We don't. We want a pretty lie so we can dress it up in fancy clothes and call it truth."

Addie's head was swimming, and not from the drinks. She made an effort to catch on to their original argument, to bring it back to something she could understand.

"But this"——Addie made a gesture that encompassed the crowded garden, the bright lights, the gaily dressed dancers——"all this is a lie, then, too. If you're so sick of lies, why not be sick of this?"

"Not a lie." Frederick braced an arm against the wall above her shoulder, his face very close to hers. "A distraction. You might even call it a digression. A momentary pause in man's beastliness to man. Shouldn't we enjoy it while it lasts?"

"What if—" The stone of the wall was rough against her bare back, rough and cold. Her eyes were on a level with Frederick's bow tie. She lifted them to his face, saturnine in the glow of the lanterns. "What if I don't believe that man is that beastly?"

His eyes dwelled deliberately on her lips. "Don't you find me beastly?"

"Not most of the time, no," she said tartly.

She shocked him into a laugh. He pushed away from the wall, miming applause. "Well played, my dear, well played."

She hated it when he sounded like that. She watched him reach into his pocket from his flask and said sharply, "You're inebriated."

Frederick uncorked his flask. "No. I'm drunk. And I intend to get drunker." He looked down at her and his voice softened with something very like tenderness. "Go home, Addie. You're not meant to be here."

"Only if you'll come away, too," she said impulsively. "You'll thank me in the morning."

"A rescue mission?" He gave an ugly laugh. "I shouldn't bother if I were you. Do you want to know the truth? I *am* beastly. We all are. If you're wise, my girl, you'll find yourself a nice little cloister somewhere. Get thee to a nunnery, Addie. And stay there. You're too good for this wicked world. Out went the candle and we all were left darkling."

"You're mixing your Shakespeare," said Addie, "and talking nonsense."

"Not nonsense. It's the truest truth I've spoke yet. I'd have said it before if I weren't such a self-indulgent ass. There was a time when I deluded myself—but never mind that." He shooed her with the flask. "Get shot of me, Addie. Slough me off like a snake's skin. In layman's terms, stay away."

"Fine," said Addie, gathering up her wrap. "If you want to drink yourself into oblivion, I won't interfere."

"That's not what I meant." He grabbed her by the shoulders, his fingers biting into her bare skin. "This is it, Addie. The end. No more. For months now, I've tried— I can't play nursery games with you anymore."

"Nursery games?" she repeated indignantly.

"I can't batten off your belief. 'I eat the air, promised crammed; you cannot feed capons so.' It doesn't work. I'll only suck you dry, like Stoker's vampire, and leave you as much of a husk as I am. What's the point of it?" His voice was as raw as the December air, a despairing denial of the prospect of spring. "I can't offer you sweet whispers in the moonlight or prospects of domestic bliss."

Addie felt her cheeks going red. "I never asked—I never thought—"

For a moment, his hands cupped her bare shoulders, sliding down her arms in a caress, a caress that made the music and laughter recede into the distance, someplace far, far away. "Didn't you?"

Addie looked up at him, prepared to protest, to deny it, but his mouth cut off her angry words, cut off thought, cut off everything but the scent of the flowers and the taste of alchohol and tobacco on his tongue, all the forbidden fruits, making her cold skin burn wherever he touched, her head spin. The music was only a distant thrumming in her ears.

She'd liked to have thought that she raised her arms to push him away, but they wrapped around his neck instead. This . . . this was what it was about . . . the illicit pleasures at which the poets hinted, of which the moralists warned, why people abandoned propriety and fortune for a hurried encounter in a hired room.

His arms pressed her hard against him, molding her pliant form to his. But only for a moment. He released her so rapidly that she nearly fell, catching at the end of the table to steady herself.

He was breathing as rapidly as she was, her lipstick smeared on his lips, staring at her as though—as though he were afraid of her.

Cruelly, deliberately, he scooped up his jacket from the floor, turning away from her, turning away so that she couldn't see his face. But she could hear his words, every painful one of them, enunciated with horrible clarity as he shook a cigarette from its case with hands that weren't entirely steady.

"Go home, Mouse. And pretend you never met me."

New York, 1999

Jon met her at the airport.

He had to jostle her elbow before she noticed him. Clemmie was in her own private fog, her head an alphabet soup of anxieties, worries surfacing and submerging against the murky background of her mind. Her BlackBerry was buzzing; there was already a list of e-mails from Paul that stretched all the way to the bottom of the screen.

Paul had been furious when she announced that she was leaving. They had meetings scheduled tomorrow with more of the PharmaNet top brass; she was supposed to be taking interviews, preparing fact sheets. *There are outlines for everything*, she had told him. *Harold can handle it.* Harold looked like he didn't know whether to be flattered or terrified. *My grandmother is dying*, she said flatly, feeling like she was lying, hoping she was lying. *I haven't taken a vacation day in three years.*

Fine, Paul had said, and she'd known he was going to take it out of her later, with some assignment that didn't need doing, or grunt work that could have been given to a contract attorney, that he didn't think a grandparent— too far down in the food chain—was worth this dereliction of duty.

It had taken nearly twelve hours to get back to New York, twelve excruciating hours. There had been snow, delicate, storybook flakes that sent Heathrow into an uproar, delaying departures, turning Terminal Four into an ad hoc dormitory. The airport had only one deicer. How could an airport in a cold climate have only one deicer? But she was one of the lucky ones. Her plane had taken off, albeit four hours late.

Her BlackBerry started buzzing the moment she turned it on after customs. *Buzz, buzz, buzz.* She marched head down through the baggage claim, scrolling through messages, trailing her suitcase behind her. She'd meant to get a cab, but someone jostled her arm and there was Jon, waiting among the ranks of taxi and livery drivers who always queued up by the end of the baggage claim.

"I thought of making a sign that said 'EVANS' with two Ns ..." he said as he gave her the statutory one-armed hug, the proper cousinly greeting. "But you look like you wouldn't remember your own name right now."

"What is my name again?" Clemmie leaned into him a little longer and harder than necessary. He smelled of starch and the sort of detergent that promised spring freshness. Reluctantly, she extracted herself, clipping her BlackBerry back to her belt. She'd deal with Paul later. "Thanks, Jon. You really didn't have to. I was going to get a cab."

He shrugged. "No problem. Besides, I thought it might be good to prepare you a bit before we get there. This all you have?"

He took the handle of her suitcase from her before she could ask him just what he meant by "prepare."

He kept his hand under her elbow as he ushered her out the sliding glass doors, pulling her back as a car skidded past, driving perilously close to the curb.

"Asshole," he said without heat. "That wasn't his light."

"Isn't the cab line that way?" Clemmie tugged on his arm, but he shook his head.

"This way," he said, pointing to one of the short-term parking lots. Given that he had her bag, there was little choice but to follow. He clicked something on his key chain and the lights of a battered blue Mazda blinked into life.

Clemmie allowed herself to be deposited into the passenger seat, her heel snagging on a tear in the carpeting.

"Caitlin didn't get the car?" she croaked as Jon inserted himself neatly into the driver's seat, clicking his seat belt into place.

He gave her a wry look. "It was North Carolina. We had two cars."

"Oh," said Clemmie, because she couldn't think of anything else to say to it. The simple phrase carried with it a picture of domesticity she hadn't yet managed to achieve with anyone, anywhere. She and Dan hadn't even shared a coffeemaker.

"You have your license yet?" asked Jon, setting the car into gear.

"Who drives when there are cabs in the world?" said Clemmie. She shifted in her seat, the seat belt cutting painfully into her chest. "Granny Addie. You haven't told me—"

"Christ, Clemmie, don't do that!" Jon slammed on the brakes just in time to avoid rear-ending a cab that had cut in front of him. He gave her a weak smile. "Not until we're out of the airport, anyway, okay? I'm not used to New York drivers yet."

"Okay, but—"

Jon flipped on the radio to 1010 WINS, the automotive equivalent of white noise. A canned voice informed her that there were delays on the GW Bridge, but the Throgs Neck looked clear. "You might want to nap a bit. You look like crap."

"I'd like to see how fresh you look after two transatlantic flights and three days in the same suit," said Clemmie, stung.

There was a complicated tangle in front of them involving two cabs and a livery car. Jon pulled over into a space on the side, twisting in his seat to look at Clemmie.

"For once, don't fight me on this? It's going to be rough enough for you without the sleep deprivation factor." He started ticking off items on one hand. "The Greenwich cousins keep calling, wanting to know if she's dead yet. Your mother and Anna are at each other's throats. The lawyer is hovering like a vulture. And then—there's Granny Addie." He cleared his throat, his eyes shifting away. "Don't kid yourself. You're going to need all your strength when we get there."

"What about you?" she asked guardedly.

Jon shrugged and turned the key in the ignition. "I haven't been on two transatlantic flights. And I don't wear suits."

"Wait." Clemmie put a hand on his arm. The engine died down into a low rattle. "I get it. I'll close my eyes and be quiet and whatever. But before we go, I need to know. What happened?" Her voice broke on the last word, all the frustration of the last ten hours seeping through.

Jon pressed his eyes closed and opened them again. When he spoke, he looked at the windshield, not at Clemmie. "Donna found her on the floor next to the bed," he said in a monotone. "She had hit her head on the edge of her night-table drawer. They think she might have been reaching for something, overbalanced, and fallen."

"But—it's just a knock on the head?" Even as Clemmie was saying it, she knew there was no "just" when it came to a woman of ninety-nine.

Jon shook his head helplessly. "That's it. They don't know. They think she might have had a heart attack and then fallen or that she might have fallen, hit her head, and had a heart attack. We just don't know." He sounded as frustrated and angry as Clemmie felt. Remembering himself, he said quickly, "But they're doing everything they can, Clemmie. It's a good hospital. And your mother wouldn't let them do otherwise."

"Mmm-hmm," said Clemmie. Her mother could be a bulldog when she wanted to, entirely mono-minded. But Clemmie's mind was on other things, picturing Granny Addie lying crumpled beside the bed, on the pale-blue flowered carpet, her night-table drawer open, Bea's black-and-white face staring sightless at the white plaster ceiling. "How long was she there for? Before they found her?"

Jon took off his glasses, rubbing them on the hem of his shirt. It was a blue and yellow polo shirt and beginning to look nearly as worn as Clemmie's suit. "It couldn't have been more than half an hour," he said wearily. "Donna checks up on her at regular intervals ever since that incident last summer."

"What incident?" Clemmie twisted so far that her seat belt rebounded against her.

If he'd said, Don't you know? she might have punched him. Instead, he said, "She was on her own watching TV, didn't like what came on, reached for the remote, and overbalanced. Debbie was in the kitchen making dinner and didn't hear her." He slapped a palm against the steering wheel, taking out his frustration on the one thing in reach. "That apartment is too damn big."

"No one told me," said Clemmie, tight-lipped. Jon had been living in a different state, and he knew. She was all of forty blocks away, and she hadn't.

"Maybe you didn't ask," said Jon, and put the car back into gear. "Damn. I'm sorry, Clemmie. That was crappy of me. It's just been . . ." He groped for words. "It's just been a long two days."

"No need to apologize." Clemmie leaned stiffly back against her seat, staring up at the folded sun shield. There was no need to apologize when it was true. "I'll just take that nap, okay?"

"Clem—"

"It's fine," she said quickly, keeping her eyes closed. "Just drive."

At her waist, her BlackBerry buzzed and buzzed again.

THIRTEEN

New York, 1999

Y ou can't stay here."

"Huh?" said Clemmie blearily. She must have fallen asleep under her desk again. "I didn't mean—I'll be just a—"

Her heel scrabbled against a tiled floor and she came fully, unpleasantly awake. Her mouth felt gummy and her back hurt.

This wasn't her office. It took her a moment to remember where she was, cramped in an awkward chair, in a gray room whose fluorescent lights only contrived to make it look grayer. A dusty poinsettia sat on a side table and tinsel drooped along the top of the window frame. It had come unmoored on one corner, one side drifting dispiritedly down. There was an electronic menorah on a side table, unplugged. One of the bulbs was missing. Someone had taped paper angels and snowflakes to the window, but the white paper had already turned a dirty gray.

Her contacts had glued themselves to the corners of her eyes. Blinking, she saw two Jons, both of them blurry.

"You were asleep," he said unnecessarily.

Behind him, between the paper snowflakes, Clemmie could see twilight streaking the sky above the park. Evening again. She had been here for more than twenty-four hours and Granny Addie hadn't once woken up. There had, from time to time, been vague flurries of activity involving machines and things that beeped, but, in the end, the official word was always the same: no change.

"What time is it?" she croaked. She scrabbled at the arms of her chair. "Has anything—"

"No," he said quickly. "Nothing like that."

A sudden, unreasoning wave of panic cut through the fog of fatigue. The last she remembered, her mother had been pacing one side of the room while Aunt Anna sat elegantly in a chair on the other, idly flipping through a magazine, the sort of magazine so strongly scented that Clemmie had been able to smell the perfume clear across the room. Now Aunt Anna's chair was empty, Clemmie's mother's, too. Even the phantom smell of perfume had gone.

Clemmie struggled upright, the vinyl padding squeaking in protest. "Where's Aunt Anna?"

"She's right outside. She went out to take a call."

Clemmie regarded Jon suspiciously. "And my mother?"

"Badgering the nurses." Jon regarded her with something dangerously close to pity. Clemmie scowled at him. He said gently, "They've got it under control, Clemmie. Take a break. Go home."

Home. Her cluttered box of an apartment on West 52nd Street, where she hadn't even bothered to put up drapes. What was the point? She was hardly ever there. That wasn't home. Home was Granny Addie's apartment, with the brocade drapes with the tassels, with the ink stain on the carpet where Clemmie had dropped a calligraphy pen when she was ten, with its familiar smells of potpourri and lemon oil and Lancôme liquid foundation.

"Go home," Jon repeated. "You look wiped. You're not doing anyone any favors by wearing yourself out. They'll call you if . . . if there's any reason to."

Clemmie shook her head. Her apartment was all the way across the park in midtown; Rockefeller Center was virtually impassable in tourist season, even if one could find a cab, which one probably couldn't.

"My apartment is too far away," she said bleakly. "What if something happens?"

She didn't have to elaborate on what she meant by "something." She wasn't sure she could.

"Then come to my place," said Jon reasonably. "It's closer. You'll be able to get back here in five minutes. You can nap on my couch."

"What? No bed?"

"And let you get too comfortable?" His voice was gently mocking. "That would ruin the whole martyr routine."

Clemmie shot up in her chair. "That's not fair."

"Made you move," he said. "Look. You're dead on your feet. And how long have you been wearing that suit?"

Clemmie didn't even bother to try to count. "Since the Ice Age. I think of it as my pelt."

"Yeah, and it's starting to look like one, too. I can't offer designer clothing, but I can offer a shower and some shrunken T-shirts." He held out both hands, palms up. "Take it or leave it."

Clemmie's shirt felt suddenly very itchy. She caught herself scratching and made herself stop. The idea of clean clothing—not to mention clean hair—was sinfully tempting.

"Are you sure it's only ten minutes?" she asked warily.

Jon knew when he'd gotten her. "Less by cab," he said. "I'm right over on IIIth and Amsterdam."

"Let me check with Mother." Clemmie hauled herself painfully to her feet, using the armrest to propel herself up. The metal handles felt sticky to the touch. Her legs felt as unfamiliar and inconvenient as those of the baby fawns' in *Bambi*, wobbling at the knees and trying to go the wrong way. A wave of dizziness made her sway.

"Whoa, there!" Jon caught her by the arm.

Clemmie wiggled away. "I'm fine. Really, I am."

Jon cautiously let go. "There's no need to be Superwoman all the time."

Clemmie let out a snort. "Ha! I'm not even Batgirl." Batgirl had always struck her as a singularly ineffectual superperson. But what could you expect when she was called girl? "Wait here?"

"I'm not going anywhere," said Jon.

By now, Clemmie could have found the way to Granny Addie's room blind-folded. She opened the door cautiously, but the machines that surrounded her grandmother seemed to be silent, nothing bleeping or squawking. Granny Addie lay as still as an effigy on a tomb, her body incredibly shrunken and small even in the narrow hospital bed. Clemmie's mother sat beside her, at the slight remove necessitated by the wires and tubes, all the apparatus keeping Granny Addie tenuously tied to life. The heartbeat measured on the monitor seemed to Clemmie's untrained eyes to be perilously faint.

There was a book in her mother's lap, a Dorothy Sayers mystery—her mother had always liked mysteries; Clemmie had hurriedly purchased a pile for her at the bookstore at Heathrow, just in case—but she wasn't reading. She wasn't sleeping either. She was just sitting there, staring into space, her shoulders slightly hunched beneath the jacket of her gray tweed suit.

"Mother?" Clemmie ventured, and the woman in the chair turned abruptly.

The harsh light seemed to strip the skin from her face, peeling her down to the bone, emphasizing the sagging flesh at neck and chin.

She looked, Clemmie realized with sudden fear, old. That, of course, was wrong; she was Clemmie's mother; she wasn't supposed to age, not as the rest of the world aged. She had always been old, in that she was older than Clemmie's friends' mothers, always solidly rooted in middle age, even when Clemmie was little. She was middle-aged and she had stayed that way, with the same hairstyle, the same clothes, the same heavy foundation and subdued lipstick, the same blouses with bows at the neck and skirts made of variations of tweed and plaid for winter, beige linen for summer.

"Mother?" Clemmie repeated with concern.

Her mother leaned back in her chair. "You startled me," she said shakily. "You look so like her. So like—" Breaking off, she shook her head, as if to clear it. "What time is it?"

"It's five forty-five." Clemmie kept her voice low. "Jon suggested I go back to his place to wash up. He says it's only ten minutes away. I think he's afraid of being downwind of me."

Her mother nodded without looking at her, pressing her fingers to her temples. "All right."

"I can stay with you—if you like." Clemmie edged closer, wanting to comfort her but not sure how. They had never been a physically affectionate family. It seemed almost a breach of etiquette to reach out to her, a kind of presumption, although it was so very clear that she was hurting, hurting badly, with no one to talk to. "If I can help—"

Her mother's shoulders stiffened. "Go with Jon. The last thing I need is you getting sick now." Brusquely she added, "I told Jon not to call you. There's no point in everyone being here."

But she wasn't everyone. She was—and there Clemmie stuck. It wasn't as though Granny Addie didn't have other grandchildren, but Clemmie had been the one on the spot, always. Well, almost always. But she couldn't exactly come out and announce, I know Granny Addie loved me best, especially not now, when it sounded so petty and pointless. And if she felt this way, how must her mother feel? Clemmie had never really thought about her mother and Granny Addie in those terms—Granny Addie was always somehow peculiarly hers, her mentor, her second mother—but she was her mother's mother. There were years and years and years there of which Clemmie knew nothing. Her mother, always so fiercely independent, had relied on Granny Addie more than any of them liked to acknowledge.

Clemmie wished Mother and Aunt Anna were closer; that might have made it easier for them, to have someone to talk to, to comfort each other in a way that Clemmie couldn't.

As if that were ever going to happen.

"You will call me if anything changes?" Clemmie pressed. "If Granny wakes up, or . . ."

"Yes! Yes." The book slipped from her mother's lap and she grabbed for it just before it fell.

"I'll be at Jon's if you need me."

"That's fine," said her mother, and went back to her lonely vigil.

In her hospital bed, Granny Addie said nothing at all.

London, 1920

"Darling, what's wrong?" Bea caught up to Addie just outside the cloakroom.

"I've had enough, that's all." Addie struggled into her coat, jamming an arm into a sleeve and looking as though she were about to burst into tears. "I *hate* nightclubs. I'm going home."

"But the night's just begun." Bea held out Addie's sleeve for her. "It's that Desborough, isn't it? What did he do?"

"Nothing, really, Bea. He's just—oh. I feel like such a fool! Never mind. I just want to go home."

"You're not taking a taxi by yourself." Bea collared Geordie Pillbrook, still sporting his ill-gotten helmet. "My cousin's not feeling well. See her home, won't you, darling?"

Like most men, he responded well to direct orders. It was a pity it didn't work on Marcus anymore.

Bea didn't want to think about Marcus. It was much more satisfying to fight someone else's battles. Yes, that was she, a regular—what was that goddess' name? The one in the breastplate with the spear, usually seen posing fetchingly on people's ceilings. Addie would know.

What *had* the bounder said to her to make her look like that?

It wasn't hard to find Mr. Desborough. He was propped against the wall like an illustration of dissolution, glass in one hand, cigarette in the other. Smoke drifted up around his face as he lifted the cigarette to his lips.

"*Such* an inspiring image of British manhood," said Bea acidly. Drawing a cigarette out of its silver case, Bea fitted it into her holder. "What did you say to Addie? She looks like death. If you hurt her, I'll have your eyes out."

His eyes lingered on her red-lacquered fingertips. "You have the nails for it. Don't worry. I've only been cruel to be kind." He obligingly produced his lighter but paused before clicking it into light, holding it just beneath Bea's cigarette. "You set this up, didn't you? You've been waiting for this."

"Right now," said Bea, shaking back her shingled hair, "I'm waiting for a light."

He clicked the lighter, producing a flame that shuddered in the breeze. He cupped it with one hand. "Don't play games. Do you know what I think?"

Bea leaned into the flame. "I suspect you intend to tell me."

He clicked the lighter shut, shoving it back in his pocket. "I think you were jealous."

Taken aback, Bea coughed on an indrawn breath. She hastily blotted her tearing eyes before she smeared her kohl. "Really, Mr. Desborough! Don't flatter yourself."

He wasn't rattled by it. "Not that way," he said, and she noticed that his speech was just a little too careful, the enunciation a little too correct. "The other way around. You'd never had a real rival for her affections before, had you?"

"You are making yourself tedious, Mr. Desborough," said Bea coldly. "Be a dear and go off and bore someone else? That is," she added cattily, "if you can remove yourself from that wall without toppling over. I shouldn't like to see you go splat."

Mr. Desborough leaned back against the wall. "Don't worry. You've won. I've removed myself from the lists. I've fallen on my own lance in the most gentlemanly way. I've used up my last chivalric instinct and I am left darkling."

He was talking sheer gibberish. Bea raised her eyebrows at his empty glass. "Someone's been sampling a little too much of the old Adam and Eve."

"If you mean original sin? I'm wallowing in it. If you mean the drink? That, too. It's a fallen world and I intend to be prone before the end of the evening."

"Don't let me impede you," said Bea, but instead of walking away as she ought, she looked at him curiously. Where most of her set were boys, oversized boys, still redolent of the playing fields of Eton, as exuberant and mannerless as puppies, Desborough usually gave the impression of being effortlessly in control of himself and his surroundings.

Not tonight. His evening togs were still impeccable, his bow tie tied, but his hair was rumpled where he had leaned against the wall and there was a tremor to his wrist as he took a glass off a passing tray.

Bea snagged another, watching as he downed half of his in one smooth slug. "You're not usually sloppy. What cast you over the edge? Don't tell me it's unrequited love."

Fleetingly she remembered Addie's pale face and felt a pang of guilt. Infatuation, she told herself. That was all. Addie was better off out of it. She'd thank Bea for this someday.

"Men have died and worms have eaten them, but not for love." Desborough pitched his cigarette onto the flagstones, grinding it into the ground with one quick, efficient motion. "Did you know Kenneth Cartwright?"

"Not to speak to." She did know the name, though. He'd been in her brother Edward's house at Eton. Edward had thought him a frightful wet. "He wrote poetry, didn't he?"

"You use the past tense advisedly. He wrote, now to write no more. 'For Lycidas is dead, dead ere his prime, / Young Lycidas, and hath not left his peer. / Who would not sing for Lycidas?'" At Bea's look, he said, "He's killed himself. Stuck his head in the oven and turned on the gas. He survived the gas in the trenches only to gas himself in his own bloody oven. How's that for poetic irony?"

"I'm sorry." It sounded painfully inadequate.

"I am, too," he said. "It's a bloody waste. The War got into his head. He couldn't stick it. So he stuck his head in an oven instead."

Bea couldn't think of anything at all to say.

"God help poor old Cartwright." Desborough shook his head and the rest of his body swayed with him. "He wanted to translate Dante. Instead, he found himself in Inferno, without a Beatrice to help him find his way out." He looked meaningfully at Bea.

Bea wasn't entirely sure what he was talking about, but one thing was very clear. "Don't look to me to rescue you," she said tartly. "I'm too busy making a muck of my own affairs to bother with ruining anyone else's."

Desborough raised a brow. "With one notable exception. Your cousin."

That was different; Addie was Bea's in a way that no one else was hers. Addie needed her, had needed her ever since that night she had been presented to the nursery at Ashford, all tousled hair and confusion. She'd needed Bea to tell her how to get on then and she still needed Bea to tell her how to get on now.

Not that it was any of Desborough's business, with his ridiculous ideas about jealousy. As if she were jealous of Addie's friends! Addie was the one who relied on her, not the other way around. She'd be delighted if Addie found someone, someone nice and kind and patient who'd take care of her, a schoolmaster, perhaps, or a budding parson. Addie would make an excellent vicar's wife. Not now, of course, but by and by.

"Isn't there something about the exception that proves the rule?" Bea said flippantly. "Addie hasn't anyone else to look after her. I'll need at least one good deed if I'm to get into heaven."

"And she's your good deed? She might resent that."

Bea bristled. "She certainly can't be trusted to look after herself. She hasn't a worldly bone in her body, poor darling."

Mr. Desborough leaned back against the wall, regarding her with open amusement. "So you've set yourself up as guardian of her virtue?"

Bea frowned at him. "You make it sound positively medieval. Let's just say that I help to weed out the rotters."

That took the smug look off his face. "Meaning me."

Bea shrugged her bare shoulders. "You said it, not I."

He raised his brows. "You have more wit than you pretend."

"Thank you for your glorious condescension." Bea blew out a long plume of smoke. "Speaking of my cousin, you appear to have given her a crashing headache. What *did* you say to her?"

"I told her to get shot of me. I told her I was a bad lot. In short, I performed your office for you."

"How surprisingly accommodating of you." Bea leaned one shoulder against the wall. "Why?"

He rested the back of his head against the wall and stared out above the dancers. "Call it a lingering trace of decency. When I'm with her, I feel like one of those poor beggars trying to warm themselves by someone else's fire, scrounging for a bit of borrowed light. There are no dark corners to her soul. She just is what she is and that's all. She believes in things."

"Mmm," said Bea. If what he meant was that Addie had failed to master the use of maquillage and joined various groups for the support or the prevention of this and that, well, then, yes, all that was true.

Mr. Desborough was off in his own reverie. "When I talk to her, I feel like an undergraduate again, back when everything was simple and the world made sense. She almost makes me believe in the things I used to believe in. Before." He gave a bitter laugh. "But that's an illusion, a dangerous one. I don't know that I'll stick my head in an oven, like old Ken, but one of these days something is going to crack."

"And you don't want it to crack near her." Bea felt as though she were glimpsing something she hadn't suspected existed, like a primordial beast lifting its head out of a swamp. There was something vaguely unsettling about it. "How terribly chivalric of you."

Mr. Desborough went on without seeming to hear her. "She has so much bloody faith. Do you know, she really believes you can bring peace to the world with poetry? Then there's that bally magazine of hers—"

"That what?" Bea asked sharply.

Mr. Desborough looked at her as though just seeing her. "She didn't tell you? Then it's not for me." He cocked an eyebrow. "She might have thought you wouldn't be interested."

Touché. Bea shrugged, pretending a nonchalance she didn't feel. "To each her own."

And to each his own. From their vantage point, she had a clear view of the table where Marcus and Bunny sat with Euan and Barbie Wallace. Bunny turned up her face to Marcus, and he brushed his lips across hers, right there, in public.

There was a waiter passing with a tray. Bea helped herself to another drink. "That used to be my own," she said indistinctly.

"What?" said Mr. Desborough, leaning forward and overbalancing slightly.

Bea caught his arm to steady him, or herself, she wasn't sure which. How many cocktails had she had? She'd lost track. She might, just might, be a little tipsier than she'd thought.

"Over there," she said thickly. "No, that table, the other one, behind the potted apple tree. Do you know who that is?"

"Lord Kitchener?"

"My husband. In theory." Bea upended her drink and looked about for another one. Mr. Desborough obligingly handed her his. "In practice, he's not much of one."

"Who's the woman?" asked Desborough.

Their little alcove felt a bit like a confessional, quiet and dark. And if she was this drunk, Bea told herself, Frederick Desborough had to be drunker. He wouldn't remember a thing she had said in the morning. And it was such a relief to be able to say something to someone, instead of pretending to be happy, happy, happy all the time.

"Bunny ffoulkes," said Bea. "Her older sister Lavinia made a go for him, but I won. But then Bunny moved in. . . ."

Who would have thought this could happen? They were married. Married. That was supposed to mean something, not eternal devotion, Bea didn't believe in that, but at least a modicum of discretion in conducting one's affairs; that was what her parents' generation had practiced. One could borrow someone else's spouse, but one always returned him in the end; the rules were very clear about that. But now . . . But now . . .

"She means to marry him," said Bea abruptly. "It's quite clear."

"Shouldn't you have her eyes out, then?" She could feel Mr. Desborough's breath as a puff against her ear, not unpleasantly scented with gin.

"Too obvious. Besides, it would only engender sympathy. I'd be the Belle Dame sans Merci while she'd be all pure and lily white." Bea shook out her blue silk skirt with unnecessary vehemence. "Vile little vamp. It's too, too sick making."

"You're going about it all wrong," said Mr. Desborough.

"And you would know how?" Bea gave him a superior look. "Is this another one of your chi-ch-valric impulses?" It might have come out better if she hadn't stammered over "chivalric."

"Who am I to resist a damsel in distress?" There were, magically, more drinks. Mr. Desborough took a swig before turning back to Bea. "It's all about jealousy. His, not yours. You have to make him jealous."

Bea stumbled a little on the Louis heel of her blue silk shoes. "Didn't you see me out there, flirting with Geordie? If that didn't make him jealous—"

"Why should it? It's quite obvious you're not the least bit attracted to Geordie."

"That's presumptuous."

"It's plain to anyone with eyes. If you want to make—" He looked inquisitively at Bea.

"Marcus," Bea provided.

"If you want to make Marcus jealous, you have to give him cause. Genuine cause," he said with emphasis.

Something about the way he said it made the hairs on Bea's arms prickle. Genuine cause. Not just a flirtation on a dance floor, but the real thing: someone's lips on hers, hands in her hair, bare skin against bare skin; the thrill of sneaking off a dance floor to a secluded hallway; hurried meetings in the middle of the day; the exhilaration of eluding capture. She remembered Marcus hustling her out of a formal dinner in France, the madness of making love on a balcony, the incredible rush of it all.

How long had it been since he'd touched her? Six months, at least. No, more. At first, it was chalked up to being considerate. She'd lost his baby; she was delicate, or at least that was what the doctor said. Shock over Poppy, a mild case of influenza, miscarriage.

But Marcus had stayed away and he'd stayed away and now he was kissing Bunny and Bea was sick of being left to molder and rot as though she were someone's maiden aunt. Why should she just stand here and wait for him to divorce her? Why should she let Marcus have all the fun?

Hands . . . lips . . . hushed laughter . . . Oh, she wanted it.

She raised her eyebrows at Mr. Desborough. "Sauce for the goose, you mean?" she said huskily.

Mr. Desborough gave her a long, assessing look. "It seems to me the goose is saucy enough already."

Bea exhaled smoke. "I can't tell if that's a compliment . . . or a condemnation."

He braced a hand on the wall behind her. "Which would you like it to be?"

He was very close to her, close and warm and very, very different from Marcus, wiry where Marcus was broad, dark where Marcus was fair. Bea wondered what his hair would feel like beneath her fingers, whether it would be soft or stiff with gel, what the prickles on his jaw would feel like against her skin. Would his kiss be different from Marcus' kiss?

Bea touched a finger to the top stud of his shirt. "Is that a proposition?"

With her heels, they were nearly the same height. His breath was warm on her cheek. "I thought you'd decided I'm a bad lot."

"Yes," said Bea, and her voice came out much more steadily than she would have thought. "But I'm a bad lot, too."

She had to be, to be contemplating what she was contemplating. She had cultivated a shell of worldliness, but never like this before. Before it had been all in play, but this was real.

Bea thought fleetingly of Addie, gone home with a headache. Addie need never know. This was separate, this was different; Mr. Desborough had already severed their connection. A nice parson—she'd find Addie a nice parson, someone reliable and dependable, without this whiff of brimstone about him, this dangerously attractive whiff of brimstone.

In fact, Bea told herself, she'd be doing Addie a favor, keeping Mr. Desborough away from her. Hadn't he himself said that he was bad for her?

"You want distraction," she said huskily. "I want revenge. Don't you think we might help one another?"

He picked up her hand where it rested against his chest. His thumb stroked gently against her palm. "Two lost souls, fiddling while Rome burns?" he said softly, and lifted her hand to kiss the pale blue veins at the base of her wrist.

"Something like that," said Bea breathlessly. She wasn't sure about Rome, but his lips burned against her wrist; she felt uncomfortable and squirmy in her own skin, restless and reckless, as though she were burning from the inside out. "If we're going to burn anyway, why not enjoy the trip?"

Mr. Desborough's fingers locked through hers. "A woman after my own heart."

Bea tilted her head archly. "I thought you didn't have one."

" 'I would I had no heart for I fear it is a hard heart,' " he said rapidly. Poetry, again. He stepped back, looking at her with hooded green eyes. "Shall I see you home?"

Bea looked over her shoulder at Marcus. He was nose to nose with Bunny, his forehead resting familiarly against hers.

"I can see you home," said Mr. Desborough—no, Frederick. He was watching Bea watch Marcus. "Or I can see you home. Either way, the choice is yours."

Bea leaned against Frederick, chest to chest, hip to hip, thigh to thigh.

"Not my home," she said huskily. Addie was there. And Marcus might come back. She slid a hand across his back, feeling the warmth of his skin through his shirt. "I'd much rather see yours."

FOURTEEN

New York, 1999

H ome, sweet home," said Jon, flipping on the light in the front hall.
     The single bulb illuminated a wilderness of cardboard boxes and
framed posters still in their packing cases. A pile of unopened mail sat on
one of the boxes, bills and solicitations and slippery catalogs spilling over
the side. The walls were a pale cream color, contrasting with the white
wainscoting, although the paint along the baseboards was beginning to
flake.

"It's nice," said Clemmie, unwinding her scarf.

"You mean it could be nice. Hold on to that for a second." Bending over,
Jon shifted a pile of posters leaning against what turned out to be a closet
door. It opened with a creak and a grunt. Inside hung a beige raincoat and
a battered black overcoat.

Clemmie handed over her coat and scarf. "It's nicer than my place."

"That's the benefit of renting all the way up here." The empty hangers
clanked against each other as Jon hung up Clemmie's old cloth coat. "More
bang for your buck. And we get a housing subsidy."

"Is this Columbia housing?" The building was pre-war, mellow, and
lovely, with weathered pink bricks striped in pale stone. The floors might

have been scraped, but they were real, long slats of honey-colored wood laid out in a repeating pattern.

"No, but most of the building seems to be Columbia related. It's like a dorm for professors."

"Keggers in the lobby?"

Jon gave her a look. "I said 'dorm,' not 'frat.' Bathroom's through there." He pointed her to the left, towards what was clearly the bedroom. Clemmie cleverly deduced this by the presence of a mattress on the floor, sporting rumpled sheets and a blanket. "Don't be afraid of the towels. I just washed them."

"You're not going to give me the tour?"

"There's not much to tour. Bedroom to the left, study straight ahead, living room and kitchen to the right. It's your standard rectangle."

Belatedly Clemmie remembered that he had had a house with Caitlin, a house with a yard and two cars in the driveway and, for all she knew, 2.5 cats and a dog. She knew that at one point, a very long time ago, she'd lived in a house with both her parents and her two older brothers, but that had been so long ago that the memory had faded to something like the print in a children's picture book, flat and unidimensional. She'd been an apartment dweller for as long as she could remember.

That had been another fight with Dan. He'd wanted a house, eventually. She couldn't imagine living not surrounded by floor upon floor of miscellaneous strangers. The goal wasn't to get out of the box but to be able to afford a larger, grander one.

Clemmie trailed after Jon into the bedroom. "Hey, at least you have a rectangle. Mine's a square. A very small square."

The bedroom was decorated in a style that could best be described as early cardboard box. A reading lamp stood on one cardboard box, Jon's alarm clock, a novel, and a spare pair of glasses on another. A few pairs of pants and dress shirts hung in the closet, but the rest of Jon's belongings appeared to be living in boxes still, all bearing the same, nondescript label: BEDROOM.

Jon rummaged in one of the boxes. "T-shirt and boxers okay?"

"Perfect," said Clemmie.

There were no shades on the windows. It was a back apartment looking out onto the narrow shaft between buildings. The people on the other side of the street had their shades drawn, little slivers of light showing between the slats. The apartment had that strange, dusty empty-apartment smell, the smell of open floor and exposed woodwork. The light reflected strangely off the bare walls and empty floors, making the room seem dimmer, rather than brighter.

"They're clean," said Jon, and Clemmie realized he'd been holding the clothes out to her, waiting for her to take them. "I just don't have a dresser yet."

Clemmie blinked. "Sorry. Just had a moment of total phaseout." She bundled the clothes clumsily into her arms. "Thanks, really. Even if they weren't clean, they have to be better than what I have on."

Jon made a deprecatory gesture. "Sorry I don't have a washing machine. . . ."

"No, really, it's fine, great." She backed away, feeling strangely shy. "Shower through here, right? Thanks."

The shower curtain was stiffly new, clear, with a pattern of slightly dyspectic rubber ducks. It smelled strongly of plastic. Clemmie showered quickly, rubbing his two-in-one Head & Shoulders into her strange, short hair, turning up the heat as high as she could stand. She felt as though she were fumigating herself, purging away the last few days, London, the hospital, everything.

The T-shirt and shorts Jon had left her were clearly his and not Caitlin's leftovers. Jon wasn't much taller, but he was broader. Clemmie had to hitch his old gym shorts to keep them from falling down. The shirt clung damply to Clemmie's chest, faded from multiple washings. She could put her bra back on—but it was as grimy as the rest of her clothes. And Jon had certainly seen her in less. She dropped it back onto the bundle of discarded clothes.

Combing her damp hair with her fingers, Clemmie wandered into the living room. "Jon?"

There were built-in bookcases along one wall, with a fireplace in the middle, but the books were currently all still in boxes, with hand-scrawled labels saying things like TUDOR-STUART or 19TH C. POLIT. HIST. or WAR POETS. There was a television on the floor next to the fireplace, not plugged in, and one of the chairs that, in college, Clemmie had heard vulgarly referred to as a "flip and fuck." That was the sum total of the furnishings.

The ancient radiator clanged, filling the room with steamy warmth and a slightly sulfurous smell.

"In here." From the kitchen, a kettle whistled. The sound abruptly stopped and Jon poked his head around the partition. "Tea? Or something stronger?"

"Stronger."

"Good. I hate drinking alone." Jon's head disappeared back into the kitchen. There were miscellaneous rumbles and thumps.

Clemmie hovered in the opening. "Can I help?'

"There's nothing to help with." Jon was cracking ice out of a battered tray into a surprisingly elegant ice bucket, with a ring on either side held in the mouth of a stylized lion.

"Nice ice bucket," Clemmie commented.

"Wedding loot," he said tersely, and Clemmie looked away, flustered.

She toyed with the dishcloth hanging from the fridge door. It was printed with faded images of Big Ben and bright red phone booths. "I have a friend who only gives edible gifts for weddings—fudge, Cake of the Month Club, that kind of thing. She says it saves the divvying up later on."

"Smart woman," said Jon shortly. He dumped pretzels into a bowl. "Take these into the study?"

Clemmie took them. The bowl was so new it still had a sticker on the bottom: CRATE & BARREL, $3.95. Jon had gotten the ice bucket, but Caitlin must have gotten the dishes. Why had she had to comment on the stupid ice bucket? She should have realized— But how was one supposed to deal with these things? Make a joke out of it? Pretend it had never happened? There was no easy way to deal with a divorce.

She should count herself grateful, she supposed, that she and Dan had never been married. Their dissolution had been pitifully easy in contrast, odds and ends of clothing and assorted toiletries, hardly enough to fill a tote bag. There had been nothing that had been theirs; it was still his and hers.

Clemmie set the bowl of pretzels down on Jon's desk, next to his computer and a stack of manila file folders. Unlike the living room, the study already looked lived in. It was a nook of a room, just large enough for Jon's desk, a file cabinet, and a squishy red love seat with red plaid cushions and a battered old afghan draped across the top. Shelves had been bolted above the desk, already half-filled with books, most of them about England and the English.

Folders littered the side of the desk, each labeled in Jon's angular printing. DIVORCE was scrawled across the front of the folder on top.

"That's for the book." Jon set down a tray with a bowl, a bottle, and two glasses, nudging the pretzels out of the way.

Clemmie started, clamping a hand down on the folder before it could fall off the desk. She hadn't intended . . . Anyway.

"The book you're working on now?" she said brightly.

Jon raised a brow at her. Damn him. He knew exactly what she'd thought. "There's a chapter on the rise of divorce post-war, as another example of the fragmentation of the pre-war codes that maintained the cohesion and power of the Edwardian ruling class." Jon slopped scotch into a glass and held it out to her. "Cheers."

"Thanks." Clemmie took her glass and sank down on the sofa. It was surprisingly comfortable. At the desk, Jon poured himself a slug of scotch. While she was showering, he'd changed from button-down and khakis into T-shirt and jeans. "You're being really decent," she said.

"Are you going soft on me?" The sofa creaked as he lowered himself down next to her, settling back against the battered plaid cushions. More gently he said, "I know this is a tough time for you. We can resume our usual hostilities later."

Clemmie looked at him sideways, at the purple smudges underneath his eyes, the new complex of lines around his lips. He wasn't, she realized with some surprise, the arrogant boy she'd known, always faster, taller, just a few steps ahead. That boy was gone, and in his place was a man who looked as bone weary as she did.

"Not just a tough time for me," she said. "How are you holding up?"

Jon gave her a look of mingled surprise and gratification. "It's . . . tough."

Clemmie nodded meaningfully, indicating that, yes, she got it. And she sort of did. Almost. Insomuch as a broken engagement could be compared to a divorce.

Jon leaned his head back against the back of the couch. "Addie—she did a lot for me. She meant a lot to me."

Huh? Clemmie had meant the divorce, not Granny. She caught herself just before she blurted that out, confining herself to another nod, repressing the urge to point out that that wasn't what she'd meant, that it wasn't his grandmother.

Which meant what? That he had no right to mourn?

Jon propped himself up on one elbow. "Do you know she's the reason I went to grad school?"

Clemmie shook her head over her glass. "No."

Jon stared at the brace of the bookshelf, a reminiscent expression on his face. "I was right out of Yale. I couldn't figure out what I wanted to do. I took that consulting job, remember?"

"Yeah." That, she remembered. "That was why you were in Rome."

She wasn't sure where that had come from. They never talked about Rome. It was one of those unwritten rules.

Jon glanced at her searchingly. Clemmie looked hastily down, locking her fingers around her glass. "Anyway"—the couch cushions shifted, rocking her closer to him—"I'd been planning to apply to either law school or business school after, just because everyone else was. I told Addie, and she said, 'What do *you* want to do?' Just like that."

Clemmie kept her eyes on her drink. "That sounds like her."

"She told me there was no point in making myself miserable just because I thought the world thought I should, that values and mores changed over time and I should do something that genuinely intrigued me, because, in the end, any job has its downsides and you have a better shot sticking it out if you like it in the first place."

"I wish she'd told that to me," murmured Clemmie.

She'd never doubted Granny had been proud that she'd gone to law school. Granny was very open in deploring her own lack of formal education, less open, although no less obvious, in her disapproval of Clemmie's mother having gone straight from school to marriage. It had been taken for granted that Clemmie would make good on the opportunities her grandmother had never had and that her mother had passed up; she had taken her success as one for the team. But there had never been anything about making oneself happy or thumbing one's nose in the teeth of the world to do so.

Of course, as Jon was so fond of saying, maybe it was just because she had never asked.

Jon smiled faintly, lost in memory. "She gave me that lecture—you know the one—"

"The 'when the crops were failing in Kenya' lecture?"

"That's the one." They shared a look of mutual amusement. "'If we had let ourselves be discouraged . . .' You know the rest."

It was Granny's equivalent of the traditional "when I was your age, I had to milk the cows and walk fifteen miles to school," only it involved the farm nearly failing and everyone having to pitch in to bring it back. They'd both heard that lecture far too many times, usually when whining about work they didn't want to do. It basically boiled down to "pick what you want and then stick with it," something that, so far, none of them other than Granny Addie had had any particular success at doing.

Jon stretched out his legs and balanced his glass on his stomach. "You know, she made that up? There wasn't a coffee-bean blight in 1935. I looked it up a few years ago."

"She was probably conflating events. People do that." Clemmie snuggled down into the couch, curling her legs up underneath her. "I'd always thought of it less as history and more as a fairy tale. You know, one of the ones with a moral lesson, like the one where the girl who takes all the apples off the tree and the cakes out of the oven is rewarded and the one who doesn't is sentenced to spit toads every time she speaks, or something like that."

"I don't think I read that one," said Jon. "But I'll take your word for it." He joggled his drink, watching the amber liquid make patterns on the inside of the glass. "What was your Grandpa Frederick like?"

"Didn't you—? I forgot. You only met him towards the end."

Jon smiled crookedly. "That's right. I came around late."

"But you stuck." Clemmie held out her glass for a refill.

"Like a bad penny." Jon hoisted the bottle up from its resting place on the floor next to the couch and obligingly poured another tot.

"Aren't pennies by their very nature good?" It was less of a tot and more of a jigger. "That's good. Thanks."

Jon topped off his own glass somewhat more sparingly than hers. "I got the sense you didn't exactly feel that way at the time," he said carefully, setting the bottle back down next to the couch. He didn't meet her eyes. "About my being around."

The scotch made Clemmie's lips feel numb. Not just her lips, all of her. She looked down into her glass. "I was jealous."

Jon choked on his scotch. "You were jealous of *me*? Why? They were your family. I would have given my eyeteeth to fit it. If I knew what eyeteeth were," he added as an afterthought.

"Yes, but . . ." Clemmie shifted in her seat, navigating around a lump in the cushion. "I was a responsibility. They had to deal with me. You were there because they liked you."

"I was there because my father married your aunt," corrected Jon. "It's not the same thing."

"I thought you were so lucky." Clemmie twisted the fringe of the afghan through her fingers. "Aunt Anna was so much *fun*. Mother was always working all the time, and when she wasn't I wished she was. And there you were, with Aunt Anna and Uncle Leonard in that cool apartment on the West Side with the twisty staircase—"

"Listening to them throw crockery and wondering how long it was going to be before it was all over."

Clemmie stared at him.

Jon leaned his head back against the back of the couch, staring dreamily up at the ceiling. "They fought. All the time. Why do you think I spent so much time at Addie's? It was the only place I could get my homework done without risking accidental concussion."

Clemmie swiped her wet hair out of her face. Jon's father had been a famous—and famously temperamental—playwright. Clemmie didn't remember much of him. He wasn't the sort who showed up for family occasions. "I didn't— I had no idea. . . ."

"Whoa, Clem! Don't look at me like that. It wasn't that bad." For a moment he looked like the supercilious prep-school boy she remembered, smirking at the world. "You were right. Anna was fun," he said judiciously. "When she was around. She was like that. I'd be her favorite hobby for about three days, and then she'd be off again, doing something else. Correction: doing *someone* else. She was sleeping around on my dad."

Clemmie stared at him.

"Of course, odds were Dad was sleeping with someone else first." Jon sampled his scotch. "It was . . . messy."

"Why didn't you say anything?"

"What was I going to say? We weren't exactly best buddies at the time, as I recall. Besides, it was a point of honor for Anna not to let your mother know. Your mother has this disapproving look—"

"I know," said Clemmie quickly. "Trust me, I know."

Jon leaned his head back against the back of the couch, balancing his glass on his stomach. His shirt rode up, showing a slice of well-muscled chest, still tanned from the Carolina sun. "What a goddamned mess. Your parents, my parents, Anna." He gave a short, humorless laugh. He sat up abruptly, catching his glass just before it fell. "No wonder none of us can make a marriage work."

"Hey!" Clemmie wasn't sure why she minded, but she did. "You don't know that. Besides, there's Granny Addie and Grandpa Frederick."

"Yeah," said Jon with a curious look on his face. "Them."

Clemmie rose to her knees on the couch. "What, you're going to give up because of one bad experience?"

Jon hand lightly skimmed hers, sending goose bumps up and down her arms. "Where's that engagement ring, again?"

Clemmie snatched her hand back, rocking back on her heels. "At least I knew when to cut my losses! Maybe if you'd had the sense to break up with Caitlin—"

She broke off, appalled. Some blows were too low. But it was too late; it had already been said.

"Do you think I haven't thought of that?" said Jon. His expression turned dark. "But what the hell. Maybe it wasn't Caitlin. Maybe it would have happened with anyone. Maybe this whole love-everlasting thing is just a sham."

"That's a cop-out," said Clemmie sharply. "But why should that surprise me? You have a long history of copping out."

Jon turned and looked at her very, very slowly. "What's that supposed to mean?"

He knew exactly what she meant. But that had been their deal all along, their unspoken deal, that there were some things they just didn't talk about. Brush it under the table, pretend it never happened, act like everything was okay.

Clemmie was sick of pretending. She'd had it up to here with brushing it under the table.

He wanted to know what she meant? Clemmie looked Jon in the eye. They were practically nose to nose, so close that she could smell the booze on his breath and the faint whiff of detergent on his clothes.

It was time to finally have it out.

"One word," she said. "Rome."

London, 1921

"When were you going to tell me? Or weren't you?"

A gentleman, Hodges had said. A gentleman to see her. Bea closed her eyes against a sudden wave of dizziness. She should have told Hodges she wasn't at home to him, but that would have caused talk among the servants and talk was the very last thing she wanted right now. One couldn't bar the door to someone without begging the question why.

She had never thought he would come here. They had been so careful, so discreet. He hadn't come here, not to Rivesdale House, not since Addie had brought him, so very long ago. But here he was, in her drawing room—no, in Marcus' drawing room—stalking towards her, a piece of cream-colored writing paper crumpled in one hand.

He brandished the paper. "Did you just mean to leave it at this?"

She'd meant that to keep him away, not conjure him like a bad fairy. Goblin fruit . . . Bea felt panic rising in her and clamped it down, clamped it down the way she did the nausea that plagued her all the time.

"Darling! What a surprise. Do come have a drink." Perhaps if she acted normal, it all would be normal; they could be sophisticated and civilized and pretend nothing had ever happened. She could close her eyes and everything would go back to the way it was meant to be, before Bunny, before Frederick, before everything. "Your usual?"

She reached for the shaker with hands that were surprisingly steady. Breeding will tell, her mother would say. Early training paid off. Her whole world would crumple around her and she could serve beverages in a hand that did not tremble. Tea and scandal, those had been the dishes in her mother's parlor. What would it be for her? Gin and ruin? The stakes had changed. Her mother had lied; nothing in Bea's early training had prepared her for this.

"Don't play games," Frederick said harshly. He held up the crumpled piece of cream-colored paper. "What do you mean by this?"

"Exactly what it says," said Bea calmly, although she felt anything but calm.

"And in a good, clear hand," he said, his dark eyes flashing. "'My dear Frederick, as entertaining an interlude as this has been, the time has come for us to say adieu. . . .'"

"Would you rather I had put it in verse?"

He wasn't amused. "You might at least have had the decency to break it off in person."

Bea shrugged. "One does get so frightfully busy—"

"Don't," he said sharply, and the intensity in his voice made her set down the shaker. "Don't."

Bea looked at him, this man who had been her lover for three whirlwind months. Three months of smoky nightclubs, hurried embraces in the backs of taxis, clandestine meetings at his flat. They had known each other's bodies, quite intimately, but in the most basic of ways he was still a stranger to her. She had never expected he would react like this. Although, to be honest, she had never thought much about how he would react at all; she had been too overcome with her own need, the need for revenge, and then, in a panic, the need to make it all go away. To make him go away.

Heavens, she felt ill.

It had been one thing to push the boundaries, to get back at Marcus for his neglect, to pay him in his own coin, a pretty little revenge, an adultery for an adultery, an affair for an affair. But this—she had never meant it to come to this, to skate so close to disaster.

Nothing had gone the way it was supposed to go; nothing had happened as planned. Marcus was meant to be bitterly jealous, to sweep her away, and they could go back to life as it was meant to be, her adored, he adoring, the smartest couple in London, her mother bragging about her daughter, the marchioness.

She wanted to make it go away; she wanted to make Frederick go away.

"Must you?" she said, and meant it honestly this time. "We never pretended our hearts were involved."

His lip twisted. "Not hearts, perhaps, but do some justice to my pride. You might have done more than send a note. Or are you that overrun with engagements?"

Another wave of sickness swept her. Bea gripped the drinks trolley with both hands. Morning sickness? More like morning, afternoon, and evening sickness. She felt ill all the time, in every possible way. The sight of a plate of eggs and bacon turned her green; the scent of gin made her stomach churn. No one had warned her that childbearing made one bilious.

"Engagements?" Bea laughed, and there was an edge of hysteria to it. "Haven't you heard, darling? I'm engaged in the greatest engagement of all."

Frederick looked blank.

"I'm with child." She smiled brittlely. "Just what everyone has been waiting for. The ceremonial bearing of the heir."

Frederick didn't say anything. He just looked at her and looked and looked and looked again, as if he were turning her inside and out. Bea's hands instinctively went to her stomach, still flat, still so hard to tell, if only the other signs weren't there. How her maid had smirked! And Marcus—how was she going to tell Marcus?

He could be made to believe; he had to be made to believe. All those nights he stumbled home, practically insensible—he'd never remember they hadn't been together, not if she swore to him they had. He'd be too proud of getting an heir to contest it, all the congratulations from his friends, his mother, her mother. He'd have to give up Bunny. It would put everything back the way it was; it had to.

The silence made her ears hurt; it was too loud, all that not saying any-thing.

"Well?" she demanded. "Aren't you going to congratulate me?"

When he spoke, his voice was low, but not so low she couldn't make out the words, the words she least wanted to hear:

"Is it mine?"

FIFTEEN

London, 1921

"Don't be abominable," snapped Bea.

Addie scarcely heard her. The only words that mattered were Frederick's.

Is it mine?

That he asked that . . . That he *could* ask that . . . Addie's stomach cramped. She had come down for her phenacetin tablets. She had given the bottle to Bea last week, and Bea had put it down on the drinks trolley, after bolting a tablet with a stiff chaser of whiskey and soda. Headache, she had said. Bea never had headaches. But Bea hadn't been at all herself these past few weeks. She had been pale and strained, snappish and easily tired. Addie had watched her anxiously. Not influenza; Addie knew the symptoms of the flu by heart.

Just a headache, that's all, Bea had said snippily. *There's no need to fuss.* Bea never had any patience with illness, with either others or herself. She was, as she herself liked to put it, healthy as a horse. The one time she'd been ill, Nanny had threatened to bolt her to the bed. Addie had begun to wonder if she would have to do the same, bolt Bea to the bed and call a physician, just to make sure there wasn't something truly wrong.

Addie had never imagined this. When she'd heard Frederick's voice, she thought he might have come for her. It had been so long since she'd seen him, not since that horrible night in December at that hideous nightclub, the least garden-like garden Addie had ever seen. There had been no more concerts together, no more lectures, no more tête-à-têtes over tea. He was gone from her life as though he had never been.

From time to time, she'd seen snaps of him in the papers. She'd never admit to anyone at the *Review* that she read the *Tatler,* but she did, flipping through guiltily, scanning for familiar faces, the girls from her deb year, the men who hadn't danced with her, their faces pitilessly illuminated by the light of the flashbulbs. And there, behind Bea, in the shadow, had been Frederick, at one of those hideous clubs. Addie had asked Bea about it, tentatively, and Bea had shrugged and said he went about with the old crowd from time to time and could Addie pass the marmalade?

Went about with the old crowd. The full extent of the betrayal buffeted her like waves against a rock, slamming into her again and again. Bea—and Frederick. Frederick—and Bea. The two of them. Together. Lying to her.

How long had it gone on? Addie's mind raced feverishly back, across all her carefully hoarded memories, all those months and months of gazing adoringly at Frederick, being so grateful to him for fetching her wraps and putting her into taxis, going with him to those nasty clubs where it was all racket and perfume, assaults on the ears and nose. Had it been going on even then? All the time he was dancing with her, had he been looking over her shoulder at Bea?

She'd thought he was so different. He was so worldly—not worldly in the way Bea's set was worldly, not shallow and superficial, but well-read, cultivated, thoughtful, everything Addie had wanted to be, everything she'd wanted him to be.

"Is it mine?" The door to the drawing room was open, just a crack, but that crack was enough. Addie could hear everything. She knew she should feel like a fool, standing with her ear to the door like a guilty maidservant, but she couldn't move, couldn't leave.

"I don't see how that's any of your affair," said Bea haughtily. Addie could just imagine her face as she said it, the tilt of her chin, the regal disdain.

She knew Bea's face as well as her own, in all of its moods. Bea wouldn't do something like this to her, surely, not when she knew how Addie had felt about Frederick. They were sisters, better than sisters, closer than sisters. Years and years and years of whispering confidences, sharing bites from the same apple, taking the blame for each other when something—usually Bea— would get them into trouble.

But if it was Bea who got them into trouble, it was always Bea who charmed their way out again, as sleek and slippery as a ferret.

Addie pressed her fist to her lips, trying not to think what she was think-ing. She closed her eyes, fighting away a terrible certainty, the certainty that what she was hearing was true, that this was Bea, that Bea had, did, and al-ways would do what she liked, regardless of the consequences, regardless even of Addie.

She had always known that about Bea, that Bea could be—well, less than entirely truthful. She had a politician's flair for expediency, twisting facts to suit her ends, making virtue whatever she wanted it to be. Addie had seen that before, again and again, Bea's way or no way. If sometimes other people's interests were harmed, there was always an excuse, so and so was too fat to want that cake anyway, she shouldn't have been dancing with him, really; Bea was doing them all a favor. It wasn't that she was lying, as such. She always believed it herself by the end, as though truth could be created in the telling.

Addie could practically hear Bea now, all golden-tongued sympathy as only Bea could be, telling her, really, darling, it was for the best, he wasn't at all what she had imagined him to be, goblin fruit, hadn't she warned her?

No. Not to her. Bea wouldn't do that to her. Bea wouldn't have—Addie scrabbled after the words to put her thoughts into, but some things were too awful for words, too awful to face in plain prose.

But it was there, right there in front of her, through the drawing room door.

"Affair," said Frederick, and Addie's chest ached at the sound of his voice, so familiar and yet so strange.

That wasn't the voice he had used with her. With her, there was always an air of reserve, as though he was holding himself back somehow, exercising special care, as if someone had set a protective guard over the blade of a knife. Now the blade was bared, his voice was all edge, razor sharp.

"Affair," Frederick repeated. "An interesting choice of words. It was my affair. Until you sent me this. The question at issue is—what else is mine?"

"Nothing," said Bea decidedly. "A child born in wedlock—"

Frederick broke in before she could complete the sentence. "When was the last time you had conjugal relations with your marquess?"

Months and months. Addie knew she wasn't supposed to know such things, but she did, everyone did, from the ladies' maids straight down to the chauffeur. Marcus had moved from Bea's bed to a cot in the dressing room long, long ago. Whether he slept in that bed was another story entirely.

"Don't." Bea's voice cracked through the room. "Just don't."

"How in the devil do you expect to convince him it's his?"

Because it is, Addie waited for Bea to say. Perhaps this was all a mistake, a misunderstanding.

"I'll think of something," said Bea, her voice rising. "I'll tell him—I'll tell him—blast it, Frederick, it's none of your concern!"

"It is—if it's mine," he said implacably. And then, "Marry me."

Addie felt herself go cold, cold clear through. She felt the way she had when Bea tried to teach her to skate on the pond at Ashford. She had fallen on the ice, the breath knocked out of her, cold straight through, the world turned upside down with the sky reflected in the ice and all of it spinning around her, Bea whirling around and around on her skates above.

"In case it hasn't escaped your attention," Bea said, in a voice that shook, "I'm already married."

"But for how long?" Frederick's voice was implacable. "How long when your Marcus finds out you're bearing another man's brat?"

"It won't come to that," said Bea obstinately, and Addie was reminded, disorientingly, of a younger Bea, in her pinafore in the nursery, putting her foot down and saying, *Shan't. Shan't, shan't, shan't*, while Nanny wrung her hands and swore she'd be the death of her. "It won't. It *won't*."

"What will your marquess say when the child is dark haired?"

Addie could hear Bea pacing, the fabric of her dress swishing across her legs, her Cuban heels tapping against the floor. "My mother is dark. And look at Addie! These things happen. Besides, we don't know that he will. We don't know that it will be a boy. It might be a girl. And it might be Marcus'," she added defiantly. "You can't know otherwise."

"Yes, but you do, don't you?"

There was a horrible silence. Addie stood frozen outside the door, her fingers biting into her palms as the silence stretched on and on and on, spreading like a stain.

"When he finds out—" began Frederick.

"If he finds out," Bea corrected him sharply, and Addie died a little inside, because there was no pretending anymore; Bea was having Frederick's child; they had lied to her, both of them.

Bea had lied to her.

The bottom of Addie's world fell out beneath her; she was falling through the ice, choking. If not Bea, then whom did she have? She'd had her dream of Frederick, and it had hurt, so very much, when he had disappeared, but she had known, on some level, that it was just a dream, however satisfying the dream might have been. She could sustain his loss, couldn't she? But not Bea. Bea was all she had, the one person in the world whom she trusted and loved, the one person who was hers and wholly hers, always, forever.

"If," Frederick said. "Have your if. If he finds out, he'll have you in front of the courts in a heartbeat. It will hurt his pride too much to keep you."

"Won't it hurt his pride more to advertise it?" Bea retorted. "Better to cover it up, brush it all under the carpet, nobody needs to know."

"Not with Bunny ffoulkes breathing in his other ear," said Frederick grimly. "She'll jump on the opportunity with both hands. She'd be a fool if she didn't." Gently he said, "It's no good, Bea." Addie hated the casual familiarity of his voice. She hated him. She hated both of them. "You'd do better to marry me."

"And give up all this?" Bea's voice had a hysterical edge. "I'm a marchioness. What do you have to offer? A horrid little flat somewhere?"

"You never found my flat horrid before."

"I wasn't living in it!" Bottles clattered as Bea's fists went crashing down on the drinks tray. She drew in a deep, ragged breath. "This is absurd, all of it. There's no point in even thinking of it. It isn't going to happen. Nothing is going to happen. Everything will stay just as it was."

"You'll pass off another man's child as your husband's," said Frederick flatly.

Bea laughed wildly. "It won't be the first time a cuckoo has borne a coronet. A cuckoo for a cuckold. Terribly fitting, don't you think?" She let out a sound that sounded suspiciously like a muffled sob. "If only he hadn't— Damn him. None of this needed to happen. Damn him, damn him, damn him. It's his own damned fault. If he'd stayed away from her—"

Addie started and stumbled as the green baize door opened. Hodges bustled through the hall, straight for the front door. She knew he saw her standing there, but he didn't look at her. A good butler didn't and Hodges was a very good butler.

"My lord," he said, opening the door.

Marcus breezed through, in evening kit already, speaking to someone over his shoulder. "I'll just grab the gramophone— Oh, hullo, Addie."

He always spoke to her as though she were slightly slow, and he must have thought she was, standing directly in front of the drawing room door for no apparent reason.

Bunny was standing behind him, just over the threshold, examining the rings on her gloved fingers. Her hair hadn't been shingled yet; she wore it pinned up in a little bun in the back with waves in front, carefully arranged to show off her earrings.

"Gramophone in the drawing room?" said Marcus, edging past her.

Addie darted instinctively to ward him off. "Um, yes. I mean, no." She cleared her throat nervously. "I think Bea left the gramophone in—"

"So that's all?" Frederick's voice cracked through the room. "I'm just to be used as a stud and then let go?"

Bunny looked up from her rings, scenting blood. Marcus looked at the door, then at Addie. "Who's in there?" he asked.

"It's no one; it's—"

"Was this your plan from the beginning?" Frederick's voice might have been etched in acid. It sliced through the door. "Should the husband fail to perform, bring in a backup?"

Bea's voice was equally acrid and equally, damnably clear. "Did you flatter yourself that I did it for you?"

Addie's eyes met Marcus'. There was disbelief in his handsome face, disbelief, shock, and the beginnings of anger. Behind him, Bunny's face was a study in excitement. Her nose was practically twitching.

"It's not—" Addie began weakly. "It's not what you—"

And Frederick said loudly, crudely, "You certainly screamed loudly enough at the time."

Marcus' nostrils flared. "Right," he said.

That was all, but something in the way he said it sent fear slicing through Addie.

Addie made a move to stop him, but he pushed past her, flinging open the drawing room door.

New York, 1999

"Rome," repeated Jon.

"Rome," agreed Clemmie. "Otherwise synonymous with 'cop-out.'"

Even after all these years, it still hurt, still stung with all the intensity of remembered rejection.

"That's not fair," said Jon.

Not fair? "Did your letter get lost in the post? Did my answering machine eat your voice mail? No. I didn't think so." Clemmie took a restorative swig of scotch. The booze burned at the back of her throat. She said hoarsely, "You couldn't even be bothered to give me the 'you're a lovely person' talk. I'd call that a cop-out, wouldn't you?"

"You really thought that was what happened." The couch creaked as Jon leaned over, reaching for the bottle of scotch. "You really thought that was it?"

Clemmie buried her face over her glass, so he wouldn't see the hurt. "I know that was what happened. I was there."

A cheap student room in Rome; the smell of stale wine and old garlic from the restaurant below; the creak of bedsprings; her dress whispering over her head; the world spinning round and round; the sound of music and laughter in the warm summer darkness.

She had been a rising senior spending a summer in Rome on a school grant, theoretically to research her senior thesis but really just because it was Rome and she could. Jon had been a second-year consultant in Rome for business. After the second bottle of grappa, very little was clear. She'd wanted so badly to impress him, to show off her Italian and show him how sophisticated she was. Instead she'd gotten sloppy drunk, so drunk she'd thrown up all over his new Italian loafers.

She'd taken him back to her room to clean him up, giggly, light-headed, still drunk. What had they called it back then? Boot and rally. She'd booted and rallied. Oh, boy, had she rallied. She'd rallied right into bed with him.

It had been—well, what she could remember was enough, years later, to bring the blood to her cheeks, confused memories of his hands and lips and Depeche Mode playing in the background on her tinny portable tape player. She'd felt like hell the next morning. She'd felt even more like hell when he'd fled with a *we'll talk later, okay?*

They hadn't.

Clemmie set down her drink with a clank. "You didn't even have the balls to call me after. You just slunk away, like . . . like . . ." Invention failed her. "A great slinking thing."

Jon sat up with the bottle, his glasses askew and his hair mussed. "You didn't get it at all, did you? Never mind. Let's just leave it."

"No. No. Let's not just leave it." She was sick of just leaving it, of people talking behind and around her. She was sick of everyone keeping secrets. "What the hell, Jon? I know you were all big and grown-up and important and I was just a little college girl, but you couldn't even *call?*"

"And say what? That I felt like an ass for taking advantage of you?"

Like she hadn't had any part in the matter? His casual assumption of responsibility made her hackles rise. "It's not like you forced yourself on me."

"You were drunk," said Jon shortly. "It's not how I wanted it to happen."

"Maybe I wanted it to happen." Her voice cracked. Maybe all twenty-one-year-olds were idiots. Maybe she'd been particularly idiotic. She could remember it like yesterday, tossing back grappa, liquid courage, so desperately wanting something to happen. She'd even worn her lucky underwear, pale pink with a rose in the middle. "If I'd known how it was going to end, I wouldn't have bothered."

Jon set the bottle down on the floor with a thunk. It rocked ominously. "If you must know," he said, "I was warned off you. Called into the study and onto the carpet."

"What in the hell are you talking about?" It wasn't just that he was start-ing to slur his words; the words themselves made no sense.

"Your Granny Addie," he said, enunciating very clearly. "She warned me away from you. Sat me down in the study and asked me what was up with us."

"How did she know? You didn't tell her—" The thought was horrible. "You didn't tell her about Rome?"

"Of course I didn't! Not about that. If you must know, I made an an-nouncement of my intentions."

Clemmie choked on her scotch. "Your intentions?"

Like his intention never to call her? His intention to disappear from her life? His intention to marry the loathsome Caitlin? That wasn't fair. Caitlin had come later, much later. Clemmie had already been dating someone else: a succession of someone elses. She'd made sure always to have a date for family events, just because. She couldn't even remember their names.

"I decided to do it the old-fashioned way. Big man that I was." Jon gri-maced at the memory. "I told her I was in love with you, that I was going to do the honorable thing and wait until you'd graduated before pressing my suit, blah, blah, blah. God, I was full of myself."

He'd what? Clemmie drove her fingernails into her palms, trying to wake herself up, trying to make herself think straight. This wasn't the history she knew.

Jon tossed back another tot of scotch. "Granny Addie set me straight. She told me you were too young, it wouldn't be fair to tie you down like that. I was traveling like crazy; you were still in college— She was right. It would have been a huge mistake. For both of us."

Clemmie had to clear her throat before she could speak. "You told her you were in love with me?"

Jon shoved his glasses back up onto his nose. "Oh, come on. Were you the only person in the New York metro area who didn't realize I had a mas-sive crush on you?"

The room felt suddenly smaller, the air charged with tension. They looked at each other, both remembering, confused, hazy, drunken memo-ries, laughter and caresses and too much wine and the tinny sound of her old tape player spooling out dark, techno-infused lyrics of lust and longing.

Drinks at the Yale Club, dances at family weddings, the knowledge of what had happened always there between them, unspoken. It was as if time had compressed, as if they were back in that ridiculous student apartment in Rome, lips tingling with booze, skin bare in the summer heat, every thought, every sensation, concentrated right here, on this moment.

"Clem—" he said.

The radiator crackled and she jumped, a whisper away from—what? Falling back into his arms? This was—she didn't even know what this was. Her skin prickled in the muggy heat of the apartment, Jon's T-shirt scratchy against her skin.

"But..." The upholstery of the couch rubbed against her bare legs. She didn't know what to say. She'd spent so many months waiting for him to call her, convinced he was blowing her off, burning him in effigy in her dorm room trash can. "Why didn't you say something?"

"I was twenty-four. We were infants. And my feelings were hurt," he admitted wryly.

"Yeah? What about mine?" What if he'd called? What if Granny Addie hadn't intervened? A whole alternate past scrolled out in front of her, a whole sea of might-have-beens.

The tips of Jon's fingers brushed her cheek lightly. "I'm sorry, Clem. I'm sorry."

"We would—we would probably have broken up, right?" she said shakily. "I mean, being so young."

"Yep," agreed Jon a little too quickly. "Probably. I would have wound up going to business school instead of grad school and you—well, you would have probably gone to law school anyway, but you would have resented me for not getting to date around. It would have been a disaster."

"A disaster," Clemmie echoed.

Her head was spinning with scotch and confusion. Her bare knee brushed his, skin to skin for the first time in years. She could feel the shock of it straight through her. So could he. She could tell.

His hazel eyes were the same color as the liquid in her glass, gold and brown.

"I wish—" she began brokenly, but she didn't have time to finish the phrase; his lips stopped her words.

What were wishes compared to this? She didn't remember consciously closing her eyes, didn't remember moving towards him. There was no thought, just sensation, the feeling of his lips, his hands, the nubby blanket beneath her knees, the feel of his bare skin under her palms as her hands slid beneath his shirt. He kissed her fiercely, demandingly, as if his kiss were his argument. She clung to him as the world tilted, a confusion of impressions, her ears ringing.

And ringing.

They stumbled clumsily apart as the phone on the desk shrilled. The world had tilted; she was sprawled on her back on the couch, Jon above her, his shirt rumpled and his hair any which way. He was breathing hard, his chest moving in and out. The phone on the desk shrilled and shrilled again.

Their eyes met, united in the same thought.

"The hospital," said Clemmie.

"Damn." Jon scrambled off the couch, stumbling on the edge of the rug and knocking over the empty bottle of scotch. He lunged for the phone, catching it just before the fourth ring. "Hello?"

Clemmie rose stiffly, trembling all over. She'd heard that was an after-effect of shock. Or maybe "shock" wasn't the right word. She yanked down her borrowed T-shirt, her movements jerky. Her elbow bumped the pile of folders, sending the one on the top slithering sideways.

Clemmie made a belated grab for it, but she was just a beat too slow. The folder slid off the side, spraying its contents across the floor.

"Anna? Anna, you're breaking up." Cordless pressed to his ear, Jon stalked out into the hallway.

Clemmie hunched down to pile the papers together, sifting them back into their folder as she strained to hear what Jon was saying outside. She shoved an early draft of a chapter into the folder, double-spaced paragraphs with lots of cross-outs and interlineations in red pen in Jon's impatient handwriting. *Chapter Five,* it said on the top. *The Great Divorce.*

"You're breaking up again! Damn." Jon hit "End" and began punching numbers into his phone. "Anna?"

Under the notes were more gray photocopies, this time with pictures, pages from magazines, featuring the young and gilded of an earlier era, women in fur-trimmed coats and men in top hats. They weren't very good photocopies; the ink left a gray film on Clemmie's fingers as she piled them into the folder, only half-seeing, surreptitiously watching Jon as he paced in the hallway, shouting over the poor cell-phone connection, guilt and confusion warring with fatigue and concern and goodness only knew what.

Her hands trembled, and a page dropped from her fingers onto the floor.

The *Tatler*, it said, in curling letters on the top, in an Art Deco frame. Beneath it was a picture of Granny's cousin Bea dressed in a smart traveling suit with fur at the throat, on what looked like a ship, her arms full of flowers, and a man, next to her, who looked, in the way that old photos did, very much like the old photos in Granny's apartment of Grandpa Frederick.

Underneath the photo a caption read: LADY BEATRICE DESBOROUGH AND THE HONOURABLE FREDERICK DESBOROUGH.

"Clemmie?"

She looked up. Jon was standing in the doorway, the cordless gripped between both hands. His knuckles were white. His face was bleak.

Clemmie dropped the paper she was holding. She rose slowly to her feet, using the corner of the couch to brace herself.

"That was Aunt Anna?" Her voice sounded strange to her own ears.

Jon nodded. He made no move to come to her, just stood there, in the doorway, holding the phone in both hands.

"I'm so sorry," he said hoarsely. "Clemmie . . . She's gone."

PART TWO

KENYA

SIXTEEN

Kenya, 1926

"hall we?" Addie moved away from Frederick, trying to hide her confusion beneath a veneer of cheerful chatter. "I'm so looking forward to seeing the farm—and the children, of course."

She wasn't sure how she managed to sound so cool. There was a whistling in her ears, like the train as it clattered along on its path, trailing black smoke, a shrill, warning sound, several thousand miles too late.

It didn't seem quite fair that Frederick should look so very much the same, a shade more tan, clad in khaki instead of tweed, but the vital bit, that spark of personality that had caught and held her firm all those years ago, in a ballroom in Kent, caught and held her just the same. She had deluded herself that his attraction had been purely a matter of circumstance. She had made a tidy story of it over the years: She had been young and naïve and fresh from the country; he had seemed to her a man of the world. He had been the first man to take any kind of interest in her, independent of her connection to Bea—or, at least, had put up a good pretense of doing so.

But here, in the unforgiving African sunlight, Addie's pretty rationalizations fell to bits. It was absurd. She ought to be proof against him now, now that she knew him for what he was: A schemer. An opportunist. And her cousin's husband.

Wiping the sweat out of her eyes with a handkerchief long since gone soggy, Addie reached blindly for the handle of the black Ford. This had been a horrible, horrible idea. She ought to have stayed home in England with David, instead of chasing after some odd notion of vindication. "Is this the car?"

"That? Oh, darling, no! That's the estate car." Bea shooed Addie towards a canary-yellow car with a flying stork on the front. She gestured towards it with palpable pride. "This is mine."

"It's very grand," said Addie. The hood seemed to go on forever.

Bea cast her husband a limpid look. "It was my anniversary present, wasn't it, darling? Five *glorious* years."

In the sun, Frederick's face seemed strangely dark. "I'll see to your trunks," he said, and turned away.

"Trunk," Addie called after him. "Just the one. I didn't bring very much with me."

Bea squeezed her arm, the familiar scent of her perfume warring with the unfamiliar smells of Africa. "It's just like the first time, isn't it? When you came to Ashford. I remember how you looked that first night in the nursery, such a little, wide-eyed thing."

"Yes, and you took me under your wing," said Addie, trying not to sound too churlish. It was true; she had owed Bea so much. But was it really necessary to revisit it now? Addie's eyes tracked Frederick as he moved easily through the crowd, shepherding the delivery of her trunk. She forced herself to look away. "I'll never forget your kindness."

"We're sisters, remember?" said Bea gaily. "You mustn't worry about a thing. We can make something over for you—fix you a whole new wardrobe. It will be such fun! I've scads of things, heaps and heaps, all but unworn. We can go through them once we get to Ashford."

"Ashford?" Addie cast her a quick, startled glance.

"That's what I call our farm. Ashford Redux. It's not at all unusual," she added defensively as Frederick rejoined them. "Lots of people call their farms after places back home. Joss Hay called his place Slains. That was their castle in Scotland."

"*Was*," contributed Frederick. "Didn't they lose it a few generations back?"

Bea bristled. "You would understand it if you had anyplace to lose. Do we have time for a drink at the club?"

"Not if we want to get back before dark." Frederick's tone was pleasant enough, but there was an undertone to it that made the short hairs on the back of Addie's neck quiver.

Bea appealed to Addie. "Wouldn't you rather stay the night at Muthaiga? It's our club," she added. "I know you're longing for a bath, and we could have a drink and you could meet some of our neighbors—we could spend the night and go up early in the morning. Early in the morning is by far the best time to travel, before the heat becomes truly ghastly."

"It gets worse?" said Addie. Already the heat was weighing on her like a second skin, beating through her inadequate hat, sending rivulets of sweat dripping down the small of her back.

Frederick chuckled softly.

Addie just managed not to scowl at him. Once, she would have been thrilled to be the source of his amusement, pathetically pleased to make him laugh, but not anymore. As far as she was concerned, he was the lowest of the low and her only interest in him was as her cousin's husband.

"I'm happy to go wherever you'd like me to go," she said to Bea. Assuming a heartiness she was far from feeling, she said, "Let's go on to—Ashford, is it? I haven't heard that name in ages. It's a little disconcerting, hearing it here."

"The natives call it Kirinyaga." She'd forgot how very green Frederick's eyes were, forgot or trained herself not to remember. "It translates roughly to 'it is glorious.'"

"How interesting," said Addie chillingly. She addressed herself deliberately to Bea. "One doesn't usually think of names as having meaning, does one? Do you think 'Ashford' meant something once?"

Bea shrugged. "I should imagine it would have something to do with a tree and a ford."

"Or some strange corruption from the French," contributed Frederick in his smooth, deep voice. Addie remembered the power a mere word from him once had over her, all their long talks, all those ridiculous lectures and conferences. She hated that the sound of his voice still had the power to raise goose bumps on her skin.

Pure habit, she told herself. Habit and memory. Nothing more.

Bea examined her gloved hands. "Yes, the French are so very accomplished at corruption, aren't they? Corruption and couture."

Bea still wore Marcus' ring, a large sapphire framed in diamonds. It gave Addie a pang, seeing it, remembering Bea at Rivesdale House, back before the world had fallen to bits around them. She wondered if Marcus minded that Bea had kept it—or, more to the point, if Frederick did.

"Aren't ash trees meant to have magical properties?" said Addie at random. "Do you remember, Bea, how Cook used to tie bits of cloth around a branch when she felt ill? I'm not entirely sure it was an ash, though. It might have been something else."

"It might have been an ash," said Frederick, entering into the conversation unbidden. "The Norse believed that the first man was formed from an ash log. It was their version of our Adam and Eve myth—without the apples."

"Would that make Ashford the Garden of Eden?" said Addie lightly. Sweat was dripping down her neck, making her back itch, and the strong sun made her head ache.

"Do you mean, since we've been expelled?" said Bea. There was a horrible, awkward silence. She yanked at the wrists of her gloves, pulling them up. "If we're not staying for a drink, we should go."

"How far is it?" Addie asked, trailing along behind Bea to the yellow car.

It was Frederick who answered, reaching past her to unlatch the passenger door. "A little over three hours."

"Yes, the way you drive," said Bea.

Frederick gestured her courteously towards the car. "I'm sure Addie would prefer not to spend her first evening in East Africa in a ditch."

"Hardly her first evening in East Africa," said Bea. "There was Mombasa, wasn't there, and then a night on the train, and that hideous little station at Voi. Not that the drive is any better than the train. You wouldn't believe the roads here, darling. They're all made of red murram—too, too dust making!—and you just lurch along from pothole to pothole. There's a trick to it, though. If you go fast enough, you simply *fly*."

"It sounds exhilarating," said Addie, wishing herself back in London, where the omnibus didn't fly, it plodded. That is, if one was lucky and it condescended to move at all.

"It is," said Bea. "Don't worry, I'll take you out when old fusspot isn't around."

The old fusspot didn't rise to the provocation. He simply held open the door, waiting for them to enter. There was, Addie knew, nothing more calculated to infuriate Bea than indifference. Addie suspected that Frederick knew it, too.

Why hadn't she had the sense to stay home?

"After you," she said to Bea, but Bea shooed her forward.

"No, no, dearest, you go in the middle. You'll have a better view that way."

"Are you sure? I don't—"

"Now that you're here, you must see the place. To get the best view, you really must go up in the air." Bea slid in beside her, neatly trapping Addie in the middle. "I'm learning to fly. It's divine. You haven't seen anything until you've gone over the Rift in an aeroplane."

"More daft than divine," said Frederick, taking the other side. The door closed behind him with a click, locking Addie in between the two, Bea's skirt whispering against her on one side, Frederick's leg pressed against hers on the other, his side against hers. His elbow bumped against her breast as he moved the clutch. "Those things are death traps. We'll take you out for a ride, Addie. You get the best view of the country that way."

"Addie hates horses," said Bea. She adjusted her hat more firmly on her sleek blond bob. "Don't you, darling?"

"I don't hate them—" hedged Addie. She caught the edge of the seat as the car lurched forward. A chicken flew squawking out of its path. "I just respect their desire not to have me on their backs."

"They can tell you're uncomfortable," said Bea, sounding much more like herself again.

"They're right." Addie wafted a hand at the red dust flying up from the road. "Remember the secret riding lessons?"

Bea winced. "I hadn't realized one person could fall off so many times! But you kept on."

"Only because you kept at me. I would have given up, otherwise." For some reason, it seemed terribly important to impress on Frederick just how thoughtful Bea had been. "Bea suborned the head groom, commandeered the gentlest old hack in the stable, and spent hour after hour walking me around the paddock. Even Dodo gave up, but Bea kept on."

"Really?" said Frederick, but he looked not at Bea but at Addie.

"You know me," said Bea flippantly. "I like a challenge. Oh, darling, do look over there. No, no, the other there. Did you see it? That was a rhino."

Addie craned behind her to see. "I missed it. Do they come right up on the road?"

"When they think they can get away with it," said Frederick. "They've had a time of it with the telegraph wires. The rhinos decided the poles made excellent scratching posts. They'd back up and rub against them. If that weren't bad enough, the giraffe would wander through and get the wires tangled about their necks. It's the devil of a nuisance when you're trying to wire for supplies and a giraffe happens across the line."

"Yes, I can see where that would pose a problem," said Addie primly, trying to shift sideways. "Are there lions?"

"They tend to leave us alone if we leave them," said Bea. "It's the monkeys that are the true pests, snatching at everything and jabbering away with that endless jabber jabber jabber like a ladies' sewing circle, you can't imagine. And the hyenas! Foul things."

"They seldom come near the house," said Frederick. "Not anymore."

"No, but you can hear them," said Bea obstinately. "Late at night you can hear them laughing, like something out of Bedlam. They feed on the flesh of corpses. Not just animals, human corpses, too. You can hear them out there at night—laughing and waiting."

Addie felt a chill down her spine despite the heat of the day. "Goodness. It sounds like something out of one of those horrid novels we used to read—do you remember?"

"Yes, but then we could close the book," said Bea, and her voice sounded so forlorn that Addie looked at her in surprise, in surprise and pity. Bea hastily rallied, raising her voice to be heard over the motor. "Do you ever see Rosita and Geordie?"

"Rosita and—? Oh." Taken aback at the complete non sequitur, Addie took a moment to figure out what Bea meant. They had been part of her old crew in those faraway nightclubbing days. Addie coughed on red road dust, wafting her hand in front of her face. "Not really, no. Our paths don't really cross. I don't go to the Ritz much these days."

"I suppose it's someplace new, then," said Bea enviously. "It always is.

What's it like being one of the New Women, on your own in the fleshpots of London?"

"Fairly staid, actually," said Addie, aware of Frederick next to her, although his eyes never left the road. "I go to a fair number of concerts—David is very musical—and plays and lectures. It would bore you to bits."

"David is Addie's intended," said Bea over Addie's head.

"Oh?" said Frederick.

"Frightfully brainy, too," added Bea. "Isn't he?"

Addie squirmed on her patch of seat. "He's a lecturer at University College. Philosophy and Political Economy and all that sort of thing."

"When is the wedding?" inquired Bea brightly.

"We haven't set a date yet." Realizing how it sounded, she added quickly, "What with David's classes and my work—well, you know. I expect we'll be married when I get back."

"St. Margaret's, Hanover Square?"

Addie laughed. "Nothing like that!" She tried to imagine David's colleagues or her more bohemian friends at a society wedding in St. Margaret's. The mind boggled. Funny to remember she had once dreamed of that, she and Bea both, clouds of tulle and orange flowers and small children to hold one's train. Bea had said she would settle for nothing less than a marquess. . . . "It will be the registry office for us."

Even that she had trouble picturing. She had no difficulty with the concept of marriage in the abstract, but it was as though she hit a dead end whenever she tried to imagine actually being married to David. Which was nonsense. He was very good to her; everyone said so. Good and kind.

And utterly boring.

Addie squelched the unworthy thought, hoping that no hint of it showed on her face.

Frederick turned his head briefly to look at her. "Congratulations," he said. "I hope he's worthy of you."

She searched for the taint of mockery but didn't find it. "Thank you," she said guardedly.

"We must make sure you enjoy your last weeks of freedom," said Bea. "You must suck every last drop out of life before we send you back to the matrimonial shackles, mustn't we, darling?"

"Perhaps she doesn't view it as a shackle," suggested Frederick.

Bea ignored him. "We may be on the outer edge of nowhere, but we do still command some little society. Dina Hay's parties are simply divvy—and not *all* of them are wicked," she added with a sideways glance at her husband. "Just the amusing ones."

Addie had heard something of those parties back in London. Garbled rumors had drifted home of cocaine-fueled orgies, random couplings in the drawing room, spousal swaps. "Are you married or do you live in Kenya?" ran the phrase back home.

"Do you dine out a great deal?" Addie asked.

"The farms are too far apart. But there is Race Week. And we do have some *lovely* Saturday to Mondays." Another one of those sidelong looks. "Frederick doesn't like to leave the girls."

"They're very young," said Frederick shortly, and pulled the car up by the side of the road at what, to Addie's eyes, looked like nothing in particular. There was no sign of a house or even a track, just a river winding along one side of the road, fringed with reeds and tufts of papyrus. A few twisted trees thrust stubbornly up from the brown grass, blazing with flowers the color of sealing wax,

"Is there something wrong with the motor?" asked Addie with a dubious glance at that long lemon-yellow hood, now liberally streaked with red dust.

"Just the climate," said Bea as Frederick collected a rusty can from the boot. "Everyone stops to water their cars here. It's the heat. It's hell on the engine. Not to mention the complexion. We might as well step out to stretch our legs," she added. "We won't have another stop until Ashford."

Addie followed Bea out of the car, her London shoes sinking into the red dust as she stepped out. "It doesn't seem to have touched yours," she said. "The heat, I mean."

"Really?" Bea looked genuinely pleased. "I feel like such an old hag these days, all dried out and shopworn."

"You look lovely. Really. As beautiful as ever." Frederick was already yards away, nearly to the stream. Lowering her voice, Addie said, "Are you all right?"

Bea turned away from her. "Why shouldn't I be? I'm in raptures to see you. It's been far too long. I should have had you out here years ago."

Years ago, Addie would have had neither the wherewithal nor the inclination to visit. As it was, the ticket for the ship over had strained her slim resources to the breaking point. David would have loaned her the money, if she'd asked—but she hadn't wanted to ask. Not for this. This was her own private pilgrimage.

Bea plucked at a tall blade of grass with gloved fingers, shredding the brown stalk into smaller and smaller bits. "My mother didn't send on a message with you, did she?" she asked with seeming carelessness.

"No." Addie tried to keep her voice light. "It's non-speakers, I'm afraid, ever since—you know."

They had blamed her for Bea's indiscretion, for introducing Frederick into the household. A cuckoo in the nest, Aunt Vera had called her, a scheming, ungrateful chit. All that and worse. She had been cut off without a penny and found herself, rather abruptly, scrabbling to make a life for herself. For the first time, she had felt truly an orphan.

If it hadn't been for Fernie, she would have been on the street. As it was, Fernie had let her stay in her tiny bed-sit, had shared what she had while Addie embarked on the quest for employment. She'd had to leave *The Bloomsbury Review*; it didn't have the money to pay her. She didn't remember much of those first six months; it was all a blur of sticky typewriting machines and weak tea and rainy days. She hadn't realized how very much she had taken for granted until she had lost it all.

"Oh," said Bea. The light had gone out of her face. She looked, thought Addie, like a lithograph of herself. "I'd thought—never mind."

Addie thought of Aunt Vera as she had seen her last, that last, awful interview, in the sterile sitting room from which all the pictures of Bea had been removed, expunged, as though Bea never was. And, yet, Addie was quite sure that Aunt Vera loved Bea, loved her more than Edward and Dodo put together. It was a strange sort of love, compounded of equal parts pride and ambition, but that was love as Aunt Vera understood it, and she had loved Bea, in her fashion, as fiercely as Pygmalion had loved his Galatea. Aunt Vera's rage over what she perceived as Bea's betrayal had been horrible to behold.

But, now, after all this time . . .

"Maybe if you wrote them?" ventured Addie.

Bea laughed, sharp and bitter. "Don't you think I've tried? There's been nothing back. I should have thought that by now——" She broke off as Frederick returned, replacing the empty can in the boot. "Heavens, that was speedy. Are we all watered and ready to go?"

Frederick held out a hand to help Addie into the car. "Ready for the final leg?" he said. "It's not much farther now."

"I don't know how you can tell," said Addie. "It all looks the same to me."

The landscape seemed to stretch on forever, with brown grasses and twisted trees and the red road that twisted on and on. Even the sky looked different, larger. There was a vastness to it that was both exhilarating and daunting.

"I imagine the Kikuyu might feel the same way about Dorset," said Frederick.

"Don't be silly," said Bea, and slipped around the other side of the car, planting herself firmly in front of the wheel. "No one dies in the desert in Dorset."

"No one dies in the desert here." Frederick took the seat on the other side of Addie. He didn't dispute Bea's possession of the wheel. "At least not this far south."

"No, only of boredom," said Bea, and started the car with a roar that sent a tiny antelope scurrying from the brush. Addie held on to the seat and watched as the scenery blurred past in a cloud of red dust and her cousin leaned low over the wheel, driving like someone fleeing demons.

They drove in awkward silence, the red dust billowing around them, until Frederick suddenly shouted, "Stop the car!"

There was a man running down the drive, holding his white robe up around his knees as he ran, the dust making little puffs around him. His white robe was streaked with red—not dust, Addie realized, but blood, and a lot of it.

Bea slammed on the brakes, the wheels skidding in a half circle that sent Addie careening into Frederick. His hands closed briefly around her shoulders. "Steady, there," he said, and vaulted out of the car without bothering to open the door.

There was a flurry of words in a language Addie didn't understand as the man in the robe began expostulating, his hands flying, his turban askew.

Frederick's face was grim. He interrupted to ask a terse question in the same language and then cursed, loudly, at the answer.

"What's wrong?" Addie asked Bea in an undertone. "Is he hurt?"

"He's all right," said Bea, and Addie realized, with surprise, that she understood whatever it was the man was saying. It shouldn't have surprised her; Bea had always been quick with languages. "It's his son. There's been an accident." Raising her voice, she said, "Where's Miss Platt?"

"Mbugwa says she's taken the girls out on their ponies," said Frederick. "They aren't back yet."

"Miss Platt is the girls' nurse," said Bea to Addie. "She deals with the scrapes and bruises. How bad is it?"

"He tried to hammer a detonator into an ornament," said Frederick tersely. "You can imagine what happened. You'll have to fetch Miss Platt back—or go for Mrs. Nimmo."

"She's gone to Nairobi. We'll never get her back in time," said Bea. "Not even with the car."

"What about me?" Addie rose to her feet in the car, holding on to the dashboard for balance.

"Oh, darling, I'm so sorry," said Bea. "I certainly didn't mean for your arrival to be like this. But we can still—"

"No," said Addie quickly. She could feel the blood thrumming through her veins, the heat and the light making her light-headed, the dry, peppery smell of the dust tickling her nose. "That's not what I meant. What about me? I have some nursing experience. Let me help."

SEVENTEEN

New York, 1999

Your grandmother was a wonderful woman."

There was a woman holding Clemmie's hand pressed between hers. Clemmie had no idea who she was. Not that that was unusual. Clemmie had been hugged, kissed, and cooed over by a whole series of strangers over the past hour, in knit suits smelling of mothballs and Chanel No. 5, and golf-ball pearls that hurt when they hugged her.

"Thank you," said Clemmie. There was no point in asking the woman's name or how she had known Granny Addie. Hers not to ask why, hers simply to press hands, murmur thanks, and feign smiles.

"They don't make them like her anymore," said the woman, shaking her teased head. And then, as an afterthought, "Happy New Year, dear."

Seriously? How happy did she think it was going to be?

Clemmie gritted her teeth and held her tongue. She couldn't take it out on this poor woman. She wasn't the one who had made the idiot decision to hold a funeral on New Year's Eve day on the eve of a new millennium, with half the world out partying and the other half huddled in bunkers, waiting for the apocalypse. In the mood Clemmie was in, she would take the bunker.

"You, too," she said gruffly. "Happy New Year."

Through the half-open windows in the living room, Clemmie could already hear the revelers gearing up for the night's festivities. It was only four, but the sky was already orange and purple. The black branches of the bare trees above the wall of the park stood out in sharp relief against the orange sky.

"She'll be missed," said a man in a gray suit, crunching Clemmie's hand.

"Thank you," said Clemmie demurely.

That was the only way to manage, she knew, to tuck the part of herself that thought and felt away in a drawer and let the remaining shell murmur the commonplaces people expected to hear. Somewhere, locked away, the real Clemmie was curled up in a ball, whimpering, but Robo-Clemmie stood at the living room door in a black sheath dress, calmly shaking hands and accepting condolences, every hair in place and mascara unsmudged.

There hadn't been any Christmas this year. None of them had been in the mood for it. Vaguely Clemmie had been aware that the rest of the world was celebrating, that there was still Christmas music in the stores and wreaths in the windows and those annoying Christmas car commercials on television. She knew, in an abstract way, that the offices had emptied as people took off the week between Christmas and New Year's, but to her it was a blur of gray slush and hospital walls and the hushed voices of those whose job was to deal with the dead. When other people had been opening presents, they'd been discussing embalming. There had been legal documents to unearth, instructions to be followed, movers and packers and appraisers to contact.

Clemmie's mother had already begun the hunt for a new apartment; she could stay at Granny Addie's until the will was probated, but the terms of the will were clear: The apartment needed to be sold to fund a trust, of which Mother and Aunt Anna would get the interest in their lifetimes, with the remainder to all of the grandchildren, divided equally.

Clemmie hated the idea of Granny's apartment being sold. This, more than anyplace else, was her home. She knew there had been a time when she had lived in California with her brothers and both parents, but she didn't remember it, not really. Her memories began and ended at Granny Addie's, in the little room they had decorated with Minnie Mouse cutouts for Clemmie, in the kitchen where there were always treats left over from parties, in the blue and white bedroom where Granny Addie had welcomed her when she had become too weak to walk. They'd already started packing up the bedroom,

Mom and Aunt Anna—but Clemmie didn't want to think about that now, not now.

"—so sorry," the person holding her hand was saying.

"Thank you, you're very kind," Clemmie murmured, and turned to the next person, automatically holding out her hand.

"Hey," said Jon, and something about the sympathy in his hazel eyes made Clemmie's carefully arranged smile start to crumble.

She drew in a long breath through her nose, fighting for composure. "Hey, yourself," she said unsteadily.

He'd been around all day, a familiar presence in a black suit, his light brown hair shining like an old penny, but they hadn't had much to do with each other. He'd been supporting Aunt Anna, quite literally, propping her up on her too-high heels, whisking her neatly out of the way of Clemmie's mother. If Mother and Aunt Anna hadn't yet come to blows, it was largely Jon's doing. The two had been snapping like small dogs all week.

Clemmie would have felt more grateful to Jon if she hadn't harbored the unworthy suspicion that keeping Aunt Anna out of Clemmie's mother's way had also provided a convenient excuse for staying out of Clemmie's.

"You holding up okay?" he said, and Clemmie didn't know whether to fling her arms around his neck and weep or kick him in the ankle. Or, preferably, both.

He was wearing his coat over his suit, a blue and gray scarf hanging around his neck, a pair of leather gloves sticking out of one pocket.

Clemmie's eyes narrowed. "You're leaving?"

He had the grace to look abashed.

"You're going to leave me to keep Mom and Aunt Anna away from each other's throats?" She tried to make it sound like a joke.

"I'm sorry I'm not staying for the cleanup. . . ." He tugged on the ends of the scarf. "I, er, have to get back to my place."

"Exciting New Year's Eve plans?" said Clemmie acidly. It wasn't fair, she knew; he had done more than his bit. But she was angry anyway.

"Hardly." There was a shadow of stubble on his chin, a patch of golden brown that he must have missed while shaving. It gave him a scruffy, down-at-the-mouth look, which, unfairly, only increased his resemblance to Indiana Jones. "You really think I feel like celebrating?"

Somehow, he had always had a knack for making her feel in the wrong. Especially when she was in the wrong. "Sorry," she said. "That wasn't fair. You've done more than your—"

"Don't," said Jon, and there was something raw in his face that shamed Clemmie into silence. "Please."

Clemmie bit her lip, not sure what to say.

Jon leaned over to peck her cheek. "Hang in there," he said. "I'll talk to you soon."

She caught his sleeve, the wool soft beneath her hand. "Look," she said. "I didn't mean to minimize—I know she mattered to you, too."

Jon's face could have been carved out of stone. "Happy New Year, Clemmie."

And he was gone, moving on to the line waiting to pay their respects to her mother at the front door.

Oh, screw it. Screw him. Clemmie abandoned her post and headed into the living room. She'd done her bit. There were only a handful of stragglers left at this point, grazing among the buffet and discussing their New Year's Eve plans. Clemmie hated them all, impartially. She hated them for scarfing all the crab cakes, for their too-strong perfume and their too-bright lipstick. She hated them for talking about Granny Addie as though they knew her.

But what did she know? What Jon had said the other night, about Granny Addie warning him away from her—she just couldn't reconcile it with the grandmother she had known, the grandmother who had told her to take her own risks and make her own choices. Clemmie took a mini quiche off a silver tray. It had long since gone cold, the cheese congealed on the top. She forced herself to chew it anyway. It tasted like rubber.

What did she know about Granny Addie, anyway? Apparently, not enough. Clemmie's mother had given the eulogy at the funeral, speaking more clearly and calmly than Clemmie would have imagined possible. Some of what her mother had said Clemmie had already known, about the farm in Kenya and her grandmother's perspicacity in breaking into the American market when many other coffee growers in Kenya were going under.

Clemmie hadn't known that her grandmother had trained as a nurse during World War I or that she had helped found a maternity hospital and a nurses' training course in Nairobi. She had never asked how they came to be in Kenya or why they had moved to New York instead of London. She hadn't known that her great-grandmother had been a novelist or that her great-grandfather had been the brother of an earl. She hadn't known any of it.

There was a portrait of Granny over the mantel, painted in the forties, not long after Granny Addie and Grandpa Frederick had moved to New York. Clemmie looked up at her, at that familiar, heart-shaped face, the hair that hadn't changed style in all the years Clemmie had known her, the double strand of pearls at the throat.

"It feels like she's still here, doesn't it?" It was Aunt Anna, on the loose at last, heading towards the bar. "Same food, same booze, same bartender . . . It's sick." Without waiting for the bartender, she reached for one of the bottles of wine and topped off her glass. "I keep waiting for her to walk back in and shout, '*Surprise!*'"

"Me, too," said Clemmie. Her throat felt dry and scratchy. She poured herself a little bit of club soda, watching the bubbles fizz themselves out. "I wish she would."

"Mmph," said Aunt Anna. "Is that all you're drinking? Here." She poured a large shot of vodka into Clemmie's soda. "Drink up, kid. Cin cin."

"Thanks—I think." Clemmie toyed with her glass, turning it around and around in her hands. "I didn't know any of that stuff about her. . . . About her nursing or her starting a hospital in Kenya . . . It's all pretty amazing."

"Yeah," said Aunt Anna dryly. "Amazing. You have to give her credit, she did a great job creating her own legend." She raised her glass to the portrait of Granny over the mantel. "Here's to Addie. The greatest spin doctor since Evita decided to go respectable. Lloyd Webber should do a musical. We could get Patti LuPone to play her. Or maybe Tyne Daly. It'd be like *Gypsy* with an English accent—and less nudity."

Even for Aunt Anna, this was a bit over-the-top. Grief made people do strange things. So did prescription medication combined with white wine.

"Would you like to sit down?" Clemmie tentatively put a hand under her aunt's arm. Damn Jon, anyway. He knew how to manage Aunt Anna better than Clemmie ever had. So much for blood being thicker. "Those shoes have to hurt."

"No." Anna shook her off. Her carefully applied makeup had cracked, revealing a network of fine lines. "I've had enough of this Saint Addie crap. All hail Addie, the great and powerful! Do you want to know what she really was?" She rocked forward, so close that Clemmie could smell the combination of perspiration and expensive powder on her cheeks. "She was a selfish, grasping bitch."

Clemmie choked on her vodka.

Aunt Anna waved a hand, yellow diamonds and white gold winking in the light. "Good, kind, wonderful Saint Addie, sitting there like a spider, weaving webs to trap other people's lives . . . She didn't steal things; she stole souls. She got her clammy little fingers in and she didn't let go. She held on and on and on."

"Um . . ." Clemmie had no idea how to deal with this. "More wine?"

"Do you know I tried to run away once?" Aunt Anna was off and rolling. "We were in boarding school in England, your mother and I. It was the perfect opportunity. *She* brought me back. She came over herself and tracked me down."

"She was probably worried about you," said Clemmie tentatively, looking around for her mother. This was the sort of thing designed to make her blood pressure rise. "If any of your kids—"

Aunt Anna slurped her wine. "I let my kids live their lives. Not that any of them were really mine—that's what your mother would say. I've heard her. I know she says it. Like it doesn't count if you didn't ruin your figure for them. Pretty fucking hypocritical when you think about it, considering."

"It isn't about the stretch marks," said Clemmie's mother sharply, making Clemmie jump. "But, then, you wouldn't understand that, would you?"

"Are the caterers okay in the kitchen?" Clemmie said desperately. She wished, desperately, that Jon were here to help. Only Jon had pecked her cheek and left. Just like last time. "Mom, maybe you should—"

Neither of the women paid the least bit of attention to her.

"Oh, you're back to that again, are you?" said Aunt Anna. She leaned back against the makeshift bar. Bottles clanked, but it didn't seem to derail her. "Why don't you just dump some more salt in the wound. Have fun with that."

"Don't play the victim with me," said Clemmie's mother. "Just because you—"

"Come on. Say it." Aunt Anna's face was as hard and cold as an old funeral mask. "Because I had an abortion. Yes, that's right," she said to Clemmie. "If you want to know what's lurking under the carpet, that's just the top of the dust pile. I had a fucking back-alley abortion and they skewered my womb. Happy now?" she said to Clemmie's mother.

"No," said Clemmie's mother, looking decidedly gray about the mouth. "No. You know I never wanted that for you. If you'd only gone to—"

"Saint Addie to the rescue?" Aunt Anna laughed wildly. "Who do you think gave me the money for it? Nothing could be allowed to upset Farve."

There was enough vitriol in her voice to make Clemmie take a step back.

Clemmie's mother came back swinging. "You were only seventeen! She was only trying to help."

"Help. Oh, yes." Aunt Anna swigged back the last of her wine. "She was so helpful. She helped herself right into everything—and everyone else out of it."

Kenya, 1926

"I can help," said Addie. "At least, I might be able to help. I do know something about nursing."

Bea could feel a headache starting, just above her left eye. This entire drive had been a nightmare from start to finish. She and Frederick hadn't spent this much time in the same space for—weeks? Months? They'd managed to avoid each other rather effectively, which was harder than one would think on five hundred acres of land. Her hangover hadn't helped. It wasn't that she drank too much—no more than anyone else—but drink hit hard at this altitude. The best way to counteract the effect of too many drinks the night before was to start again as soon as possible the following afternoon. And so it went on.

She'd been ratty when they set off and the three-hour drive into town hadn't helped, silence broken only by stilted commentary about the weather and loaded questions. They couldn't seem to speak to each other without sniping these days, she and Frederick. She didn't mean to do it, but it just came out that way, every statement a preemptive strike, hitting out at him before he could strike at her. He'd made it all too clear what he thought of her. She could feel it now, in the simmering frustration held in check only by Addie's presence. Bea knew what he was thinking, that if she were a different sort of wife, they wouldn't have to send for Miss Platt or Mrs. Nimmo, that she should be the one calling for medical kits and boiling water and all that rot.

And why? She hadn't been bloody trained for this.

Somehow, it made it worse that Addie had been. She'd forgot about that, Addie's stint as a nurse during the War.

Bea squinted against the too-bright light, saying, as brightly as she could, "Yes, but that was years ago, and you're our guest. We couldn't possibly—"

"I volunteer at St. Mary's once a week," Addie said briskly. "Surely that's better than waiting for the governess to come back. If he's as sick as they say—" She looked expressively at the bloodstains on Mbugwa's robe.

"It isn't going to be pretty," warned Frederick.

Addie stared him down, five foot nothing of sheer determination. "I've seen guts spilling out of a ruptured stomach before. These things are never pretty. Do you have a medical kit?"

Frederick didn't hesitate. "What do you need?"

"I won't know until I see him. We will need to boil water, to sterilize it. If that's possible?"

"We're hardly so primitive as that," said Bea sharply. Too sharply. Frederick frowned at her. "Why don't you see to the water?" she said to Frederick. "I'll take Addie to the *shamba*."

"Right, then," he said, giving Bea a long, hard look. She hated it when he looked at her like that. "Boiled water, medical kit—anything else?"

"Strong spirits," said Bea.

"Oh, yes!" said Addie. "To sterilize the wound."

"No, for us." Addie hadn't the slightest idea what she was getting into, what she might find in the native encampment behind the house. Bea caught her cousin's hands between her own, such small, square hands in their cheap gloves. "Darling, you don't have to do this. We can send for Miss Platt or for that hideous Scotswoman on the next farm over."

"It's all right. I don't mind at all." Addie firmly but gently drew her hands away, leaving Bea feeling, somehow, bereft. "Will you show me the way?"

Bea shrugged, swinging her long legs out of the car. "It's your funeral, darling."

"Hopefully it won't be anyone's funeral." Addie scrambled inelegantly out after her. "Who's the boy who was hurt?"

"Hardly a boy. He must be at least twenty, although it's hard to tell. They don't reckon age from birth the way we do. It's all done by circumcision year."

Addie's eyebrows rose. "Circumcision year?"

"When you ask how old a boy is, you'll be told he was of the circumcision year of the locusts, or the year when all the rains failed. They're all circumcised at puberty, boys and girls. They make a big ritual of it, feasts, dancing, slaying of cattle. Our cattle," added Bea. "Somehow, the best beasts always seem to break a leg just on the eve of a festival. Quite the coincidence."

She led Addie around the house, past the straggling acacia bushes planted by the previous owner. They'd been lucky—or so Frederick liked to tell her. Most of their peers had done a stint living in a grass hut, waiting for a house to be built. They'd got theirs already made, off a chap who had sold up to pursue a cattle-ranching proposition in Uganda. As houses went here, theirs wasn't bad. It was solid stone, built in the bungalow style, long and low with a wide porch that ran along the front of the house and a courtyard in the middle. They had plumbing, such as it was, and electricity that ran as long as nothing bumped too hard against the generator. Opulence by Kenya's standards, poverty compared to what they had left behind.

The previous owners had made some attempt at landscaping. There was a terrace at the back of the house and some overgrown rosebushes, but the scent of the roses couldn't mask the other smells, smoke and sweat and goat.

They didn't have far to get to Mbugwa's encampment, an entire settlement of round, grass-roofed huts, each leaching its own haze of blue-gray smoke through the thatch. Maize grew in neat plots around the huts, tended by slender women in leather aprons whose anklets jingled as they hacked at the weeds with their pangas. They worked all but bare in the hot sun, their arms encircled by copper wire wound so tightly that the flesh bulged on either side. Some wore babies strapped to their backs in slings; older children played in the dust outside the huts as a chicken idly scratched at the dirt.

"These are the native *shambas*—farms," Bea translated. "They squat on our land. Or we squat on their land, depending on how you look at it. It works out rather well all around. They work the coffee and we give them a place to herd their goats."

"It sounds very feudal," said Addie.

"It is." Bea nodded towards one of the huts. "That's Njombo's hut."

It was an easy guess, based on the number of people gathered around. They drew back as Bea and Addie approached, making way for them. Bea could see Addie try not to goggle at the men, dressed only in short blankets tied toga-style on one shoulder, or the women, with their shaved heads and bare breasts.

Bea had had an image of how Addie's arrival was meant to be, the house servants lined up in their white robes, drinks on a tray, the lamps lit, everything sparkling and just a touch exotic. "This isn't how I meant your visit to be."

Addie looked up at her and smiled, as if they were ten again and at Ashford, the real Ashford. "I don't mind. Did your headman say anything about the nature of the wound?"

"Gloom, doom, and general dismemberment. It usually is." In this case, though, it actually might be. "It might be bad. He tried to hammer a detonator into an ornament."

"Into a—?"

"Anything metal seems to be fair game," said Bea. "We can't keep nails; they turn them into anklets and earrings. The detonator must have looked suitably shiny. According to Mbugwa, Njombo took a rock and tried to beat the detonator into an anklet."

Addie breathed in sharply through her nose. "He's lucky to be alive."

"Do you want me to see if Platt is back? They can't have gone far."

Addie shook her head. "I'll do what I can." She poked her head into the doorway, then turned her head, blinking. "The smoke—"

"It's the cook fire," said Bea. "They're all like that."

Addie nodded and plunged into the smoke, shoulders hunched, keeping her head down below the worst of it.

"I'm here to help you," Bea heard her say in the sort of cheerful voice nurses always used, the voice that made one want to thump them with a bedpan. And, "Where does it hurt?"

Bea stood by the doorway, twiddling her thumbs and feeling generally useless, as Addie crawled on her hands and knees, making soothing noises, comforting Njombo with a hand on the side of his head. Her skirt trailed dangerously near the fire at the center of the hut. Slipping inside, Bea pushed the fabric back.

"I don't want you immolating yourself," she said gruffly. "Not with Platt not back yet."

Addie smiled her thanks. "Can you see if the water's here yet? I can't do much without it. The clotted blood needs to be sponged away before I can see how bad it is."

"Of course it does," murmured Bea. The smell in the hut was almost unbearably strong, sweat and blood and the peculiar pong of the monkey skins that were marks of status. "I'll see what's keeping them."

She seized on the excuse to duck out again, hating herself for her weakness.

No one had warned her of any of this. *Come to East Africa,* they had said. *Fortunes to be made! Reputations to be repaired! More old Etonians than Mayfair!* But they hadn't told her about this, about the very basic realities of living, about jiggers that burrowed under your toes or the flies that clustered around children's eyes or strange pests and diseases that drove horses mad before they killed them.

She hated it here.

Bea twisted Marcus' ring around on her finger. In those fairy stories Addie used to whisper to her when they were little that should summon a genie or some other spirit, and she'd be able to close her eyes and wish herself back to before, to Rivesdale House and the world before Bunny. Before Frederick. If she had known then . . . But wasn't that always the rub? At the time, Marcus' infidelity had seemed insurmountable, a slight that needed to be avenged. Now, she wished she had followed her mother's advice and looked the other way. Bea had never thought, never imagined, that it might end like this.

Marcus and Bunny had married. Bea had seen the pictures in a six-month-old *Tatler*, the blushing bride with her bevy of attendants. He hadn't wasted much time; they were engaged as soon as Bea was on the boat, married almost immediately after. They had two little boys, an heir and a spare.

Those were meant to be her children, her boys. It was unpardonably perverse of Fate to have got it so backward, to have expelled Marcus' child from her womb while the other, the cuckoo in the nest, had clung so stubbornly to life.

Marjorie, Frederick had called the cuckoo, such an ugly name, like someone's maiden aunt, but Bea had been beyond caring. She knew it wasn't fair to blame the child for the circumstances of her birth, but Bea couldn't seem to help it. She had looked at that red, squalling thing and knew it to be no part of her, this parasite who had lodged in her gut and cost her everything, her family, her home, her reputation, the man she had thought she loved.

Instead, he had married Bunny, and Bea had found herself in Kenya, a social outcast, married to a man who seemed more and more a stranger, a stranger who buried himself in agricultural journals and regarded her with thinly veiled disdain—that was, when he bothered to look at her at all.

Still, there were compensations. Idina's parties. Safaris. Race Week at Muthaiga. Raoul, who swore he'd marry her, even if his Catholic family cut him off, an empty promise, but flattering nonetheless. It was nice to know that someone still wanted to marry her, even if her husband wished he hadn't.

And, of course, Val. Val, who promised nothing, who cared about nothing. Val, who took her flying.

"Memsahib, memsahib!" It was a small boy, clothed only in a loincloth. One arm was hideously scarred, remnant of a fall into the fire in babyhood. So many of the children boasted similar injuries, scars and wounds that would have felled their counterparts back in England. "Bwana say bring."

He hoisted the old leather bag that held their store of medical supplies. Bea hadn't the foggiest notion what was in it. That was Platt's province. Behind him followed Frederick with a large bucket of steaming water held in one hand, clean cloths hanging off his arm.

"Here you go," he said. "Is there anything I can do?"

Bea stepped between Frederick and the door of the hut. "We have it in hand," she said regally.

Frederick looked over at Addie, bent over Njombo, and then back at Bea. "Yes, I can see that you do."

Bea bristled. There was certainly no magic to telling a boy to fetch water. It wasn't as though Frederick were in there, sewing the man up. She'd yet to see Frederick apply a sticking plaster, and yet he had the gall to look down his nose at her, just because she hadn't been taught something she'd never had the least idea she would have to know—and she wouldn't have had to know it if he hadn't blundered into her life at the worst possible time.

"There wasn't much call for this in Mayfair," she said defensively.

"We're not in Mayfair anymore."

"Don't you think I know it?"

"Sometimes?" Frederick raised his brows. "No."

"Oh, hullo." Addie stumbled out, her face smoke grimed, her eyes tearing. She braced one hand against the wall of the hut. "Do you have the water?"

"Water and medical kit," said Frederick, handing over the bucket and snapping his fingers at the boy, who stepped smartly forward.

"Thank you." Addie bundled the cloths over her arm. She glanced back over her shoulder into the hut. "It's not as bad as it seems. He's bled a great deal from a scalp wound. I can't promise anything, but it looks as though most of the cuts are superficial. He seems to have got scraped up with the flying rock."

"Most of the cuts?"

"He's banged up his hand rather badly. One finger is dangling by a . . . well." She pressed her lips together. "I can try to sew it together, but the odds of infection . . ."

"No one expects miracles," said Frederick.

For some reason, that seemed to annoy her. Her back straightened and she gave him what Bea could only describe as a look. "That's no reason to shirk."

She disappeared back into the smoke, taking her spoils with her. Frederick watched as she knelt by Njombo, his expression abstracted. Addie had discarded her hideous hat. Her curly hair was in disarray, her face and arms streaked with soot and worse, and yet Bea felt a strange frisson of fear. It reminded her of the first time she had seen Marcus with Bunny, seen the way his eyes lingered on her.

Nonsense, of course. But still . . .

"You forgot something," said Bea to her husband.

"What?" Frederick was too immersed in what Addie was doing to re-spond immediately. "Yes?"

"Our drinks," said Bea, putting her chin up. "Make them strong."

EIGHTEEN

New York, 1999

Y ou're drunk," said Mother to Aunt Anna.

Aunt Anna twisted away from Clemmie's mother. "I may be drunk, but in the morning I'll still be honest, and you'll still be lying through your teeth. You spent your whole life sucking up to that bitch. What about *her*? What about our mother?"

The words hung there in the air between them.

Clemmie's mother took a deep, deep breath. "Clementine, the caterers— See if they need anything."

"In a moment," said Clemmie. Someone needed to put Anna in a cab—or to bed. She was making no sense. Clemmie didn't like the way her mother looked either. Now that Granny Addie was gone, it was as though the last buffer between Clemmie's mother and mortality had been removed. She was seventy-eight and today she looked every year of it. "Aunt Anna, do you want—"

"No." Aunt Anna's long fingernails dug into Clemmie's arm. "Come with me. There's something you ought to see. You, too, Marjorie."

"See what?" Clemmie rolled her eyes at her mother as her aunt tugged her along, through the study and down the back hall.

"I thought she'd destroyed them," Aunt Anna said. "But, no, they were here all along."

She shooed Clemmie into Granny Addie's room, strangely empty now without Granny Addie in it. Aunt Anna went straight to the closet. As in so many pre-war apartments, it was an oddly shaped afterthought of a closet, a triangular bend in the wall. She came out bearing an album Clemmie had never seen before, longer and flatter than the albums Clemmie was accustomed to, with clips that held it together on one side and a cracked red leather cover.

Aunt Anna dumped it on the empty bureau. "I found this yesterday, at the back of the closet. Go on. Take a look."

Clemmie cast a puzzled look at her mother. Her mother's lips were pressed firmly together, her expression stoic.

Aunt Anna looked over her shoulder at Clemmie's mother, raising her perfectly manicured eyebrows. "What do you think, Madge? Do you think Farve kept them? Or did Addie sit here and gloat over them?"

"I think," said Clemmie's mother sharply, "that you need new tranquilizers."

Clemmie opened the album, half-expecting something to leap out and bite her. "They're pictures from Kenya," she said.

She recognized that much from the few pictures Granny Addie had had framed, the sepia images of men in mushroom-shaped hats and riding breeches and women in saggy tops and calf-length skirts. There was a curious sameness to them all, the men in their hats and suits, the women in their clothes that looked so dowdy now but were probably the height of fashion back then.

Clemmie wondered if this was what her college pictures would look like to future generations, if one woman with big hair and a denim jacket would look just like another.

She looked over her shoulder at her mother. "It's just an old album."

"Keep looking," said Aunt Anna.

Clemmie put the album on the edge of the dresser so they could all see. There were group photos with everyone standing around, looking awkward; posed shots of men next to their trophies, rifles in hand; more casual shots of people sitting on crates at a picnic, a wind-up gramophone next to them, no one paying attention except one woman looking over her shoulder.

Clemmie recognized that woman. It was the same woman she had seen hanging on the wall of the Rivesdale House hotel a million years ago, with her pointed chin and her dare-me stare. Perhaps it was the cracked sepia of the photo, but she looked older here, more world worn. "That's Granny's cousin, isn't it?"

"Mm-hmm," said Aunt Anna.

Clemmie's mother said nothing.

She'd run away, the marquis had said. What was the word he'd used? "Bolted." Well, if one was going to bolt, Clemmie supposed Africa would have been a good place to bolt to, especially if Granny Addie and Grandpa Frederick were already there.

Bea was in the next picture, too, along with three other women, one holding a banjo, one inspecting a basket, while the other two sprawled on picnic blankets. Gently, Clemmie eased it out of the small triangles that held it to the page. On the back, it read: WANJOHI, 1924 in a writing that Clemmie didn't recognize and, under that, DINA, COCKIE, ALICE, AND SELF.

There were pictures of Grandpa Frederick, too, at first sporting a silly mustache, and then later, clean-shaven, with a little girl in miniature riding breeches, standing next to something that looked almost like a deer but wasn't.

"Mom, is that you?"

Her mother nodded. "That was my pet dik-dik. Feather." Her voice sounded cracked and unsteady, as if she was trying not to cry.

There were more of Clemmie's mother—with a pony, with Grandpa Frederick, sitting on a porch with a doll with a white-robed house servant standing by. No Granny Addie. Clemmie began flipping through faster, scanning for her grandmother. There were a lot of servants: house servants, and grooms, and bearers carrying animals hanging upside down from long poles. There were more photos of safari groups and picnic parties and a series of rather opulent ones labeled RACE WEEK AT MUTHAIGA, with women dressed like something out of a *Masterpiece Theatre* special, all long pearls and feathered headdresses. Lots of Bea—Bea and friends, Bea and Frederick, Bea with a baby who had to be Aunt Anna—but still no Granny.

"Did Granny Addie take the pictures?" Clemmie asked.

"No," said Aunt Anna. She sounded very definite about it.

Clemmie flipped over the last page. Granny's cousin was decked out in full flapper chic, positioned between two men in evening dress, each with an arm around her shoulders. One looked half-blotto, his features blurred as though he'd turned at the last moment. The other smirked straight at the camera. He looked a bit like Rufus Sewell in *Cold Comfort Farm*, pure smoldering testosterone.

On the back it read: NEW YEAR'S EVE, 1926. SELF, VAL, AND R'L.

So this was Bea's album, then. But where was Granny Addie? She hadn't appeared in a single photo. The book ended with 1926. There was nothing more. Clemmie knew she had seen other photos, photos with Granny Addie and Grandpa Frederick in their coffee fields, but there were none of those here.

"Where's Granny Addie?"

Aunt Anna leaned against the wall. "Do you want to tell her, Madge? Or shall I?"

Clemmie's mother sat down heavily on a box of books. "She's not in them because she wasn't there." She knotted her hands together in her lap and looked up at Clemmie. "She first came out when I was five years old."

Kenya, 1926

Addie woke to the rhythmic swish of a twig broom brushing the path outside her window.

Light shone through the gaps between the curtains, distilled and magnified like strong spirits. Addie burrowed deeper into the linen sheets, feeling the unfamiliar slide of silk against her skin. There had been pajamas left for her on the bed last night. She had been too tired to hunt down her nightdress, so she had wiggled into the pajamas instead, flame-colored silk, the same color as the blossoms on the trees, slippery and decadent.

Addie propped herself up against the pillow, rubbing the sleep from her eyes, as last night came back in bits and pieces: Bea and Frederick's bickering, the smoky hut, the wounded man, strong drinks, a supper she barely remembered, set on a dining room table incongruously adorned with Irish crystal and Spode china, served by silent servants in white robes and bare feet. She hadn't met the children or their mysterious governess; they dined separately.

How long had she slept? The watch on her nightstand had stopped, but the household was already clearly awake. There was a pot of tea and some hard biscuits on a tray next to her bed, along with a vase with a flower she didn't recognize and a note in a hand she did. It was from Bea, and all it said was: *Gone out for a bit, back soon. Rest and enjoy!*

Addie took a sip of her tea. It was sickly sweet and stone cold. She shuddered and put it aside. During the years of austerity, she had trained herself to drink her tea unsweetened; by now, she preferred it that way.

Scratch, scratch, scratch, went the broom outside her window. She was tempted to bury her head under the pillow, in the cool dimness of her room, but that would be hiding. She'd have to go out and face the world sooner or later. By "the world," she meant Bea and Frederick. She hauled herself out of bed, her whole body feeling strangely achy, as if she were recovering from a fever. Or from a long ride in a train and a car.

At least she was clean. Last night, Bea had insisted she bathe, in a vast jade tub like something from an Oriental emperor's lascivious fantasies, scented steam rising off the top, candlelight reflecting off the murky waters. Between the gin and the jasmine-scented smoke, Addie had felt as though she'd stumbled into the Thousand and One Nights.

Addie found the bathroom with the jade bath. In the light of day, it was just a bathroom, good for cleaning one's teeth and washing one's face. Cold water and her own clothes made Addie feel more herself again. *Rest,* Bea had said, but according to the grandfather clock in the hall, Addie had rested quite long enough; it was past ten, shamefully late. At home, she would have been long out of bed by now, sitting at her desk in the office after a long and shivering Tube ride, her umbrella drying out in a battered can by the office door.

Not by inclination, though. Bea had always been the early riser, naturally alert and cheerful in the mornings, while Addie, left to her own devices, would happily stay burrowed under the covers as long as anyone would let her. It had always been a wonder to her, during their Season, that Bea could dance all night and still be awake for a ride in Hyde Park in the morning, seemingly untouched by the hectic schedule.

Addie ventured out of her room, feeling as though she had wandered into someone else's fairy tale. Outside, there were strange birds calling, bells tinkling, voices raised in languages Addie didn't understand, but the stone walls of the house buffered and transformed them into a serene hum, wrapping the house in a peculiar sort of calm, Sleeping Beauty's East African lodge.

Addie helped herself to a cup of coffee from the breakfast room, taking it out onto the verandah. The acacias around the verandah filled the air with their scent; from their petals came the drone of insects, intent on extracting nectar.

She wasn't the only one on the porch, she realized. A little girl was curled up next to the balustrade, engaged in earnest colloquy with a tattered porcelain doll. As Addie came out, the girl scrambled to her feet, looking as though she was contemplating a retreat.

"Good morning," Addie said, setting her coffee down on a wood table. "You must be Marjorie."

The little girl looked up at her over the head of her doll. Her hair was a dark blond, not as blond as Bea, but blond enough that Bea needn't have feared that Marcus would have suspected a cuckoo in the nest. Her eyes were a disconcerting pale blue. Gillecote eyes.

Addie held out a hand, unsure of the protocol. She hadn't dealt with children since she had been one. "I'm your cousin Addie. I've come for a visit."

The child kept a good grip on her doll, eying Addie from a distance. "Farve says you've come from England."

Farve? Child parlance for "Father," she guessed. "Yes, on a very big boat. And a very smoky train."

"I wanted to see the train," said the child. "Farve wouldn't take me."

"It's very noisy," said Addie. "And very dirty. You didn't miss much. It's much nicer here."

"Karanja says it's a snake," said the little girl. "A great silver snake."

Well, that was one way of looking at it. Addie hunkered down on her heels. "If it is a snake, it must be under an enchantment."

"What's 'chantment'?"

"A magical spell," Addie elaborated. Had no one told the child any fairy tales? "You'd need a magical spell to make a snake grow that big. It goes on as far as you can see and it spits out fire and smoke like a dragon. Dragons are rather like snakes," she said before the little girl could ask, "but bigger and scarier. And they can fly." Feeling like she was getting rather out of her depth, Addie pointed quickly at the doll. "Who is that you're holding?"

Marjorie contemplated her for a moment, then held out the tattered china doll. "This is Annabelle."

"Good morning, Annabelle," said Addie, since some introduction seemed to be required.

"Good morning to you, too," said an amused male voice from above Addie's head.

Addie shot to her feet so quickly that she nearly stumbled over the hem of her own skirt. "Oh, hullo. We were just—"

"Farve!" shouted Marjorie, and catapulted herself towards her father, who swung her up high in the air, her booted feet narrowly missing Addie's nose.

The little girl wrapped her arms around Frederick's neck, nestling trustingly against his shoulder. He squeezed her tight for a moment, rubbing his nose against the top of her head. They seemed so complete and entire together, so happy. Addie would never have imagined Frederick, not the Frederick she had known, as a doting father, and yet his daughter obviously adored him and he adored his daughter.

It didn't at all go with Addie's notion of an evil seducer.

Frederick set his daughter firmly down on her feet. "Lesson time for you. Miss Platt is looking for you."

"But Feather will be missing me."

"Feather is Marjorie's dik-dik," said Frederick to Addie. His expression was relaxed, amused. He looked fondly at his daughter. "After your lessons. Then you can introduce Cousin Addie to Feather."

"I shall look forward to it," said Addie. "Oh, and you won't want to forget this." She leaned over and retrieved Annabelle.

"What do you say?" said Frederick.

"Thank you," said Marjorie, and ran off back into the house.

Addie would have liked to have followed, but that would have felt too much like flight. The last time she and Frederick had been alone together had been five years ago, a continent, a marriage, two children away.

"I hate to ask," she said, "but what's a dik-dik?"

Frederick's face creased into a smile. It gave Addie a queer feeling in her chest. "It's a sort of deer. Marjorie will show you."

"Yes, I'll hold her to that."

They stood there for a very long moment, not quite looking at each other, and Addie realized, with some surprise, that he felt just as awkward as she did.

With some hesitation, he said, "I'm just going down to the coffee shed. If you like, I'll show you around the farm."

She knew it was a bad idea, but the sun was shining and the outdoors looked tempting and Bea was still nowhere to be seen. It would be like inoculation, she told herself. Exposure in the interest of indifference. "I won't be interfering with your work?"

"Not at all. When we say we work here, we really mean we have others do it for us. You'll want a hat," he added, and snagged one from a table on the verandah, dropping it onto her head. It was made of double-lined felt, beige on the outside, red on the inside, and it sagged down nearly to her eyes. "You're courting sunstroke otherwise."

As they stepped out from under the verandah, the heat shimmered in a palpable haze, like the tulle on the gowns she had worn during that awful deb year; she felt she could reach out and scrunch it up between her fingers.

To her surprise, it wasn't unpleasant, not like the stifling heat of her compartment on the train. Instead, it settled over her like a second skin, warming her straight through. She always felt cold at home, a deep cold that had settled into her bones long ago, huddling in a closet in a long-forgotten house in Bloomsbury on a rainy day in November.

Here it seemed as if no such thing as Novembers existed. The sky was bright and clear, a blue so intense it hurt the eyes.

They took a path that led the opposite way, not towards—what had Bea called them?—not towards the huts they had seen last night, but along a narrow stream, through the high, brown grass, past jagged thorn trees and twisted erythrinas with their flowers the color of Bea's pajamas. Insects sang on a high, clear note while a chameleon panted by the side of the path, its coat the same mottled green-brown as the grass around it. Addie could hear the tinkle of goat bells as a small boy, dressed in nothing at all, drove his flock, and, as Bea had warned, the chatter of monkeys conducting their own private business in the trees.

Strange flowers flared at her feet; the brush rustled with life all around them. It was fantastical, all of it, the light, the heat, the flowers, the men with their hair in a fleece of short braids, their earlobes distended by dangling ornaments, the women wound in their coils of copper wire. She felt as though she'd wandered into an illustration in an old book, *Robinson Crusoe* or something by H. Rider Haggard.

"It's like something out of a novel, isn't it?" said Frederick.

Addie frowned at him from under her hat. "You shouldn't read my mind; it's not polite."

Frederick grinned, striking ahead of him with his walking stick, a long, gnarled thing. "It wasn't mind reading, just common sense. I felt the same way when I first saw it."

"It certainly makes a change from a Bloomsbury winter," said Addie guardedly. She didn't want him rooting about in her emotions. Arm's length, that was what they would be. Polite and distant. "Marjorie is lovely."

Frederick's face lit with pride. "Isn't she? We'll need a proper governess for her soon. She reads anything you put in front of her."

Addie shifted her hat. "Should I hide my novels, then?"

The lines at the corners of Frederick's eyes crinkled. "I'd forgot your taste for scandalous literature. Are you still editing *The Mercury*?"

"*The Bloomsbury Review*," Addie corrected him. "And I was never an editor, only a lowly dogsbody. No."

That Addie, the one who had worked at *The Bloomsbury Review*, who dreamed of changing the world through poetry—the Addie who had fancied herself in love with Frederick—was a different creature entirely. She knew better now.

She said simply, "It folded three years ago. I took a job as a typist at an import-export outfit."

Frederick looked at her curiously. "What about university?"

She might as well have cried for the moon. "I wasn't going to go from one tower to another," she said. "Don't look like that; really, I like the work. It's been good for me. I wouldn't have thought it, but I'm far better at figures than I ever was at parsing poetry. My parents are probably rolling in their graves, but there it is. I seem to have a bent for business."

To her surprise, he didn't mock her. "Strange what we discover about ourselves, isn't it? I never thought I'd take to farming."

"You plant coffee?" Bea had said something the other day about coffee bushes.

"Among other things. We experimented with indigo, but that turned out to be a bust. An informative bust, but a bust nonetheless. It's still trial and error out here," he said. "You can never tell what will hit."

"It sounds very exciting."

"Exciting and maddening all at the same time. We didn't know anything about it when we came. I'd read books and thought that was enough." Frederick smiled wryly at his own expense. There was a humility about him there hadn't been before. It was not displeasing. Not at all.

"I take it that didn't work?" said Addie politely, maintaining a careful distance.

There was something very disarming about his smile. "The experts go on about soil acidity and proper growing conditions and this altitude and that fertilizer, but when it comes down to it, you don't know what will work until you try it. Then there are locusts, drought—all the things they never tell you about when they're touting the benefits of growing coffee."

"Not exactly a golden goose, then?"

"No. It's worth it, though," he added. "Despite all that. There's nothing like seeing that first crop of coffee berries and thinking, How in the hell did we manage that?"

"Like Candide," said Addie, smiling. "Cultivating your garden."

Frederick leaned on his walking stick. "In the best of all possible worlds."

She couldn't tell whether he was being sarcastic or not.

"What's that over there?" she said instead, pointing to a rectangular structure, open at the sides and roofed with closely woven fronds. "It looks like something Swiss Family Robinson might have built."

"That's the coffee nursery. It's where we keep the seedlings until they're large enough to be planted."

As he explained the workings of the nursery and the vagaries of coffee planting, Addie let his words wash over her as she looked him over, older, browner, and yet, somehow, more solid. The brooding Rochester she had fancied herself in love with in London didn't exist; it seemed as though he'd left that aspect of his nature behind along with London. She remembered him always surrounded by a cloud of smoke, in the unnatural half-light of an underground club. That man, urbane and cynical, had nothing to do with the man so enthusiastically propounding planting techniques.

It made her more than a little uneasy. She'd known—or, at least, knew now—how to deal with that man. She didn't know how to handle this one. She couldn't reconcile this Frederick with the old one; it was like seeing two photographic exposures, one imposed over the other, the outlines blurring and neither quite right.

"Sorry," he said, breaking off. "I'm boring you, aren't I? You didn't come out here for a lecture on coffee cultivation."

"Why not?" she said. "It's shameful. I've been drinking it for years with no idea where it came from. Is that the coffee? I'd never imagined the beans would be red. I always pictured them as brown."

"We call them cherries," he said. "And they do turn brown, once they've been roasted."

Addie scrounged for something else to say, something safely impersonal. "Why is it only women working in the fields?"

Frederick came to stand beside her, looking out over the fields. "We tried to recruit men when we started off here and they wouldn't come. They were all right with the ploughing and digging, but once the plants were in the ground the weeding and picking are women's work. It's very different here," he said, as Bea had said the night before.

"Yes, I can see that," said Addie. She lifted her face to the sun. In the coffee fields, the women were singing as they worked. To the far left, she could see the shadows of the mountains, purple in the distance. "But beautiful."

"It is, rather, isn't it?" Frederick looked out across his kingdom, and his expression was something like what it had been when he had looked at his daughter, fond and proud. Bracing himself on his stick, he turned to look at Addie. "I never thanked you for what you did for Njombo last night. It was very good of you."

"Anyone with the proper training would have done the same," she said quickly. "I'd seen worse, during— Well, you know."

Frederick looked out over the coffee plants, the shadowed hills in the distance. "Out here, the War feels a very long way away." He shook his head. "It *was* a very long way away. I'm surprised you remembered all that."

Addie tucked her hair back behind her ear. "I volunteer once a week at a charity hospital in the East End. It's the maternity ward," she admitted, "so it's not entirely applicable, but I do still see my share of needles and aether."

Frederick leaned against his stick. "You should talk to Joanie Grigg— Lady Grigg, I should say. She's the governor's wife. She's just launched a project to open a maternity home in Nairobi. She'd be delighted to have someone else with some experience on board."

"I'd—" Addie caught herself just in time. What was she thinking? This was only a visit, after all, a chance to see Bea. "I don't imagine I'll be staying long enough for that."

Frederick plucked up his stick. "Of course," he said. "You'll be wanting to get back to your— What was his name?"

"David." She didn't want to talk about David, not with Frederick. It made her feel somehow disloyal, although to whom and why she couldn't quite say.

Frederick started towards the coffee sheds, steps and words speeding up at the same time. "Do you mind terribly if we cut our walk short? I have some accounts to see to. It's the one bane of my life here, the bookkeeping. Well, that and the locusts, and of the two, the bookkeeping's the worse. The numbers never do add up."

"May I help?" She wasn't quite sure why she offered. Curiosity, perhaps? Or simply boredom. She'd lost the habit of leisure years ago. "I do have some bookkeeping experience."

Frederick slowed, looking down at her in a way she remembered all too well. "You're a guest," he said.

Addie shoved her too-large hat back on her head. "I do wish you and Bea would stop saying that. I like to work. I've got used to it. I'm not very good at being idle gracefully."

"In that case, I'll take you up on that offer." He raised a brow. "I warn you, you'll probably regret it. The books are on their way to being my own personal Augean stables."

Addie nodded briskly. "Take me to it and I'll see what I can do."

Frederick squinted down at her. "Is there anything you can't do? Build a submarine, translate from the Japanese?"

Addie thought for a moment and then grinned. "Stay on the back of a horse. That's Bea's forte." *Back soon,* Bea had said. It had to be nearly noon already. "Where *is* Bea?"

Frederick looked out towards the road, his expression grim.

"Riding," he said.

NINETEEN

Kenya, 1926

"Altimeter . . . Oil gauge . . ." Bea squinted at the instruments on the control panel. This was only her second time behind the controls, and, if all went well, her first solo flight. "It all seems in order."

"Seems?" drawled Val, perched on the tail behind her. "I know not 'seems.' Check it again."

Bea rolled her eyes but complied. It was his aeroplane, after all, and aeroplanes weren't exactly thick on the ground in the colony, for all that there was talk of a new airstrip and an aerodrome. By the time that aerodrome was up, she fully intended to have her A license. It took sixteen hours of airtime to earn; so far, she'd clocked one. Val had a dangerous habit of providing other distractions.

But not today. Today she was determined to get into the air. She'd woken at dawn, left a note for Addie, and made the drive to the makeshift airstrip in less than two hours, blazing down the potted red roads at a speed that would have horrified her husband. Of course, most things horrified her husband these days.

It was at times like those that she felt free, with the engine thrumming in front of her and zebra fleeing from the road into the fastness of the bush. Racing through the still-sleeping landscape, the dew still crisp on the grass, she could pretend away the past six years and be back at Ashford again, the real Ashford, with the whole world to conquer. And that was nothing to the feeling of leaving the ground behind entirely, soaring into the air, with all of Kenya spread out beneath her.

"Don't forget the control stick." She felt Val's lips on the side of her neck, expertly navigating beneath her hair. His hands slid over her shoulders, cupping the sides of her breasts.

Bea shrugged away. "Stop it, Val."

"You're here, aren't you?" His breath was warm in her ear. "Naughty, naughty, Bea."

She jerked her head away. "Not now," she said.

"Well." Val leaned back, stretching his arms out above his head. "Aren't we a little cat this morning. What's put your claws in a clamp?"

He looked feline himself, all boneless grace, with the measureless self-satisfaction afforded by knowing his ancestors had been dining off gold plate when others had still been scratching about in the dirt: the Honorable Theophilius Vaughn, the despair of an ancient line. According to his frustrated family, he had both the morals of a cat and all of its nine lives.

Val called it hypocritical of them. *We've been sinning for centuries and profiting from it, too,* he liked to say. *It's the world that's changed, not us. Why should we bow to their bourgeois morality?* It wasn't just lip service. He lived down to his creed. As far as Bea could tell, he got away with it because he was so bloody good-looking. She should have known. She'd been playing that game for years.

The difference, of course, was that he was a man. He didn't need to marry to secure his place; he didn't have to ruin his figure having babies. No one called him passé at twenty-seven. He could tell the world to go to hell and live as he liked and everyone loved him for it, professing shock at his excesses in tones of horrified admiration that were more a compliment than a condemnation. Everyone had a story about Val. Many of them were even true.

A fallen angel, that was what he was. Lucifer, in human form, as beautiful as an old statue and about a million times more carnal. He had the black hair and brilliant blue eyes of the Vaughns and something more besides, a restless carelessness that bordered on cruelty. It was all maddeningly attractive.

Most of the time.

"Nothing," said Bea shortly. "Nothing at all."

Val took a small porcelain box from his pocket and flipped it open. "If you're not going to entertain me . . ." He scattered a few grains on his wrist and sniffed, elegantly, before offering the box to her. "A vast improvement over snuff, wouldn't you agree?"

Bea waved it aside. "I'm not in the mood."

She'd partaken before, but the euphoria always faded, just like everything else. No matter how many men she took to her bed, how many fences she leaped, how much gin she downed, how many lions she stalked, it was always the same; the thrill was shorter and shorter lived, leaving her craving more. It was like trying to slake one's thirst on champagne; each sip left one more parched than before.

But flying—that was different. Up in the air, she didn't have to care about anything, not the husband who despised her, the family who had disowned her, the adoring little cousin who was neither so little nor adoring anymore.

Val snapped the lid of the snuffbox shut. "Goodness," he said. "It *must* be serious."

Bea pushed back her goggles. "You promised me a lesson."

Val was obviously in one of his provoking moods. "I promised a lesson. I never specified the kind." He ran a finger down the open collar of her shirt. "You need to be more careful when negotiating your devil's bargains."

Despite herself, she leaned into his touch, knowing too well by now just what his hands and lips could do, the temporary oblivion they provided.

"What else could you possibly have to teach me?" she demanded huskily.

Dropping his hand, Val jumped lightly off the side of the plane. "Patience, perhaps?"

Bea's chest burned where he'd touched her. She could feel her nipples pebbling under the fine linen of her shirt. From his smirk, he could see it, too.

Damn him. Damn him and damn that abominable smile of his.

Bea yanked the collar of her shirt back into place. "Weren't you the one who said patience is only a virtue when there's something worth waiting for?"

"One of my less esteemed ancestors. But close enough. Was that meant to wound me?" He pressed a hand to his heart. "I am slain. I die. Alas."

Bea wasn't in the mood. "Just take me up in the air."

"I've upset you." He cupped her face in his hand, stroking the hair back from her brow with his index finger, all tender solicitude. "My poor little earthbound angel. Still trying to get back to the heavens."

Ordinarily, she might have laughed at him, but his words cut a little too close to home. She'd so hoped that Addie would provide a bridge back to Ashford—but she'd been expelled from the Garden as firmly as Bea. It was so bloody unfair. All she'd done was do what Marcus had done, trying to get some of her own back, but she had broken the cardinal rule. She had been caught. That, not her adultery, was the unforgivable sin.

Bea batted at his hand. "Where do you get these ridiculous lines? From the talkies? You need a better script, darling. I liked you better when you were taking your lines from—oh, whoever that poet was."

"You really are appallingly ignorant," he said.

In his smoky voice, even the insult sounded like a caress. That didn't take the sting out of it, though. It was as though Fate was conspiring to assault her with her ignorance from all corners. She knew nothing about coffee farming, nothing about nursing; she couldn't quote poets or bandy philosophers.

Last night had been dreadful. It had been bad enough standing by while Addie sewed up Njombo, but dinner had been an unmitigated nightmare, Frederick picking at her, Addie speaking coolly of her job and her flat and her friends, friends who weren't Bea's friends, people who weren't in *Debrett's*, people who did things, who made things. The new order.

When had it all changed? Not so very long ago, Addie used to look to her for advice and guidance, and not just Addie. An entire season of debutantes had taken their cue from Bea, copying her dresses, aping her hairstyles. If she wore a diamond clip, a hundred diamond clips would spring up across London. It had been a glorious game. Sometimes, she would commit absurdities just for the fun of watching others copy them.

It had all gone and she didn't know how to get it back.

She felt a sudden surge of impotent rage against her mother, who had tossed her out into the world all unready. Nothing she had been taught had any bearing on this strange new world in which they lived. What did it matter that she could arrange a dinner for eighty in perfect accordance with the rules of precedence or snub an upstart baronet's wife without even bothering to open her mouth? When it came down to it, her mother's tutelage had prepared her for nothing, for nothing at all. She ought to have trained as a nurse, like Addie; read her way through the Ashford library, like Addie; gone to lectures and concerts, like Addie.

Oh, bother Addie. And bother Val, too.

"I hadn't thought it was for my mind that you wanted me," she said. "If you want a lady don, try the droopy-stocking brigade at Oxbridge. I'm sure you'll all have a heavenly time quoting at one another."

Val yawned, unconcerned. He had the thickest hide of anyone she knew. It would take nothing short of a charging rhino to pierce that armor of ego. "It was Donne, my little savage. John Donne, undone. 'License my roving hands and let them go. . . .'" He swung his legs over to the side, sliding to the ground. "Only you aren't in the mood to license anything today, are you?"

"It's my license that's at issue," she said crossly. "You're meant to be teaching me to fly."

He leaned both arms against the side of the plane. "And don't I do that?" The sun glinted blue off his black hair.

"Not that way. I'll never get my A license if I don't get this crate up in the air."

"Don't insult the Moth." Val stroked the silver siding with more care than he ever exercised with her. "She'll never fly you into the sun if you do."

"You care more about that plane than you do any person."

"But of course. People can be so tedious, with their claims, their duties, their obligations, their endless whining. All the Moth asks is a regular supply of petrol." Val leaned an elbow against the cockpit and raised a brow. "Are you going to play, pet, or shall I put you into your nice little motorcar and send you back to your family?"

"No one *sends* me anywhere." She saw the amusement in his eyes and knew he'd done it on purpose, to get a rise out of her. And she'd fallen right into it. "Damn you."

"Dearest, dearest . . . You're wasting your breath. I was damned long before I met you." With exaggerated gallantry, he lifted her hand to his lips. "Not that you wouldn't be worth a brief stint in the infernal regions, but I'm afraid you'll have to get in line."

Enough was enough. Besides, much as she hated to admit it, time was getting short. She'd meant to be back by lunchtime, before Addie and Frederick realized she was gone. It was already getting on towards ten. With an hour in the air, she'd be cutting it close.

"Take me flying," she commanded. "Or I'll go home."

"All right," he said. She should have known he was always his most dangerous when he was his most accommodating. He turned her hand over in his. She shivered as his lips grazed the inside of her wrist. "But first . . ."

She shouldn't. Ten o'clock already, and when one gave in to Val he always took it as license to press even harder the next time. . . .

He expertly turned back her sleeve, his lips moving along the inside of her arm, and Bea's brain turned to jelly.

"Unless, of course, you can't."

He looked at her disingenuously, daring her to say it, daring her to say she had to go, to admit that she was less free, shackled to a husband who didn't want her and children who baffled her. She knew if she said it, he'd pat her on the shoulder and let her go. She'd fume all the way home, squirming with sexual frustration and rage and wanting him all the more because of it.

"It's your choice," he said.

Only it wasn't, really, was it? She'd forfeited her choices years ago, when she'd got pregnant with Marjorie.

"Yes," she said defiantly, "it is."

And she dragged his mouth to hers, closing her eyes against the sky and the struts and the birds watching from the trees, kissing him as though she could suck out the secret of his marvelous unconcern and make it hers. She heard his breath quicken, felt his pulse beat faster, and felt a surge of triumph. In this, at least, she was master, not he.

There was more than one way to fly.

New York, 1999

"But I've seen the pictures," said Clemmie. "The ones of Granny and Grandpa together in Kenya."

There was the one on the table in the living room, the two of them in their coffee field together, Grandpa Frederick in a solar topee and Granny Addie in a pair of high-waisted trousers, and another that used to live on the bureau, Granny Addie and Grandpa Frederick in the same stone house Clemmie had seen in Bea's album, seated on the porch with Clemmie's mother standing on one side and a sulky-looking Aunt Anna sitting on Grandpa Frederick's lap. Clemmie was sure she'd seen others, too, if only she could remember where.

"Those are all later," said Aunt Anna. "Take a closer look at them, you'll see. She didn't come out until 1926."

Several years after Clemmie's mother was born. "Did she send you to Kenya with Grandpa Frederick?"

Clemmie had heard of children left in England while their parents went off to the colonies, but never the other way around. On the other hand, people were strange. Perhaps they'd been going through a bad patch; perhaps Granny Addie needed to stay behind for business reasons. It could have been anything.

Clemmie's mother cleared her throat and said, with difficulty, "I was born in Mombasa. Your aunt was born in Nairobi." She cast a narrow-eyed look at Aunt Anna. "What your aunt is trying to get me to tell you is that biologically, your Granny Addie wasn't my mother. Not that I can see why that should matter at this point, after so many—"

"Biologically?" Clemmie broke into her mother's tirade. "What?"

"She wasn't our mother," said Aunt Anna.

"She was in every way that counted," said Clemmie's mother stubbornly. "She was far more of a mother to us than—"

"You can't even say her name, can you? She doesn't even exist to you."

"We barely existed to her."

"Whoa," said Clemmie. She felt like Alice through the looking glass, everything upside down and topsy-turvy. "But she and Grandpa Frederick— they met when she was thirteen! She told me the whole story. With the mouse."

"There were intervening events," said her mother primly.

Aunt Anna gave her sister a look. "They were married in 1929. There's probably a marriage certificate floating around somewhere if you don't believe me. You do the math."

By 1929, Mother would have been almost eight years old, Aunt Anna five. But there, in front of her, was an album dated 1926, featuring everyone but Granny Addie.

From a very long way away, she could see a manila folder, splayed open on the floor of Jon's study, and the grainy photocopy of the cover of an old magazine. Another picture without Granny Addie. She could see the caption in front of her, ink smeared but still legible: LADY BEATRICE DESBOROUGH AND THE HONOURABLE FREDERICK DESBOROUGH.

Not Gillecote. Not Rivesdale. Desborough.

Clemmie pointed at the album. She was amazed at how steady her hand was. "It's Bea, isn't it? She's the intervening event."

It was easier to think of it that way. An intervening event was so cold and anodyne. Not a person, an intervening event.

Her mother nodded.

"She's——" Clemmie couldn't bring herself to say "my grandmother." The words choked at the back of her throat. Her grandmother had been Granny Addie. Only she wasn't. The words burst out of her. "Why didn't you tell me?"

Her mother's throat worked. "It didn't seem important."

"Not important?" Clemmie had spent her whole life trying to remake herself in the image of a grandmother who wasn't her grandmother. She was—Clemmie didn't even want to try to do the genealogical plotting. Her voice wobbled as she asked, "Was Grandpa Frederick really my grandfather? Or was that a lie, too?"

"You have his eyes," said her mother.

"You used to say I had Granny's chin," retorted Clemmie. "I just didn't realize it was the wrong granny. Why didn't you tell me?"

There was silence.

Clemmie's nails bit into her palms. "What happened to her? To my real grandmother?"

It felt like a betrayal to say it, to even think it, here in Granny Addie's room, with the ghost of Granny Addie still among them, in the pictures propped against the wall, the clothes in the boxes. Clemmie had spent so many hours in this room, bouncing on the bed that wasn't here anymore, playing dress up with the clothes that used to hang in the closet, sitting by that horrible metal hospital bed. They'd spent so much time together, she and Granny Addie.

But Granny Addie wasn't Granny Addie, and she had betrayed Clemmie, too, by keeping silent.

"Your sainted Granny Addie got rid of her," said Anna. "She came out to Kenya and everything went to hell."

"That's not fair," said Clemmie's mother sharply. "You can't blame it on Mummy. It wasn't her fault."

"Mummy?" Aunt Anna made choking noises. "God, she had you so brainwashed! You just couldn't wait to get rid of our real mother, could you?"

"You weren't old enough to remember," said Clemmie's mother with dignity. "You don't remember how it was before."

"Yes, I do." There were lines in Aunt Anna's face that Clemmie had never seen before. "I remember our mother—our real mother. I remember her perfume. I remember her laugh."

Clemmie's mother rose to her feet. "Do you remember the fighting? Do you remember how she used to disappear for weeks on end? Do you remember any of that?" She clutched the back of the chair with both hands. "I remember. I remember the way the governesses used to come and go. I remember the nights she didn't come home. You were only a baby—you wouldn't remember. She never wanted us. She never—"

"Maybe she didn't want you," Aunt Anna tossed back.

Clemmie's mother shook her head. "Addie was more a mother to both of us than she ever was."

"Oh, yes," said Anna. "She could afford to be. She got everything she wanted. Once she got rid of our mother."

Tension sizzled between them. For a moment, they looked eerily alike, not in feature, but in expression, in the hostility radiating from each.

"Stop! Stop it, both of you!" Clemmie rounded on her mother. "Were you ever going to tell me?"

"You don't understand how it was. Our own mother . . . left us." Aunt Anna made an indignant noise, but Clemmie's mother didn't let herself be diverted. She looked steadily at Clemmie. "Your grandmother was my mother in every way that counted. She was my mother for seventy years. She's the mother I would have chosen if I'd have the chance to choose."

"She wasn't my grandmother," said Clemmie. Her mother's voice was a buzz in her ears, her arguments going past her, making no sense. "If she wasn't your mother, she couldn't be my grandmother."

"She didn't think of it that way," said Clemmie's mother. "It would have hurt her to hear you talking like that. Your Granny Addie loved you,"

"She wasn't my Granny Addie." Clemmie felt as though she'd been pummeled. Every muscle in her body hurt. She felt slow and stupid. "She was my—what? My cousin two times removed? How could you keep that from me?"

"What good would it have done to tell you?" Her mother's voice was almost pleading. "You had a grandmother, a real grandmother. Why would I take that away from you?"

"You should have told me," Clemmie said stubbornly. She couldn't get past the injustice of it, the not being told, the not knowing. A horrible thought struck her. "Did Dad know?"

"Yes," said her mother.

"Bob? Bill?"

"No."

It ought to have made her feel better that her brothers were equally ignorant, but it didn't. They wouldn't care, either of them. They'd always belonged more to her dad's side. They'd known their other grandmother, Dad's mother, who had died before Clemmie was born. It was Clemmie who had come to New York after the divorce, who had lived day in and day out in Granny Addie's house, constantly being told how much alike they were, how much she was following in her grandmother's footsteps.

Which grandmother?

"Jon knew, too, didn't he?"

Clemmie didn't even have to wait for the answering nod. It was so obvious. All of that about not digging too deep, letting sleeping dogs lie, et cetera, et cetera. She didn't know whom she wanted to punch more, but one thing was clear: She couldn't punch her seventy-eight-year-old mother.

Clemmie ran a shaking hand through her hair, Bea's hair, short, and straight, and cut like a flapper's. "I'll talk to you later." Guilt forced her to add, "If you need me for anything, with the apartment, let me know."

"Where are you going?" her mother asked.

Away. Just away. Away where she could fume in peace. If she stayed—what was the good of staying? They would just go round and round and round and someone would wind up saying something horrible that couldn't be unsaid.

You lied to me. You lied to me. You lied to me.

She wasn't sure if she was saying it to her mother or Granny Addie, but either way, she needed out.

"Out," she said shortly. "Just out."

TWENTY

New York, 1999

"Clemmie! I thought you were the Chinese food."

Jon stood in the doorway, his body blocking the entrance. He didn't look entirely thrilled to see her. Good. Let him be afraid. Let him be very afraid.

She'd meant to go home. But once she started walking, her feet had turned her right instead of left, uptown towards Harlem. All around her, cabs with their lights off carried loads of revelers to their New Year's celebrations. She knew from experience, it was nearly impossible to get a cab on New Year's Eve. But Clemmie didn't mind. She wanted to walk; she needed to walk. She'd left her gloves upstairs at Granny Addie's—at Addie's. There was no way she was going back for them, so she'd tucked her cold hands in her pockets, tucked her head down into her collar, and plowed into the park, picking her way over slick leaves and fallen branches. There had been a dusting of snow earlier, frozen now into a fine crust. She could hear it crunching under her heels as she walked, faster and faster, her breath coming in sharp bursts, misting the air in front of her.

Her mother would have been horrified at the idea of her walking through the park. The park had been no-man's-land when she was little. That was one of the rules: no park after dark, no going above 96th Street, no West

Side. Rules, rules, rules and she'd obeyed them all, Mother's rules, Granny Addie's rules, unquestioning. She'd worked so hard to please them—and for what? Clemmie's inappropriate heels skidded on a thin layer of ice. She caught herself just in time. Let a mugger try to take her on; she'd have his balls for breakfast. Hell, she'd welcome it. She was spoiling for a fight, for something; the blood boiled in her veins. She should have been cold, but she wasn't. She was seething, burning up from within.

No sensible mugger would take her on. She was muttering to herself, rehearsing arguments, practicing recriminations. The things she should have said to her mother! And Granny Addie—Granny Addie who wasn't Granny Addie, who had spent all those years pretending and died before she could explain. Had she meant to tell her? Was that why she'd started with those stories? Maybe if Clemmie had been around more—

Guilt warred with anger, combining into a bilious brew of self-righteousness, doubt, and hurt feelings. Fine. What about all those other years? What about the hours she'd spent after school in Granny Addie's apartment? What about all the Christmases and Thanksgivings? Their special grandmother-granddaughter trip to London together? Why had she never sat her down and said, By the way . . .

The park spat her out near 96th Street, on the West Side. She could have gotten on the 1, gone back to her own place to defrost and fume. Instead, Clemmie turned north. She didn't remember the number of Jon's building, but she remembered the block, or thought she did. She went down two wrong blocks before she found it, her adrenaline rising with every loop. There it was, Jon's name on the buzzer, in block capitals in black ink on a piece of masking tape, unevenly applied over the name of the former tenant. By the time Jon's crackly voice came on the intercom, she didn't even bother to identify herself; she just barged right on through, stomping her way up the stairs, blood pumping, cheeks numb, hair standing straight up with static.

"Why didn't you tell me?" Clemmie's voice came out in little pants. It had been too long since she'd been to the gym.

Surprise, guilt, and confusion chased across Jon's face. He glanced back over his shoulder. "I only just . . ."

"Bullshit." Anger felt good. Clemmie stepped forward, forcing Jon to move back, opening the door wider. "All that crap about letting sleeping dogs lie. You knew all along. Did you enjoy it? Being able to put one over on me?"

A curious expression passed across Jon's face. "Your grandmother," he said slowly. "That's what this is about."

"*Not* my grandmother," Clemmie corrected him. "How long did you know?'

Jon pressed his eyes shut. "Not that long," he said. "Only just a few years. Listen, Clemmie—"

"Just a few years," Clemmie repeated flatly.

How many was a few? Jon was a historian; he dealt with decades at a time. Had he known in Rome? She knew, logically, the one didn't have anything to do with the other, but somehow the thought made her even angrier. Sleeping with her, bad; lying to her while he was sleeping with her, unforgivable. Screwed and screwed over.

"How long?" she demanded.

Jon let out a short, frustrated breath. "I did some poking around when I was doing my dissertation research. You do the math. Look, Clemmie—" He blocked the doorway with his body, speaking quickly, "What difference does it make? Your grandmother was your grandmother. She loved you. I've always thought Bea sounded like a bitch."

The very fact that he'd known Bea existed, that he'd had time to develop theories about her, made Clemmie see red.

"Great," said Clemmie bitingly. "If she's a strong woman, she must be a bitch."

"I never said that! I wouldn't say Addie was a bitch—would you call her weak?"

She didn't know what to call her at all.

Jon was off on his own line of thought. "It's the weak who have to resort to bitchiness, not the strong, like a cornered animal. It's a defense mechanism."

Lovely. Just what she needed. "Thanks for the fortune-cookie philosophy. Can I have some chow mein with that?"

Jon held up both hands, propping open the door with his back. "You want someone to take this out on? Fine. Knock yourself out. But what good does it do? It was what it was. At least you had someone to call grandmother. Be grateful."

"Easy for you to say," Clemmie shot back.

"Because it's not my family?" Jon smiled crookedly. "Thanks. I'd wondered when that was going to come up."

He had some nerve. "Because you're not the one who's been lied to for the past—forever!"

Clemmie's voice cracked, and she realized she was dangerously close to tears.

She struggled for composure. Anger was okay; crying wasn't. She couldn't lose it all over Jon, not now. It had just been such an awful, awful day: the forced piety of the church service, the empty space where Granny's bed used to be, lipstick on the teeth of the party guests. . . It all came crashing together. And now here she was, on Jon's doorstep—not even in the f-ing foyer, for Christ's sake—throwing a temper tantrum like a spoiled five-year-old who hadn't gotten her cupcake.

She tried to speak but couldn't find the words. If she said anything, she was going to burst into tears, and that was the very last thing she wanted. She'd thought having it out with someone would make her feel better. Instead, she wanted to crawl into a hole and bawl.

Jon's expression softened. "I'm sorry, Clemmie. I mean it. I should have told you. Look, why don't you go home. Sleep on it."

Clemmie wordlessly shook her head, her lips pressed tightly together.

"I'll go down with you and put you in a cab." Jon put a hand on her arm, steering her back around. His voice was low and soothing. "We'll talk tomorrow. I promise, I'll tell you everything I can—everything I know," he amended. "No more secrets."

Clemmie looked up at him, green-brown eyes behind gold-rimmed glasses; the small scar by the side of his mouth from the time he'd taken her roller-skating in Wollman Rink in eighth grade and tripped over a daredevil six-year-old; the bits of gray just beginning to show at his temples.

The crazy adrenaline rush that had driven her through the park dropped away, leaving her tired and cold and shaky. She felt like a melted snowman, all the fight drained out of her. She felt hollow and very, very tired. It was good to be able to lean on Jon, good to have someone to hold on to. She wondered, abstractedly, if the cab ride back to her place might be more than just a cab ride, if they would finish what they'd started last week, blotting out everything that had happened since, the funeral, the relevations, the lies. They could burn the slate clean and start over, skin to skin, in her ridiculous little shoe box of an apartment.

"Okay," she croaked.

Jon squeezed her arm. "Let's get you—"

There was a noise in the foyer. The old floorboards creaked as a female voice said, "Hey."

Clemmie felt a strange wave of vertigo. The hallway seemed to shimmer in front of her, or maybe that was just her eyes, still stinging from the cold. The cold, that was all. She looked up at Jon, trying to make sense of this latest development and failing utterly.

Jon's Adam's apple bobbed up and down. In a low, urgent voice, he said, "I meant to tell you—"

"Hi!" There was a woman standing on the other side of the door. Her hair was still damp from the shower, twisted half up with bits sticking out on top. She wore a pair of yoga pants, a UNC tank top, and she looked very much at home.

The last time Clemmie had seen her, she'd been wearing a big white dress, a veil, and a whole lot more makeup.

"Jon! Why didn't you tell me we had company?" Caitlin padded forward on bare feet. "Hi. Have I met you?"

Kenya, 1927

"Quite a spectacle, isn't it?" Frederick joined Addie at the base of the terrace.

Above them, on the verandah, Addie could hear the clink of ice against a shaker and the high-pitched clatter of sophisticated conversation. The real spectacle, though, lay ahead, where the Kikuyu were throwing a celebration in honor of the marriage of Njombo. Having patched him up all those months before, Addie felt somewhat of a proprietary interest in the proceedings.

She'd been told that a *ngomo* was a thing to behold, but she hadn't realized quite what was meant until dark fell and, with the torches flaring, the dancing began. The men she knew as farmhands had transformed into warriors, their bodies oiled and decorated with intricate designs in white chalk and red ochre, feathered spears in their hands, clappers at the ankles and ornaments in their ears. Their headdresses were more elaborate than anything she had ever seen in the nightclubs and ballrooms of London, bursting with beads and feathers.

And then there were the women, oiled, too, decked with beads, bare but for the briefest triangle of grass fore and aft. They swayed unabashedly to the music, hips undulating, breasts bobbing, oiled bodies glinting in the light of the bonfire as the elders sat in their own section, looking on. And all the while the drums beat a primal rhythm as the dancers leaped and swayed, their elongated shadows twisting and swaying, too, all echoed in the movement of the long grass and the branches of the trees, so that all the world seemed swept up in their dance, bending and rolling to the rhythm of the drums, drums, drums.

"Listen to those drums," said Frederick quietly, but Addie could feel the words resonating through and around her, everything somehow more pronounced, more vivid, in the light of the flames. "You can feel them beating all the way through you. Can't you?"

"It's . . . fascinating," said Addie. Such a drab, safe little word. She felt as though she'd been caught out in some sort of voyeuristic indulgence, there was something so sensual, so erotic about the dance. Frederick was right. The music got right into one, throbbing like a second heart, promising all sorts of illicit pleasures. She hadn't been drinking, but she felt as though she had, her cheeks flushed, her hands unsteady.

"Let's go for a walk," said Frederick. She was amazed by the urgency in his voice. Addie turned to look at him, the flames playing across his face.

"But," she said weakly, "the party . . ."

Frederick glanced back over his shoulder, at the verandah where Bea was holding court, playing her admirers off one against the other. Addie was reasonably sure at least one of them was her lover, possibly more. She had missed the cues back in Mayfair, but now she was more sophisticated, she knew the signs.

"They're all well entertained," Frederick said, and held out a hand to her. "Shall we?"

It was a dreadful idea, she knew, a dreadful, dreadful idea. She and

Frederick spent scads of time together—in the coffee shed, in the nursery with the children, walking the fields—but always in daylight and never alone.

It had been six months since she had come to Kenya, six months of working together, talking together, planning together. Addie had been so smug in their friendship. She had congratulated herself on their maturity in being able to put the past behind them, be the friends they had never been in London, equals now, as they had never been before.

She had willfully ignored the signs: the extra hours in the field, just to steal a few more moments together; the accidental brush of a hand over a ledger; looking back over her shoulder as she said good night to find Frederick's eyes on her, his gaze following her as she walked from the room.

It meant nothing, of course. They were friends, weren't they? Friends.

She could tell herself that over and over, as if repetition might blot out the truth: that she had fallen again, and fallen hard, not for a mirage this time, but for the man himself, the man she saw day after day, wrestling with the books, playing with his children. The very thought of it made her heart ache. She didn't want to think of it, not any of it; if she didn't acknowledge it, it wasn't true.

The drums urged her forward, to the shelter of the laughing darkness. "Just—just a short walk," she said. "It's so warm near the bonfire."

It wasn't just the bonfire heating her blood. It was a sort of madness. She itched to move as the dancers moved, to throw herself into the middle of that fiery circle and sway, bobbing in and out of the light of the fire, dancing past the crackling flames.

Frederick's hand closed around hers, drawing her forward, and she followed, along the garden paths, past an acacia that dropped pale blossoms onto the gravel path. Behind them, the message of the drums followed, a steady thrum, like the beating of her heart, faster and faster, the air scented with rich perfumes, and Frederick's arm around her shoulders, drawing her into the darkness, beyond the terrace, past the bonfire, where the trees rustled with the breeze and strange birds calling, urging them on.

They left the group on the verandah far behind, the sound of sophisticated conversation and glass clanking in cocktail glasses. They might have been anywhere, thousands of years before, the first man and the first woman, cushioned in the warm darkness with only the faint echo of the drums to set their pace.

She wasn't sure how it happened, a stumble on the dark path, a pause, but they weren't walking anymore; she was in his arms, his lips on her hair, her cheek, her lips, clinging together with all the urgency of the past six months of thwarted desire, working together, dining together, hiding her feelings behind a polite social smile and a briskness she was far, so very far, from feeling.

"Addie," he whispered into her hair. The crepe de chine of Bea's old dress felt like gauze and gossamer, scarcely a barrier; she could feel the press of his hands straight through the fabric, warm on her back, her waist, his lips against her neck. "Addie . . ."

Above them, in the trees, a branch cracked, a harsh, unlovely sound. Addie wrenched herself away. "What are we doing?"

Frederick caught her around the waist, his voice like velvet in the darkness. "Exactly what we've been wanting to do for months—years." She hated herself for swaying towards him, for leaning into the touch of his hands. She hated him for being right. "Why else did you come out here with me?"

Something about the surety of that statement irked her, especially since it was true. But to admit to it meant—oh, so many betrayals! "For a walk," she said sharply. "Just a walk!"

"Don't lie," said Frederick. She wished she could see his face, but it was shrouded in shadow. "Lie to yourself if you have to, but not to me."

"We can't—I can't— You're married!"

"So what?" Frederick's voice crackled with frustration. Even in the dark, she could picture his face, chart each iteration of his expression. She knew him so horribly, painfully well. He jerked a thumb in the direction of the house. "So are half the people back there."

"Is that it?" Pain wrenched through her, horrible, searing, wrenching pain. Bad enough to love and love unrequitedly, but worse, so very much worse, to be a tool for revenge. Her voice came out too loud and too shrill. "Just because we're in Kenya, it makes it all cricket? You may be able to take your marriage vows that lightly, but I can't. I won't be—I won't be your revenge against Bea. I won't be your plaything."

"You little fool," said Frederick softly. They shouldn't have, but the words sounded like a caress. He advanced towards her, shoes crunching on the gravel. "Do you really think that's what this is? Do you really think I hold you so cheap?"

"I don't know what to think." That much, at least, was true. "We should go back—we shouldn't be out here. No good can come—"

"Addie." Frederick's voice cut her off. The words tore out of him, harsh and raw. "Addie . . . in England . . . five years ago . . . I made a damnable mistake."

Addie stood frozen, wanting to hear, not wanting to hear. What good could it do?

Don't . . . Her lips formed the word, but no sound came out.

Moonlight shone off Frederick's tortured face. "I was ten times a fool, and don't you think I know it? Don't you think I've paid the price for it, over and over and over again?" He laughed, low and humorless. "Do you know what it's been to have you here, in front of me, and know I can't touch you?"

Addie stared at him, mouth ajar.

"Trust me," said Frederick viciously. "No one has been served a more fitting punishment for a moment's extreme stupidity."

"More than a moment," Addie heard herself saying. Old hurts rushed to the fore. "If you really felt that way, if you really wanted me then—"

"Don't you understand?" His hands were on her shoulders, his voice compelling. "It was all wrong back then, everything. The whole world was topsy-turvy. I didn't want to drag you down with me. I was just a step away from sticking a pistol in my mouth and pulling the trigger, but then there was Marjorie and all this"—his gesture encompassed the sleeping fields—"and I woke up from my bout of insanity and wondered what in the hell I'd done. I thought I could make the best of it, but then you came back. And now—"

"There is no now!" Addie's voice came out more harshly than she'd intended. She felt as though her emotions were scraped raw, all the might-have-beens dancing in front of her—if she'd never introduced him to Bea, but she had, and he had acted on it, and how could she believe him? How could she believe any of it? "There can't be."

"Dammit, Addie." He sounded so indignant she might have laughed if she weren't so close to tears. "I'm trying to tell you I love you."

"How can I believe you?" Her voice was thick with tears. She tried to pull away, but his hands on her arms held her tight.

"I love you. I love you," he repeated, like an incantation. "I love the way you slurp your tea—"

Addie's head shot up. "I don't slurp my tea!"

"Yes, you do," said Frederick tenderly. "You slurp your tea and you twist your hair when you're nervous and you get starchy when you're angry. I love you for all of it. I love you for being you. I loved you then, when I barely knew you—even if I was too much of a fool to own it—and that emotion is the mere shadow of a shadow to what I feel for you now. We're meant for each other, you and I, whether you admit it or not."

This was a whole new kind of hell, a thousand times worse than hiding her love behind the guise of friendship. This—to bring it out into the open like this—

"This is cruel," she said angrily. "I should never have—"

"Are you telling me you don't feel the same way?"

Addie's hands balled into fists, her nails biting into her palms.

She hated that she couldn't answer, that her principles, all the years of pounding propriety into her, bone by bone, all those years of Aunt Vera's precepts faded before this one, primal need. She wanted him so very badly. It was true, there had been times, these past few months, when Bea was off jaunting, that Addie had pretended it was all hers, that this was their coffee farm, that Marjorie and Anna were their children, that they would have the right to sit on the porch with the owls hooting, her head against his shoulder and his lips in her hair.

"You see?" said Frederick, his voice low and triumphant.

"But it's *wrong!*" It was all she had left to cling to, that last vestige of principle.

Frederick cupped her face in his hands. "Right, wrong . . . What does it matter out here?" There was something so terribly seductive about that notion, thousands of miles away from other people's strictures, here, in the wilderness, with the drums pounding around them. "Tell me this isn't right."

For a moment, she clung to him, his lips on hers, putting all her tortured feelings into that kiss, all the wishes and wants and might-have-beens. She could feel his body molded against hers, limb by limb, and knew that this was what original sin must have felt like; there was no turning back the clock. No matter what, no matter where she went, she would always remember this, the feeling of this moment. She would never be able to look at him without knowing what his body felt like against hers, his hands in her hair, dizzying and urgent.

"I'm going home." Addie pulled away, disheveled and panting, her lips leaving his with an audible popping sound. "I'm going home to England."

Home. What a lie! England wasn't home, not Ashford, not her old rented flat. Home was here, with Frederick. But it wasn't her home. It had never been her home. She had only pretended it awhile, stolen crumbs from someone else's life.

"I'm leaving," she repeated, "as soon as I can get passage."

Frederick stared at her, his chest going in and out, laboring for breath. "You mean you're running away."

The words stung, stung horribly. And who was he to judge? If he hadn't slept with Bea all those years before . . .

"I can't do this—not to Bea, not to David." She'd hardly thought about David, not since being here, but now she held him up like a shield. "I can't go on pretending to be your friend, pretending nothing's changed, not after this. I'm going home."

Blindly Addie turned on her heel. The delicate fabric of Bea's old frock snagged on an acacia bush, releasing a shower of pale petals.

"Don't tell me you mean to marry him?" Frederick's voice was harsh, incredulous.

"Why not? After all"—the words came out unbidden—"you married Bea."

Addie yanked at her skirt, not caring when she heard the fabric rip, and fled back to the house, slippers slapping against the gravel.

TWENTY-ONE

Kenya, 1927

"Your cousin is so deliciously prim," commented Val.

She didn't look prim now. Bea watched Addie coming around the side of the house. Her face was flushed, her hair mussed. Clandestine assignations behind the acacia bushes? How terribly out of character.

There was a man striding around the side of the house, hurrying after Addie. Bea couldn't see who it was at first; the flickering firelight played strange tricks. He said something, but Addie shook her head and kept going, leaving him standing alone, near the cookhouse. He turned and Bea recognized him, not by his features, but by his stance, the way he held his shoulders, the angle of his chin.

She should know. It was her husband.

"So charmingly untouched," mused Val, trailing his fingers along the bare curve of Bea's spine. "Like a flower quivering on the cusp of awakening."

Bea turned away, leaning her back against the balustrade. "Don't, Val," she said shortly. "She's not the type."

She took a long drag on her jade cigarette holder, feeling the familiar grate of the smoke against the back of her throat, drawing strength from the nicotine.

Val leaned forward, holding out his cigarette in two fingers. "Jealous?"

Bea mustered a convincing laugh. "Darling, you *are* joking, aren't you?" She was jealous, but not in the way Val meant. She doubted he could understand it; she wasn't sure she understood it herself. "Raoul, darling, there you are! And with bubbly! What an angel you are."

"I shine only in the reflected light of your divinity," he said. Unlike Val, he didn't say it superciliously.

"The reflected light of your divinity?" Val raised a brow. "Does that make you the moon or simply a rather large hurricane lamp?"

"Better than quivering petals on the cusp of awakening," retorted Bea, more sharply than she ought.

"Meow," murmured Val. "Is someone feeling overblown?"

"Hardly." Never show weakness, that was the rule with Val. "Merely bored by present company. Do come entertain me, Raoul. I need you."

"Of course." He took her arm and led her away, sending a glower in Val's direction for good measure. Val merely smiled in return. Of course he would. Nothing ever flustered Val. He was impervious to all the normal human emotions. Whereas she . . .

In just two weeks it would be her birthday. She was almost twenty-eight. Twenty-eight! Just a whisper away from thirty and her life wasn't anything like what it had been meant to be.

Everyone had always told her that she was born for greatness. They had told her that her lineage and her beauty were her destiny, and so it had seemed, back in the heady days of her first Season, with all the sons of her parents' friends tripping over their own feet to dance with her. She didn't need to stoop to conquer; she conquered simply by virtue of being what she was. At twenty, she had been a prize; by twenty-two, she was ruined. And here she was, at almost twenty-eight, hunted by everyone except her husband.

She hadn't expected Frederick to remain faithful. But if he had to stray, why did it have to be with Addie?

"I wish you meant it," muttered Raoul.

"Meant what, darling?" asked Bea absently. Addie was climbing the stairs to the terrace, keeping her eyes carefully on the treads. She wore Bea's old frock, a green crepe de chine, two Seasons out of date.

"That you needed me." Raoul grasped her hands, forcing her to face him. "That you needed me as I need you."

"*Darling*," said Bea. Such a wonderful, multipurpose word, designed to mean anything one needed it to mean while promising nothing at all.

Raoul's eyes glinted in the reflected light of the fires. "Come away with me. Come away with me from all this. They"—his sweeping gesture encompassed the terrace, the dancers, Frederick—"they do not deserve you." His fingers bit into her arm. "You know it is true. You cannot deny it."

No, she couldn't. Even before tonight, she'd seen it happening, week by week, seen it and pretended she didn't.

"Come away with me to Carmagnac," Raoul urged. Raoul. It was so easy to forget he was there, like a puppy at one's feet, constantly licking one's toes. "You shall be feted as a queen—as an empress!"

She was tempted, so very tempted. Comtesse de Fontaine. It had an attractive ring to it. It was also about as likely to happen as a jaunt around the moon. Raoul's Catholic family would hardly be thrilled to receive an Anglican, and a twice-divorced one at that.

"Isn't there a cousin you're meant to be marrying?"

"Adele." Raoul shrugged her off as immaterial. "Her affections are no more engaged than mine. She will not feel the loss."

"Even so, I can't imagine your family will be all too pleased if you break it off."

"They will adore you as I do," said Raoul with all the supreme confidence of twenty-three. "There can be no question."

There could be a great deal of question, indeed, but Bea was too tired to point that out to him. She needed his confidence, his youth; they were a sop to her wounded ego.

All she had was her beauty, but even that was bound to desert her, burned away by the relentless Kenyan sun, stretched out of her by successive pregnancies. She'd kept her figure so far, but there were lines and sags where there hadn't been before and freckles that had to be relentlessly kept at bay with patent lotions.

What happened when her beauty went? What then?

"You doubt me," said Raoul. "Do you really believe that I would allow anyone to stand in the way of our eternal happiness?"

God, he was young. She wanted, so very badly, to believe him, but experience—and Val—had a way of implying otherwise.

She could just see it now, another embarrassing divorce, another spate of *Tatler* headlines. They'd marry, in some dreary civil ceremony, only to have his parents pronounce it no true marriage at all. Out the cousin would come from the wings, and there Bea would be again, fallen lower than before.

"Not allow, precisely," said Bea, "but families have a way of intruding just the same." Val had moved to intercept Addie, purely to annoy her, she was sure.

Now if it had been Val asking her to run away with him . . .

"Let me convince you." Raoul lowered his voice, leaning closer. "I have a plan—"

"Later." Bea squeezed his hand and let him go. "I must rescue my cousin. She's no match for Val."

"Vaughn is no match for you," said Raoul darkly, but he followed her all the same, scooping up her scarf for her, trotting along with it like a page boy following behind his mistress. A pity that such slavish devotion seldom lasted.

Addie didn't seem as delighted to see her as one might wish. Bea's sharp eyes noticed the instinctive move back, the quick tucking of a strand of hair behind one ear. Addie always did that when she was nervous.

Bea swooped down on her. "Darling! Are you enjoying yourself?"

"Yes. Very much so." Her smile was too bright and rather crooked around the edges. "It makes a grand send-off."

"A send-off?" Bea looked keenly at her cousin, but Addie's head was down.

"Yes." Addie fiddled with the clasp of her bracelet, another loan from Bea. "I've stayed too long already. Six months! I hadn't realized how long it had been."

"You can't possibly leave until you go on safari," said Val, looking so innocent that Bea knew he had to be plotting something. "Don't you agree?"

Addie shook her ahead. "I'm afraid there won't be time. I've stayed away from England too long as it is."

"You hadn't said anything about leaving before," said Bea as neutrally as she could, her eyes scanning the terrace for her husband. Something had happened, something between them; she ought to have seen it brewing, months and months of it, but she had been so busy with Val, Val and Raoul . . .

"Don't you want a soft pelt for your bed?" said Val. "You could recline on the skin, like Elinor Glyn. There's nothing like the feel of a tiger rug beneath your skin—isn't that right, Bea?"

"If anyone is to acquire you a skin," Raoul said to Bea, "I shall. That one couldn't shoot a cat in a barrel."

"Why would I want to go shooting cats in barrels?" Val stretched, lithe as a panther. "There's no sport in that. It's like seducing bored wives."

Val had a talent for making her feel cheap. But wasn't she? Twice discarded, first by one husband, now by another. "I'd never think to hear you advocating anything requiring effort," retorted Bea.

Val smiled lazily. "For myself? No. But it amuses me to observe it in others. I shall derive a great deal of pleasure from it on our safari."

"There won't *be* a safari," said Addie stubbornly. "Not on my account. I'm quite happy to leave the animals alone as long as they leave me."

Raoul looked at her in confusion. "You have fellow feeling for the leopardess?"

"No," said Addie frankly. "But I have a hearty distaste for the prospect of being mauled." She looked to Bea for confirmation. "Wouldn't you agree?"

"Nonsense!" Bea didn't meet Val's eyes—or Addie's. The vague outlines of a plan began to form in her mind, less a plan and more a series of prospects. One made one's own fate, wasn't that what Addie always said? Bea was sick of being buffeted. "You can't possibly leave Africa without going on safari, darling! What would people say? No. Val is right. We must arrange . . . something."

"In that case," said Raoul belligerently, "I also shall go on safari."

Bea looked at him limpidly, but her mind was churning, weighing and discarding possibilities. "You didn't think I'd leave you behind?" she cooed.

"Splendid," said Val coolly. "I'll speak to Budgie. He doesn't have anything booked next month."

Addie stepped between them. "You really needn't—"

"Yes," said Bea firmly, "we do. We'll all go. You and I and Val and Raoul and Budgie—and Frederick."

The name crackled like a dead leaf on her tongue, dead and desiccated. He'd had done with her—and she with him. That much was clear.

Addie looked anxiously over her shoulder, scrambling for excuses. "But what about the girls? Oughtn't someone to stay with them?"

Bea smiled without humor. "That's what we have a nanny for."

Addie grasped her final straw. "Aren't safaris terribly dangerous?"

Bea raised her glass, watching reflected flames dance along the edge. "Darling, that's the point."

New York, 2000

Clemmie went back to the office on Monday.

Nothing had changed in the two weeks she'd been away, but it all felt strangely out of proportion, the beige walls narrower, the moss-green carpets darker, the long, brown desks in the hallway, at which the secretaries sat, higher than usual, like a familiar object seen in a fun-house mirror. Clemmie's metal in-box, positioned precariously in front of her secretary's workstation, was so full that it had tipped over backward.

Clemmie had walked these halls month after month, year after year, but she felt like she was seeing them through the eyes of a stranger, everything twisted and unfamiliar.

Helen, her secretary, put a hand over the mouthpiece of the phone. "Welcome back! Happy New Year!"

"Happy New Year," echoed Clemmie, even though it felt anything but.

Forty-odd hours later, she still felt dazed, uncomfortable in her own skin. She kept expecting to see someone else in every reflective surface she passed, someone who looked different. She didn't know whether to be confused or relieved when it was always still just her, the same pale eyebrows, the same flapper-cut hair, the same chicken pox scar just to the left of her lips.

She'd spent the weekend huddled up in her apartment, in her oldest pair of pajamas, watching *Twilight Zone* reruns on her tiny television, if "watching" was really the word. It was more that she had stared sightlessly at the screen as the pictures went by, sitting in a sort of waking doze, jarred awake from time to time by the shrill ring of the phone.

Jon had called. And her mother. And Jon again, saying, *Hey, Clemmie, I know you're there. Pick up.* She hadn't. She couldn't stop replaying that awful moment when Caitlin had stepped out behind him. No more secrets? So much for that. No wonder he had been so eager to hustle her out of the apartment.

She'd wanted to throw up. She'd wanted to take a machete to him. Instead, she'd murmured something inane, something about just being on her way, and blundered out, out into the almost-January night, her head aching and her stomach churning.

Bastard.

"Wait, there's more mail for you," said Helen, and dug under her desk for a pile wrapped in a rubber band.

"Thanks," said Clemmie, flipping through it as she wandered toward her office. It didn't look like anything earth-shattering. There was the internal firm newsletter, with garishly colored photos from the staff Christmas party, a solicitation letter from the New York State Bar Association begging her to take advantage of their special New Year's dues offer, and a copy of the *ABA Journal*.

The one thing she was waiting for, the memo announcing the election of new partners, wasn't there yet.

Clemmie shouldered open the door of her office, flipping through one more time, just to make sure. Nope, no memo. She was pretty sure the committee had met already. Among the oddsmakers she knew she was counted a good bet. And why wouldn't she be? She'd spent most of the last seven years in here. As a third year, she'd graduated from a shared office to this one, her own little cubby, with open shelves crammed with black binders and a narrow closet with room for just her coat and a spare suit. She'd spent Christmas in here, Valentine's Day, New Year's Eve. She'd worked through Labor Day weekends when everyone else was out at a pool, and Fourth of July, with the fireworks exploding over the Hudson River in the distance.

She might not know who her grandmother was, but Clemmie knew this: She'd worked her ass off for this firm.

She dumped her mail and pulled out her desk chair, the dark fabric splotched with old coffee stains. Her desk seemed strangely empty without its usual litter of half-empty coffee cups. She'd have to get started on that. There was nothing like crappy coffee to start the day off right.

The phone rang before she could make her escape to the pantry. Not Paul already. The only time he came in this early was when he'd had a fight with his wife. Not fun for anyone.

She checked the display on the phone. It was an external number. Jon? She didn't think he had her office number, but it wouldn't be hard to find.

"Clementine Evans," she said crisply.

It wasn't Jon. The voice on the other end was very, very cautious and very, very British. "This is Tony Lawton. Er, Rivesdale."

Okay, her secretary was really going to have to start doing a better job of filtering her calls. Sorting through papers with the phone tucked under her ear, Clemmie said, "I'm sorry, I'm afraid—"

The hesitant voice cut in while managing to sound like he wasn't. "You did me the honor of staying with us a few weeks back?"

Rivesdale. Crested stationery. A man with cocker spaniel eyes and an endearing stutter.

"Oh, right! Hi." Clemmie dropped her sheaf of papers on the desk, setting her feet down flat on the floor in her surprise. "You were the one who was so kind to me."

"Not at all," said the warm voice on the other end. "Not at all. I only hope the situation resolved itself."

If one could call death a resolution. In this case, it wasn't, but she couldn't say that to the marquess. Rivesdale. Tony. Whatever. "Thanks to you, I made it onto a flight back," said Clemmie brightly. "I can't thank you enough." Damn. There were already new e-mails popping up on her computer screen, some of them flagged in red. "It's very sweet of you to check in. . . ."

"Well, that is to say . . ." The hemming and hawing went on for some little while. "I had rather an ulterior motive."

"That sounds sinister." Helen had popped her head around the door, trying to get Clemmie's attention.

"I should hope you don't think so. That is, during a renovation, I came across some items that I thought might be of interest to you—about your cousin. Beatrice Gillecote. You did say she was—?"

"A relative." He had no idea. Clemmie choked down a slightly hysterical laugh. He had no idea because she had no idea. She had no idea who this woman was, this Bea. Cousin, grandmother, bolter. "You might say that."

"Well, if you might be interested, I happen to be in the States. On business. I brought the file with me—on the off chance, you see."

"That was very kind of you." Her voice came out rough and hoarse. She took a deep breath, striving for something more like her normal tone. Whatever this file was, she wasn't sure she wanted to see it. She wasn't sure she wanted to know more. Easier just to hide herself behind the familiarity of her file folders and stained coffee cups and pretend none of it had ever happened. "If you want to leave it . . ."

"I'd thought perhaps we might look at it together. Over dinner, perhaps?"

"Um . . ." From outside the door her secretary was making frantic hand-waving motions. Line two began blinking madly.

"Or a coffee," the marquess said hastily. "I'm in town until Thursday week."

"Yeah, sure, that would be nice." Helen was going through contortions and the phone was lighting up like the Fourth of July. "I'm sorry, but I really have to—"

"Tomorrow night, perhaps?"

"Sounds great." Nothing sounded great right now, but maybe if she said it often enough it would start to be true. And she'd liked the marquess— Tony. Whatever. "Just e-mail me the details—cevans@cpm. I'm so sorry, but I really have to go. Work. You know. Bye!"

It was only as Clemmie jabbed the button to activate the other line that it occurred to her to wonder whether the marquess had been asking her out.

Not likely.

On the other hand, she wasn't the best at picking up these cues. It had taken her half the evening to realize that her first dinner with Dan was a date. Maybe because she hadn't particularly wanted that dinner with Dan to be a date? As for the marquess—Clemmie pushed those thoughts aside. There was work to be dealt with. And Paul.

The number on line two was an internal number, Paul's secretary, Joan. "Hi, Joan, happy New Year."

"Hi, Clemmie." Joan's voice sounded like someone talking through a handkerchief on a pay phone, low and gravely. She said it was something to do with her tonsils. Clemmie thought it had more to do with her pack a day. "Welcome back."

"Thanks." Amenities concluded, she tipped her chair back and said, "What's up?"

"Paul wants to see you. Can you come now?" The question was pure formality; Joan knew as well as Clemmie that there was no saying no.

Clemmie rolled her eyes at her corkboard. "I'll be right there."

It was classic Paul. Rather than simply call his associates with assignments or, heaven forbid, e-mail them, he liked to summon them into his office. Because, really, walking up and down that flight of stairs was the best use of her time. Once, it had been to ask what she thought of the color of his new tie. She'd gone running from a conference call for that. One of these days, someone was going to bludgeon Paul to death with a yellow legal pad.

All the same, there was something rather comforting about his pettiness. The world might have gone mad in every other aspect of her life, but here it was still turning on its normal, sadistic axis.

Clemmie grabbed up a yellow legal pad. This was good. Paul would pile ridiculous quantities of work on her and she could go back to being stressed out about normal things, things she could do something about. That was just what she needed, a few all-nighters in the office with the crumbs from last night's takeout scattered under the desk and a confusion of half-empty white paper cups spilling curdled coffee onto her files.

As an afterthought, she asked, "Should I bring the PharmaNet files?"

"No." Joan's voice sounded strangely subdued. "Just bring yourself."

TWENTY-TWO

Kenya, 1927

Out in the bush, an animal called. Addie had no idea what it was, but it sounded close. And hungry.

Stepping out of her tent, she looked about for the others. There were servants everywhere, a ridiculous number of servants for six people, and Budgie, their safari leader, cleaning his rifle by the fire, but that was all. Thank goodness for that. The atmosphere in the camp had gone from bad to worse, tensions degenerating dangerously close to open hostilities.

Vaughn seemed to take active delight in taunting Raoul de Fontaine, who, in turn, clung close to Bea, who retaliated by flirting with Vaughn. They'd come close to blows the night before. De Fontaine was incensed, Frederick withdrawn, Vaughn insufferable, Addie miserable. Of the lot of them, Bea was the only one in high spirits, fueled, Addie was quite sure, from the little porcelain snuffbox that Vaughn kept constantly in his pocket. Even that, Addie was quite sure, was a front. She'd seen Bea watching Frederick out of the corners of her eyes. Watching Frederick—and Addie.

It was no use trying to speak to Bea about it, though. She'd very effectively avoided all private communication, responding, when cornered, with a breezy *Do try to enjoy yourself, darling*, that did nothing to alleviate any of Addie's concerns.

Shivering, Addie pulled her wrap closer around her. The nights were cold once the sun fell. It fell quickly here. Too quickly. Out in the dark . . .

According to Val Vaughn, all it took was a couple of hours for the animals to entirely devour a body. It boggled Addie's mind that the vestiges of the human form could be so completely eliminated, from something to nothing, in the time it would take them to have tea. She would have thought that Vaughn was exaggerating for effect but for the fact that Budgie, their guide, had backed him up.

One of the bearers whistled, long and low. He turned and called to Budgie, "Sigilisi!" followed by a spate of Swahili too rapid for Addie to follow, for all her lessons. Her smattering of kitchen Swahili was little use here in the wilderness.

"What is it?" she asked, moving to join Budgie on the edge of the fire. She felt safer next to Budgie. He might have had a drink in his hand, but his gun was well within reach, his ammunition in the two large pockets on either side of his vest. Hard and soft, he'd told her. Hard for big game, soft for lions, leopards, and other things that snarled in the night. "What did he say?"

Budgie obligingly made room for her on the packing crate that doubled as a chair. "He said that Simba is hungry tonight." The sun was barely down, but Budgie's breath already smelled strongly of gin. He claimed it was the only way to keep his malaria at bay. "It's a lion. There it is again. Do you hear it?"

"No," said Addie. For her, all of the sounds of the bush melded into one threatening murmur, the cries of the animals, the rustle of the leaves in the wind, the slithering of snakes in the long, dry grass. She hated snakes.

"You have to know how to listen for it." Budgie took a swig from the flask he kept at his belt. He offered the flask to Addie, who shook her head in refusal. Neat gin wasn't her tipple of choice. "He's quite close."

Addie instinctively pulled her legs close to the crate. "Is it dangerous?"

Budgie smiled a gap-toothed smile. "It's always dangerous. Otherwise, why would we be here?" He peered at her through rheumy eyes. "Out here, one sees all sorts of strange things. The Nandi people tell of a creature like nothing you can imagine. He's part man, part bird, but nothing like either. He feasts on brains from the cracked skulls of the animals he kills, and those unlucky enough to stumble upon him say that his mouth shines red in the dark like a lamp made of infernal fire."

Sparks crackled on the fire and Addie involuntarily flinched. "That sounds unpleasant," she said. "What do they call it?"

Budgie refreshed himself from his flask. "When they speak of him, they call him the chemosit—although few have lived to tell the tale."

"Not that old yarn." Dry grass crunched underfoot as Frederick joined them, a pair of scuffed boots next to her crate, scuffed boots and khaki breeches and the buckle of an old brown belt.

"That yarn is older than either of us," said Budgie, tipping back on the crate. "There are more things in heaven and earth and all that."

"It's sheer bunk," Frederick said unkindly. "Nothing more than nonsense to frighten children."

"Would you say the same to the Loch Ness monster?" inquired Budgie, shamelessly enjoying himself.

"I'll let you know if I meet him," said Frederick.

"You do that." Budgie heaved himself off the crate, neatly snagging his gun. "I'd best go and chivvy the troops. It's well past time for cocktails."

"Funny," muttered Frederick, just over Addie's head. "I could have sworn he'd started already. Or was that just his cologne?"

Addie looked up at him. "There's no call to be unkind to poor Budgie."

"Poor Budgie, my ass," said Frederick ungraciously. "You do realize that he uses that ridiculous chemosit story to frighten women into his bed. It works, too, half the time."

"Budgie?" Addie couldn't help laughing. Fifty if he was a day, with a paunch and sagging jowls, Budgie was more an amiable alcoholic uncle than a Casanova. "He's no Val Vaughn."

"You'd be surprised." But Frederick's grumpy expression lightened. This was always the hardest, looking away from the tenderness in his eyes. Why couldn't he be the cad she had once believed him to be? Why did he have to be so damnably—Frederick? "I'm sorry. I'm being an ass, aren't I?"

"Yes," she said. "You are."

He held out a hand to her, and, against her better judgment, she took it, letting him help her off the crate. This was what her days had become, a dozen small tests and trials. It was exhausting her, trying to keep away from him.

Frederick held on to her hand for just a moment too long. When he spoke, his words echoed her thoughts. "We can't go on like this."

Addie clasped her hands together, knuckles white. "I know."

On the other side of camp, there was the familiar bump and snick of a record being placed on the gramophone. The familiar strains of Mozart's clarinet concerto in A blasted out into the wilderness, Budgie's favorite record, playing night after night, again and again. There was a scratch on the record, making it skip every few bars, but Budgie played it anyway, again and again, around and around.

Frederick swore savagely. "I wish someone would smash the bloody thing and have done with it already. I'll do it, if no one else will."

"Don't." She wasn't talking about the record.

Frederick lowered his head, breathing in deeply through his nose. "It's damnable, the whole situation. Damnable."

"It will be over soon," said Addie in a low voice. "I leave in two weeks. If we live through this hideous safari."

She tried to make a joke of it, but the words felt flat.

Out in the wilderness, a hyena howled with wild laughter, sending chills down Addie's spine.

Frederick dug his fingers into his temples. "This is ridiculous." He looked down at her, his eyes intent on her face. "You can't go back to England. That farm—it's as much yours as mine. You've learned more about coffee than I'll ever know."

It was true, she'd never been happier than on the farm. She loved the daily challenge of it, the books, the machinery, the songs the women sang as they hacked at the weeds with their pangas. The idea of going back to England— away from Frederick—was impossibly dreary.

But the alternative was worse. The past few weeks had made that more than clear. It had been sheer hell seeing Frederick go into the tent he shared with Bea every night. Somehow, at Ashford, it had been easier to pretend. Frederick kept his own room there, next to Bea's, yes, but separate. Here Addie was constantly reminded, night after night, that he belonged to Bea. She couldn't go on like this.

Neither could he.

She could feel it in the air, like an impending storm, something ready to break.

Addie's throat was tight. "Mbugwa is an excellent headman. I'm sure you'll manage without me."

Frederick caught her by the shoulder. "What about the girls? They'll miss you. They need you." His voice dropped. "I need you."

Addie's nails bit into her palms. "I can't stay. You know that."

"You mean you won't."

"I mean I can't." Addie's voice rose dangerously. She was sick of being strong, sick of pretending, sick of having to watch him with Bea, always on the outside of the tent. "I can't do this, do you hear me? I can't. It's enough."

"You belong here." Frederick's voice crackled with impatience. "With me."

"With you—and Bea?"

She saw him flinch, knew the shot had hit home. "To hell with Bea!"

"You married her," said Addie wearily. "There's no way around it."

"I'd unmarry her in a second." Frederick straightened, his eyes brightening. "If I were to divorce her . . ."

"Not for me," Addie said quickly. How could she do that to Bea—to the girls? She couldn't forget the girls. "I'm not going to be the cause of your divorce."

Frederick's eyes were unnaturally bright. "You don't need to be—there's Val Vaughn; there's Raoul de Fontaine. I could name half a dozen others. Think of it. We could be together."

It was so painfully tempting. Together. Working on the farm together, playing with the girls together, slipping out into the gardens together at night, with the heady scent of exotic flowers thick around him. Not having to sneak or skulk.

But there were other, older loyalties to contend with, the shade of a little girl in a white nightdress teaching her to ride, protecting her from Aunt Vera.

"Would you really do that to her? Drag her through the courts again? It was bad enough the last time."

"You're so concerned with her happiness; what about ours?" Frederick caught her hands, and it was all she could do not to fold herself against him, to lean into him, to agree to anything he wanted. "No one told her to go running off with Val Vaughn or Raoul. She made her own choices."

"Not entirely." Addie hated to say it, but she had to. "You can't say you played no part. Last time, you were the one. If you hadn't—well, you know—she might still be with Marcus."

"Or she might have gone off with someone else," said Frederick quickly. "She was ripe for it. I just happened to be there."

"You were there and you acted on it."

"Is that what this is? I'm to be punished for the rest of my life for the sake of a few months' indiscretion?" Frederick dropped her hands and stepped away, his face dark with frustration. "That's not justice; that's revenge. Are you angry at me for being such a fool before? If you are, it's your right, but don't cast it in moral terms."

"It's not like that!" She hated that they were fighting; she hated all of this. "You can't have it both ways. Either neither of you is at fault or you both are."

"Addie—" He held out a hand to her, but she wrenched away.

"Oh, what does it matter? Either way, there's nothing any of us can do about it. Not without making an even bigger muddle of it." She pressed her eyes together, fighting against the stinging. "We've made our beds."

"You mean I made them," said Frederick, his voice low and savage.

"We all did." She blinked back tears. "You can't exonerate me either. And I've only made it worse by staying on."

"I won't have you blaming yourself. It's rotten luck. Rotten luck and stupidity. *My* stupidity. If I could turn back the clock—"

"But you can't. And how do you know you wouldn't want to turn back the clock five years after me? You might feel just the same way. You might resent me as you do Bea."

"Never." He spoke without a moment's hesitation. Addie looked up at him to find him looking at her, looking at her as though memorizing her every feature. His voice dropped. "This is different. This is— I don't want anyone but you. Ever."

It would have been easier to argue with him if she hadn't felt the same way. It had never been like this with David. She couldn't marry David; she knew that now. Perhaps, someday, there might be someone else. . . . But he wouldn't be Frederick. It was a hideous, hideous thought.

Frederick voiced the thought she hadn't dared to think. "If there were no Bea—"

In Budgie's tent, the record hiccupped and the clarinets squawked. Addie could already hear other voices, closer to camp now, Bea's husky alto, Vaughn's drawl.

"It must be nearly supper time," said Addie in a small, tight voice. She started to hold out a hand and then thought better of it. "Are you coming?"

"Not yet. I'm going to stay here for a bit." A shadow fell across his face like a mask. "I need to think."

Kenya, 1927

Addie woke with a headache.

She drew her elbows close, burrowing down into her cot, but it was no use. The light blazing through the canvas and the clattering noises outside her tent flap indicated it was past time to face a new day. One of the many disagreeable aspects of the safari was that the hunters rose so early in the morning. Addie had never liked either dawn or hunting, but there was very little getting away from it here.

There seemed to be even more clanking and clattering than usual this morning, bearers calling to one another in Swahili, someone singing, the cook banging pots about. The sounds hammered against her skull.

Addie rose reluctantly, wiggling into a pair of trousers and a loose blouse, standard gear on safari, although she still felt awkward and exposed in trousers rather than a skirt. She'd slept poorly last night. Frederick had stayed away for a very long time, and when he did reappear he was silent and brooding, hardly participating at all in the conversation at supper. There'd been dancing after, but Frederick had disappeared. Bea had disappeared, too, soon after, with Val Vaughn, reappearing an hour later, more animated than before. Raoul had been livid. He'd done his best to pick a fight with Vaughn, who responded by telling him to cool down and tossing a gin fizz in his face "to help."

Addie hadn't seen what happened after that. She'd gone to bed, thoroughly disgusted with everyone, including herself.

She hadn't slept, though. Instead, she'd lain awake, debating futilely with herself over the moral merits of staying or going. The man or the tiger? For five blissful minutes she would convince herself that divorce was really quite common these days and Bea would be happier without Frederick anyway. Then she'd think of the girls, of the papers, of the scandal, of Bea, in braids and breeches, teaching her to ride, and she'd be right back where she started.

She'd finally drifted off to sleep in the wee hours, only to be awakened again by the sound of voices, angry voices, just barely hushed below the shouting level. It was Frederick's voice, speaking fast and furious, and, in response, Bea's tinkling laugh, and the sound of glass smashing.

Addie had waited breathlessly, but there'd been nothing more after that. By the time she got up the nerve to creep out of the tent, their light had gone out. Their voices had been just muffled enough that she couldn't hear what they were fighting about. Raoul? Vaughn? Her? She'd curled into a ball, feeling sick to her stomach with resentment and guilt.

The sun stung her eyes as she lifted the flap of her tent. It must have been later than she'd thought. The morning mist had already lifted from the ground and the sun was strong and clear.

"Have you seen Bea?" Raoul was pacing back and forth in front of the fire, his boots painfully shiny in the morning light. "She's not with you?"

"Why would she be?" Addie held up a hand, shading her eyes. She felt even blearier than usual this morning, her head heavy, her mouth like cotton wool. "Isn't she up?"

Budgie looked up from the gun he was cleaning. "Not a sign of her." He raised his eyebrows significantly. "Nor Val."

"He's meant to be reconnoitering today, isn't he?" Trying to think was like slogging through treacle. Addie stifled a yawn. "Perhaps Bea went with him."

Raoul muttered something rather nasty in French.

Budgie looked apologetically at Addie. "We three were meant to go out this morning. A bit late for it now, though."

"I'm sure she just forgot," said Addie as soothingly as she could. The sound of tinkling glass clattered in her memory. Bea in a rage was a volatile thing. Much as Addie loved her, she was beginning to lose patience.

Or was she just trying to justify wanting to steal Bea's husband?

The flap of Frederick and Bea's tent was flung upon and Frederick staggered through, into the light. He hadn't shaved yet; there was dark growth on his chin, and a long, vicious-looking scratch down one cheek. Bea's doing? Addie felt sick to her stomach.

"You look like all kinds of hell," said Budgie cheerfully.

Frederick winced at the sunlight. "That good? Then I must look better than I feel. Good Lord, what was in those drinks last night?" He looked significantly at the silver coffeepot. "Is there coffee?"

Budgie waved at the table. "Help yourself."

Addie made a move towards the table and made herself stop. There was no reason for her to pour Frederick's coffee for him. It was gestures like that that gave her away.

Frederick carried a cup over to her. "You look like you need this."

It was tea, not coffee, made just as she liked it, brick red with a dash of cream, no sugar. She wanted to howl with frustration. She wanted to fling the cup across the clearing and hear it crash against a tree. She wanted to storm and rage and break crockery like Bea.

Addie took the cup from him in hands that were surprisingly steady. "Thank you," she said primly.

"Is that coffee?" Val Vaughn strolled into the clearing, unwinding his scarf from around his neck.

"Where's Bea?" asked Frederick.

"Why would I know?" Vaughn helped himself from the pot on the table. "Is there any food left, or have you all scarfed it?"

"Didn't Bea fly out with you?" asked Addie.

"Not this morning." Vaughn lounged against the table, his leather flying jacket open over a white linen shirt. "I just did a quick loop to see which way the game was wending. Is the old girl still snoring away on her cot?"

"You're lying," said Raoul hotly. "You've run off with her."

Vaughn eyed him askance. "I hate to point this out, de Fontaine, but to have run off with Bea, I would have to have run off. Unless you are all the victims of a rather convincing hallucination, I appear to be rather palpably present. Wouldn't you agree?"

"I wouldn't agree if you told me the grass was green," retorted de Fontaine furiously.

"Wise lad," said Vaughn. "It isn't. It's more of a beigy brown."

De Fontaine made a wordless noise of frustration.

"Bea's gone missing," said Frederick to Vaughn.

Vaughn looked at the scratch on Frederick's face but said nothing.

"Maybe she went for a walk?" suggested Addie. Bea had never been the walking type, but, as Vaughn had pointed out, it would be rather hard for her to have run off when anyone with whom she might have run off was right here in the clearing. Or, more likely— "Are all the cars here?"

"As far as I can tell," said Vaughn. "I had the Hispano-Suiza, and the two Fords are in the clearing."

Budgie set down his rag and cracked the pieces of his gun back into place with one swift, efficient movement. "This isn't Sussex. It isn't safe to wander about alone. Desborough. Come with me?"

"I'll go," said Raoul.

"Not by yourself," said Budgie. "Dammit, man, I don't need to lose two of you. Come with us. If she's gone to bag something by herself, I'll have a piece of her hide."

He stalked off, and the other two followed, leaving Addie sitting on her crate and Vaughn standing by the table, looking contemplatively after them.

"Did you see anything from the aeroplane?" Addie asked tentatively.

Vaughn's head turned sharply. He drained his coffee, waiting until the last drop was gone before he responded carelessly, "I was looking for elephants. They're on a rather different scale." He put down his empty coffee cup. "Shall we? We can't let the Frog have all the fun."

Vaughn always sounded as though he was speaking in subtext, but there was an odd undercurrent to his words that made Addie distinctly uneasy. The idea that he was willing to join the search at all was disturbing enough. She would have expected him to pour another cup of coffee, stretch out his legs, and announce it was no affair of his.

Addie heard herself asking, "Do you think she's all right?"

Vaughn gazed out across the brush, his blue eyes hooded. "That depends."

"On what?"

Vaughn looked down at her. "On how many of her nine lives she's already used up."

There was a shout from up ahead, and a burst of excitable French. Addie abandoned Vaughn, thrashing forward through the brush. All the men seemed to be talking at once, talking and expostulating.

Raoul held something up, waving it in the air, a creeper of some kind, long and brown and twisted.

"What is it? Is that——" Addie skidded to a stop next to Frederick and felt her breath catch in her throat.

That wasn't a creeper Raoul was holding up. It was a scarf. A long chiffon scarf. It had once been a pale green, but now it was stained through, streaked with something that had dyed it a rusty brown.

"Call the bearers," said Budgie sharply. "We need everyone to search. *Now.*"

TWENTY-THREE

New York, 2000

"Come in and close the door."

Paul was waiting for her, kicked back in his massive magenta desk chair behind a glossy mahogany desk that looked like Paul had nabbed it from J. P. Morgan. He didn't stand when she entered; he never did. It was part of the power play.

Behind Paul, on the credenza, sat the framed photos of Paul's hypothetical children—hypothetical because Clemmie had never seen any hard evidence of their existence. The glass-covered shelves behind him were stocked with law books—no plebeian binders for Paul. Those were kept in Joan's cubicle, along with all the rest of the actual apparatus of legal productivity.

Following his instructions, Clemmie closed the door gently behind her, holding her yellow legal pad under one arm, a black pen clipped to the top. Paul's pens were for Paul only. Many an associate had learned that the hard way.

"I hope you had a good holiday," he said in the false cheerful voice he used when he was trying to be chummy.

Clemmie stared at him. Really? He knew her grandmother had died; he'd bitched enough about Clemmie missing work for it.

She swallowed her snarky comment and crossed the office to her usual chair across from Paul's desk. Deep breaths. Just suck it up. That was the only way to deal with Paul. In a day or so, the partnership announcement would be out and she'd never have to kowtow to the Pauls of the firm again. Instead, she'd be sitting with him at the partners' lunch table and he could just lump it.

Yes, good image. She'd just hold on to that one. Once someone made partner, there was no way to unmake them. She could be as snarky to Paul as she liked and there'd be nothing he could do about it. It was a remarkably soothing thought.

Clemmie sat, balancing her yellow legal pad on the slippery polyester of her pin-striped skirt. "Joan said you wanted to see me?"

There was a plastic football Paul kept on his desk, a little novelty one. He tossed it up in the air and caught it again. "Yes."

Up the football went again. And down. Clemmie waited. And waited. Meanwhile, her BlackBerry, attached to her waistband by its own special clip, buzzed and buzzed again.

Any year now . . .

"You're probably wondering why I wanted to see you," said Paul.

Clemmie sat up straighter in her chair. It was faux Louis XIV, with slippery satin upholstery. "If it's about PharmaNet, I've been coordinating with Harold while I've been away," she said briskly. "I have the latest copies of the internal reports as well as an indexed binder excerpting the pertinent testimony."

Two paralegals had given up their New Year's Eve for that.

"No, no." Paul frowned. "Although now that you mention it—Joan!"

"Yes?" The suspiciously regular rattle of typing cut off and Joan popped her head around the door.

Clemmie had to hand it to her; Joan had put up with a daily dose of Paul for nearly five years now, even if she had gone on a bender at last year's Christmas party and used a couple of cocktail franks to rather graphically illustrate just what she'd like to do to him if he made her retype his f-ing briefs one more time. No one had wanted to eat the cocktail franks after that.

Paul leaned sideways. "Tell Harold I want to see him once I'm done with Clementine. In, say . . . five minutes."

"Gotcha." Joan disappeared around the door.

Paul settled back in his chair, kicking it back. "Where were we?"

Clemmie had no idea. All she knew was that she needed coffee and she needed it now. "PharmaNet?"

Paul steepled his fingers. "I suppose you could say this does have to do with PharmaNet," he said thoughtfully. "You are aware that you left us in a difficult position in London, leaving without warning."

"I told you as soon as I—"

"Hmph." Paul hushed her with a hand gesture. "It didn't look good. Gordon wasn't pleased. We'd told him we'd have a senior associate present and we walked in with a first year. Not good."

"I certainly didn't intend—"

"It was a highly awkward situation," said Paul. "It's not the sort of image we like to project."

Awkward? It had been a hell of a lot more than awkward for her.

"My grandmother was dying," said Clemmie flatly.

"Yes, you mentioned." Paul waved that aside. "Even before that, though, some of your comments about PharmaNet's marketing practices—I know you meant them just for our ears, Clementine, but you never know who might be listening. That was very unwise."

Clemmie struggled to remember. Was this all because she had questioned their off-label marketing of drugs to the elderly? "I was trying to protect the best interests of the client."

Paul shook his head sadly. "That's just the problem, Clementine. If it had been an accident—but that sort of choice goes to your judgment."

He looked at her intently, as though waiting for her to say something. Clemmie had no idea what he was waiting for.

"Sometimes," she said, "reasonable people disagree."

Paul looked at her pityingly. "In a law-school hypothetical, perhaps." He took up the football, squeezing the plastic seams. Clemmie resisted the urge to snatch it away from him. She hated that damn thing. "As I'm sure you know, the partnership committee met last week. The announcement will be made tomorrow."

"Yes," Clemmie said warily. "I had heard something to that effect."

Paul leaned back in his chair, narrowly missing conking his head on a studio picture of his theoretical offspring. "As your team leader, I wanted to speak to you personally before the memo went out."

"Thank you?" said Clemmie.

Paul settled the football on the desk, leaning both hands on it. "I want you to know that everyone on the committee spoke very highly of the work that you've done here."

Since it felt redundant to say thank you again, Clemmie just nodded. Please, just get this done, she thought, please say congratulations and let me leave. No more torture. No more plastic football.

"But there were some concerns voiced. About your commitment"—Paul looked meaningfully at her—"and your judgment."

What? Clemmie nearly lost her grip on her yellow legal pad. She grabbed at it just before it slid off her lap. She could feel the sweat beginning under her armpits, prickling against the nylon of her Banana Republic blouse.

"In the end, the committee decided that it just wasn't a chance we could take. It was a tough decision," he added. "We do want you to know that."

Tough? Clemmie's mouth opened, but nothing came out. Tough? She'd spent twenty hours a day, seven days a week, in this building. She'd blown off her family, her friends. She had no idea what was on television because she hadn't watched it since law school. She hadn't read a book since—well, did they still make them out of parchment? She'd missed her own god-daughter's christening because of a fire drill that turned out to be a false alarm. She'd broken off her fucking engagement for the firm. He had to be kidding.

"You aren't serious."

Paul did his best to look concerned and understanding. "We all think very highly of your abilities as an associate, Clementine—but what makes a good associate isn't necessarily what makes a good partner. There are certain qualities we look for in a CPM partner."

"Qualities like yours?" Clemmie couldn't believe what she was hearing. This wasn't happening. It wasn't.

Sarcasm wasn't Paul's strong suit. "Precisely," he said, looking pleased.

So, basically, if she'd been a raging asshole with no managerial skills, she'd be fine?

"This isn't happening," she muttered.

She was asleep, she was hallucinating, she was—she didn't know, but this couldn't be real. She had busted her butt for so long, never put a foot out of line, always put the firm first . . .

"Naturally," said Paul, "we hope you'll consider staying on as a senior associate. Everyone admires your output and we'd love to keep you here at the firm if we can. It's not your work product anyone has issues with," he said kindly, "just your judgment."

"Thanks." She was going to be ill. She felt like throwing up, if there'd been anything in her stomach to go. All she'd had this morning was half a cup of cold coffee, the dregs of her cut-price coffee machine.

"If you do decide to go elsewhere, we hope you'll think fondly of CPM. I know several of our clients would be happy to have you on board their in-house teams—"

She couldn't take this. Seven years. Seven years she had given up so she could be told she didn't have the right *qualities*? Paul's voice went on and on, in-house work, client relationships, giving work back to CPM, blah, blah, blah. As if she were meant to be grateful. Grateful for what? For kissing his ass for two years? For never taking a holiday off? For spending her birthday doing twenty-two hours of doc review and sleeping the remaining two under her desk next to the frayed bits of lettuce from the previous night's salad? Yeah, right, sure.

Clutching the carved arm of the chair, Clemmie heaved herself upright. The yellow legal pad slid off her lap, onto the faux Aubusson rug that covered the industrial green carpet. It didn't make a sound. Neither did she.

"Clementine?" Paul broke off in confusion.

Her legs felt wobbly. She took a deep breath and straightened her spine. She didn't have to do this anymore. Screw Paul. Screw CPM.

"Clementine!"

Clemmie ignored him. She did what she should have done years ago. She turned around and walked out.

Kenya, 1927

"When was the last time you saw Mrs. Desborough?"

"On Wednesday night. I don't recall the time." Addie sat with her legs crossed at the ankles, her hands folded in her lap, perched on the edge of a narrow metal chair in a tent that had been turned into a temporary headquarters for the superintendent of the Chania CID.

It was Budgie who had radioed to the police when the initial search for Bea proved fruitless. *We don't have the manpower*, he had said when Raoul demanded to know why. Frederick had been silent, staring at that scarf, that ominously stained scarf. As for Val Vaughn, goodness only knew what he thought. He had stalked off to the makeshift landing strip, taking his plane out, for the aerial view, he said, although Addie didn't imagine one could spot a woman as one could a herd of elephants. There was a distinct difference in scale.

Perhaps, she thought, it helped him to be doing something, anything. The sitting about was maddening. Addie didn't know whether to be terrified or furious. Terrified for Bea's safety, out in the bush alone, furious at her putting herself into this position in the first place. It would be just like Bea to storm out, planning to teach them all a lesson by staying away until they were good and worried—she'd done something similar when she and Addie were young, seeking revenge on Nanny for some minor slight. She'd sauntered back after dark, having had a perfectly pleasant time taking tea with the head gamekeeper while the nursery was turned upside down and all of them were sent to bed without supper.

As for the scarf, Addie had lost a good year of her life over that until she'd remembered that breaking noise, something smashing. Bea had probably cut her hand on that broken whatever it was and wrapped her hand in her scarf until it stopped bleeding. It all made perfect sense, and any moment now Bea should come strolling back in with a nonchalant, Miss me?

Only she hadn't.

The superintendent had appeared on Thursday, bringing with him a complement of *askaris*, native police officers. They had fanned out over the surrounding area, searching. For all their combined efforts, there had been no sign of Bea. Instead, all they had of Bea was a pitifully small pile of objects gathered on a rickety table on the side of the room, labeled like exhibits in a museum. Item: one diamond clip, worn by Mrs. Frederick Desborough on the shoulder of her gown. Item: one chiffon scarf, stained. Item: one blue silk evening slipper.

Like the scarf, there were stains on the shoe, ugly, dark stains. It had been found about five yards away from the shoe, on an incline down towards a narrow stream, as though Bea, fleeing, had lost first her scarf and then her shoe. An *askari* had found the brooch glittering on the ground not far away.

The shoe bothered Addie. It nagged at the back of her memory. She could have sworn that Bea was wearing green that night, not blue. Addie hadn't seen her in blue since that horrible party at Ashford where Val Vaughn had brought up a safari and started them all on the path to this fiasco. Bea was always so careful with her attire; she would never wear blue slippers with a green frock. That was the sort of thing Addie might do absentmindedly, but never Bea. She was too particular about her appearance.

But had it been a green dress that last night? Addie had thought so, but it had been dark, the light uncertain. She'd had other things on her mind. Her attention had been for Frederick, silent and brooding, not for Bea, blithely playing Val and Raoul against each other, one on each side, while Budgie slid further and further into his traditional evening stupor. Bea's shoes might have been crimson for all Addie would have noticed.

A pale blue crepe de chine didn't look all that different from green chiffon in the candlelight.

"Can you tell me roughly when that might have been?" asked the superintendent. He had a flat, strange accent. Canadian, he had told her when he first called her in for a statement, three days before. Since then, his expression had become more harried, the lines between his nose had deepened, and his questions had become markedly more pointed.

"We didn't take much note of the time," Addie said, "not out here. It felt late, but with the early sunset it's so very hard to tell. It might have been any time between nine and midnight. I'm sorry. That's all I can say."

"That's all right." The superintendent made a note with his pencil.

Addie was beginning to hate those notes. She had been in and out of this tent for days now, for seemingly random inquiries, scratch, scratch, scratching with that abominable pencil in that absurd little notebook. In the meantime, Bea was still out there somewhere, lost, confused, possibly hurt. . . .

"No," said Addie forcefully, startling the superintendent into snapping his pencil point, "it's *not* all right. What are you doing to find my cousin?"

The superintendent looked up, surprised. "Miss Gillecote—"

"She's been missing for four days now. That's four days in which she might have been found. We have no idea where she is, and as far as I can tell we aren't any closer to having any idea. She might have hit her head. She might be wandering, confused."

Addie could picture her, thin, dirty, scratched by thorns, wandering in the bush, drinking from streams, disoriented and alone.

Fear made Addie imperious. She stood, leaning both hands on the superintendant's makeshift desk. "Instead of being out there, looking for her, you're sitting in here, asking the same questions over and over. Frankly, I just don't see how this is any use at all." The superintendent opened his mouth to speak, but Addie swept on. "I fully appreciate the need for a full and complete record, but shouldn't you attend to the ministerial duties *after* you've found my cousin?"

The superintendent put down his pencil. "Miss Gillecote—" He broke off, massaging the muscles of his right hand with his left. "At this point, the odds of recovering your cousin are . . . slim. If she were to be found, we would have found her."

In the complete silence of the tent, Addie could hear the monotonous drone of a fly. Outside a bird chirped. A drop of sweat worked its way slowly down her spine, under the band of her brassiere. She could feel the itch of the stitching on the straps against her skin.

The idea that Bea wasn't to be found, that Bea might be . . . gone. It was unthinkable. Nine lives, Val Vaughn had said.

Yes, but how many had she used up?

Addie sat bolt upright in her chair. "That makes no sense at all," she said with a sniff worthy of Aunt Vera. "If my cousin were . . . were dead, shouldn't we have recovered a body?"

The superintendent looked at her with something very like pity. "Not necessarily. In fact, it would be highly unlikely. The animals—"

"Take care of their own." Addie's voice came out strangely high-pitched.

The superintendent looked at her strangely. Addie shook her head. "Sorry. Just something someone said."

"Whoever it was, he was right. The animals make short work of bodies out here." Something in her face must have caught him. He set down his pencil and said apologetically, "I am sorry, Miss Gillecote. I had thought you knew."

Addie shook her head wordlessly. He was wrong; he had to be. Not Bea, Bea who was always so full of life, so resourceful.

So careless.

"What was your cousin's relationship like with her husband?"

The use of the past tense stung her. Her head snapped up. "What has that to do with anything?"

The superintendent tapped the blunt end of his pencil against the table. "We need to examine every aspect of the situation." Leaning back in his chair, he subjected her to a long, assessing stare. "We can't rule out the possibility of foul play."

"Foul play?" echoed Addie. "You mean— Murder?" She could hardly bring herself to say it. It was too absurd.

The superintendent neither confirmed nor denied it. "We would be remiss if we did not examine every possibility."

Then what about the possibility that Bea was still alive? Addie couldn't, though. She could see the pity in his eyes and resented it. He'd dismiss her as hysterical. He'd already made up his mind. Bea had been murdered.

Murder. It was something that happened to other people, in penny thrillers or in newsreels, not real people, not people one knew. It was all a horrible, horrible mistake. It had to be.

Tight-lipped, she said, "I see." She sat back down, taking care rearranging her skirt, smoothing it down so that it didn't bunch up beneath her.

The superintendent shuffled a pile of papers. "I know this is difficult, Miss Gillecote—"

Difficult? No. Difficult was a jigger under one's toenail or a broken belt on the coffee dryer. That was difficult.

"—but the evidence all points to the possibility of . . . unpleasantness. We have a missing woman and we have a scarf and a shoe, both with blood on them. You seem like a sensible woman, Miss Gillecote. If you had come into this from the outside, what conclusions would you draw?"

She knew he was deliberately manipulating her, attempting to play her with that patronizing nod to her common sense, but the question ate at her all the same. From the outside, it all looked rather damning, and even more damning if one factored in the bits he didn't know about: Raoul's jealous outbursts, Vaughn's odd behavior. Frederick.

She could hear his voice that last night, the strange expression on his face as she left him by the fire. The sound of raised voices and glass shattering.

"Did your cousin have anyone who might wish to harm her?"

The question cut too close to Addie's own train of thought for comfort. "Everyone loved Bea." Except when they didn't. "She was always much in demand."

The superintendent's eyes narrowed. He said deliberately, "Monsieur de Fontaine tells us that Mrs. Desborough planned to run away with him. He said they were planning their departure that night."

"That's nonsense!" Addie's surprise was unfeigned. "It can't be. She would have—"

Told me, she almost said. But would Bea? She had been so distant towards the end, hinting at secrets, veering oddly between cool reserve and strange rushes of affection, mocking one moment, embarking on a round of *do you remember?* the next.

"I merely repeat what Monsieur de Fontaine told us." The superintendent's voice was neutral, but his eyes watched Addie keenly. "She never said anything to you?"

Addie gathered her scrambled wits together. "Monsieur de Fontaine did fancy himself in love with my cousin—but she would never just run off like that. She has two daughters," she added by way of explanation.

Oh, Lord. If Bea was gone, how were they going to break it to Marjorie and Anna? How could she tell them that their mother was never coming home? It wasn't going to happen, she tried to tell herself, but her faith was wearing thinner and thinner. In her imagination, she could hear the hyenas howling.

"Was Mr. Desborough aware of Monsieur de Fontaine's feelings for his wife?"

Addie didn't like the way this was going. "We all were," she said flatly. "It would have been hard to ignore it. But we all assumed it was, oh, a certain amount of Gallic excess. There was nothing the least bit serious about it."

The superintendent made a note.

Addie drew herself up. "My cousin was a woman of the world, Superintendent. She had admirers and she had flirtations, but there was certainly nothing the least bit suspect or clandestine about it! It would have been odd if she hadn't." She looked him straight in the eye. "Everyone knew the rules."

They weren't her rules, but they had been Bea's and those of Bea's set and that was what counted.

The superintendent's gaze strayed to the bloodstained shoe. "Unless someone was playing by a different set of rules." He gave her a moment to allow that to sink in and then said briskly, "Thank you, Miss Gillecote. You've been very helpful."

It was clearly a dismissal. Addie wasn't ready to be dismissed. She had a hundred questions she wanted to ask—but she couldn't, not without giving away information that the superintendent might twist or bend to fit whatever theories he was forming. He had a theory, she was quite sure of it, and equally sure she wouldn't like it.

She stood, smoothing her gloves over her wrists. "Do keep me apprised of developments, Superintendent. If there's anything I can do . . ."

"Thank you, Miss Gillecote. Wait," he added with studied casualness. "There is one last thing."

"Yes?" Addie's nerves were stretched to the breaking point, but she did her best to keep her face expressionless.

The superintendent consulted his notes. "Mr. Desborough informed us that you intended to return to England after the safari."

"Yes," said Addie slowly. That seemed like a million years ago. She'd meant to go away to keep from hurting Bea. Bea . . . Bea couldn't be dead; it was absurd. "I was going to make the arrangements as soon as we returned. I had—I have commitments in England."

The superintendent chose his words carefully. "We would appreciate if you would stay. Just until we finish our inquiries. A formality, you understand."

They couldn't think that she—no. "Yes," said Addie. "Certainly. But it won't be necessary. I'm sure Bea will—will turn up."

"Let us hope so, Miss Gillecote." The superintendent courteously held open the flap of the tent for her. "But, in the meantime, do keep us apprised of your plans."

TWENTY-FOUR

New York, 2000

Out of his natural habitat, the marquess looked even more like Hugh Grant.

Not the marquess. Tony, Clemmie reminded herself. When she'd met him at the Oak Room, he'd told her to call him Tony, as his friends did. It was very strange thinking of him by his first name rather than his title. Paul would be appalled.

Clemmie reminded herself that she didn't have to care what Paul thought anymore. Not since yesterday.

They'd managed to secure a small round table all to themselves, near the window, beating out a couple of Russian businessmen and their dates.

"Is this all right?" Tony asked. He needed a haircut. His hair flopped endearingly over his forehead, giving him a misleadingly boyish air, at odds with the formality of his dark blue suit and the inherent courtliness of his manner. His eyes were as warm and brown as she remembered. Kind. She could use a little kindness right now.

"It's great." Maybe it was like whistling a happy tune: If she feigned enthusiasm, she would eventually feel it. Right now, all she felt was numb.

She hadn't gone into work until well past noon today. She'd slept in instead, ignoring her alarm, ignoring the light creeping through her unshaded windows, pulling the pillow over her head as she lingered in that gray realm between sleep and waking, not so much because she was tired, but because there was no impetus to get out of bed, nothing she wanted to get out of bed for.

She wasn't speaking to her mother, she hadn't returned Jon's calls, she didn't have a grandmother anymore, and the firm had just made clear that she wasn't one of their own. Sure, they were still paying her. If she disappeared for long enough, they might send someone from HR to track her down, but it would take them awhile. She'd only mattered while she was partner track.

Once in the office, she'd closed the door firmly behind her, pulling a solid layer of wood between her secretary's condolences and the curious, pitying stares of her fellow associates. She could hear the whispers following her in the hallways, the news spreading, office to office. She'd collapsed into her chair, staring unseeing at the monitor of her computer, watching the messages pop up on e-mail, like the moles in Whac-A-Mole, just waiting to be knocked down so another could pop up. She couldn't muster the energy to deal with any of them, not the administrative ones, not the client ones, not the ones flagged with those annoying red exclamation marks. Who gave a flying fuck whether the firm wanted her to help host a summer associate reception in April? What did they expect her to tell them? Come to CPM, work like a dog, and then get kicked to the curb! Woo-hoo!

Harold wanted help with a memo; the scared fourth-year associate wanted reassurance on a brief. Well, screw it. Let them go to Paul.

All of the things she believed gave her meaning—her job, her family—had dissolved, like a dream, like a hypnotist's illusion. She'd always felt so buffered from the world, in the high walls of Worldwide Plaza in her claustrophobic office or in Granny's living room. There was always somewhere she was meant to be, people who needed her. Slumped in her desk chair, in the office that was no longer really hers, she felt stripped bare, nothing left but the bare physical reality of her, a tallish woman in a cheap suit with coffee stains on the sleeves, an impractical pair of high-heeled black pumps, and stockings with a run in them.

She'd unclipped the BlackBerry from her belt. She'd put on her coat and her scarf and gone back home, leaving the angry beeping of the BlackBerry behind her. She'd taken a long, hot shower, standing under the spray long enough to scrub every last trace of Cromwell, Polk & Moore from her skin, as if she could wash away the last seven years with a little bit of Pantene and Irish Spring. After some rummaging, she'd finally dug an old dress out of the back of her closet, black, knit, clingy. It had been so long since she'd worn anything other than a suit that she'd forgotten what it felt like. She'd forgotten what it felt like to dress for a date, to take time with her makeup.

It took her a moment to recognize herself in the mirrored wall of the lobby as she'd hurried downstairs. She'd looked once, then again, trying to reconcile the woman in the mirror with the Clemmie she knew. The black dress clung in all the right places, emphasizing curves she'd forgotten she had. The high-heeled black boots didn't hurt either; they clung to her calves, adding a strut to her walk. It felt very different from her usual hurried hunch, head down, shoulders braced against the wind.

Clemmie found herself slowing down a bit. Sauntering, even. Her hair had started to grow out. It swished pleasingly just shy of her shoulders, fashion-model blond against the black knit. Clemmie wasn't quite sure who this woman in the mirror was, but whoever she was, she looked sexy. Sophisticated.

She could tell the marquess—Tony—appreciated her efforts. He was surveying her with frank appreciation. She could tell by the way he quickly dropped his eyes and pretended to be studying the menu.

How long had it been since someone had looked at her like that? Clemmie tried to remember. Her suits had become a sort of armor; she'd all but forgotten how to flirt. With Jon—well, with Jon it hadn't been an issue; he'd seen her in everything and nothing over the past twenty-odd years. The last time she'd dressed up for him had been in Rome, that cheap sundress that had been her favorite that year and a pair of perilously high sandals. The memory made her feel hollow and more than a little bit sad.

Or maybe that was just the not having eaten all day.

She crossed one booted leg over the other and watched as Tony looked and pretended not to be looking. It was a rather heady sensation, playing the game again—especially after seeing Jon with Caitlin. Not that Jon and Caitlin had anything to do with anything, she hastily told herself, taking a sip of water. She was just out for drinks with an interesting acquaintance, that was all.

Jon would be green if he knew she was having drinks with the descendant of his research subjects.

"I can't tell you how pleased I am that you were able to make the time for a drink," Tony said, doing an admirable, if not entirely successful, job of trying to look at her face, rather than her Wonderbra. He cleared his throat. "I'd have thought you'd be chained to your desk."

"Not anymore," said Clemmie. "I'm clipping my shackles. I'm thinking of leaving the firm," she translated.

"From what I saw of Mr. Dietrich, I can't say I blame you," said Tony, and just as quickly caught himself. "Sorry. None of my lookout."

"Not at all." Clemmie leaned forward, making her dress stretch, and smiled her most seductive smile. "You were absolutely right. Mr. Dietrich is a raging asshole."

Tony blinked. She wasn't sure whether it was the cleavage or the language. "Well, then," he said, recovering himself with remarkable aplomb. "You're best out of it."

Clemmie nodded briskly. "I couldn't agree more. What are we drinking?"

It felt incredibly decadent to be contemplating booze at five o'clock in the evening. Vodka from an airplane miniature in one's desk drawer didn't count. She frowned at the drinks menu, consulted gravely with Tony on the relative merits of gin versus vodka martinis, contemplated various interesting concoctions made with Godiva liqueur, and settled on a plain old gin and tonic.

Once the issue of drinks was dealt with, and the proper polite questions about Tony's stay in New York, his business meetings, and his accommodation, she leaned her elbows on the table and said, "The real problem is what to do next."

"Will you, er, find another job?" It sounded a bit like he was translating from a foreign language, trying to speak American. It was rather endearing.

"Maybe," said Clemmie. Inevitably, yes. She didn't have the wherewithal to be unemployed for any length of time. She'd only just paid off her law-school loans, and the unlovely apartment on 52nd Street drained away an ungodly amount of cash per month. But she couldn't tell that to the Marquess of Rivesdale. "At the moment, I'm just enjoying my newfound freedom."

Tony set his drinks menu aside, that one lock of brown hair flopping over his eye. "There's always room for you at Rivesdale House."

Clemmie grinned at him. "That sounds like an advertising slogan. You could post it up on the Tube with a picture of all the happy house staff."

"It's not meant to be advertising." Clemmie felt her cheeks warming as Tony's eyes met hers, frankly admiring. "We'd love to have you—as a guest. A proper guest."

Clemmie wondered who the other part of the "we" was. A business partner? A non-business partner? "Thanks," she said, playing it cool. "If I find myself back in London, I'll let you know."

"Please do," he said warmly. "It's not every day I find an almost cousin."

Clemmie leaned her elbows on the table. "I'm surprised they're not battering down your door."

The marquess—Tony—made a deprecatory gesture. "They wouldn't if they knew the size of our overdraft."

Clemmie laughed huskily. Amazing what one could do once one didn't care anymore. She briefly toyed with the image of the look on Paul's face if she told him she was out with the Marquess of Rivesdale. He would, as the phrase so elegantly went, be shitting bricks. That really would be a great big up-yours, if she followed in the path of her grandmother and married a Marquess of Rivesdale. Everything solved for her, no one asking her why she'd left CPM—who would when there was a handsome Brit in the picture? They could ride off into the London smog, happily every after.

Whoa. What in the hell was she thinking? The word of the day, folks, is rebound, she told herself, and took another swig of her water. Not rebound from Dan—that had been over long ago—but rebound from the firm.

"Besides," Tony said, "how many of them would be artwork come to life? I always rather fancied her," he added. "The lady in the portrait."

He was smiling still, but Clemmie's imagination painted his smile in sinister colors. There was something a little too gothic about it all, the man in love with the painting on the wall.

"She's nothing more than canvas and pigment," Clemmie protested, "an image on a wall."

"She was a real person once," said the marquess. "A rather smashing one, actually."

Smashing hearts. Clemmie thought of her mother and Aunt Anna, of

Granny Addie. Whoever this Bea was, she'd left them all shattered in her wake.

"We don't look that much alike," Clemmie said shrilly.

"No, you don't," said Tony disarmingly. He leaned back in his chair, propping one ankle on the opposite knee. "There's something very different about you. Something . . ."

"American?" suggested Clemmie.

He grinned at her and she felt herself relaxing. "Yes, that's most likely it. Your features are very like, but—" He scrutinized her face, not rudely, but with an almost childlike curiosity. "You don't look at all the same, somehow."

"My teeth are probably better," said Clemmie before wondering whether one should really make dentistry jokes to a Brit. Not that Tony's teeth were that bad, just slightly yellower than she was used to.

Tony shifted in his chair, rummaging in a leather portfolio case. He drew out a handful of yellowed newspaper clippings. "Those papers I wanted to show you—they're about her, actually. There were wedged away in the back of a drawer. At first, I thought they were just lining, but then I took a closer look, and—well, I thought you might be interested."

With a courtly gesture, he handed the clippings across the table. Clemmie's breath caught in her throat. Uncrossing her legs, she leaned forward, fanning the papers out across the table, feeling the old paper crackle and break.

Marchioness Murdered! blazed one headline.

Peer's Daughter Missing ran another, more circumspect.

"Good Lord," said Clemmie. Bea stared out at her from the yellowing print, smirking at the camera in a fox fur stole that went up right beneath her chin. Clemmie quickly shuffled through, scanning for the relevant bits, oblivious to the man sitting across from her, the social chatter at the neighboring tables.

No wonder Granny Addie had kept it all quiet all these years. They weren't just talking spouse swapping.

Lady Beatrice Desborough had gone missing from a safari in Kenya in 1927, missing, believed dead. Her husband was suspected . . . suspected. . . . No. Clemmie didn't believe it, wouldn't believe it.

Not Grandpa Frederick. That was Grandpa Frederick's grainy face in that picture, and there was another, a copy of the picture of Bea and Grandpa Frederick on the ship. A HUSBAND SCORNED? ran the caption.

In the very, very small print, it mentioned that the deceased's sister had stayed behind to look after her orphaned children. They'd gotten Granny's name wrong as well as their relationship; they had her as Adele rather than Adeline. Miss Adele Gillcott.

"Are you all right?" asked Tony. "You look rather pale."

"Where's that drink?" Clemmie all but grabbed her gin and tonic off the waitress' tray. She took a fortifying swig. "No, it's just—wow. I didn't know things like this happened."

"It's not the only famous murder to have happened in Kenya," said Tony helpfully. "There was also the Earl of Errol."

He went on, outlining the circumstances of that case and the book based on it while Clemmie stared at the clippings, trying to make sense of them, trying to reconcile what had happened in Kenya decades before she was born with the people she had known, the people who had kept the shampoo out of her eyes and helped her with her homework.

There were ten clippings in all, each successively smaller as it became clearer and clearer that the police weren't about to make an arrest.

Death by misadventure was the final verdict.

"They never solved it, did they?" She broke into his monologue.

Tony looked quizzically up at her. "The Earl of Erroll?"

"No, this one." Clemmie tapped the clippings with one bitten nail. "The Desborough murder."

"I don't believe so," said Tony, slightly disconcerted. A smile spread across his face. "They needed that Belgian chap on the case."

"Or Miss Marple," said Clemmie abstractedly. "Who do you think did it? Not the Errol murder—this one."

"Well," said Tony, making an effort to play along, "the most likely suspect would have been my grandmother, but she was back home in England— and she'd probably have gone in for poison, nothing quite so messy as wild animals."

Clemmie mustered a feeble smile, since one seemed to be required. "Of the people on the scene?"

Tony tilted his head, making his hair go flop. "My money is on the husband. They're nearly as bad as butlers when it comes to committing murders."

The husband. Clemmie remembered Grandpa Frederick in his old fedora and tweed jacket, with that ridiculous walking stick, standing at the base of a rock in Central Park, watching her as she clambered up, holding on to her ice cream for her.

"They do say the spouse is always the first suspect, don't they?" she said a little wildly.

"It sounds like he had motive," said Tony. "All those other chaps and all that."

Impossible to suspect Grandpa Frederick of murder. On the other hand, what did she really know of him? What did she know of anyone? They'd all been lying to her for years. Clemmie swallowed hard against the lump in her throat.

"I prefer the Frenchman," she said, trying to keep her voice light. "Do you know what happened to him?"

Tony frowned. "I believe he went off to France and married the woman his parents chose for him. I did do a bit of poking around, out of curiosity," he confessed. "It gave me something to do while the plumber was unstopping the downstairs loo."

"And what about the other potential murderer—this Vaughn person?"

"He died in a plane crash not long after." Tony looked thoughtfully at the condensation rings left by his drink. "They didn't come to a happy end, that lot."

Clemmie remembered Granny Addie and Grandpa Frederick sitting with their heads together by the old black-and-white television in the den, arguing politics together. She remembered the way Granny Addie slipped the best pieces of meat onto Grandpa Frederick's plate, the way Grandpa Frederick had held the door for Granny Addie. They'd always been Clemmie's image of the perfect couple. They'd always seemed so happy.

Clemmie stared down at her hands, bare of rings, unadorned except for her watch. She was, she realized, more than a little bit tipsy on the one G&T. Not having eaten since yesterday might have something to do with it. She hadn't been hungry.

"Perhaps some of them did. Eventually." She looked up at Tony, the marquess. "My mother was one of their little girls."

Confusion chased across the marquess' face. "But I'd thought you'd said she was a sort of cousin."

"It's a long story. But no. She was my grandmother. The one who was murdered." It felt bizarre saying it, claiming her. Clemmie would have thought it would have given her a sense of ownership; instead, it just felt empty.

"Oh," said Tony, and his drink slopped over the sides of the martini glass. He looked at her and she wondered what he was seeing. The woman in the portrait? Or an American woman well on her way to getting sloshed on one G&T? "Well, that does make us rather more closely related, doesn't it? Your grandmother might have been my grandmother."

If she hadn't died in Kenya. But she had died in Kenya and Addie had come to New York and somehow everything had gone all topsy-turvy. For the better, Clemmie's mother had said. For the worse, said Aunt Anna. Clemmie didn't know whom or what to believe.

Murder, screamed the headlines of the articles.

"Here's to grandmothers," said Clemmie, and clinked her glass against the marquess'. "Whoever they may be. I don't know about you, but I could use a second round."

Obligingly Tony raised his hand and ordered another round of drinks.

Kenya, 1927

Addie woke in the wee hours.

The covers were twisted around her, damp with sweat. Addie lay blinking in the dark, shaking off the last vestiges of a dream. She had been with Bea. They were in Nairobi, but it was a Nairobi that didn't look at all like the Nairobi Addie knew, more of an Eastern bazaar out of a book, with lush tents and rolls of silk and lamps hanging from chains. There were people tugging on their dresses, chanting, "Come buy, come buy."

She turned to look for Bea, but Bea had gone, slipped off into the bazaar. Addie tried to follow, but there were hands plucking at her skirt, her sleeve, her belt, holding her back. "Come buy, come buy." Ahead, she could see, faintly, the flounce of Bea's skirt, whisking around a corner. She could hear Bea's laugh, like silver bells.

Addie pulled free, desperately twisting and winding, Bea's laugh always just ahead, always just ahead of her. . . .

Addie struggled up into a sitting position, shivering in the midnight cold. It was useless to try to sleep now; she knew that from experience. It seemed bizarre that outside the rest of the world went on, the crickets chirped, an owl hooted, an animal called. Out in the fields, the coffee was growing; in the huts, babies cried and men snored; and yet Bea was dead and would wake no more.

Addie drew her dressing gown around her. It was cold at night, so cold. She had never noticed it before—probably because, before, there had been no impetus to wander the night, listening to the lonely calls of nightjars and the squawk of a small animal in the most dire of distress.

She wasn't the only one who walked the night. There was a light where there oughtn't have been, coming from the dining room. Addie padded to the doorway in her bare feet, tying the sash of her dressing gown over the silk pajamas that had been Bea's gift to her, made to Bea's own design.

In the dining room, Frederick sat at the long table by himself, a crystal glass in front of him, a decanter in easy reach. The generator went off every night at midnight and the electric lights with it. Frederick had lit the heavy silver candelabra that stood in the center of the table. The candles cast a flickering light across his face, dancing over the stubble on his chin, hiding some shadows and creating new ones.

He reached for the decanter, drawing out the stopper.

"You should go to bed," Addie said softly.

The stopper clattered against the neck of the bottle. "Good God. You scared the life out of me."

The decanter had been nearly full when Addie went to bed. Now it was down below the halfway mark. "You've had enough for one night."

"Enough? There isn't enough whiskey in the world." Addie watched from the door as he splashed more into his glass. "All the whiskey in the world couldn't wash me clean."

He was talking gibberish. "You need your rest. For the girls."

"The girls." Frederick turned the glass around in his hand, watching the candlelight play off the amber liquid. "They're going to take them away from me, Addie."

Addie ventured into the circle of candlelight. "What on earth are you talking about?"

Frederick lifted his head. "They think I did it. That detective. He's going to pin Bea's death on me." He blinked at her, having trouble focusing. She hadn't seen him this sloshed since England, since those nightmare night-clubs. She didn't like it. "If they hang me—you'll take the girls, won't you? Don't let them go to Bea's witch of a mother. I wouldn't let her near a dog."

"No one is taking the girls away. Frederick." Addie slipped into the chair beside him, leaning forward along the polished table. "Frederick, look at me. They can't hang you for something you didn't do."

Frederick's elbow knocked the decanter. Addie caught it just before it went over. "Why not? It's happened before. Our own local Lestrade over in Chania has decided it. He thinks I conked Bea over the head and strangled her with her scarf, then dumped her for the animals to eat her."

Addie couldn't think of anything to say. She was speechless.

"It's a nice little plot, when you think about it." Whiskey sloshed as the glass swayed in his unsteady hand. "Crime of passion and all that rot. I saw Bea carrying on with Vaughn and Fontaine and I made plans to bump her off. I shared the tent with her. I had the best opportunity. Motive and means all in one. Get out the black cap and build the scaffold."

Addie shook herself free of the image of Bea, senseless, being dragged through the woods. It was all nonsense, sheer nonsense.

"And you're just going to let them do that?" Addie said sharply. "For heaven's sake, Frederick, enough! This is pure self-indulgence. If you don't care to defend yourself, do it for—do it for the people who care about you. If you had motive, so did Vaughn and Fontaine. Are you so anxious to pro-tect them?"

Frederick blinked at her. "The inspector . . ."

"Has nothing. Nothing but speculation. You didn't do it," Addie said firmly. "That's the important thing. Don't go turning yourself in for some-thing you didn't do. That's not nobility; it's stupidity."

Frederick shook his head, as though trying to clear it. "We fought that night. The inspector knows about it. I told him. Had to. Didn't want it to look like I was trying to hide."

Addie leaned forward, the sash of her dressing gown biting into her waist. "Frederick, what happened that night? What really happened?"

It had been eating at her since that night, the look on Frederick's face at dinner, the sound of their raised voices, the scratch on Frederick's face. She didn't, couldn't, believe he would have been so cold-blooded as to hurt Bea—at least, not intentionally. There had been that horrible crash. If Bea had cut herself, if she had been badly hurt, if it had been an accident—it was too horrible to be thought of, but she had to think of it. She had to know. They couldn't go on like this, starting at shadows.

"I heard you fighting. And something smashed."

"A looking glass," said Frederick dully. "Bea threw her looking glass at me. The one with the silver backing. It smashed against my trunk. Seven years' bad luck."

"Why did she throw a looking glass at you?"

"Why did Bea do anything?" Frederick swayed in his chair. Addie put out a hand, but he caught himself. "It was late. She'd come in around three in the morning. She'd been with someone—I could smell it on her. I don't know whether it was Vaughn or de Fontaine. It might have been both for all I cared."

Addie schooled herself not to react, her heart aching for both of them, for Bea and for Frederick.

"She taunted me with it." Frederick stared out into the darkness. Addie wondered what he saw there. Bea? "She'd never done that before. Oh, she'd had affairs, certainly, but she didn't rub my nose in them." He shook his head, confused. "It was almost as though she wanted to make me angry."

"And she succeeded?" Addie said softly.

Frederick's grim expression was all the answer she needed. "I told her I wanted a divorce. I told her that I could divorce her, or she could divorce me, I didn't much care which. I told her I was in love with you."

Addie's nails cut into her palms. She forced herself to unclench her hands finger by finger. "What did Bea say?"

"She laughed." Frederick put his hands to his temples. "I can still hear her now, laughing, laughing. . . . And she said, she said"—his voice rose in a vicious mimic of Bea's—"'I've already tried divorce, darling. It's a dead bore.'"

The only sound in the room was the ticking of the clock.

"It deteriorated from there." Frederick's voice was flat. He reached to pour himself another shot of whiskey. This time, Addie didn't object. "I told her I'd divorce her whether she liked it or not. She told me she'd like to see me try. I—"

"Yes?"

"I called her a lying whore." Frederick's face twisted with self-loathing. "I told her that she was no better than a cat in heat and that no court in the world would back her against me. I told her that the girls would be better off without her."

"Oh." Addie's hand rose to her lips. "Oh."

Frederick went grimly on. "I told her they'd be better off with no mother than a mother such as she. And Bea—and Bea said—" He drew a long, shuddering breath. "She said that she'd be only too happy to oblige."

Addie's mouth opened, but no sound came out. There was nothing to say.

"I can't get that out of my head. You know what Bea was when she got an idea in her head. And that night—she was high on something anyway. Gin, cocaine. God only knows. She laughed at me. She laughed and said she'd be only too happy." Frederick set down his glass with a clatter. "I killed her. I didn't do it with a cudgel—or that bloody scarf!—but I killed her all the same. I drove her out there."

"No." Addie found her voice. She clutched at Frederick's hand, squeezing it as hard as she could. "No, you didn't! Bea wouldn't have—Bea would never—" What did she know about what Bea would or wouldn't? She was beginning to think she hadn't known her cousin at all. But she couldn't say that to Frederick, not now. "This was an accident, a horrible, awful accident. It wasn't your fault."

"The things I said to her—" He looked up at Addie, his face haggard. "Do you know the worst of it? I meant every word. I can't even say I didn't mean it. I did."

Addie's hand tightened around his. She felt so feeble in the face of his grief, so incapable of doing anything at all. "Frederick—"

"All I wanted was to be rid of her. But not like this! Never like this." Frederick's eyes were bloodshot, his face haunted. "I didn't love her, but I didn't want her dead."

"I know," said Addie brokenly. "I know."

It had been eating away at her for the past month, the same horrible guilt. She'd wanted Frederick, but she'd never wanted Bea gone, not gone gone.

"I wanted us to be together, but not like this. It's all ruined. After this—you must despise me." Frederick grasped both of her hands with feverish strength. "Go back to England. It's the only thing for you. Take the girls. Don't let me drag you down."

"Stop being an idiot!" Addie's voice cracked through the room. In a low, earnest voice she said, "I let you drive me away once before, and look what happened. I'm not going anywhere. We'll see this through together."

Frederick made a strange noise deep in his throat. He shook his head, murmuring something indistinct.

"Frederick?" His head was bowed, his shoulders shaking.

It took Addie a moment to realize that he was crying, in gut-wrenched, soundless sobs that shook his whole body.

"Oh, darling." Addie slid off her chair, wrapping her arms around him, pressing his head against her breast. She could feel his tears soaking through the thin fabric of her wrap. "It will be all right, I promise. We'll all be all right."

Except Bea. It tore at her, the idea that there would never again be a Bea flitting in with that impish smile of hers, dispensing charm and worldly wisdom, making everything brighter just by walking into the room.

She pushed the thought away, wrapping her arms more tightly around her cousin's husband. "You're not getting rid of me that easily."

She stroked his head, where the dark hair was beginning to thin. There were silver stands in the candlelight, gray that hadn't been there before. Her eyes were damp with tears, but she tried to keep her own voice steady. She had to be strong for both of them, for all of them, for Marjorie and Anna, too. She might have failed Bea in everything else, but she'd take care of her girls.

"I'm staying right here with you. For as long as you need me."

Frederick looked up, his eyes red, his face ravaged with tears. "Don't leave me," he said hoarsely. His hands reached up to frame her face. "Promise you won't leave me."

"Never," she promised, but the word was lost against his lips as he drew her face down to his.

TWENTY-FIVE

New York, 2000

Aunt Anna's apartment looked much smaller without Jon in it.

This time, it was Aunt Anna who met Clemmie at the door, casually elegant in a brightly patterned dress that looked like—and probably was—vintage Pucci. Jon and his snowmen seemed like half a lifetime ago.

"Thanks for having me over," Clemmie said, trying not to wince at the brightness of the colors. She had the hangover to end all hangovers. She hadn't had one this bad since law school.

Aunt Anna led her past the study, into a small, rectangular living room with built-in bookcases on two sides of a small, glassed-in fireplace. Some of the shelves held books; most were filled with pictures, pictures of Aunt Anna's stepchildren and pets. Clemmie recognized the late, lamented Shoo-Shoo.

"I wondered when you'd be over," said Aunt Anna, not realizing that her voice had the effect of a buzz saw. "Coffee? Or something stronger?"

"Coffee," said Clemmie with feeling. "But that's okay, you don't need to—"

"It will take two minutes. Sit."

Clemmie didn't sit. Instead, she wandered over to the bookcases. Jon's wedding picture was still there, Jon in a tux, Caitlin in a traditional meringue of a dress. It suddenly struck Clemmie that she wouldn't want to be in Caitlin's shoes, married to a man who didn't know if he could believe in love. It was a strange feeling, feeling sorry for Caitlin, but she did. It made a nice change from bitterly resenting her.

Was Jon right? Were they all too screwed up to ever love anyone properly? Clemmie didn't want to believe that. Surely that was what self-determination was all about, taking responsibility for one's own destiny. Just because their parents' marriages had been screwed up didn't mean theirs needed to be.

She just wished she could be as comfortable with anyone as she was with Jon, could feel as alive bickering with someone. Tony was a nice guy, but talking to him felt like an exercise in translation. What was it someone had called the Americans and the Brits? Divided by a common language? It was that and more than that. She hadn't quite been able to shake off that slight feeling of the creeps she'd gotten when he'd told her he'd had a crush on her grandmother's portrait. They'd had a good time last night, especially after the third round of drinks, but any little spark she might have felt was long since gone.

She'd been glad when they parted with a wobbly kiss on the cheek. They'd parted friends, she was fairly sure. He'd reiterated his invitation to come stay at Rivesdale House. *And not because of the portrait,* he said, and she'd thanked him with an effusiveness born of booze.

Clemmie winced in the afternoon sunlight reflecting off Aunt Anna's blindingly white bookshelves. Tony must think she was slightly unstable.

She was slightly unstable. She felt off-balance, and not just because of the hangover. No law firm—no Granny Addie—all the familiar paving stones of Clemmie's life had been dug up and dumped away, leaving her on highly uncertain ground.

There were so many familiar family pictures on Aunt Anna's shelves, but Clemmie looked at them differently now, trying to figure out who was really related to whom, scrutinizing Uncle Teddy for any resemblance to Granny Addie. Clemmie had thought her mother looked like Granny Addie, but it must have been simply a trick of expression.

"Here you go." Aunt Anna came back into the room carrying two heavy ceramic mugs.

Clemmie turned away from the pictures. "Was Uncle Teddy Granny Addie's or Bea's?" she asked.

"Addie's," said Aunt Anna promptly. "He was the only one of us who was." Dropping gracefully onto the couch, Aunt Anna reached for a crumpled pack of Benson & Hedges. "God, I miss him. It's been almost thirty years now—can you believe it?"

"I remember his funeral," said Clemmie, and she did, vaguely. She remembered the hushed tones and the dark clothes and her mother's red eyes and feeling obscurely guilty for taking such pleasure in her new black velvet dress. "It was the first time I met Jon."

"Jon." Aunt Anna held up her orange plastic lighter. Her eyes took on a very particular gleam. "Speaking of Jon—"

"I gather Caitlin's back in town," said Clemmie quickly.

Frowning, Aunt Anna held the flame to her cigarette and breathed in, making the point glow red. "I hadn't heard anything about that."

"Well, anyway," Clemmie said quickly, before they could wander further down that alleyway, "what I really wanted to talk to you about was—"

"I know. Your grandmother." She didn't specify which one. Aunt Anna stretched out comfortably on the couch. She still, Clemmie noted, had amazing legs for a septuagenarian. "I'm glad you called me. I wanted to tell you years ago, you know."

"Thanks," said Clemmie, and sipped her coffee. It was one of the powdered, flavored varieties, thick and cloying. It made Clemmie's stomach churn. She set it aside.

"Your mother was against it. She didn't want to screw up your relationship with Addie." Anna's expression amply betrayed what she thought of that.

Clemmie sat on the edge of her chair. "I've seen the newspaper clippings," she said bluntly. "About Bea's death."

Aunt Anna's manicured eyebrows rose. "You have been a busy little bee, haven't you? You always did do your homework."

Clemmie wasn't in the mood to play games. "What happened?"

"That's the million-dollar question. Wouldn't we all like to know?" Aunt Anna flicked ash into a silver ashtray. "The short answer is that no one really knows. My mother, my father, and Addie went on safari. My mother didn't come back. You do the math."

"Couldn't it have been a horrible accident?" Clemmie wasn't sure why it mattered quite so much, but it did. A grieving widower remarrying was one thing. The other possibilities weren't to be contemplated. "The way Granny spoke about Bea—she sounded like she loved her."

"She might have," said Aunt Anna coolly. "Once. But she loved my father more."

There was no arguing with that. Granny Addie and Grandpa Frederick's love for each other had been legendary. Clemmie could remember them together when she was little, still entirely wound up in each other, finishing each other's sentences, leaning on each other for support—although it had always seemed that Grandpa Frederick leaned a little more. Which made sense. He had been older and frailer, already suffering from the first stages of the esophageal cancer that later killed him.

"Once she had him," said Aunt Anna, breaking into Clemmie's thoughts, "she would have done anything to keep him."

"Not murder," said Clemmie stubbornly. This was the woman who had bandaged her childhood cuts and supervised her homework. Addie might have lied to her, but Clemmie couldn't believe her capable of that. Not even for love, love with a capital L, the kind of love Clemmie sometimes doubted existed.

"No," agreed Aunt Anna, and there was a decidedly odd expression on her face. "Not murder."

Clemmie felt some of the tightness in her chest release.

Until Aunt Anna added, "I don't think my mother was dead. And I'm fairly sure Addie knew it."

"That's—" Clemmie choked on sickly sweet coffee, her eyes watering. "That's insane."

"Is it?" Aunt Anna sipped her coffee, smoke curling up from the cigarette balanced in the ashtray. "All they found was a scarf, a shoe, and a diamond clip. The party line was that my mother wandered away from camp and was eaten by animals. There were certainly plenty of people with a motive for murder—my father and Aunt Addie among them—but nothing was ever proved. One way or the other." She added, almost as an afterthought, "They never found the body."

Clemmie looked up sharply at her. "But she was declared dead. She would have to have been for—"

"For Addie to marry my father. Yes. They married two years later, as soon as my mother was declared legally dead. Legally dead and dead are two very different things."

"But wouldn't they have had to have proof—"

"What proof? All they needed to do was wait it out. There was never any proof. There was never any body." Anna leaned forward, her face intent. "I saw her. In Nairobi."

Aunt Anna rose from the couch, pacing restlessly across the room, years of pent-up energy, pent-up anger, in her stance.

"I was seven years old, and there she was, in the bazaar. I tried to find her, but Addie caught me and brought me back. They told me I was imagining things." After all these years, the hurt and rage still came through. "As if I would imagine that! They sent us off to school in England not long after that," she added bitterly. "Addie saw her, too. I'm sure of it."

Clemmie looked up at her, not sure where to even begin. "Wouldn't Addie"—she stumbled over the name, strange on her tongue without the usual honorific—"have said something? Done something?"

"And risk blowing everything? Are you kidding? With my mother out of the picture, she had it all—the farm, Farve. And then there was Teddy. If Mummy showed up out of the blue—" Aunt Anna gestured expressively. "Marriage might have been a loose concept in Kenya, but they still frowned on bigamy."

"Even though she—your mother—had been declared dead?"

"You're the lawyer," said Anna. "I don't know. But it would have been a legal mess and a huge scandal. Addie didn't like scandal."

That much was true. Granny Addie had been very much of the shovel-it-under-the-carpet variety. Clemmie's mother had inherited that in spades.

"But couldn't they have just gotten a divorce? Your mother and Grandpa Frederick, I mean?" Clemmie was floundering. "If they divorced and Granny Addie and Grandpa Frederick remarried—"

"There was still Teddy," said Aunt Anna. "Teddy would have been one or two at the time. The laws regarding legitimacy didn't change until 1976. Until then, even if the parents married each other after, the child was still legally a bastard." She spoke with the grim certainty of someone who had studied her subject. "So you see, Addie had a reason for making sure Bea stayed lost."

"But what about Bea?" Clemmie asked logically. "If she were alive, wouldn't she have tried to get back to you?"

"Unless Addie paid her off—or threatened her. Who knows? But I know my mother was there, in Nairobi, that day. I know she tried to come back to us."

Something about the way she said it sent a shiver down Clemmie's spine.

"I was too young, then, to do anything about it. My father and Addie had the final say." Aunt Anna stared out over Clemmie's shoulder, a million miles and sixty years away. "But I always knew my mother was out there, somewhere. I went looking for her, later."

Clemmie looked at her aunt. "Did you ever find her?"

"No." Aunt Anna ground her cigarette into the ashtray. "No."

TWENTY-SIX

New York, 1971

T hank you, you're very kind."

If one more person told her how sorry he was, Addie would scream. She would scream and scream until the china ornaments on the mantel shattered and the glass in the pictures cracked, until the windows dissolved into tiny pools of sand and salt and the wind howled through the open apertures from the park beyond.

Her son was dead. Her baby boy. How was that right or fair or just? It had been a heart attack, they said, on Metro-North. One moment he was sitting there, with his briefcase and his paper; the next he was flat out on the floor, gasping for help that didn't come, his own body turned against him.

Why Teddy? He was one of life's golden creatures, good-natured to a fault, open and kind. Admittedly, he had married a creature of quite staggering vapidity, but that wasn't the sort of mistake that killed; one didn't die of boredom or suffer heart attacks from it. He'd been a big, bluff, hearty man, Teddy, fond of his drink, but equally fond of the golf course and the tennis court. He should have outlived them all.

Who had ever heard of heart trouble in their family? Addie's was still going strong, for all that it felt like breaking. As for her own father and mother, they hadn't lived long enough to tell. It was staggering to think that they, forever old in her imagination, had been younger than Teddy when they died. It crawled over her like a creeping chill, the knowledge that she was older than her parents had ever been, older than her son would ever be, her son, her son, the only child of her body.

"At least you have something to remind you of him," said the particularly vapid wife of Addie's stockbroker, looking sentimentally at Teddy's children, arranged prettily around their mother, the girls in neat black dresses, Ed in a black suit that looked as though it pinched.

"Yes," said Addie. "They're a great comfort."

They reminded her of Teddy not at all. They were all Patty's. Addie had never liked Patty.

She liked her just as little now, although one would think they'd be linked in their common grief, if nothing else. But Patty's wailings had set Addie's teeth on edge, nothing about Teddy, about his loss to the world, but all her own woes; how was she to survive, how was she to live, now that Teddy had gone? Addie had patted Patty's hand mechanically, blotting out her selfish cries, the endless repetition of "me," "I," "me." Such a selfish kind of grief.

Addie's grief was selfish, too, she supposed. All grief was, in the end.

She grieved for all the things Teddy might have done and hadn't: the grandchildren he would never dandle, the tennis matches he would never play, the stars that would never shine for him again. She grieved for the children who had never been, the younger siblings Teddy had never known, two of them, one after the other, barely formed, not even recognizable as babies, too early for headstones, bundled out of the house and buried in the garden. Teddy had only been told that Mummy was sick; he'd sat on the edge of her bed and babbled at her in his own childish patois while she'd tried not to let him see how she was weeping, the tears seeping soundlessly down the side of her face.

After the last miscarriage, the doctors in Nairobi had told her she couldn't have other children. She'd told Frederick she didn't mind; three was more than enough for them, what with school fees and the like. They had their two girls and a boy; anything else would be sheer excess.

Their girls. They were always very careful to treat all the children equally.

At least, they tried. It wasn't an effort on Frederick's part; he loved them all equally, his children, although Addie had always suspected that he had a special place in his heart for Anna, his wild child.

Anna had come back from Hawaii for the funeral, bringing with her the latest husband, a playwright of some sort, with a bristly reddish brown mustache and a mustard-colored velvet blazer over wide-legged tweed pants. His skin was violently sunburned beneath the extraneous facial hair, a relic of their barefoot beach wedding.

On Anna, the sun didn't burn so much as kiss; she was a fashionable pale biscuit color, her hair strikingly blond against her tanned face. Her minidress wasn't at all the thing for a funeral, but at least she'd worn black. Addie had wondered if she would. Anna liked to provoke, sometimes just to provoke, but she had known better this time.

Addie's heart felt as though it would crack, as though everything in it would leak out through the broken shards until there was nothing more than a puddle on the hardwood floor, a puddle and a confusion of black clothes and Bea's diamond clip sparkling in the midst of it all.

Anna murmured something in the playwright's ear. In her ridiculously high shoes, she was tall enough that she had to lean to speak in his ear. She had Frederick's height, Anna—Frederick's and Bea's. Next to them, Addie had always felt like a charwoman who had strayed into Olympus. Even now, her stepdaughter could make her feel the same way.

They'd brought the playwright's son, nine and solemn, with a bowl haircut and a bow tie. Seeing him made Addie think painfully of Teddy at that age. Not that Teddy had ever been quiet or solemn; he had always been outgoing and assured. But, then, Teddy had had the advantage of two parents who openly adored him, sisters who cosseted him, not like this poor boy, dragged willy-nilly into an alien tribe, caressed and cooed at by a mother he had known for a month.

Anna stroked the boy's head in a careless caress. She played at mother the way small girls played house, dropping the doll as soon as a more entertaining toy came along. Addie would have thought that Anna, of all people, would have known better, would have remembered how much it hurt to be left behind.

Perhaps it might have been different if Anna had had one of her own; perhaps then her mothering instinct might have been more, well, steady. Addie wondered about that, from time to time.

At the time, it had seemed so simple.

Anna had come to her in confidence. The father was married, she said. One of her professors. She hadn't apologized, she'd simply stated the facts, and Addie had been reminded, again, of Bea, who was always most brazen when she knew herself most likely in the wrong. Anna wanted the child "taken care of" and she assumed that Addie, with her connections to natal hospitals, would be able to help—without telling Frederick.

She had arranged it all: the flight to Switzerland, the clinic. Frederick had thought Anna was skiing with friends. It had hurt Addie terribly, lying to him—he was her other half, a piece of herself—but Anna had been adamant; her father wasn't to know. If Addie wouldn't promise, Anna would take care of matters herself. So Addie had promised, telling herself that it was for the best, that it freed Addie to have the chances that Bea hadn't. Besides, there would always be more children, children with the right person.

But there had been no children after that. Anna had dropped out of art school and grad school and the curatorial training program at Sotheby's. She had flitted from career to career, setting herself up as an interior decorator one month, a fashion designer the next. Mostly, she did exactly what her mother had done. She married and married and married again.

Addie wondered how long this one would last. Anna had made short work of the first four. In the case of the last one, the divorce had taken longer than the actual marriage.

And then there was Marjorie, moving efficiently through the crowd with her tray of canapés, making sure glasses were placed on coasters and used napkins discarded. She was a fighter, Marjorie. Addie just wished she hadn't had to fight quite so much. She had wanted so much more for her, for both Bea's girls. At least Marjorie was back in New York now, not out in California with that dreadful Bill. And she had brought Clemmie with her.

Clemmie was holding out a tray of canapés, her mother's chosen delegate. "Would you like a cheese puff, Granny Addie?"

For a moment, Clemmie looked so like Bea that it staggered her, not Bea as she had been at the end, but Bea as she had first met her. They'd had velvet dresses like that for best, she and Bea, black velvet with a broad white lace collar and thick stockings underneath. Nanny had tied back their hair at the sides with broad velvet bows.

"Granny?" Clemmie said, and the accent was wrong, American, slightly nasal, not Bea's cut-glass tones, not Bea at all, but Clemmie.

"No, thank you, darling," Addie said. "Have you brought one to Grandpa?"

Clemmie dutifully trotted off, holding the tray very carefully, making sure the cheese puffs didn't skid. She took her duties as passer of hors d'oeuvres very seriously. She took everything seriously, not at all like Bea, who, even in her and Addie's childhood, had blazed through life with careless panache.

Addie watched as Clemmie held out the tray to Frederick, and the expression of love on his face made her heart twist. He bent, painfully, to take a cheese puff from the tray. He never could say no to any of the grandchildren.

He looked so old, her Frederick. Those lines, when had they had the time to etch themselves so deeply in his face? When had his back begun to stoop, his chin begun to sag? She hadn't noticed it until now, until Teddy's death took the certainty from Frederick's step and the smile from his face. It was like viewing a distorted mirror, on the one side the Frederick she remembered, forever twenty-one, a young man in evening togs holding out a mouse, on the other side this strange old man, twisted and gaunt, bent double with a hacking cough that wouldn't go away. She'd tried to get him to see a doctor, but he'd sworn it was nothing, it would clear up soon enough. Cough and cough and cough, all through the long, sleepless night.

Overnight, they were old, truly old. It boggled the mind to think that if Bea had lived, she would have been old now, too. Addie remembered how panicked Bea had been, at the ripe old age of twenty-eight, to be losing her bloom. Perhaps it was kinder that she hadn't lived, hadn't lived to see her skin sag under her chin, as Addie's did, hadn't lived to see her belly crease with babies who were never born, hadn't lived to see her children die before her, a pain almost beyond bearing.

Over the long, prosperous years, Addie had felt sorry for Bea, for all she had missed—sorry and a little bit afraid, as though, if she weren't careful, she might glance over her shoulder and find Bea following her, come to demand her forfeit, her price for all those years of happiness Addie had stolen from her, her husband, her children.

Was Teddy the price?

She was being absurd. It was only in Victorian fairy tales that one found such direct equivalencies, a child for a child, a loss for a loss. It did seem frighteningly neat, though; she had been so scared for Teddy's sake, all those years, chivvying her family from Nairobi to New York, always afraid for Teddy, for Teddy's place in the world. She had felt so guilty sometimes, so guilty for being grateful that her cousin was dead, her cousin whom she had once loved more than anyone else in the world; she had felt guilty for the thrill of panic she had felt when Anna called Bea's name in the Nairobi bazaar, for the late-night pacing and planning that followed. Addie had refused to entertain the very possibility; she had shut her eyes and her ears—for Teddy, for Teddy's sake.

But Teddy was gone.

She wondered what Bea would look like now, what sort of lines life might have driven into her face, lines from joys and griefs and everything in between. Would she have grown into herself eventually? Would she have quieted, in her older age, from that madcap thing she had become? Or would she have gone the route of so many of her friends, taking ever younger and younger lovers, her elegance a thing of paint and illusion, addicted to the drugs that had once been playthings?

It was nothing but speculation, of course. Bea had been gone forty-four years now: three years longer than Teddy had been alive.

But Addie couldn't stop remembering, after all these years, a child's cry in the Nairobi bazaar and a discarded shoe that ought to have been green instead of blue.

New York, 2000

Clemmie loitered outside the faculty offices in Fayerweather Hall, pretending interest in a bulletin board that advertised historical Pictionary for grad students, extra tutoring for undergrads, and ten bucks a pop for inclusion in someone's psych experiment.

In her heavy jeans and sweater she felt like she was unsuccessfully undercover. Male and female alike seemed to wear the same uniform of jeans and sweatshirt, women with their hair twisted into scrunchy buns, a handful of the men sporting the goatee du jour. A harried grad student, dressed all in black, coffee cup in one hand, armload of papers in the other, hurried along the hallway, miraculously managing to keep her coffee upright while juggling fifty-odd midterms.

The door in front of Clemmie was a careful inch ajar, just far enough that she could hear the murmur of voices, one young and very unhappy. The card on the door read: JONATHAN SCHWARTZ, and under it, in smaller letters, ASSISTANT PROFESSOR.

The door opened and an undergrad trudged out, L.L. Bean backpack hanging from one shoulder. She didn't look at Clemmie. Her stacked loafers scuffed against the floor of the hallway.

Clemmie waited until the undergrad was halfway down the hall and then knocked gently on the door.

"Come in," said Jon's voice, sounding very authoritative and un-Jon-like.

It wasn't a large office. What there was appeared to be composed entirely of books, books slapped onto shelves seemingly haphazardly, some with plastic bindings, others with the faded faux leather of earlier editions. Jon sat at a large desk in the middle of it all, papers scattered in front of him. With his glasses on, surrounded by the tools of his trade, he looked more like Indiana Jones than ever. Minus the hat and whip, of course.

"Come in and take a seat," he said in a monotone, making a final note in a ledger. He looked up and his whole expression changed. "Clemmie! Hey!" He looked pleased, she thought, pleased and a little bit wary. He jumped up and waved her in. "Is this about my grade on your midterm?"

Clemmie nudged a pile of books out of the way with her boot. "Is it midterm season already?"

"High midterm season." Jon moved around her to shut the door before hurrying to shovel off a chair for her. "They got their grades back this morning. Since then, I've been the subject of an inventive mix of threats and cajolery."

Standing in front of the desk, Clemmie pursed her lips. "Cajolery. Nice word. Any of it work?"

Jon forced a grin. "I was tempted by the bottle of wine, but figured that would count against me when it came to tenure decisions, so I told him to bring it to the department chair instead."

Clemmie idly turned over a paper on Jon's desk, a printout of a book review from a periodical called *Past & Present*. It looked more past than present. "What did you give the guy?"

"A B minus."

The Ivy League equivalent of an F. "Ouch."

"Trust me, it was deserved." Jon leaned across the desk, just a little too eagerly. "Please. Sit down. Can I get you anything? A soda, some coffee? The department machine ain't much, but it's vaguely potable."

"No, no, really, I'm fine. I pre-caffeinated. See? Full sentences."

Jon sank back down into his chair. "That one wasn't."

Clemmie made a face at him. "Picky, picky."

"Sit down at least. It's good to see you." There was a question tacked on, a question Clemmie wasn't sure how to answer. He quickly added, "What are you doing out in the middle of the day?"

"The official story is that I'm taking some vacation time." Clemmie dropped into the chair in front of his desk. It was vaguely eggshell shaped and made her recline farther than she would have liked. "The real story is that I didn't make partner."

"I'm sorry."

"Don't be." Clemmie squirmed upward, pushing against the pull of the chair. She planted her feet firmly on the floor. "I'm looking at some other options. One of our clients has already offered me a job in-house."

It had been PharmaNet, of all people, PharmaNet, who had complained about her to Paul. Not that Paul had needed much impetus to blackball her. He'd disliked her from day one. The PharmaNet people had told her they liked her spunk and they wanted her on board. It wasn't what she had planned, but she was intrigued, all the same. She could have a hand in shaping some of the policies that had bothered her; she would be on track for a general counsel job at a large corporation. Not to mention some other benefits of a slightly pettier nature.

"The plus side," said Clemmie, "is that I'd get to give orders to my old boss. Oh, and it's in London."

"Are you going to take it?"

Clemmie settled back in the eggshell chair. "I might. It's tempting." She'd already spoken to her new friend, Tony, about possibly spending a few days at Rivesdale House while looking for a flat. She wished she were more romantically interested in Tony. It would tie everything up so neatly. "I've never lived in London, or anyplace other than New York. The longest I ever stayed anywhere else was—"

"Rome," Jon filled in for her.

Their eyes met across the pile of papers.

"Mm-hmm," Clemmie said quickly. "And that was just one semester. Anyway, it's about time, don't you think?"

Jon's hand stilled on the handle of his coffee mug. His hazel eyes were steady on her face. "So is this a good-bye visit?"

"No! Nothing like that. Nothing's decided yet." Although PharmaNet was pressing her for an answer. "I had something else I wanted to talk to you about. Are you sure I'm not keeping you from your undergrads?"

"Quite sure." He leaned forward, pushing miscellaneous papers out of the way. "I had something I wanted to talk to you about, too. On New Year's Eve—I owe you an explanation—"

"No you don't." The chair creaked as Clemmie pushed it back. "Really, no explanations required. If you and Caitlin are back together, that's great."

"Together?" Jon rescued his coffee just in time to keep it from splashing onto someone's midterm. The cup had a faded history department logo on it, now severely coffee stained. "We're not back together. Caitlin just had a layover in New York. She needed someplace to stay. That's all."

It hadn't looked like that was all. "It doesn't matter," said Clemmie with forced cheer. "As long as you're happy—"

"We're not back together," Jon repeated more forcefully, then glanced guiltily over his shoulder. "She caught a plane to Paris the next day and that was that."

Clemmie knew she should change the subject, but she couldn't quite resist saying, "You looked pretty cozy."

"We were married for three years," said Jon. Looking down, he played with his cup, creating a pattern of overlapping coffee stains. "It had been a tough day. The idea of being with someone from a completely different part of my life was tempting—for about five minutes. It was just so easy. Until it wasn't. We're not right for each other and we never will be."

Clemmie hated herself for how happy that made her. "I thought you'd decided no one would ever be right for you. The whole too screwed up to love thing."

Jon winced. "It wasn't a good time. I— Let's just say seeing Caitlin helped clear some stuff up."

"Hmm." Clemmie decided to let it go for the moment. This wasn't the time or the place. She crossed one leg over the other, against the general will of the chair. "Anyhoo," she said, striving for cool, "I don't want to waste your time during midterm season. I really came here to ask you a favor."

Papers crunched under Jon's elbows. So that was why academics liked to wear leather patches on their sleeves. "What kind of favor?"

"A research favor." Clemmie took a deep breath. "I met up with Aunt Anna last week. She has a theory; that is, she thinks . . . that her mother— her real mother—didn't die in Kenya."

"Ah," said Jon.

"Ah?" She didn't like the sound of that "ah." "You know about this."

"I've heard her story," Jon said carefully. "The death that wasn't, all that sort of thing."

"You don't believe it."

"I don't have sufficient information to believe or disbelieve."

Clemmie rolled her eyes. "That's a cop-out." With more force than she'd intended, she said, "I can't believe that Grandpa Frederick murdered her. Or Granny Addie."

"No," said Jon, "neither can I. But"—she knew she wasn't going to like that "but"—"you can't rule out pure accident. They were on safari; it was dangerous. People died that way and the bodies were never found. People still die that way."

"But what if she didn't?"

"So what?" Jon lifted his glasses to rub his eyes. "Even if she were alive then, she'd be dead now. Long dead. She was older than your grandmother— than Addie, I mean. What does it matter whether she died then or later?" In a gentler voice he added, "You can't find a replacement for Addie that way."

"I'm not trying to find a replacement!" Catching herself, Clemmie eased back in her chair. "I just want to know what happened."

"I don't want to be a downer—" said Jon.

"A downer?"

"—but you might never know that." Jon ignored the slur on his undergrad slang. "The sources might not be there. Or even if they are, they might be open to multiple interpretations. The facts might lead in multiple, inconclusive directions. That's one of the downsides of professional history," he added. "Most of the time, there is no truth, only various levels of interpretation. Fact is a construct we provide to the public."

"Welcome to my life," said Clemmie. "What do you think I do every day? I weave fact into argument. There are two stories for every single set of facts. In this case, though, there's a simple answer. She died or she didn't. If she didn't, I want to know what happened."

Jon held her gaze. "Why?"

She knew what he was fishing for and he was wrong. She wasn't looking for a replacement for Granny Addie—well, not entirely. But this woman, this stranger, was a part of Clemmie somehow. She wanted to know what had happened to her. She wanted to know why her mother never spoke about her. She just wanted to know. And if it was as simple as it seemed, if she really had been eaten by a lion on safari, then that was that.

In some ways, that would be the easiest answer. It would mean that there had been no foul play and no betrayal, just the awkward circumstance of a woman marrying her cousin's bereaved husband. Was that what Clemmie wanted? Maybe. It would give her Granny Addie back, not as a blood relation, but as the person she'd known and perceived her to be, not the sort of person who would maintain a bigamous marriage or threaten away her stepdaughters' mother.

Clemmie couldn't explain it to Jon when she wasn't quite sure she understood it herself, so she just said, "Why does anyone try to solve unsolved mysteries? It's not like most people have any personal stake in the Princes in the Tower or the Lost Dauphin, but they worry about their fates anyway. For that matter, why do you do what you do? It's the same idea. You're solving puzzles, finding out what happened."

Jon glanced down at the muddle of papers and exams on his desk. "Right now, I'm grading a bunch of semi-illiterates." He looked up and a slow smile broke across his face. "Okay. I'm in. Why do I feel like we should pinky swear or something?"

Clemmie grinned at him, giddy with relief. It felt so good to be part of a team, to know she wasn't on her own. "Don't go all Hardy Boys on me."

The corners of Jon's eyes crinkled. "I always preferred Nancy Drew." Getting down to business, he said, "Anna inherited a bunch of papers from Addie. She hasn't touched them."

"Out of principle?" That was some serious grudge holding going on there.

"Something like that. I'll take a look through, and if there's nothing there I'll start working some other angles. I have a few ideas. In the meantime . . ." He paused, as though debating with himself.

"Yes?" Clemmie prompted.

Jon cocked his head. "Have you considered talking to your mother?"

TWENTY-SEVEN

New York, 2000

Clemmie picked up a bunch of flowers on the way over to see her mother. She wasn't sure what they were, but they were long stemmed, with delicate purple and white petals, and they created a nice weight on her arm, all wrapped up in a cone of stiffened paper with the petals poking out of the top. The air smelled of spring, cool and moist, warm enough to walk with her coat unbuttoned and her gloves in her pockets, even if there was still just enough of a nip to the air to remind her that there had been snowstorms in March before.

She felt strangely lighthearted and free, walking through the city with her coat open and the breeze blowing her hair into her eyes. Jon had called to tell her that he'd been through a pile of Granny Addie's papers and hadn't found anything yet, just ledgers from the early days of the coffee plantation and Anna's school reports. He was saving them, he said, to blackmail Anna at the next family dinner. The memory of the conversation made Clemmie smile.

It felt good having Jon back. Possibly too good.

Her mother's new apartment was just off 1st Avenue, in the lower 70s. Clemmie walked up along 1st, past delis and drugstores and boutiques with SALE signs in the windows. There were old redbrick houses and newer, post-war constructions, tall buildings with wide windows and balconies, their pale bricks blindingly white in the sunshine. Her mother's new building was one of those white-brick buildings, with a long awning that led down from the street into a busy lobby with a wide desk manned by no fewer than three doormen.

Clemmie was expected, they confirmed, and sent her up to 17C in a narrow elevator with mirrored walls that reflected her own red-nosed face back to her with unflattering accuracy. The walk had brought pink to her cheeks and turned her hair into something resembling a scrub brush.

"Clementine." Her mother greeted her with a press of the cheek.

Clemmie was struck, for the first time, by how much she had to lean down to embrace her. "Sorry, I'm all cold," she said. She brandished the flowers. "Oh, and these are for you."

"You didn't have to." Somehow, when her mother said that, it really sounded as though she shouldn't have.

"I know, but I wanted to." Clemmie followed her mother through a narrow entrance hall into the living room, making sure to scrape her shoes on the mat along the way. "It's finally starting to feel like spring."

"I'll put these in water and get the tea." Her mother disappeared into the galley kitchen, closed off in the middle, but with a door out to the living room on one side and a small, mirror-walled dining nook on the other.

"Can I help?" From her vantage point, Clemmie could just see a very shiny metal garbage can, the dishwasher, and white cabinets with silver handles, but she could hear the sound of china clattering and the click of her mother's electric kettle switching off. She must have put the water on as soon as the doormen had called up to say Clemmie was on her way. Clemmie was oddly touched by that.

Clatter, clank, swish. "No, just sit down."

Clemmie sat. The couch was white, made up of multiple sections, stretching around in an L shape. It wasn't at all what she would have expected of her mother, whose taste in interior decoration could best be described as *Masterpiece Theatre* meets Buckingham Palace, with lots of chintz and petit point and Dresden miniatures.

There wasn't a Dresden shepherdess in sight. Instead, everything was light and modern and surprisingly functional, a white couch, a glass coffee table, a pale blue carpet, and abstract seascapes—Clemmie thought they were seascapes—on the walls. There were sliding doors off the far end of the living room onto a minuscule balcony furnished with a metal table and chairs. The entire effect was light and airy and uncluttered.

Her mother came out with an entire tea ensemble on a lacquered tray, china pot and teacups, silver strainer, cookies on a plate, and tiny napkins folded into triangles.

"The new place looks great," Clemmie offered.

Her mother set down the tray on the glass coffee table. "It's rather nice finally having a place of one's own," she said, surveying her domain with something like satisfaction. "I'd never bought my own furniture before."

"Not even with Dad?" The words were out before Clemmie had a chance to rethink them. Her father was generally a verboten topic. But that was what this was about, wasn't it? Getting rid of those old taboos.

Instead of shooting her down, her mother simply said, "Your father had very firm tastes. And with two young boys, there really wasn't much I could do other than try to make sure there wasn't anything too breakable."

Her mother began setting out the tea things, turning the cups right side up on their saucers, lifting the lid to check the progress of the tea in the pot. She wasn't wearing her wedding ring. There was still a pale mark where the ring had been. Curiouser and curiouser. Clearly, more than interior decoration had been going on in the past few months.

"I owe you an apology," Clemmie's mother said. Clemmie gaped at her as she set a silver strainer over the cup nearer to Clemmie. "I should have told you about your grandmother before. That was wrong of me."

Clemmie blinked at the patch of sunshine on the carpet. The world really had turned upside down. She'd thought she was going to have to drag the conversation to Granny.

"Thanks," she said in surprise. "That's what I wanted to talk to you about—I mean part of what I wanted to talk to you about," she added quickly, before she could open herself up to charges of bad daughter–dom. "I've been trying to put the pieces together, about Granny Addie and your mother."

"There aren't that many pieces," said her mother in her usual brisk way. "Tea?"

"Yes, please." Clemmie watched as the steaming liquid poured out of the pot, brewed rich and dark. That was the one familiar item in her mother's new world, Granny Addie's teapot. It was French, Limoges, with gold edging and tiny blue and purple flowers. She had seen Granny Addie pouring tea from that pot a thousand times in the dining room back at 85th and 5th.

Her mother moved the strainer from Clemmie's cup to her own. "I'm sure Anna's told you her own version."

"Yes," said Clemmie. There was no point in trying to hide it. Aunt Anna must have told Clemmie's mother that they'd met. Mother's relationship with Aunt Anna had always baffled Clemmie. They couldn't stand each other, but they spoke weekly. "She thinks Granny Addie kept your mother away. Or something like that."

Her mother shook her head. "Poor Anna," she said, surprisingly. "She hurts herself so. The truth is that our mother left us."

Clemmie looked up sharply from her tea. "You mean—"

"No, not like that. At least, not that I know. Like Anna, I've always wondered." She tipped some milk into her tea. On the milk before versus milk after debate, Clemmie's mother felt very strongly about milk after. "What I meant was that she'd left us long before. If it hadn't been that accident on safari, she would have run off with someone, probably within the year. I was old enough to see it all. People do tend to talk in front of children."

"You didn't," pointed out Clemmie. Her parents' divorce had come out of the blue. One moment they were living with Dad outside L.A.; the next they were packing up her mother's old car and driving cross-country and Clemmie wasn't supposed to talk about Daddy or ask about Daddy. What she knew she had picked up later on, piece by piece, eavesdropping on adult conversations she wasn't meant to overhear.

Her mother sighed. "I wanted to protect you from it. We conducted our fights behind closed doors, after you were asleep. My parents—" She took a neat sip of tea and set the cup firmly back on the saucer. "They did not conduct their fights privately."

"You mean your real parents," Clemmie clarified. Granny Addie and Grandpa Frederick had "discussions" that occasionally verged on the snippy, but Clemmie couldn't remember either of them ever raising their voices. They weren't the fighting kind.

Her mother nodded. "My mother hated the farm. She missed London. She had been a debutante—which meant a very different thing then than it does now. She'd had a title, servants, her picture constantly in the papers. She went from that to being mewed up with two children in a remote farm in a remote country with a husband who was more interested in agriculture than in her. That's how she saw it." She took another sip of tea, cup perfectly balanced, back perfectly straight. "I don't think she liked any of us very much."

Ouch. Clemmie didn't know how to respond to that. She resisted the urge to ask whether her mother had liked her own children; that wasn't the point. Clemmie thought her mother liked her. Most of the time.

"But particularly me," her mother said, adding delicately, "I was the reason they had to marry."

It took Clemmie a moment for the meaning to click. "Oh. You mean—"

Her mother nodded. "I remember my mother throwing that up to my father. She accused him of ruining her life." Her lips twisted. "He held his own, though. He called her all sorts of things, horrible things. It wasn't the sort of thing a child should hear."

They sat in silence for a moment, steam curling from the teacups, cookies sitting forgotten on their plate.

"You never told me any of this," said Clemmie, feeling a bit lost. She'd never thought of her mother as a child, other than the obvious, the stories about the farm and the pet dik-dik, a sort of *Leave It to Beaver* meets *Out of Africa*. She'd never thought of her mother as an accidental child, unwanted.

The way Clemmie had been. Not that her mother had ever made her feel unwanted, but, as her mother had said, children knew. Sometimes, Clemmie wondered whether her parents would still have been married if she hadn't intruded, a noisy intrusion into their otherwise empty nest.

Of course, there had also been Jennifer-the-Journalist, so maybe it wasn't all Clemmie.

"Why would I?" Her mother reached for a Petit Ecolier, dark chocolate over a butter biscuit. "It was all so long ago. There was no need. Not to mention," she added, "that I was far more concerned about you and keeping a roof over your head."

The classic maternal one-two punch. "Fair point," Clemmie muttered.

"I know that Anna thinks that Addie ruined everything and broke up our happy home, but it was really quite the opposite. We didn't have much of a home until Addie came."

Clemmie watched her mother munching her biscuit and blurted out, "Do you think she was still alive? Your mother?"

Her mother set down the decapitated Ecolier. "If she was," she said, her voice like steel, "then staying away was the kindest thing she ever did for us."

All righty, then. "Wow," said Clemmie.

Her mother gave her a patient look. "I'm not saying your grandmother—your adopted grandmother—was a saint. She wasn't. She could be stubborn and overbearing and meddlesome. But she did what she did out of love." She looked pointedly at Clemmie. "I just want you to remember that when you tell your daughter about me. Intentions matter."

"If I have a daughter," Clemmie murmured.

Her mother was silent for a moment. "I was so concerned about your marrying too young. It never occurred to me that—" She broke off. "I didn't want you to make the same mistakes I made." She looked up at Clemmie. "Your Granny Addie tried to stop me marrying your father, you know. She was furious about it. We didn't speak for years."

Clemmie hadn't known that either. "Do you wish you'd listened?" she asked tentatively.

Her mother folded her napkin and set it back on the tray. "You can't look at it that way. If I had it to do over—no, your father wasn't the man for me. I was too young. It was a bad idea, all around. But if I hadn't married him, I wouldn't have you or your brothers. You can't take the one without the other."

She rose to her feet. The interview was clearly over.

Clemmie stood, too. "Can I help you clean up?"

"No, that's all right. Leave it." She glanced at her watch. "I have an engagement this evening. I should get dressed."

"An engagement?" There was something about the way she said it that gave Clemmie pause. "You mean a date?"

"Clementine!" Ah, the joy of an older-generation parent. Her mother had never submitted to the kind of familiarity her friends' Baby Boomer parents encouraged. Pert, she called it. This time, though, she surprised Clemmie by saying, "Yes, actually."

"Seriously? I mean, that's great. Really. Who is it?"

Was her mother blushing? No, it had to be just a trick of the light. Her mother busied herself collecting teacups. "Just a gentleman I met at the Mostly Mozart series. You really should join us one of these days. The music is excellent."

Clemmie shrugged into her coat, grappling with the bizarre image of her mother picking up men at Lincoln Center. "Sounds like it."

Her mother gave her a look. Someone was being pert.

Her mother's face cleared. "I nearly forgot. Your grandmother wanted you to have these."

"Have what?"

Clemmie trailed along after her mother into the hallway as her mother disappeared into the bedroom.

"These." She came out holding three framed prints piled on top of one another. They were the pictures that used to hang in Granny Addie's bedroom. "You'll need a bag. . . ."

Clemmie slid her arms under the stack, grappling for a good angle. "That's all right. I'll just take a cab." She leaned over to kiss her mother's cheek, accidentally bumping the wall with one of the frames. "This was really . . . nice."

Her mother pressed her cheek to Clemmie's. "Don't stay away so long."

Clemmie hitched the pile of pictures against her hip. "I won't."

Her mother frowned at the unwieldy stack of pictures. "It would only take a moment to wrap those up properly. Are you sure you don't—"

That was the parent she knew. "No, I'll manage. Don't fuss." She waited until the door was almost closed before adding, "Have fun tonight!"

She could have sworn she heard a "Clementine!"

Her mother dating. Good for her. The divorce had been final nearly thirty years ago now. That was a long time to wait. Unless, of course, there had been other people in the interim. There might have been. Clemmie hoped there had been. But she rather suspected otherwise. The wedding ring had never come off before. The new man seemed to go with the new apartment and the new, sleeker haircut.

The top picture slipped and Clemmie grabbed for it, staggering to keep from dropping the whole pile. Damn, damn, damn. Her mother had been right. Clemmie inelegantly braced the stack against the wall, trying to wedge them between the wall and her body. There were three, and her mother had turned them so that the ones on the top and the bottom were glass side in, less likely to break that way. Clemmie jabbed at the elevator call button, trying not to lose her grip on the pictures.

The backing was tearing off the one on the top. It was nothing expensive, just plain black matting, graying with age and beginning to peel. Beneath it, she could see the shiny back of the picture, photo paper with something written on it in a narrow, spidery hand.

The elevator pinged open. Clemmie ignored it. Carefully, as carefully as she could, she set the pile of pictures down on the ground. Kneeling down beside them, she peeled back the black paper.

DOVE MOUNTAIN, it read. And under that, 1976.

It was the same handwriting she had seen on the photos in Granny Addie's bedroom.

Arizona, 1972

"Where are you from?" The cabdriver had been trying to strike up a conversation with her since Tucson.

"New York," said Addie, watching out the window as the familiar urban sprawl gave way to a landscape of the sort she had never seen before, red mountains, stark and imposing, presiding over long stretches dotted by scrub and brush.

"You don't sound like you're from New York."

Addie smiled politely into the rearview mirror and returned to her window, hoping that would effectively repress further conversation.

This was one of those times when she wished she were capable of driving herself. She had never learned to drive, not properly. Living in New York, she hadn't needed to. Usually, when she needed to be driven somewhere, Marjorie took her. After all those years in California, Marjorie was entirely proficient behind the wheel.

But she couldn't ask Marjorie to drive her this time. Not where she was going.

"It's a long way from New York," the cabdriver tried again.

Poor man. It wasn't his fault that she wanted to be left alone with her thoughts, wanted time to compose herself, as if the eight hours on an airplane and the night in a Tucson hotel room hadn't been time enough.

"Yes," said Addie. "Yes, it is."

Sunlight beat down on the cab, through the windows, making her skin prickle. Even with the air-conditioning on, wheezing away in the front, she could feel the heat.

She had dressed carefully for the occasion, in a lemon-yellow sheath with matching shoes and hat. The skirt was already crumpled from sitting on it, her jacket sweat stained, her gloves grubby. The yellow leather pumps had given her a blister.

Dimly, she remembered feeling like this before, on a train from Mombasa, with the red dust of Kenya staining her suit and sweat beading beneath the band of her cloche hat. She had been so young then, in retrospect, so young and untried. For a moment, the jolting of the cab became the jolting of the train and she was twenty-six again, in a pearl-colored suit, on her way to see Frederick.

Frederick . . .

"Are you visiting family?" The cabdriver's voice startled her back into the present.

Had she been dozing? She wasn't old enough to drop off like that; she was only seventy-two, hardly at the dozy, rocking-chair stage.

Addie pulled herself together. "How much farther is it?"

The red roads went on and on and on.

The people at the hotel had told her it should take about an hour. Not much traffic out that way, they had said, and Addie had wondered what they had meant by that. Now she thought she understood better. There was not much of anything out here, traffic or otherwise, just endless brush and scrub and the red, red mountains that towered over it all.

The cabdriver consulted his map, spread out on the passenger seat. "We should be there any moment now. You've never been here before?"

"No," Addie said, and left it at that, repressing the urge to babble nervously, to say that this was her first trip to Arizona, to make idiotic observations about the cacti. "It's certainly an impressive landscape."

"Hot, too," said the cabdriver, and grinned at her in the rearview mirror. He jerked a thumb towards the window. "That'll be the house, down there."

"That one?" It was a silly question. There was only the one, although she had to strain to see it. It had been cunningly constructed to blend into the landscape, built of a reddish brown clay of some kind that mimicked the color of the ground. It was a long, low, rambling house, built all on one level, sprawling out in either direction, in the shadow of the cactus-studded hills. As they drove along the winding drive, Addie spotted a paddock with two horses in it, one brown, the other piebald, swishing their tails as they browsed idly among the brown grasses. There were outbuildings, too: a barn, a garage, a series of miscellaneous sheds. She caught a glimpse of the artificially blue water of a swimming pool.

The driveway brought them to a stone path, which crept its way along between round agave plants to the front door of the house.

The driver pulled the cab to a stop and killed the engine. "Do you want me to wait for you?" he asked.

She couldn't blame him for sounding so doubtful; the house had an abandoned, Sleeping Beauty air to it, dozing in the sunshine. But there must be someone here, someone who fed the horses and kept the pool so sparkling and clear.

Someone. Not necessarily the someone she was seeking.

"Would you?" Now that she was out here, the whole project seemed absurd, foolish. She had fought the urge last night, in her wide hotel bed in Tucson, to turn around and go home. Now she wished she had. What if it was the wrong person? What if there was no one there?

Even worse, what if there was?

Addie pulled her gloves back on, snapped her purse shut, and waited as the driver came around to open her door. "I won't be long," she said crisply.

The heat slammed into her as she emerged from the comparative cool of the car. How did people live here? The plants around the house were all variants on the desert theme, spiky agave, cacti shaped like barrels with odd yellow flowers sticking up on top, the ocotillo with its spindly limbs, covered in thorns like something out of a fairy story. The stones of the path bit into her feet through her thin-soled shoes and the sun stung her eyes. She should have thought to bring sunglasses or a hat with something more of a brim.

There were stained-glass inserts on either side of the door, bold, primary colors in an abstract pattern. Addie pressed the bell. She could hear it chiming inside, and the slap of flat-soled shoes against a hard-tiled hall.

There was a sound of a latch being drawn, and the door opened. "Yes?"

There was a woman standing in the doorway, dressed in white linen slacks and an open-collared blouse. Her hair was silver, coiffed close to her face, highlighting the elegance of bones laid bare by age. She wore large earrings, big chunks of raw turquoise framed in silver, and a necklace of the same, filling in the open collar of her shirt.

It was like looking at an old picture, a picture faded with time, crumpled and smoothed out again, cracked and lined but still unmistakably the same image.

"Hello, Bea," said Addie.

TWENTY-EIGHT

New York, 2000

Clemmie wasn't quite sure how she got home, but it involved a cab.

Somehow, she got herself into and out of it without incident, although she wasn't sure whether the bill she'd handed over for the fare was a ten or a twenty. She had other things on her mind. She kept peeling back that little flap of paper, reading again, DOVE MOUNTAIN, 1976.

Dove Mountain. Arizona? It looked like Arizona, all reds and browns and cacti. She'd gone to Arizona to take a deposition once, on a case of alleged securities fraud. The landscape through her cab window had looked like that, like something out of an old Western movie, just one step removed from the OK Corral.

She waited until she got home to inspect the other pictures, spreading them out on her kitchen table. She had never looked at the pictures very closely before. She had assumed, if she had thought about them at all, that they were prints. They looked like it, the sort of glossy art shots decorators used to brighten up a wall. One featured a jagged mountainside, with cacti sticking out along the sides. Another showed a sprawling house, circled by those mountains, with a blue, blue sky above. The last was a cactus close-up.

She peeled off the backing on each but found only the same thing: DOVE MOUNTAIN, 1976.

There were no names this time. Well, that made sense. There were no people in the photos. She didn't need names. She knew that handwriting.

The phone rang. Clemmie let it go to the answering machine. 1976. She had been eleven. There was no second-guessing the dating; the style of the photo and the colors used all looked 1970s, certainly not much earlier than that. It would take an expert to determine that for sure.

"Clemmie?" Jon's voice came through the answering machine. "Clemmie, are you there? Pick up."

She pushed aside the picture and grabbed for the phone. "Jon?"

"Guess what?" His voice was taut with excitement. "I can't believe it, but—I think I've found her. I found Bea."

Clemmie glanced down at the pictures on the table. DOVE MOUNTAIN, 1976. "So have I."

Jon arrived thirty minutes later, bearing a large file folder.

"That was speedy!"

"Well, you know, the subway . . ." He looked as though he had run the rest of the way from the subway. His hair was tousled and his cheeks were flushed. There was something rather endearingly boyish about it.

Clemmie stood aside to let him in. "Deep breaths," she said, following her own advice. "Here, give me your coat."

"Thanks." Jon relinquished his jacket but not the folder. Underneath, he wore a button-down shirt that clung damply to his chest. Heat rolled off him in waves. "It's very . . . cozy."

Clemmie released the door, which swung shut a little too emphatically. She winced at the sound of metal hitting wood. "It's a place to sleep."

"Hmm," said Jon, his eyes taking in the sleeping alcove, the tangle of sheets on the unmade bed, the silk pajama top in a crumpled heap on the floor. There was something sybaritic about that unmade bed, dappled with late afternoon sunlight, rumpled sheets spilling over onto the floor.

Maybe having Jon over hadn't been the best idea after all. They should have met in a coffee shop, in a bar, someplace safe and neutral. She was still wearing the wrap dress she had worn for tea with her mother. It felt absurdly dressy for her cluttered and dusty apartment.

"I'll be moving to London in a month anyway," Clemmie said, dumping Jon's coat over the back of a chair. "You know. That job I told you about. PharmaNet."

Jon set his file folder down on her messy kitchen table, his eyes intent on her face. "So you're really going."

Clemmie nodded. "They want me to start on April 1. It's a good offer. Lots of responsibility, benefits, the works."

"In London," said Jon.

"Why not?" said Clemmie flippantly. "There's not much to hold me here in New York right now. No more CPM, no more Granny Addie—and can you believe my mother seems to be dating?"

He didn't return her smile. He didn't match her light tone. Instead, he braced both hands on her kitchen chair, and said, in a voice that sounded like it had been scratched from the very bottom of his throat, "Don't go."

Clemmie could feel her body go into fight-or-flight mode, every nerve on edge. She tried to keep her voice light. "Can you give me a good reason to stay?"

"Stay for me," Jon said.

She stared at him, her hands closing convulsively on the edge of the table.

Jon smiled a crooked smile. "It sounds impossibly arrogant, doesn't it? Don't stay for me. Stay for this." He reached for her, and somehow, it seemed like the most natural thing in the world to go to him. He bent his head so she could feel the whisper of his words tickling her cheek, brushing against her lips. "Stay for us."

Outside, the cab horns and the piano scales faded into nothing as he kissed her, kissed her as though they were making up for the past fifteen years, for all the kisses they hadn't had. Clemmie could feel the linen of his shirt crisp beneath her fingers, the small hairs on the back of his neck, the brush of the stubble on his chin against her cheek. It was, she reflected hazily, the first time they had kissed while sober. No excuses, no plausible deniability, no numbing alcoholic blur, even if her head was spinning as though she'd been tossing back tequila shots.

But she'd felt like this before, hadn't she? In Rome. When she'd thought it would be all champagne and roses and happily ever after for them.

She said, breathlessly, "What us? There hasn't been an us."

Jon leaned his forehead against hers. She could feel his heart beating, his breath against her cheek. "Hasn't there?" he said quietly. "Or are you going to tell me it was all on my side?"

"Don't be an idiot!" said Clemmie unthinkingly, and watched as his face lit. "That is—what I mean is—oh, hell."

"I know," he said, locking his hands around her waist, his lips against her ear. She could hear the amusement in his voice. "I know. We've both been idiots. We could have a contest for which of us was more idiotic. But don't you think it's time to wise up?"

Wise had nothing to do with it. Clemmie did her best to gather her scattered wits together. She pulled back just enough to see his face.

"About that . . ." Clemmie took a long, deep breath. "I know this is a weird time for you. Are you sure you're not—I mean, that I'm not— Crap."

"Do you really think you're a rebound? If anyone was the rebound, it was poor Caitlin." Jon leaned forward, framing her face in his hands. "It's always been you. You're the pot to my kettle."

"Wow," said Clemmie, with something that was almost a laugh, "you say the most romantic things."

"Would you prefer I say that you're as much a part of me as breathing? That I can't imagine a world without you in it? That no matter what, no matter where I've been, all roads lead back to you?" There was no mockery in his voice. For once, he was dead serious. He was stripped bare, without mask or pretense. "I guess what I'm trying to say is that I love you. I have loved you. I will love you."

His honesty humbled her. Clemmie rested her forehead against his. "Our timing sucks."

It was an admission, and he knew it.

Jon slipped his fingers beneath her chin, tilting her face up to his. "I think timing is what you make of it. If it's meant to work, it will. Look at your grandmother."

Clemmie made a face. "Which one?"

Jon laughed. "Either—but I was thinking of Addie. That was the best marriage I've ever seen, however it started."

Everyone always talked about how things started. There were all those cute "how we met" stories, like Granny Addie and her mouse. But what if it wasn't the starting that counted? What if it was the things that happened in the middle? It made a less tidy story that way, but possibly a happier one.

"They got their second chance," Clemmie said slowly.

"And they made the most of it," said Jon. "Why shouldn't we?"

Because she was afraid. That was what it boiled down to in the end. She was afraid of being hurt, afraid of losing the dream of what they might be for the reality of it.

Clemmie twisted away, fiddling with the sash of her dress. She moved around the side of the table, putting a safe length of faux wood veneer between them. "Speaking of which . . . didn't you have something to show me?"

For a moment, he looked as though he might push the point, but he didn't. He knew her that well.

"Yes," he said instead. "Take a look at this. It's a private investigator's report. About Bea. I found it in the papers she left to Anna." He busied himself with the file folder, turning it so she could see better, including the letterhead on the top of the first page. *Dear Mrs. Desborough,* the letter began. *Pursuant to your inquiry . . .*

Clemmie felt a little shiver go down her spine. She'd known when she saw the writing on the pictures, but, somehow, this was more real. There it all was, in hard black and white, facts, dates, details. "Granny Addie hired him?"

Jon nodded, leafing through the pages. "Right after your grandfather died." He looked up at her, and there was a depth of concern in his expression that made Clemmie's chest tight. "Are you sure you want to hear this?"

"I already know." Clemmie took a shaky breath. "Bea was still alive in 1972 and living in Arizona, in a place called Dove Mountain."

Jon's eyebrows hit his hairline. "Want to loan me that crystal ball? I could make a fortune on the lottery."

"It's not a crystal ball." Fetching a picture at random, Clemmie handed it over to Jon. Her hand tingled where it brushed his in passing. "This was one of the pictures from Granny Addie's bedroom. Look at the back."

"'Dove Mountain, 1976,'" he read. "But how did you know—"

"The handwriting," said Clemmie. "I'd seen it before on a bunch of Bea's old pictures. It's a little shakier here, but still pretty much the same."

Jon regarded her with frank admiration. "Points to you. That's some good sleuthing."

"Not such good sleuthing," said Clemmie. "The batting on the back was ripped. It practically jumped out at me."

Jon fingered the tear on the back of the frame. "This doesn't look torn," he said. "This looks cut."

"Now who sounds all Nancy Drew?" Clemmie mocked before the meaning of what he was saying hit her. "Jon—do you think—Mom told me she left them to me. Specially."

Jon lifted the file in his lap. "She made sure this was left to Anna."

Their eyes met over the sheaf of papers. "I don't know if that counts as amends or a taunt," said Clemmie. "To know that she'd known all that time and never told her. . . ."

"We don't know that that was Addie's choice," Jon pointed out. "Bea might have had some say in it as well. She'd made herself into a completely different person by then—in every possible way. She might have had some trouble explaining away a prior family to her new family."

"Okay, so who was she?" Clemmie wasn't sure if she was asking the right question. It was more a matter of what was she, this woman who was part of her, but not.

Jon consulted his papers. "In 1972, Beatrice Desborough was living under the name Eliza Goldsmith. She was a Canadian citizen married to an American named Carl Goldsmith. They were married in 1946."

The facts sounded so spare put like that, just names and dates. "Was there anything about how she got there?"

"Not much," said Jon. "She did have a war record—she flew for the Royal Canadian Airforce Women's Division in World War II. But that's it. Nothing about how she got from Kenya to Canada."

And nothing about how she felt about it, nothing about what drove a woman to pick up and leave her husband and children behind. "Did she ever have other children?"

Jon shook his head. "No. Just stepchildren."

Something in the way he said it touched a nerve. "Hey." Clemmie touched his hand. "Jon—"

"There's more," he said quickly. "Check this out."

Drawing his hand away, he extracted a photograph from between the pages of the report. It was a normal three-and-a-half-by-five print, a snapshot, taken on an inexpensive camera. The photo hadn't aged well. It had been overexposed, making the whole strangely orange tinted, the people indistinct. But she could still make out the scene. It was a poolside, with two women on lounges, one wearing a sort of caftan and a floppy hat, the other in a bathing suit with a little skirt on it. There was a small table between them with drinks and books.

Clemmie flipped it over. There were no names, just DOVE MOUNTAIN, 1974.

The prints on the wall had been labeled 1976. "Granny used to go to a spa in Arizona every year."

"Mm-hmm," said Jon. "I think you found her spa."

Clemmie looked at the picture, at the two women lying so companionably on their lounges in the Arizona sun. Bea's floppy hat hid her face. Granny Addie's was obscured by the shadow of the beach umbrella. There was nothing to say how they'd felt, what they were thinking. But Clemmie thought, if she squinted hard enough, that the two women were smiling.

Year after year Granny Addie had gone off to Arizona in February, on the anniversary of Grandpa Frederick's death. It was her alone time. Better than Florida, she had joked.

The trips had stopped while Clemmie was in college—possibly right around the time she was throwing up on Jon's shoes in Rome. She hadn't thought anything of it. Granny Addie was in her mid-eighties by then, and long plane trips weren't a good idea. Besides, Clemmie had had other things on her mind. Midterms and job interviews and Jon.

Clemmie held up the photo, tilting it to try to get a better view. "All those years and she never told."

"It would have been pretty awkward. She'd have to explain why you had an extra grandmother."

"And Aunt Anna would have gone ballistic." Clemmie wished she could see Bea better. That hat was maddening. "She was so convinced that Granny Addie was deliberately keeping her mother from her."

"Well, now we know," said Jon practically. "She didn't know until 1972."

The two women looked so happy together on their lounge chairs. *Bea* . . .

Granny had said. Clemmie remembered the way Granny had spoken of Bea as a child, with so much love. "I'm glad they found each other again."

She heard the slide of papers as Jon pushed the folder back on the table, felt the warmth of Jon's hand against the small of her back, ready to hold her up if she needed it. "You okay?"

Clemmie looked at the taller woman, the one in the caftan and floppy hat. Her grandmother. Beatrice Gillecote Rivesdale Desborough Goldsmith. This was the face she might see in the mirror in forty-odd years. And she felt no connection to her at all. Just idle curiosity.

She looked up at Jon. "It just—I don't know. It doesn't seem to matter anymore. I'd thought I'd feel something else—I should be feeling hurt that she left or that she was alive and never came back—but it's just not there. It's like she's a character out of a novel."

"Her life certainly reads like one," said Jon. "And we'll never know all of it."

At the poolside, the two women looked like one of those comical post-cards, the ones with conversation bubbles, two elderly ladies taking the sun. "They really lived, didn't they?" said Clemmie. "Not just Bea, both of them."

"Those were dramatic times," said Jon. "The twilight of the aristocracy, two world wars—we're kind of tame in comparison."

"More than kind of tame." Clemmie looked around the apartment that she had never liked. It was so small. Not just small in space, but in scope. The books on the shelves were books she'd read in college, nothing more recent. There were no recent photos, no albums, no souvenirs. It was the sterile record of a life lived in a cocoon. These women, in their crazy bathing outfits, had experienced so much more in their lives than she ever would. They'd traveled the world, swapped husbands, flown planes, run companies.

Clemmie looked at Jon's familiar face, at the streaks of gray in his brown hair, at the laugh lines around his eyes. "I'm tired of playing it safe," she said.

Those laugh lines deepened as he took both her hands in his. "Would you like to start a farm in Kenya?"

"I think a new job in a new country should do it," Clemmie said, choosing her words very carefully. She squeezed Jon's hands, hard. "I think we both need some time. Just a little bit. You still have a divorce to finalize. And papers to grade. And I—I need prove I can stand on my own for bit."

"A bit?" said Jon, but she knew that what he was asking was something else entirely.

Clemmie braced herself. "I love you. I do." Amazing how difficult it was to throw the caution of years aside and say the words, even now. Getting them out there made her feel slightly giddy, as if a large weight had lifted. "I love you. And I don't doubt that we're—"

"Soul mates?" suggested Jon, cocking one brow. "Destined?"

"Something like that." Why was it that the most important things always sounded the most cheesy? "But if we're going to do this, let's do it right this time, nothing rushed, nothing hurried. No mixed messages, no miscommunication."

Jon studied her face for a long, long time. "All right," he said, and Clemmie thought how much she liked that about him, his innate sense of fairness, his ability to see a story from all sides. "Fair enough. I take a lot of research trips to London."

Clemmie felt her heart lift. "And PharmaNet has a New York office. I'm pretty sure I can find a lot of excuses to come back here. I'll need someplace to stay, though, since I'm giving up my apartment."

Jon gave the matter deep thought. "There's a fairly reasonably priced hostel on 111th Street, if you're interested." He gave her a look that could only be termed smoldering. "You may have to share a bed though."

Clemmie's body tingled. "I think—I think I can manage the hardship."

"Oh, yeah?" Jon drew her to him for a long, thorough kiss. "And when the time is up?"

Clemmie grinned at him. "I'll meet you in Rome."

The New York Times, March 25, 2001

WEDDINGS

Clementine Evans, Jonathan Schwartz

Clementine Evans was married Saturday evening to Jonathan Schwartz at the Metropolitan Club in New York. The bride's stepfather, the Honorable Carl Sandberg, a District Judge for the Southern District of New York, officiated at the ceremony.

The bride, 35, is a director in the legal department of the New York office of PharmaNet, the London-based pharmaceuticals firm. She graduated from Harvard cum laude and received a J.D. magna cum laude from Columbia Law School. The bride's father, William Evans, retired after a career in real estate development. The bride's mother, Marjorie Desborough Evans Sandberg, is a docent at the Metropolitan Museum of Art.

The bridegroom, 38, is an associate professor in the History Department at Columbia University. He is also the author of *Decline and Fall? The Twilight of the English Aristocracy in the Aftermath of the Great War*. He graduated from Yale magna cum laude and received a Ph.D. from Stanford University. The groom's father, the late Leonard Schwartz, was one of America's foremost playwrights of the 1960s and '70s.

The couple intends to honeymoon in Kenya.

ACKNOWLEDGMENTS

This is my tenth book, but, in many ways, it felt like my first: both exhilarating and terrifying. I owe a huge debt of gratitude to Jennifer Weis for traveling with Addie from the initial train ride to Nairobi all the way through several sets of revisions; to Mollie Traver and the rest of the team at St. Martin's for shepherding the manuscript from idea to book; and to my agent, Joe Veltre, for waving the pom-poms and urging me on when I broached the notion of leaving my Napoleonic spies for a new century and a new continent.

This book wouldn't be here but for my friend Christina Bost-Seaton, who loaned me her copy of *The Bolter*, and inadvertently set off a chain of "what if. . . ." Thanks also to Susan Pedersen for hiring me, years ago, as her TF for Second British Empire and showing me that there was more to twentieth-century Kenya than *Out of Africa*, and to the wonderful Deanna Raybourn for so generously sharing her Kenya sources with me and not dropping her drink on me when we discovered that we were both writing books set not only in the same place but in the same year.

Hugs and thanks go to Liz Mellyn, who spent hours walking along the Arno with me last spring, rethinking the nature of the Addie and Bea relationship, and to Alison Pace for our Writing Thursdays, where much coffee was consumed and very little writing written. Sometimes, you just need to talk the book through to someone. (Or, as my little sister prefers to phrase it "at" someone.)

The biggest thanks of all goes to my family for bringing me up on a diet of *Masterpiece Theatre* and British classics, for supporting me in all things, and for being nothing like Clemmie's family. Thanks, Mom, Dad, Spencer, and Brooke, for being you and for always being there. Last but not least, to James, who puts up with manuscript pages on the couch, imaginary people at dinner, and copyedits in lieu of wedding planning. I love you more than I can say.